SECRETS AND RUIN

JACKY LEON BOOK NINE

K.N. BANET

CHAPTER ONE

APRIL 17TH, 2023

I t was four in the morning when the alarm started going off. With a groan, I reached out and hit it, knowing I wouldn't be able to keep my eyes closed until the next one went off. The man next to me, my fiancé, was already rolling out of bed, as if he had been summoned to war or some emergency was happening.

There was no war, at least not today. There wasn't an emergency, either. I was sure of it.

No, today was an early morning because we were driving Dirk to the airport, and I wasn't ready for that. If I could keep sleeping and pretend it wasn't happening, I would.

"Jacky, he'll be here any minute," Heath murmured in my ear.

I growled into my pillow but pushed myself up. Bleary-eyed, I looked around the room. My eyes landed on him, the black-haired, blue-eyed werewolf I was going to marry one day. Somehow, he was already dressed.

"Did you go to sleep in that?" I was almost certain he hadn't.

"The alarm went off thirty minutes ago," he said, smiling down at me.

Groaning, I knew I needed to get moving. He was right when he said Dirk was going to be here any minute. I got into the shower quickly, not fiddling with the temperature. Cold water would wake me up, which was what I needed. Hissing and moving fast, I got myself clean enough to get through the trip to the airport. I put my hair in a wet ponytail and stalked through the bedroom and closet until I found something acceptable to wear.

By the time I made my way downstairs, I could smell food. Dirk was already there, his suitcases in my living room, and there were bags of fast food.

"Thanks for doing this," he said, smiling at me for a moment before it disappeared. "Bad morning?"

"Early morning," Heath said, chuckling. "She stayed up a bit too late. I tried to warn her."

I went for the bags, finding bacon, egg, and cheese things to devour while they stood around. The moment I had those in hand, Heath pushed coffee at me, and I took it with me to sit down.

"I couldn't sleep," I explained as I unwrapped the first breakfast sandwich. "Thanks for the food."

"I wasn't going to show up empty-handed," Dirk said, sitting across from me with his own food. "Seriously, though, thanks for driving me today."

"Landon didn't want to see you off from here?" I

looked around but couldn't smell Heath's son. It worried me a little because he and Dirk were in a relationship and lived together. Was this going to cause some sort of fallout?

"He said goodbye to me when I left earlier. He's trying not to follow me. It's the same reason he's not taking me to the airport." Dirk chuckled softly. "He doesn't want to test his strength of will. If we give him a chance, he might buy a ticket to follow me."

"You brought his keys with you, right?" Heath reached out as he walked by, and Dirk handed them over. Heath hung them up with our keys, then sat beside me.

"Well, now we know he'll have to walk if he wants to go anywhere," I said, shaking my head. Like that would stop Landon if he really wanted to get to the airport to follow Dirk to Germany. He was trying to support this trip for Dirk and do it from afar instead of pushing himself into the situation, which was a positive. I knew what was at stake with Dirk's trip, and Landon following him there could be the spark for the powder keg.

"I'll give him back his keys once you land," Heath said to Dirk, ignoring my comment with a smile. "He'll be in a better place once you land, and we know Niko hasn't killed you on sight. You still have a plan for trouble, right?" We had gone over every variation and possibility. There were backup plans for the backup plans.

"I have a ticket just in case it doesn't go well," Dirk said, chuckling sadly. I could smell his fear. "If there's any sign he and I can't talk about this, I'll just turn around and get on a plane back."

"Yeah, he won't attack in an airport," I said softly, the reality of this weighing heavily on me. I wanted to keep him here and protect him from even the possibility of Niko rejecting him. I wanted to send him home and tell him to go back to bed with Landon because it was too early. I wanted to go with him to make sure Niko couldn't get the wrong idea.

In my heart, Dirk was mine. My head told a different story as logic warred with emotion. He was Niko's. My brother had raised him and loved him as a father loves a son.

There are some things I can't protect him from. No matter how much I want to, I can't protect him from Niko. I have to trust both of them. And Zuri. Zuri said this would be fine, and I have to have some faith in that.

Dirk's identity as a werewolf was too big to keep a secret forever, so this trip had to happen to free him, me, and so many others from the potential of exposing it in the wrong way. Dirk needed his father to support him, and every time it was brought up, I could see on his face that he *wanted* his father's support.

We finished breakfast and loaded into my vehicle. I didn't drive. Too tired to want to be behind the wheel. It was a long drive to the airport.

"While we're at the airport, do you finally want to make a decision about the private—" .

"No," I mumbled, shaking my head as I cut Heath off. "It can sit in whatever storage it's taking up for now." There were a good number of things I had won in my 'war' against the Dallas pack a year ago. Their private plane was one of those things, and one I wasn't sure what to do with. I knew I could sell it, but I didn't pull the trigger. After we defeated the pack, I asked Heath to make sure its paperwork was updated with me and him as the new owners, but that was as far as I got.

"Then I'll keep it as is." Heath wasn't bothered by my reply. "As it stands, if you want to use it, it'll take about two hours to mobilize the crew required to fly it, and during that time, the flight plans and everything would be worked out."

"Do you really see me..." I didn't finish the question. There was a real chance that I would end up needing to use it at a moment's notice. That was why I couldn't bring myself to get rid of it even though it was excess and wasteful. "We should have forced Dirk to use it."

"Then I would lose the crowd of humans to protect me if Niko decides to react violently to my new werewolf identity," Dirk reminded me.

"That's right," I said, inhaling deeply as I silently fretted and freaked out. There was only one way for anyone to know how Niko would react before Dirk landed, and that was my only role in this. One I dreaded but was willing to take on for both of them.

"There's always a chance he doesn't show up at the airport because of how he reacts to my call," I pointed out. "That would be nice."

"Or he thinks he can handle it, but the moment he catches my scent, he can't," Dirk countered.

"Let's stop thinking about the worst-case scenarios, please," Heath ordered, clearly losing his patience. "This is Niko we're talking about. He's by far one of the most well-mannered members of your family."

"I'm a werewolf, and he fought a war against us," Dirk reminded us.

"He was born to a werewolf pack, and the only reason he didn't become one was due to a betrayal by other werewolves, not his own family," Heath fired back. "He's not entirely close-minded. He's never tried to attack me for what I am, and I'm not related to him. You're his son, and I can promise that's more important than what you turn into during a full moon."

I reached out and touched Heath's thigh, glad he was willing to look on the bright side. Dirk and I were having trouble finding it. Without a doubt, I needed to be more positive, but I couldn't find it in me. I was scared for Dirk, and that was overriding everything.

Reaching the airport without further conversation, we unloaded Dirk's suitcases from my car onto a cart.

I was antsy and uncomfortable with how close this was. The day had snuck up on me, and I dreaded it. I didn't want to see him go. I didn't want to open the can of worms we were about to open. I was steeped in trouble everywhere I turned, and now I was sending Dirk off into the unknown to handle something without me, more trouble I had caused.

He wouldn't be a werewolf if it wasn't for me. I know that. Niko will know that. He could have died... and I had promised to keep him safe. Niko will know that.

It was more than a bit selfish to think of it like that, but I had made a promise to Niko to keep Dirk safe, and I hadn't. Instead, Dirk had to throw himself in front of danger to help protect others and paid the price. It was only Dirk's relative okay-ness with his situation that kept me from the gnawing guilt most days, but it had grown every second as this very trip came closer. Only months ago, I had been steady in my resolve that this would turn out okay. That had eroded to a desperate hope, and it was quickly waning.

"Jacky, you need to relax," Heath murmured in my ear as I clung to the suitcase I had been trying to put down. "He'll be fine. This will turn out okay in the end."

"Yeah. Even if he's mad, it'll wear off," Dirk said, leaning on the rest of his things.

"After Niko is Hasan. After Hasan, are the rest of your aunts and uncles," I reminded him.

"Zuri handled it well," Dirk reminded me.

"Zuri and Mischa aren't the same," I countered. Mischa was a volatile werecat, her moods swinging from joy to rage and back again before anyone could figure out how to handle her. She was harboring some sort of mean grudge right now, too. I hadn't spoken to her in months, not since last November when I had hosted werecats for political discussions with Zuri.

"No, they aren't," Dirk agreed, sighing. "But Niko is my father, and I have to trust he'll back me up... that he'll back you up. If Zuri can back us up, he definitely can as well."

I only nodded to appease Dirk on that front. Niko didn't support me, not publicly. He was a silent source of *maybe*. As the family tried to figure out how to deal with my relationship with Heath and now his pack's residence in my territory, Niko never spoke up. We all understood why. He was in a difficult position. If he supported me, he could turn half the family against himself, purely thanks to his background.

"Dirk, if you need anything, call. Help will come, no matter what," Heath said.

I looked up to see them hug. A growing relationship of trust and friendship was really beginning to bloom. I could see the way Dirk looked at Heath with respect and admiration as he agreed to do just that.

I hugged Dirk next, feeling like I was trapped by a bear. I was stronger than him, but Dirk was big, and the hug felt all-encompassing.

"I'll call him once I get home," I promised.

"Thanks. I know it's a weird situation, but if you warn him now, then he can decide before I land what he wants...."

"I know, I know." I squeezed until he grunted, then released him. "Go, get on the plane before I buy a ticket and follow you."

He chuckled and started pushing his things inside, waving at us until he disappeared into the airport.

"Shit," I mumbled, rubbing my eyes. "I hope Niko is going to be okay with all of this."

"You'll find out once you get home," Heath said, guiding me with an arm around my waist to get back into the car.

"Yeah, I will," I said, sighing heavily.

CHAPTER TWO

At home, I sat down in my office, watching the clock tick by, knowing I had to prepare for the inevitable conversation. I had scheduled a meeting with Niko over a week before. My brother knew Dirk was on his way and had assumed this was about that before I ever mentioned something to him.

How had he said it? A status report on what to expect after being in America for so long?

Oh, Niko, you have no idea...

I turned on my computer and fiddled with programs and settings until I was satisfied and completely out of time. Heath hovered in the doorway, his eyes stormy with worry, not for Dirk but for me.

"He could hate me for this," I whispered.

"I know."

"It doesn't matter if he's okay with Dirk being a werewolf or not... Once he finds out how it happened, he could hate me. I risked his son's life and didn't protect him like I had promised." I was preparing myself for that conclusion.

After everything I had been through with this family, it was easier to expect the worst than to hope for the best. Hope had me trying to prove to Hasan that Heath was a good man but failing at every turn because my werecat father refused to see what was as clear as day. It only led to mean comments, arguments, and a father who hoped I would fail.

I was tired of hoping for the best when expecting the worst at least prepared me.

"I know. Jacky, it's the last thing I want, but if you... don't have them, you'll always have me. You'll always have Dirk, Landon, and Carey. It's not any consolation for losing your family because of their hate and unwillingness to see how wonderful you are, but you won't be alone."

I gave him a weak smile, cherishing every word. He was right. Niko could be angry, and I might lose him as a brother, but I would have the patchwork family I had built here. I would probably still have Zuri, too. I wouldn't be alone.

"Time for you to go," I said, keeping that smile. "I'll call you in if Niko wants to talk to you as Dirk's Alpha."

"Okay." He came over and swooped in for a kiss, then he was gone.

Calling Niko right on schedule, he picked up in less than two seconds, showing up on my wall-mounted monitor. His smile was bright, his excitement to see his son clear.

Niko was a wiry man. There was something that said rockstar about him. A little too thin in places for me, but I bet women fell over themselves for him. His hair was just past his shoulders, but that couldn't hide his cheekbones. His German heredity wasn't the most obvious because I didn't know how to identify that sort of thing, but he was clearly a European white guy.

"Hey, Jacky! Dirk's flight just took off on time. Now, all we do is wait." Niko's smile was infectious, but I lost it quickly.

"Yeah, all we do now is wait," I agreed. "You were right about what this phone call is about, you know. There's some stuff Dirk and I wanted you to know before he landed in Berlin, so you had a moment to come to terms with it."

"Yeah, I was expecting something like it. You've mentioned that he's been a valued member of your team there. How's he getting along with everyone? You have a lot of supernaturals in your territory now."

"He, uh..." I tried to think about Dirk and the pack. He and Ranger were finally settling into something acceptable, no longer going for each other's necks to pick fights. Dirk was more comfortable with his position in the pack, but that was tentative at best. It was only a temporary thing for any werewolf. It only mattered how long temporary was for each werewolf and the pack they were in. Dirk got along with most, but he also kept his distance because he was my nephew and in a relationship with Landon. He didn't have solid friends among the werewolves, but Heath never made it a big deal.

"Well?"

"He's still a pretty solitary man," I said at Niko's questioning. "He's private, you know? Quiet. Does his thing and only speaks up when he feels it's necessary. He's reliable, though. He doesn't let the other supernaturals push him around. He's certainly not afraid of them."

"Good. I never wanted him to be afraid. Smart, cautious, but not fearful."

"Yeah..." Nodding, I could understand why Niko wanted that the same way Heath didn't want Carey to fear him or Landon.

"You seem a bit out of it. Miss him already?"

"More than you know. I guess I should cut to the chase. No reason to let you interrogate me when you don't know...." I took a deep breath, reading the confusion on Niko's face. "Dirk is a werewolf."

His jaw dropped open as I watched him process that. I wondered if he believed me as I watched his expression turn disbelieving before he pushed away from his desk, rolling backward as he looked around. For what, I didn't know, but he was clearly processing, so I didn't try to guess. Instead, I started telling him what else he needed to hear.

"You must remember the attack on my territory this time last year, Carey's fifteenth birthday. He was supposed to go to a safe room with the other humans still on the property, Carey and Oliver. He didn't. While I was trying to head off the majority of the attackers outside the house, Heath and Landon were preparing to take on any who made their way inside. Dirk decided he would sit at the top of the stairs and shoot anything he could see. He killed a lot of werewolves that night, but one finally took him off guard towards the end of the assault."

Niko was shaking his head as if he couldn't believe anything I was saying. He was still staring into the distance, not looking at me.

"He could have been killed, but Oliver and Carey heard what was happening to him and opened the safe room door. Oliver killed the wolf."

"You said... you said there were no—"

"I said there were no casualties on our side nor injuries that couldn't be recovered from," I said, reminding him of exactly how I had phrased it when I told everyone. All in an effort to protect what had happened to Dirk.

"He can't... recover from being a werewolf," Niko growled softly.

"It's not an injury," I murmured, knowing my deceit. I had lied by omission, letting everyone believe one thing when I had meant another. "It's a curse."

"I don't need an explanation for how you fooled me. My son was Changed into a werewolf without his consent... and you waited a year to tell me," he continued, growling through every word. "A *year*, Jacky."

"He wanted time to adjust," I said weakly, knowing I could have gone against Dirk's wishes any time and told his father. The man who trusted me to keep his son safe, my brother, a member of our fucked up supernatural family, which was already dealing with the strain of too many secrets and revelations in the last few years. "I honored his request for privacy and secrecy until he was ready."

"Is he... happy?" Niko asked, his Adam's apple bobbing as he swallowed between words.

"He's as happy as I have ever seen him, though it's not entirely because he's a werewolf. There's a lot he needs to tell you about his life when he arrives... if you want to see him."

"What does that mean?" he snarled, finally turning back to the webcam. His eyes seemed to reach over the vast distance and found my soul. They were no longer human but feline eyes, telling me that it was for the best that he and I were several thousand miles away from each other.

"Dirk has a second ticket to leave Berlin if you aren't there to pick him up... so he can fly back without troubling you. That's why he had me tell you now. I can let him know if you won't be there. Also, if you think you might get violent—"

"There are a lot of people I would be violent with right now. Dirk is not on that list," he growled.

"I'm sorry I failed you in regard to his protection," I whispered, lowering my head. "The wolf that attacked him is dead. The pack is long destroyed... I hope it's enough."

"I'll decide what's enough," he snapped. "Right when I think that there can't possibly be anything more wrong with this family, you come out and tell me Dirk has been a werewolf for an entire fucking year, and I didn't know. Damn it, Jacky! How did you hide it from Zuri? She was in your territory!"

"I didn't," I admitted softly.

"Of course. of fucking course, Zuri knows another secret in this family that wasn't hers to know, but for some reason...." He started ranting in German.

While I didn't understand the language yet, I was starting to pick up on several words I heard from Dirk's mouth all too often. Niko jumped up and started pacing, his hands flailing about while he ranted. Eventually, he settled and stopped in front of the webcam again.

"What's his status? Lone wolf?"

"No. He's a member of Heath's pack," I answered, having no idea what Niko would have wanted for Dirk in that regard or how he would react. "Heath and Landon said it was better for new werewolves to have a pack, and Heath is the only werewolf I would ever trust to be his Alpha. He and Landon have been close for some time, and Dirk didn't have a problem with it."

"Heath was right, but he's also Callahan's worst enemy, a Rogue Alpha with a pack that doesn't report to him. Hasan hates him for being with you. I'm not sure what would be worse, actually. My son being forced to learn how to be a werewolf as a lone wolf or... getting caught in that situation as another rogue with your fiancé."

"It was the best we could—"

"The best you could have done was send him *home*," Niko snarled.

I finally felt some fire and glared at Niko in return.

"In my opinion, he was home," I growled back. Niko's scoff only added fuel to my sudden shift in temper. "From where I'm sitting, he's left home to visit a place he left behind years ago. As for the situation I'm in with Heath? Dirk was already caught up in it. He's my security guy, the person who helps protect my home. He's in it, Niko, just like *you* taught him to be. If you didn't want him involved, you would have sent him to get a normal education instead of raising him to be an immortal. Now he is one!" I stood up. "Now you need to tell me if I should call him back home."

"You don't need to do that," he said, shaking his head. "You're right about one thing. My son is an immortal now, and I plan on spending as much time with him as possible. Here's my request, though. Don't ever fucking call me again unless it's about his health or happiness, which I hope is never in your hands again."

He hung up on me.

My office door opened slowly.

"He's just angry," Heath said gently as he came in. "He'll come around."

"Will he?" I asked, sinking back into my chair in defeat. "He's fine with Dirk, the werewolf. He hates that I kept a secret from him."

"It wasn't your secret to give," Heath said kindly, coming around my desk.

"Wasn't it? If Landon had something terrible happen and asked me to keep it a secret, would you expect me to?" I searched his expression as he went to a knee in front of me.

The conflict was there as he tried to process the question and figure out his answer.

"Or Carey, though that's different. She's a minor."

"Carey, yes. Landon..." Heath sighed heavily. "I think I would be emotionally angry but would logically understand that Landon is a grown man who can make his own choices, but... I've never been in that position."

"See?"

"That means Niko may be dealing with the same thing, and once he talks to Dirk, he'll cool off and things will be okay again."

"I hope so, but hope is getting harder, Heath. It really is."

"Life has been really hard on us recently, but we'll get through it," he murmured. He stood up, a hand stretched out, an offering of support I took before I even knew where it would lead me. "Want to do something to get your mind off it?"

"What's your plan for today?"

"I'm going to do house visits for the pack," he answered. "You can tag along if you think it'll help you think of something else."

"I would like that, actually." Nodding, I got up, our fingers entwining as we left my office. Closing the door softly, I left my family troubles locked inside. So long as Niko intended on continuing to love and support Dirk, there was nothing else I felt like fighting about. In the end, that at least was a victory. I had to take it and let the rest lie for now.

"One step at a time, right?" I said as I went to the garage with Heath. "This was just step one."

"That's right, and you're not walking alone."

Leaning on his shoulder for a moment, I knew that.

"Who's first?"

"Landon."

If there was anyone in the state of Texas that was probably feeling worse than me, it would be that werewolf.

3

CHAPTER THREE

"At least Teagan could take Carey to school today," I said as we drove towards Landon's home. "I mean, he does most days, but it's nice of him, and we should pay him more."

"I agree he should be paid more, but his time driving kids to school is going to be over sooner rather than later. She'll be getting her provisional driver's license in about a month. Thanks for doing all of that stuff with her learner license with me. It would never have gotten done without you. With her and Benjamin both being able to drive, they can haul Arlo around until his probation is over." Heath grinned at me. "Maybe I should find some way to backpay you for teaching Carey."

"I couldn't help but remember how I felt getting my first car and driving on my own, so there was no way I was going to make her wait longer than necessary," I said, smiling a little. Those hours behind the wheel, getting her to driver's ed classes, studying the book... It had all been one of the most miserable experiences of my life, but I knew life would be better once Carey had the freedom to drive herself to school or the movies. She was planning on volunteering over the summer or picking up a summer job to give her some experience working, and I knew Heath and I would be too busy to drive her back and forth for those sorts of things. While it was terrifying to think of her driving places alone, I knew it was worth it.

"You're going to put a tracker on whatever car we buy her, right?" I asked softly.

"Obviously," Heath said without missing a beat, not shocked at all by my suggestion. "We're not going to stalk my daughter, though."

"No, of course not." I couldn't stop a laugh. "We won't let Landon have access to it. It's only in case she's in danger, you know?"

"I do," he said, clearing his throat as we both faced the reality of the situation.

Carey deserved to have a normal life, regardless of what dangers the world held. To drive a car, to have a job, to grow up. On the other hand, being human didn't stop her from being his daughter or my future stepdaughter.

We always worried about Carey's safety. We always worried about Dirk's. And Oliver's. We worried about each other. We also worried about ourselves because dying wasn't conducive to planning a wedding that almost no one wanted to happen.

Nothing had really happened since I had invited the werecats to my state to talk, but things just seemed to get heavier, regardless. The growing silence between me and my father, the head of the family, was part of it. So was the trip Dirk was taking to Germany.

We pulled into Landon's driveway without saying anything else. It was close to noon, so I was reasonably certain he would be awake and moving around. With the three hours to the airport and back, then waiting on my call with Niko, half the day was already gone. Landon was never the type to sleep for very long, even after a full moon. Landon didn't know how to rest, even when it seemed like he was doing nothing.

However, all the lights were off.

"Is he up?" I asked, frowning at the house Landon had bought to share with Dirk.

"He will be," Heath replied, getting out of the truck.

I followed, staying behind Heath because I didn't want a cranky Landon to see me first.

Heath didn't knock. He used his key and went inside first. I hovered on the threshold, not willing to barge into Landon's house without welcome. I knew he was home. My territory magic told me that much, but he wasn't moving around.

Or he wasn't until he realized people had entered his house. I didn't need my magic to know he barged into the living room and growled at his father, though. My eyes and ears told me that.

"What the fuck are you doing in my house?" he demanded of his father, who sat down on the recliner, ignoring the comfortable-looking couch. No one sat on the couch except for the men who occupied the house.

"Checking on you. I'm doing rounds today," Heath

K.N. BANET

said lightly, putting his feet on an ottoman I was certain was a newer addition to the space.

"Ah, the tried-and-true Heath Everson coping mechanism," Landon muttered, shaking his head. He caught sight of me and sighed. "Come in, sit down. I'll get you two a drink."

"How are you holding up?" I asked, closing the front door. I wasn't surprised by what he said about Heath. Heath took care of things he could when others were out of his hands. Of course, he was trying to cope with Dirk heading for unknown territory. He was going to make sure all the other werewolves were okay to keep his mind off the one he couldn't hover over.

Landon snorted but didn't give any sort of real answer until he was handing me a soda and sitting down on the couch. I went to the safe loveseat, also avoiding the couch.

"I hate that he's dealing with his father on his own," Landon said, staring at his open can as if it held answers to the world's greatest mysteries. "I know all the plans for his safety. I helped make them... but it doesn't make the distance easier. It doesn't make me comfortable knowing he's doing it alone."

"Well, his father knows he's a werewolf now, and... he's not mad at Dirk," I said, trying to smile. "They should be fine."

"Blamed you, did he?" Landon grunted, his annoyance filling the room. "Your family likes doing that."

"He had some good points. I got snappy with him. He hung up on me. It happens."

"Stop pretending like he didn't rip your heart out and stomp on it," Landon growled. "It pisses me off when you try to play nice with them. They practically never do it for you."

"He was angry I didn't keep Dirk safe and didn't tell him about the life-changing event Dirk was forced to go through. He's Dirk's father. He had the right to be mad at me, his sister." I didn't need this, not from Landon. I didn't need a temperamental wolf feeding into my temper. Landon was one of three werewolves in the pack I could lose against if we decided to take our feelings out on each other. It was unlikely we would ever do that, but I was in enough of a mood to think about it.

I'm mad because he's right. Just like Niko is right. And I'm right.

And we're all wrong, too, and there's nothing we can do to fix that. It's Dirk's life, and we're all passengers to his decisions about his future. We just have to weather the storm, no matter how it makes us feel about ourselves or each other.

I wasn't bitter about Dirk's decision for secrecy. I fully supported his choice and understood it all too well. In some ways, I agreed with Landon. I was always the one at fault in my family, always the one picking someone over someone else or prioritizing the wrong thing in everyone's eyes.

Everyone is an exaggeration I can't allow myself to make. It's not everyone. It's just enough of them.

I also agreed with Niko. Knowing Heath would probably react the same way, what else was I supposed to do than take the blame assigned to me?

"You two aren't going to get anywhere talking about this," Heath warned. "It's a family matter, and family matters are complicated. There's no real right or wrong answer and getting into it won't help anything. You should drop it."

"She just lets them continue to—"

"I don't let them do anything," I growled. "Niko's stance is reasonable, and I'm not going to push back when it comes to his son. He's rightfully angry. This isn't a situation like Mischa, who's an angry bitch who just treats me and everyone else as though she's mad at shit. Mischa's not justified. Niko is." I glared at Landon, daring him to challenge that. If he thought Niko and Mischa were the same, then he needed his head readjusted, and I was willing to do it.

"What about Ha—"

"Enough," Heath snarled, and his power rippled through the room. Like always, it slid around me, ignoring me, unable to exert itself on my will. Landon, though, was definitely put in his place and sank deeper into his couch.

"Apologies, Father," he mumbled.

"Don't put your nose where it doesn't belong. You should be focused on one thing and one thing only. Dirk is, as far as we can tell right now, safe around Niko. That has to be enough. Let it be enough, Landon."

"Yes, sir," he said very softly, looking away from us. "I'm glad Dirk is safe."

"Apology accepted," Heath said with finality, then stood. "If you want to mope, then mope. I'm going to continue checking in with the other members of the pack."

"I'll join you for dinner... if you'll have me," Landon said, like a boy who knew if he stepped over the line again, he was going to get a wooden spoon to his knuckles or an old-school ass whooping.

I wasn't entirely comfortable with it.

"You're always welcome at my home for any reason," I said quickly, then stood and walked out. Heath said something, but I didn't listen. Landon was always welcome at my table, and even though Heath lived with me, it was still *my* table.

I got into Heath's truck and waited ten minutes for him to meet me there.

"What's wrong?" he asked as he pulled out of the driveway.

"You really snapped at Landon, and I didn't like it," I said, not holding back because that wasn't how Heath and I did things. He wanted my honest opinion, and I gave it to him. "He seemed like a kid for a minute, ready to get spanked."

"Ah... it wasn't that, but I guess our relationship would make it...." With a sigh, Heath turned down the next road, heading for the next home. "He's my second, and he crossed a line. His response to me was a werewolf showing enough submission I wasn't going to snap again."

"I can handle my own with Landon. You don't need—"

"No, I don't need to, Jacky, but at the end of the day, he's my son. I'll be damned if he hurts you because his head is too far shoved up his own ass. He was pushing too hard on a discussion that doesn't involve him. While you can absolutely handle your own against my son in a verbal debate, I wasn't in the mood. I asked him to drop it, and he didn't. I put my foot down. It was insulting. You and I both know you don't let your family treat you poorly.

"We both know you fight against them at every chance because you want to prove yourself to them, but most of them keep pushing you back down. I certainly wasn't going to let him say you haven't done enough or anything about Hasan. It's not your job or responsibility to make Hasan think, feel, or believe anything. You aren't responsible for making him change. You stand your ground, and he digs his heels in the mud."

I didn't know how to reply to any of that. Family matters were complicated.

"Who are we checking on next?" I asked as we drove.

"Teagan while all the kids are in class. The boys are ours after classes today, so we'll see them later. Teagan has some work coming up that will keep him in Dallas for a few nights, so I want to check in with him about who he's taking with him. Plus, after Landon, I'd like to be around his energy."

"Shit, that's right. Has he picked his protection?" None of the werewolves left the territory without at least one other werewolf as backup, and usually, it was two or three. We let them pick their groups, and if Heath wasn't satisfied, he would add another, just in case.

"Shamus, Ranger, and Fenris," he answered.

I didn't like the idea of those three today. Shamus was Heath's third, a fun-loving father. His two adult children were also members of the pack. Ranger was our resident disabled werewolf, missing a leg, thanks to me.

Fenris was... Fenris. He always went with Teagan to the office when Teagan needed to go. It worked well for them, giving Fenris some time out of my territory with a werewolf he would rely on.

But this is an overnight trip... What would happen if Shamus wanted to take everyone to a bar for a fun night out? Fenris could start a brawl, and Ranger would be totally into it. Teagan isn't dominant enough to stop any of them, and if someone accidentally hurt Teagan, we could see bodies piling up.

It was three werewolves I would never put together in a room for Teagan's protection. Their temperaments didn't match, and with werewolves, that could be a disaster. There was only one way for it to be an even worse mix of werewolves.

"Maybe you should send Landon and make it a real party," I mumbled, feeling chaotic.

Heath had the balls to laugh as if it wasn't the most terrifying thing the pack could muster.

4

CHAPTER FOUR

After he was done laughing, Heath wiped his eyes while he kept trying to drive.

"You're right, and I already made some adjustments, I promise," he said, still holding back laughter as he tried to speak. "You asked if he had picked his protection, and those were who he picked."

"What changes did you make? I know I don't technically run the pack or anything, but...."

"It's fine. I let him keep Fenris because he wants Fenris. Teagan knows he's calming enough on the mad wolf to let him off his leash sometimes, and I won't deny that Teagan is really good with him. We're going to be talking to him later today, too."

"It was wild to find out he spoke German...." I admitted.

Talk about a night of horrible thoughts running through my head after a long fucking week. Heath and I had both jumped up and tried to figure out what to do as quickly as we could. We decided to give it a night since Fenris hadn't acted on anything he might have heard, then talked to him the next day. Heath had been his Alpha for a not short amount of time in Dallas, but German had never reported as one of Fenris's languages. Not even Teagan had known he could speak it. All of that was normally written down by Alphas when werewolves were transferred.

"It really threw us for a loop, didn't it? He didn't hear anything from Dirk, though, so we were in the clear. Fenris wasn't lying, and he doesn't have the Talent or personality to try."

"Yeah," I said, sighing. "Though he's getting better and better since he's been here. A mistake on his paperwork because he so rarely used the language...." I shook my head. That was what Fenris had said, and to him, it was the truth.

"Callahan was the one who filled it out," Heath repeated, the same thing he had explained when we had questioned Fenris about being a fluent German speaker.

"I wonder what other little things Fenris can do that never got onto the paperwork," I said, snorting. "Callahan is personally invested in him. I can't help but wonder why."

"It's all very strange, but so long as Fenris doesn't lie to us, we have to trust him. I can't tolerate continuing to treat him like he's broken when you're right about one thing... he's improving. He's done really well. How he helped last year, even with the other werecats around?

That was something I could have never asked him to do a decade ago."

"Less than that. He attacked me in 2018 when I was helping you. That was only four and a half years ago, five years this August or September. No, I'm not saying we should lock him up here. I was just thinking about how he gave me that spook."

"It was certainly that. Now, you wanted to know the new roster for Teagan's work trip back to the city?"

"I did!"

"Aside from Fenris, I've asked him to take Carlos and Jenny. They're a fierce team and can handle damn near anything when they're working together."

"Not bad." I didn't talk much with Carlos and Jenny, but they never gave me any reason to think they couldn't handle something like this. Generally, we said polite hellos and went on our way. I had work, and so did they. They were probably the two werewolves who showed up at home the least on top of that.

"Exactly. Now we get to see how he feels about it."

Turning onto his driveway, we parked in front of Teagan's house on the large property he'd bought to finish raising his two wards. He walked outside right as we were getting out of the car.

"A house visit?" Teagan's amused chuckle carried as he hopped down his front steps. "Don't tell me the boys are in trouble for something."

"No, not at all," Heath said, shaking Teagan's hand in greeting. I gave him a half-wave. "We're just doing some house visits so I can check up on everyone. Dirk is on a plane, and Jacky needed to move around. You're just the second stop of many."

"Well, come on in, and we'll chat. With the boys at school, we'll be able to have a real discussion since the walls won't be rattling from their music."

I snorted because I understood the pain. Thankfully, Carey didn't play loud music. Regretfully, I was a werecat and had some of the most sensitive hearing in the supernatural world. It didn't matter how quiet her music was. I would hear it if there was nothing else. I got good at ignoring music and conversations through the walls, though. I didn't want to invade anyone's privacy.

We sat down at a round breakfast table in the kitchen nook that Teagan used instead of a more formal dining table. The dining room was used as a game room, with different televisions and monitors for the boys to play together.

"Did you see my roster for your Dallas trip?" Heath asked as Teagan put a drink in front of him. I politely declined because if I got a drink at every house, I would need to use all of their bathrooms. Teagan put a glass of water in front of me, anyway.

"I did," he finally said, sitting down with a cup of coffee. "I was hoping to take Ranger and Shamus for the same reason as Fenris, you know. Shamus still deals with his children every day, even though they're grown, and Ranger just needs more activity. He's still fussy about driving his truck and doesn't get out enough." Teagan didn't seem hurt, but that he could immediately offer that explanation told me he had put a lot of thought into his plan.

"I figured, but it's not a good group of personalities. Plus, you deal with stakes that could piss one or all three of them off. You need two cooler heads who don't feel the need to push their way into situations. Shamus and Ranger aren't the werewolves for that. They'll want to get involved and have opinions. By that rationale, Fenris isn't a good choice, either, but you're one of the few werewolves I can send him out with."

"He's become a staple at the offices," Teagan confirmed. "He enjoys it. The offices are quiet, and even when people get heated, there's very little to worry about in terms of violence. Nothing sets him off, you know? I was hoping Shamus and Ranger could enjoy it, but I understand what you're saying. Both of them are used to being some of the most important people in the room, present company excluded. They would have comments...."

"Does Fenris sit quietly through meetings?" I wasn't sure I could believe that. I didn't pry about everyone's work lives, but it was fascinating to hear about Fenris sitting in a law office and listening to someone prattle on about property values and insurance or whatever Teagan dealt with.

"He does, actually. I think he falls asleep through half of them. Sometimes, he'll ask a question, but Fenris isn't uneducated. He knows what to ask." Teagan shrugged. "I can take Jenny and Carlos. My new condo has the space for them."

I smiled hearing those two words—new condo. When we'd moved to Dallas, Teagan was the only person we could safely reach out to. He had been in a smaller apartment while trying to handle two teenage boys. It had taken convincing, but Heath worked tirelessly to get Teagan to finally treat himself nicely with the new condo in the city. He had the money but preferred simpler living. Teagan was just like that.

"Do you like it?" I asked, leaning in. "The new condo."

"Yes, I do. It's perfect for these overnight visits and lets me put my feet up when I have downtime on the days I'm in the city. It helps that it's in the building next to the office."

"Good, good," I said, nodding happily. "I still have that awful mansion, too, if you need the space."

"I spend months renovating it, cleaning out all the evidence of the Dallas pack, spend thousands of dollars of her money and mine... and she calls the entire building awful," Heath said, his face blank at the end.

Teagan laughed, and Heath joined him while I eyed the side of my fiancé's head, wondering if his children wanted it to stay attached to the rest of his body.

"Maybe if we put people in it, I wouldn't think it's a waste of real estate, but it just sits empty and spends my money in the form of property taxes right now." I crossed my arms, daring him to argue. We hadn't used it since the gathering last year, and I had no plans to use it any time soon. Just like the jet, it sat around, reminding me of events I didn't want to think about and didn't want to deal with.

"I think you designed it so your family could come visit you, and that makes it worthwhile," Heath replied, a loving smile softening everything.

"Good point, and one that might be more valid if my family actually wanted to visit me," I mumbled.

"Don't feel alone in that. I understand all too well. My family doesn't visit me either," Teagan said kindly. "And they never will, so long as I throw my support behind Heath. I'm not sure there's any way for me to fix that now. It's okay, though. I have the boys, Fenris, both of you, and this pack."

"You have family out there?" I wasn't the person who asked. Heath was just as surprised as I was, and the words left him faster than I could summon them.

"A couple of siblings and a cousin," Teagan said with a mysterious smile. "Jacky, you know I'm an expert in Tribunal Law, right?"

"I do..."

"My last few relatives are members of Corissa's pack," he said. "Which I left some centuries ago, but not before the Tribunal was formed. I was the person who spent time memorizing every line, every nuance, every little piece I could. Corissa and Callahan leaned on me for a time, but the entire thing became too much, so I left for a quieter life, away from all that."

"Wow." I leaned back, thinking. "I can't imagine why you don't tell that to people."

Teagan laughed, nodding in agreement. My sarcasm landed exactly as I'd hoped.

"I tend to avoid talking about it because of the obvious implications. I never wanted Alphas coming to me to get them a conversation with Corissa through my family because that meant I would have to talk to my family. Before you ask, I wasn't important. Corissa and Callahan didn't use me as a confidant. I was someone good at understanding the fine print. It was also a peace treaty in the beginning. I wasn't the only person asked as counsel to get insight on the writing. They had dozens of other werewolves they discussed things with." Teagan shrugged. "I left for personal reasons a very long time ago. Cut my ties with the pack entirely. Even before I joined a rogue pack, my family didn't speak to me."

"I'm sorry to hear that," Heath murmured. "I've been your Alpha for decades, and...."

"They don't acknowledge me, and I don't acknowledge them. It's better that way. We might as well not be related," Teagan said with his characteristic gentle smile. "Now, enough about me. Maybe later, I'll tell you more stories, but you should probably get on with your day. Heath, I'm fine with the new group. I understand your reasoning. Maybe next time, I can leave Fenris at home and get Shamus and Ranger out."

"I like that plan. I already asked Jenny and Carlos to make sure they were free. Thank you for not giving me any trouble over this."

"There's no reason for trouble. I hope you two have a

nice day," Teagan said, picking up our drinks and taking them to the sink as Heath and I left.

"He's an interesting guy. I wish he was more open," I said as we got into the truck once again.

"This is the most open I've ever seen him," Heath said as he put the truck in reverse and pulled away from the country home. "There's no world in which I thought he would ever start talking about the life he had before coming to Dallas. He arrived shortly before Fenris after I took over the pack. His file from his previous pack was sparse, but it was enough that I didn't dig. I was still restructuring the pack from my takeover, and having an older Beta like him was a good addition. Someone calm and experienced helped me smooth over the rough edges of the transition."

"It wasn't an easy transition?"

"Not at all," Heath murmured. "The smoothest part was Landon claiming his position as my second."

There was a faraway expression I knew too well. Everyone got it when they thought of distant memories, especially the unpleasant ones.

"Do you want to talk about it?" I asked softly.

"Not today. There's only one thing I could say about it. When I tell people I will do anything to protect my children, I mean it."

I didn't bring the topic up again for the short drive to Fenris's home.

CHAPTER FIVE

Fenris didn't hear us coming as Teagan had. Teagan had modern security that would alert him when someone was entering or leaving his property. Fenris had none of that. I knocked while Heath looked around the property, standing on the drive as he inspected. Fenris didn't live in squalor. There were no dead decades-old vehicles sitting in the fields, but there was something run down about his property. It wasn't refurbished the way Teagan had cleaned up his home. There were no new coats of paint or someone consistently maintaining the fields, which were now overgrown to the point of going wild.

Beyond all that, I saw he had a well-cared-for riding lawn mower, and his actual yard was clear and clean. His driveway had fresh gravel, leveled, so there were no potholes. Everything within fifty feet of his home was cared for, A small area of very specific care, indicative of the man who owned the property.

We had a complicated relationship. He annoyed me with his jokes, oftentimes inappropriate in their nature, timing, and delivery. He scared the shit out of me sometimes because I knew he was unstable. His instability was one of the highlights of our initial meeting years ago.

I also liked him, understanding he held a deep pain inside him. I understood being the outcast of my own kind, and Fenris was certainly an outcast among his own. Like Landon, he was considered a fundamentally broken werewolf. He couldn't manage the community nature the way most werewolves did. He didn't crave it. In fact, like Landon, he didn't trust it. Most werewolves needed their community. Not those two.

The door swung open with a growl from the feral werewolf.

"Huh? What are you doing here?" he asked when he saw me.

"She's with me," Heath called, heading towards us. "She's joining me on my rounds."

"Ah…" Fenris nodded, looking at Heath for only a second before staring intently at me. "Is this where I have to be polite and invite you inside for drinks?"

"Do you not want me at your house?" I asked, frowning a little, but I kept something teasing in my tone. He was at my house fairly often, but this was my first time at his. "Are you afraid I'm going to break something? Or perhaps I'll make asinine comments about your choices in furniture. Or art. Or—"

"Yeah, yeah, I fuckin' get it," Fenris grumbled, but he couldn't turn away before I saw him smile. "Damn cat."

"I've heard that turnabout is fair play," I said, chuckling. "What if we just sit on the porch? I don't need to go inside."

"I like that." Fenris nodded, looking back inside. "I think I got some... lemonade or whatever."

"That would be wonderful." I had felt safe rejecting Teagan's offer. Fenris offering a drink was something I couldn't bring myself to decline. He hated my kind with a passion that led him to violently attack the moment he saw me when he had never met me before. However, we had bonded over problems and fought together to save the Dallas pack and Heath when he had been captured by the witches trying to use the pack for their own means. I had been the one who let him out of the cage, then he had saved me from being taken down by the gas that had rendered Heath vulnerable.

As he went inside to get the lemonade, I realized Heath hadn't said anything more. I looked at him, and he was moving the patio furniture around so we could sit in the way he would like.

"Does this work for you?" I asked, hoping I hadn't overstepped.

"This more than works for me," he said, smiling at me before going back to trying to dust off the table.

I opened up the front door, only peeking in to yell down the hall.

"Can you bring a washcloth or paper towels?"

"Yeah!"

I went to sit down, knowing Heath heard that confirmation as well as I did. When Fenris came out, I took the washcloth from him to finish wiping down the table while he poured each of us a glass of store-bought lemonade.

"So, the pup is off for his vacation, and you're all sad without your favorite member of the pack, so Heath brought you out to harass the rest of us, huh?"

"You think Dirk is my favorite? I'm engaged to this one." I nodded towards Heath, who chuckled.

Fenris snorted.

"Heath, I got a question for you." Fenris sat down, stretching his legs out, but I noticed he didn't try to put them in our way. Heath did that sometimes, using small things to physically take up space and make people work to get their own. It was really only on display when he was pissed off or needed to posture with another strong werewolf.

"Yes?"

"Landon is your wolf. Teagan, me, Ranger, Shamus... all your wolves? Is Dirk one of your wolves?"

Frowning, I looked between them. Dirk was in the pack. He was one of Heath's wolves.

"He's a respectful member of the pack who follows orders and is close to my son on an emotional level. He is Jacky's wolf," Heath answered calmly. "I've never thought any differently."

"Yeah, he's loyal to the pack, but like, we all know if you and Jacky had a falling out, he would stay with Jacky.

We'd all leave with you. He and Landon would have to make things work, but he would stay here."

"Um... that's interesting to hear, but that doesn't make him my favorite." I had never chosen a favorite.

"Kids come before lovers," Fenris said, smirking. "If you had to save Heath's life or Dirk's, we both know the obvious. You try to save both, but let's be honest... if you had time for one, you would save Dirk."

"He's right," Heath said, shrugging. "And I don't expect any different nor make a judgment about it. Just like we'd both save Carey before each other."

"Yeah..." I couldn't argue with that. Heath had age and experience Dirk didn't. "Still doesn't mean he's my favorite."

"Okay, let's take the Alpha you're fucking out of the equation," Fenris said, now getting more than a little annoyed with me.

"Okay, then he is," I concede with a chuckle. "Landon is third. He was second, then Dirk became a werewolf."

"I'll let my son, who absolutely won't care, know he has lost esteem in your eyes." Heath was trying not to laugh.

"You think Landon doesn't care about her opinion?" Fenris did laugh, not bothering to hold back how funny he thought Heath's statement was. "That fucking boy would die for her. He cares more for her opinion than he ever did the entire fucking pack in Dallas."

"He wouldn't care that he went down in her rankings for Dirk," Heath countered.

"Ah, well. He's got that love thing fucking going for him, doesn't he? That would be like Landon or Carey saying they like Jacky more than you. Would you really care?"

"They *do* like Jacky more than me," Heath said, not seeming bothered by it at all, and this time, I was the one laughing. "And no, I don't care."

The conversation drifted away from favorites and rankings to the property.

"Do you think you'll clean up and use these fields for anything one day?" Heath pointed at the fields we could see, the ones that surrounded Fenris's driveway.

"Nah, I like it this way. Wish I had more trees, though. Might try to scrounge up the money for that."

"Scrounge? Callahan set up a trust for you centuries ago. You have money."

"Yeah, but I haven't looked at it since I bought this place. I was pretty fucking amazed he hadn't revoked access yet. He might have taken it from me now."

"He doesn't have the legal power to do it, but where there's a will...." Heath sighed heavily. "It would be an awful thing for him to do to you."

"I don't care. Rich or poor, I never gave a damn." Fenris shrugged, then swiftly changed the topic from his financial situation. "So, I'm keeping it like this."

"It might make the neighbors talk," Heath said in a gentle way that told me he needed to mention it, but he understood Fenris's direction and didn't really want him to change it.

"I want it a little wild, Heath. It's nice when the full

moon comes up, and I get to Change in the tall grass then run to the pack. The wildlife is coming back to my fields. I see deer in the mornings. The wilder I let it get, the more I see. I couldn't find a nice little cabin in the woods that you thought was livable enough, so I'm doing this. I'm really fucking happy to be out of the big city."

"The rest of the working farmers around you might not appreciate the local wildlife," Heath said, a deep frown beginning to form. "Maybe clean up half of it but let one area go back to the wild."

"I think it's fine, but maybe fence off a piece of the closest field and trim it down. Start a garden. It's something for you to do," I said. "You sit around here all the time because you don't have a job. Get a hobby. Sell stuff at the farmer's market and make some money if that's a problem."

"A garden?" Fenris laughed harder than I had ever seen, and when it finally died down, he was wiping his eyes. "You are something else. A fucking garden."

"Do it," Heath ordered, but it lacked the power he'd used with Landon earlier. "Try it, Fenris. Do something. I don't like the idea of you stewing here, and the only thing you do is go with Teagan when he can take you. He's trying to get other werewolves some time away from the territory, but not all of them can go with you."

"Yeah, yeah," Fenris said with a roll of his eyes. "I'll do it. Just you two, don't tell anyone about it, though."

"Don't Arlo and Benjamin come over to help out around here? Won't they see it?" I was curious as to how he would hide it from the teenagers who lived within walking distance.

"They're not stupid enough to give me shit over it. Teagan and I would just put them to work. Actually, that's a good idea. Instead of just... mowing the yard or whatever. Gardening would take more time and care...."

"Aw, look at you, thinking of the boys." Smiling, I sipped the extremely sweet lemonade with more sugar than lemon.

"Aw, look at you thinking about us werewolves," he fired back with a toothy grin. "Everyone's favorite werecat, you are. There's no competition."

"I wouldn't say everyone's," I said, clearing my throat as Niko's face flashed through my mind, followed by dozens of others, many of whom either tried to kill me or made it clear they would if they ever found the chance.

"Everyone who doesn't like you is fucking stupid," Fenris said, shaking his head. "A lot of bad shit in this world, but you aren't part of it. You get in the way of everyone else being shitty. A rebel. No..." Fenris seemed to ponder. "More like a revolutionary. Rebels don't have causes and all that. You do. Plus, you're sleeping with a real revolutionary if I remember my American history."

"You're correct, but I hate how you somehow connected all that." Heath didn't seem angry, though. More bemused, as though he enjoyed just sitting here and listening to how Fenris's mind worked.

I was in the same boat, seeing the connections Fenris made, hating how he phrased it, but it was funny, too.

"Well, this has been fun, but if you're making rounds,

you don't need to sit here with me all afternoon," Fenris suddenly declared. "Hey, if I start this garden, you two have to buy what I grow. Make me that deal. Help me fucking make waves at the farmer's market." He snorted at the end as he smiled.

I was struggling to keep from laughing as a grin spread over my face. The image of Fenris trying to sell anything to normal people, humans just going about their day, was insanity I was more than willing to be a part of.

"You will have to come over to dinner and behave during it," Heath said, clearly beginning a bargain to get Fenris for more proper socialization. "So, we can best review your wares and provide feedback, of course."

"Damn straight. That's even better than free food. I'll get paid to eat."

"Good. We'll leave you be, then. Actually, one more thing. Mark where you want the garden, and I'll bring Arlo and Benjamin out here to help clear it, get it done while you're in the city with Teagan. I won't do anything else to the other fields. I just want to help you get started." Heath stood, and I followed his lead, only half a second behind him.

"I can mark it out today. Maybe I should check on the trust fund, too...." Fenris's frown was deep. "Haven't looked at that stupid thing in months."

"You used to get a monthly stipend deposited. Did those stop coming?"

Fenris shrugged in silence.

"Fenris." Heath's tone was a demand for anything more.

"I'll figure it out and let you know. Maybe while I'm in Dallas with Teagan, he can spare an hour or two helping me see what's wrong."

"How are you eating?" I suddenly asked.

"Oh, I still had plenty in the bank. I'm good for a few years just on what I've saved. You don't need to worry about me. Been a wolf for a long time. This isn't the first time Callahan and I have stopped talking to each other. I always make sure to have a shoebox full of cash, too."

"Okay then." With that handled and him seeming comfortable, I finished the tooth-rotting lemonade and left his patio. He waved at Heath and I as we got back into Heath's truck and pulled away.

"He's doing really well, isn't he?" I couldn't help but ask, hoping I wasn't the only person who had the growing sensation that things were changing for the better on this one front.

"He is," Heath confirmed. "I'm really proud of him. Getting him out of a large pack, letting him have some freedom... It's been really healthy for him."

I couldn't help but smile.

"Exactly. I hope he continues to get comfortable, maybe finally open up to us. I still wonder about what his real name is."

It was one thing Heath and I hadn't asked about, trying to respect the privacy of the old werewolf. He wasn't as old as Teagan by any means, but Fenris carried the weight and trauma of his eight hundred years so much more than Teagan did. When we questioned him about being fluent in German, we had decided not to pry beyond that specific detail. I knew there was something about Fenris we all decided to ignore. I had only seen it that once, hearing him tell the matriarch of that malicious witch family that Fenris wasn't his real name. It was a limited sample size from a bad night when I had been dealing with a lot of shit happening all at once. Some of it still gave me nightmares, not frequently, but I would never forget my fear as that witch captured my will.

"We'll give him the time he needs to feel comfortable and hope one day, he'll trust us with it," Heath said, his tone telling me he was looking on the bright side.

"I hope so. I bet it's something super proper. I mean, why else would he decide on a name that harkens to Fenrir, the apocalyptic wolf of Norse mythology? It's probably the exact opposite."

Heath's chuckle at my theory brought my smile back as we headed to our next stop.

6

CHAPTER SIX

As we made the rounds, Heath listened to Rose complain about the job market, and Ranger bitched about his stairs. Shamus was trying to convince his children he didn't need them hovering, and I tried to step in, Heath laughing as I did.

For all the respect they had for their father, Stacy and Kody thought he was a walking disaster. Stacy finally dropped it and left for her apartment while Kody stuck around, not having found his own way in the world yet. He still lived with Shamus, and we were all wondering what he would finally decide on and when.

I couldn't worry about Kody as much as I wanted to because when Heath and I were finally done with seeing everyone, we found the three youngest members of our little community in our living room. Carey didn't look up as she walked Arlo through what seemed to be a nasty little piece of work for a math problem. I made a face as I listened to her describe it, glad I wasn't in school anymore. Benjamin tried to help, but he was a quiet young man, and Arlo was hitting adulthood and could be intimidating as he grew into his dominance.

"Look at them," I said softly. "The future."

"Getting sentimental?" Heath asked as he finished putting away our small load of groceries, then leaned on the bar next to me.

"A bit," I admitted. "Probably because I miss Dirk."

"Yeah..." Heath touched my lower back as he planted a kiss on my cheek. "But you don't have to miss him forever. It'll be fine."

"Where did Dirk go?" Arlo asked loudly, his head popping up, curiosity lighting up his eyes. "I keep hearing about how he was going somewhere, but no one wants to say more."

"Don't eavesdrop," Carey snapped. "And stay focused on this. I don't want to be doing my homework for another hour because you keep getting distracted."

I watched as Arlo's lip began to twitch before one side rolled up in a silent growl. It was a perfectly natural response for a werewolf coming into his own, his hormones making his temper harder to control. I could even smell it, Arlo's indignant rage at how she talked to him, the more dominant werewolf in the group. She didn't even rank as a human.

But not in my house and not directed at Carey.

"Don't," I whispered softly, an order I didn't feel needed to be loud. Heath's back was turned to them, but in the corner of my eye, I saw his eyes shift from human to wolf, becoming the ice blue I knew well. He didn't need to know who I had just said that to, only that I said it.

Arlo sank, his face going blank as he focused on his homework again.

"Teenagers," Heath said, his tone not matching the fury in his eyes. He was doing his best, too. There was only one thing Arlo or Benjamin could ever do to earn Heath's ire—not his annoyance, not his disappointment, but his anger.

If they ever threatened Carey, he would no longer treat them as young men who weren't fully adults. He would fight them as if they were genuine threats to his family. They were. Any werewolf or werecat was. While Heath and I could handle our own protection, we trusted Arlo and Benjamin with Carey. If they lost control and bit her, she would have to survive the Change or die. It was the only rule that made the boys equal to the adult werewolves around them.

"Hormones," I agreed, nodding lightly. Arlo seemed to have already cooled, knowing he had crossed a line. Even though the growl was probably instinct over intention, it was important to learn to control those impulses.

Working on something for the teens to eat, an easy snack, until Heath and I decided on dinner, I watched as Carey slowly found a way to shift away from Arlo, and because she did that, Heath steadily calmed down until his eyes went back to normal. It was a deft play on Carey's part. At sixteen, she knew how to deal with the predators around her better than some of the predators themselves. Heath eventually left, heading outside, comfortable everyone in the room was calm and safe again.

"All right, mine is done. You can get the rest of your own done," Carey announced.

"But..." Arlo looked as if he wanted to ask for more help but quickly thought better. "Thanks for helping with the harder ones. I can get it from here."

"Cool, because I can't do your homework for you," she said as she stuffed her books away. "Benjamin, don't help him, either."

"Do you want to play something?" Benjamin asked, smiling at her as she stood up. "I'm done with mine, too."

"Yeah!" Carey grinned as they left the living room and ducked into her room. The door was left open for Heath's peace of mind.

Arlo looked annoyed as he kept working, throwing glances at Carey's room every time he heard her laugh. When I walked by to get something, the scent of his jealousy was thick in the air, so was his attraction. I had always wondered if one of the boys would fall for her, and it almost fit that it was Arlo.

But there was a problem I noticed while walking by.

There was also a faint bit of Benjamin's own crush hidden under Arlo's stronger scent, which Arlo would have caught.

Oh, no. No, no. We can't have this.

I wanted to laugh even as I realized the problem we faced.

"Snacks are done!" I called out, then looked around,

wondering where my fiancé had wandered off to. I'd put together a platter of veggies and dips, adding some fruits and cheese for anyone who wanted those instead. I could have gotten a store-bought tray, but I enjoyed the process of setting it up while watching everyone moving around the house. I could still close it up and save it for another day or later if I wanted a late-night snack.

"Thanks, Jacky," Carey said as she grabbed a carrot.

"You're welcome," I said as I walked past her, heading outside to see where Heath had gone. I found him easily enough, sitting in the security building.

"Just looking for a private place to get away from them or spying on all of us?" The screens were on, rotating through the different camera angles for maximum coverage of my property.

"Somewhere quiet to get the scents out of my nose," he explained. "Arlo isn't doing poorly. I reacted strongly."

"He growled at her. You handled it well enough, letting me tell him to quit it." I stood in front of him, blocking his view of the screens. "He handled it well by immediately realizing he wasn't in control and adjusting his behavior."

"It's only going to get harder with him, you know. It'll get harder before it gets easier." Heath groaned softly. "In a couple more years, he'll have the right to challenge others in the pack. We say Dirk is the lowest-ranking member, but he's an adult. Technically, Arlo and Benjamin are lower, even under Teagan. Once Arlo is allowed to challenge someone, he could get hurt or could hurt someone. He'll get temperamental, a lot like Dirk's and Ranger's issues. They've calmed down, he will as well, but it's a storm I'm not excited to weather."

"How has Kody gotten through it without that sort of problem?" Shamus's younger son was still in his early twenties, but I couldn't remember seeing anything like what Heath was describing. "Or Stacy. This can't only be a male problem."

"It's not. Shamus is old enough and dominant enough to keep him in his place until Kody is truly ready. He'll get to be more like his father, I bet, but Shamus knows how to guide him. Stacy is not so dominant as to want to fight for her place, not until she has to." Heath sighed, one of exhaustion. "Teagan loves those boys with everything he has, and he's the father they both deserve. One who will just love them where adults have failed them before. But when it comes to Arlo's maturity as a werewolf, that will come to me... sooner rather than later."

"Are you worried?" I asked gently.

"No, not about Arlo growing up. He's an honorable young man, only battling the same monster we all do," Heath said, shaking his head slowly. "I'm uncomfortable with myself. I don't like when I have to fight my own instincts around the boys. I don't want to ever be in the position of wanting to fight them, wolf to wolf. I have a hard boundary with Carey's safety, but I never want to have to enforce it. I stepped out once I felt comfortable enough to do that to clear my head."

I felt immense guilt about why I had come to find my fiancé, knowing what I knew now.

"I trust you," I murmured as I sat in his lap, wrapping my arms around him. His arms became a vice around my waist, not too tight but firm enough to make sure I felt secure. "With Arlo and Benjamin. I think everyone in the pack does."

"Thank you." He kissed my neck. "Did you need something, or were you just checking on me?"

"Now, you have to promise me you won't react poorly if I tell you something interesting I learned after you left the house," I said, not really answering his question.

"Jacky..."

"Promise."

"I promise. Whatever it is, you can handle it, and I won't react to it poorly." He was telling the truth, his scent surrounding me with love and worry.

"Arlo and Benjamin are both crushing on Carey," I said, deciding to be blunt. "I caught their scents as I was grabbing something from the living room and had to pass by Arlo."

"Fuck," Heath groaned, his head becoming deadweight on my shoulder. "No..."

"Yeah."

"Landon is going to fucking kill one of them."

"I bet it's been brewing for a while, and we've been too busy to notice," I said, trying to theorize why I only noticed today. "I mean, looking at how the boys hang out with her and their limited availability in a friend group...."

"I think you have the right of it," Heath said, lifting his head. "They've been spending a lot of time together, and we've been busy with other stuff, like getting Dirk safely to his father's. I don't doubt others might know and didn't feel the need to say anything."

"You won't do anything, right?"

"I won't do anything. I'll watch for any signs a fight might break out, but I don't think Arlo has it in him to attack Benjamin unless Benjamin pushes him, and Benjamin would never."

"If they fight, Carey will never date either of them," I pointed out. Carey had yet to have a proper boyfriend, go on a real date, or anything similar. She almost had that chance once, just a year ago, with a human boy from her school. She didn't have the patience for werewolf bullshit, though, so I didn't have much hope for Benjamin, much less Arlo.

Beyond the werewolf part of the equation, I had a feeling about who Carey might have a crush on. Carey spent most of her time with a boy in Mozambique, talking all day and night by any means necessary—Jabari's son, Makalo. I didn't ask her about Makalo because I didn't want confirmation. She didn't bring him up to me or anyone else. We all knew they spent a lot of time together, the physical distance not hampering their friendship at all.

"You're right. They need to learn to deal with this sort of thing. Emotions like that are a natural part of life. Carey will need to learn to establish boundaries if one of them asks her out or causes trouble with the other." He wouldn't get involved outside of safety reasons. There were only two things Heath wanted for Carey that truly mattered. One was that she enjoyed a normal life—we had to settle for as normal as we could give her. The second was her safety.

"I think we can trust her," I murmured, kissing his forehead. "And if she needs help with those boundaries, we'll be there to back her up."

"If Benjamin or Arlo try to test any of those boundaries, they're going to learn exactly how long I can make an order stick," Heath huffed, but I knew he would be fine.

The more I saw him with the other werewolves, the more sides I saw of him, though that didn't change him in my eyes. Everything he did always went back to the root of who he was. He was a man who would do anything for his family, but *anything* still had its limits. He wasn't unreasonable. His responses always felt appropriate for the situation, and I knew that came from his years of experience. He wasn't perfect, but he tried his best. Today was evidence of that. He'd lost his temper more than he wanted but hadn't acted on it.

"I love you," I whispered in his ear before nipping his ear lobe.

"I love you, too," he murmured, pulling me closer. He was silent for a moment, then chuckled.

"What?"

"Teenagers. Somehow, some way, they always end up the center of attention and distract us by giving us more to worry about."

I laughed. If that wasn't true, I didn't know what could be.

"I have a feeling I'm going to miss Dirk even more in a few days when it sinks in that we'll only have the teens around," I said as my laughter came to its end. By Heath's blank face, he'd already figured that out. We still had Landon, but he was going to be moping for most of the next two weeks.

"Maybe we can adopt them out," I said pragmatically, wondering if there was anyone who would be willing to do it.

"We'll drop them on Landon."

"I like that plan...." It would keep Landon busy and might keep from other problems with Arlo and Benjamin. Maybe. I knew we'd have to warn him before he figured it out. I was willing to deal with all of that, though, for one important reason.

"We might finally get some alone time..."

Heath finally gave me his wolfish smile, a glint in his eye.

"Exactly."

7

CHAPTER SEVEN

I stared at my phone, knowing Dirk would be calling any second. He'd promised. After Heath and I did the house visits and dealt with our pack of teenagers, we got to work on things around the house, going our separate ways. It was life stuff. I budgeted for the next two weeks, handled payroll Oliver had left for me, and answered emails, one from Zuri, wondering if she could tell Jabari yet.

Soon, Zuri. Just waiting on Dirk's call.

I knew why she was anxious. She wanted to prepare him for the fallout as quickly as possible. I knew I would stand by Dirk, and if she trusted Jabari, I would, too. There may not be any fallout, but we prepared for the worst-case scenario, not the best.

I woke up my computer to see the flight's estimated arrival time in Berlin, hoping everything was still on track and the plane hadn't crashed or anything crazy like that. During his layover, I texted Dirk to tell him that Niko would be there, and he'd replied, but I needed to hear from him once he landed, not only for Zuri but for me. I needed to know if he was still okay doing this by himself. I needed to know if Niko followed through and arrived to pick him up. If he didn't, I would bring Dirk home, and Niko would never see him again.

"Any word?" Heath asked as he peeked into the office.

"Not yet, but his flight is ten minutes away from landing. Soon," I answered, putting my phone down and looking away from the computer. "He's been flying or dealing with layovers for fourteen hours, so it probably won't be a long conversation, but...."

"I know," he said gently. "Want me to leave you to it, or would you like me here in case he wants to talk to me?"

"He'll reach out to you if he needs you," I said, smiling. "But you can sit in here with me all you want."

Smiling, he closed us in the office and sat down in the armchair near my windows. He grabbed a book, one I believed he had already read, and focused on it, leaving me with silent comfort. There was no expectation on me for conversation. He would be there if I needed him.

The minutes ticked by slowly, but the moment my phone buzzed, I frantically grabbed it and answered, my mind barely registering that Dirk's name was on my screen.

"Hey! How were the flights?" I asked before he could even say hello.

"Exhausting but I'm here. Walking towards luggage

claim now. Let's hope he didn't convince himself not to show...."

"He's your father. He'll be there." I wasn't sure I believed my words or that I hid my trepidation well enough.

"He's Niko," Dirk said softly. "No matter how well you know him, he can still be a mystery."

Coming from Dirk, that spoke volumes. I knew my brother in Germany was one of the most shadowy of my siblings. He hid a lot of his personal life from everyone, including the siblings he'd had for centuries. It was always like that with him. He didn't offer much about himself, and what he usually explained to me was something the rest of the family already knew.

He got angry with me over secrets, but I bet he has hundreds...

"He loves you. Trust me. I already talked to him," I said, sighing.

"Why don't I like the way you said that?"

"Bad phrasing," I said quickly. "Look, he's going to be there. He'll probably be at baggage claim. I wish I could give you advice, but I can't. Are you still on board with me letting Zuri get Jabari up to speed?"

"Yeah, don't change the plans with anyone else. Steps, right? Tell Niko, let Zuri tell Jabari, then we figure out how to... tell everyone else." He paused, clearing his throat. "How's Landon?"

"He's missing you, but he'll be fine. Call him next when you have the chance. If you want, tell him how your trip is going, and he'll tell only me what you think I need to know or hear."

"I might do that...." Dirk chuckled. "Since we both know you're hovering right now,. I got to sleep on both flights, not a lot of sleep, but enough. You should probably get some yourself."

"I'll be fine. How far until baggage claim?"

"I'll let you know when I'm there."

We talked about airplane food until that moment.

"Okay... now I need to find—"

"When did you get such an American accent?" Niko asked, the phone picking it up.

Startled, I nearly dropped my cell phone.

"Damn it, Niko, don't fucking scare me like that," Dirk said as I struggled to keep my phone from hitting the desk.

"Welcome to Berlin," Niko said, sounding stiff. "Who is that?"

Dirk said something in German, and Niko replied in kind.

I'm learning German.

"Well, he's here," Dirk said, his accent now as thick as I'd ever heard it. "Talk to you later, Jacky."

"Let me talk to my sister," Niko said, and I could see him holding out his hand. "While you get your things."

"Jacky?" Dirk didn't need to ask.

"Let him on," I said, sighing heavily.

There was quiet for a moment. I could hear the activity around the airport, but nothing else. I waited, wondering if Niko was actually going to say anything.

"Now that he's distracted... he looks good... comfortable."

"He's had time to adjust. He needed that time."

"We all do... but that's not why I wanted to speak to you. I've had time to think, and I wanted to ask something of you."

"I'm all ears...." *And full of worry.*

"I would like to request that you keep Heath from contacting him while he's visiting me. Heath is his Alpha, and I would prefer not to have him calling to order Dirk to do anything, even if it's something simple. I don't dislike him, but from this moment, he's here as my son, and I won't have pack business getting in the way of that time."

I looked at Heath, who was still staring at his book, but I knew he was listening intently. When he looked up, his eyes were ice blue, but he nodded, silently agreeing with the request.

"That won't be a problem," I told my brother. "Dirk knows to call us if he needs anything, and if there's something Dirk needs to know while he's gone, it'll come from me, not his Alpha."

"Perfect." He said something in German and didn't translate. "With that settled, goodbye, Jacky. I will let you know if something happens."

I said my goodbye as Niko hung up. With a heavy sigh, I looked at Heath as he closed his book and held it in his lap.

"Remind me to start taking German lessons soon."

"I'll join you," he said with a knowing smile. "How do you feel?"

"Nervous as hell, but he's there. They're together. Niko will probably drive Dirk back to his territory, or maybe they'll spend a day in Berlin first. I don't know. Are you sure you're okay with that request from Niko?"

"Well, it wasn't a request for me. He was telling you he wanted you to play interference, but he didn't need to. I have no problem with it. There's nothing I could think to order Dirk to do while he's visiting his father except to stay safe and... I'm not going to order people to do that. If there's trouble, Dirk will make his choices, and I hope he at least calls you if there is."

"Or Landon. There was no stipulation about Landon, but I bet that's because Niko doesn't know about them yet. Hopefully, Dirk finds a moment to reach out to Landon before things get too busy. I don't think there's anything planned for the trip, but... people invent ways to be busy on these sorts of trips."

"Of course. Dirk's gone back to where he grew up. He'll probably want to visit old friends, see favorite places, do stuff with Niko." Heath shrugged. "Landon knows that. Don't worry about him. If Landon wants to talk to Dirk, he'll reach out, and I'm sure Dirk will put aside some time." He put his book down on the small table beside the recliner. "What's next for you? Telling Zuri she's in the clear?"

"That's easy enough, then I'm going to bed," I said, sending Zuri an email to let her know both that she could tell Jabari and that I was going to sleep. She got back quickly, telling me she would try to keep Jabari from calling for more information so I could sleep.

"And with that...." I stood, Heath doing the same. We didn't head straight for bed, though. Going outside barefoot, I walked into the grass around my home and stared at the trees, my own form of meditation. A few minutes of this and I knew I would finally be able to relax and sleep.

It was nearly perfect until I heard a howl.

"Who was that?" I asked Heath, knowing he'd stayed on the front porch. "Someone in the pack just out tonight for a run?"

"None of mine," he answered. "It wasn't close, though."

"Yeah, I don't feel any new werewolves in my territory," I said, frowning at the sky. "We must have someone wandering around. This is the fourth time since the beginning of the year. A spy wouldn't reveal themselves with a howl or anything, right?"

"There's a chance they're trying to keep us on edge. Or maybe it's someone looking for me, a lone wolf looking to join the pack. It could just be lone wolves running by, announcing themselves as they pass since they know I'm in the region. If the pack caught a wolf who didn't, it would be a fight. I'll call Shamus and ask if he and Kody can run the edge of your territory—"

"No...." Shaking my head, I knew what I wanted to do. If I couldn't get my moment of peace standing in my yard, I could do what any other smart werecat would.

I haven't gone on a solo run in a long time.

"Go inside and read your book," I said, beginning to strip off my clothes. "I'm going for a run of my border."

"You'll be careful, right? It's probably nothing, but...." His concern was reasonable. Baiting a werecat to the edge of their territory was a smart way for werewolves to create ambushes.

With a nod, I finished getting undressed and began to Change, letting it roll through me. A quick but painful thirty seconds as my body transitioned between forms until I was the five-hundred-pound cat I had become nearly fifteen years ago.

Heath stayed on the porch as I ran into the trees. Sniffing, I caught the patrol path the pack would take when they decided to do night watches, but there was no one out tonight. I could feel them all, knowing they were all at home. If any of them had howled, they would have sounded closer, but I always first asked Heath if they were one of the pack because assumptions could kill.

Running for the edge, I kept alert as I reached the edge of my border but didn't cross it. Without stopping, I turned and began to run at full speed, catching thousands of scents along the way. None of them were werewolves I didn't recognize, though, and there was no second howl.

I would have been bothered with Dirk having just left, but this wasn't the first time another supernatural came close to the territory, and nothing happened. It probably wouldn't be the last. I had rogue werecats coming close, though none had tested my border in some time. I or one of my werewolves would catch their scents near the border, but none ever tried to take my territory.

The howl tonight could have been as simple as what Heath said. When werewolves passed through claimed territory, they would try to speak to someone from the pack to keep there from being any trouble if they didn't want it.

I moved fast, not because I wanted to go home quickly, but to stretch my legs and exhaust myself so I couldn't think anymore. Maybe with that, I could get to sleep just a bit faster once I got home. By the time I got back, my legs were tired. Heath had taken my clothes inside and left a robe on the patio. Changing back into my human form, I wrapped it around myself and went inside.

He was already in the bedroom, in bed with that book that was quickly put down as I walked in.

"Feeling better?"

"Yeah, I don't think the werewolf came within a hundred feet of the territory," I said, dropping the robe and crawling into bed.

Heath's wolfish smile told me if I wanted, I could get even more exhausted before closing my eyes.

I took him up on his offer.

CHAPTER EIGHT

"Jacky!"

I blinked several times, trying to wake myself up. I looked down, trying to remember what I had been doing.

Oh, accounting... no wonder I fell asleep at my desk.

With a yawn, I got up to find out why Carey was calling my name. It wasn't urgent. I knew what that sounded like. I found her in the kitchen and wondered why it looked like someone had dumped flour on her head. A small smile began to form as I saw the mess. It looked like a bakery had exploded in my kitchen.

"Carey..." I reached out and ran a finger over one of my counters. With a small lick, I tasted sugar, flour, and I was certain there was some cocoa in it as well. "What happened?"

"I've been trying to make something, and I'm following the recipe, but it's not... working." She huffed and ran her hand through her hair just like her father did.

Except when he did it, he wasn't standing in the middle of a baking crime against humanity.

"Let me see it," I said, chuckling. "Explain the problem while I read."

She started telling me how the mixture wasn't turning out the way the recipe said. I wasn't one to bake from scratch, but I could get by if I followed clear instructions from a good recipe. I had cheats, like cookies from a cake mix.

As she told me about it, I read through what she was trying to do. It was a devil's food cake, a classic chocolate, but it was a recipe credited to the 1800s and had icing I had never heard of. I pulled out my phone to figure out what boiled icing was, only to discover it was normally called Italian meringue.

"Who are you making this for?" I asked, chuckling. "It has you making Italian meringue for the icing. I've never done that before."

"It's Landon's favorite cake. I know he's down since Dirk left and I wanted to do something nice for him." Carey groaned. "But it's a disaster. He'll be over for dinner tonight, and it's just... It's not going to be ready if I don't figure it out now! I was hoping to surprise him by bringing it out for dessert!"

Oh, it's Friday already? Where did my week go? Dirk left on Monday.

"He might be late. He went to Dallas to check on the group there, so we should have time." I put the recipe down, throwing myself into it with her. It was a sweet gesture, so I wasn't going to question it. She wanted to make this cake, so we were going to make this cake.

"That's right. Him and Dad, yeah? I mean, Dad has his own stuff, too. So does Landon."

"Yeah, but they're using the excuse of errands to make sure Teagan is handling everyone with him well enough."

"You know, it's Friday. Shouldn't Teagan be off work today and coming back?"

"I don't know Teagan's schedule, but I think there's some work going through the weekend, and he won't be back until Sunday." With a shrug, I started reorganizing the kitchen, trying to get the ingredients where I needed them. "It's not my business to know what the pack's involved with, not in their personal lives."

"I don't know how Dad does it, keeping track of everyone all the time. It seems like a lot of work," Carey huffed. "But he does, no matter what. He knows who has a work thing or an anniversary or a birthday. He knows when they need time off or should be somewhere they aren't. Or when they are somewhere they shouldn't be. It's crazy."

"He's... particularly talented at it," I agreed pragmatically. "I think he likes it. He seems comfortable when he's managing all of his werewolves."

"And us."

"You. He doesn't manage me," I countered, smiling as I started measuring things out. Carey joined in, and I caught on to her problem quickly. "Carey, the measurements have to be exact. You can't just scoop as much or as little as you want."

"But I want it to taste extra chocolatey. I think he'll like that."

"It ruins the mix because the dry ingredients and the wet ingredients need to be balanced. That's why recipes exist, so we don't need to figure out what that balance is. Someone else already has. Baking is chemistry, and I know you're good at chemistry. You don't throw in whatever you want while you're doing stuff in the school's lab, do you?"

She emptied the double helping of cocoa and got the proper amount. She didn't answer my question, which worried me a little, but I let it go.

We got the mix on the first time this time, and I was able to get it into the oven before starting on the icing.

"Now, the hard part," I mumbled. Carey nodded as we both stared at the ingredients for the Italian meringue. "You ready for this?"

"Not at all, but I've got you. I think we can make something decent."

With a grin, I got to work, loving that she trusted me like that. She had me, so we could make this happen. She had me, so she could face any challenge.

In my heart, she was already my daughter even though Heath and I hadn't tied any knots or walked down any aisles yet.

We haven't even started planning a wedding... but it doesn't matter.

We worked together, an experienced team as we tried

to get the cake ready for the inevitable judgment of Landon Everson. Since it was from his sister, I had hope he would go easy on her if it wasn't the best-tasting cake he'd ever had. If he learned I had a hand in it, the judgment would probably be laid at my feet. Landon had a funny way of showing he liked me.

We finished only thirty minutes before the men got back, Heath coming in first. Carey disappeared the moment we were finished, and it was tucked away in the fridge. I was glad I cleaned up quickly, or it would have been exposed as Landon walked in behind him, sniffing the air. Seeming satisfied with something, Landon elbowed his father.

"See? She's not a housewife. She didn't sit here and cook dinner for you just because you weren't here. Aren't you glad I put in an order for dinner?"

"Thank you," Heath said, chuckling as he shook his head. His eyes were on me, and I could tell he wasn't upset or disappointed. "But I could have texted her to make sure. What if she had something for herself and Carey since we were running later than intended?"

Landon only shrugged and walked back out.

"What's going on?" I asked, crossing my arms.

"Landon got something for us to eat from his favorite steakhouse. When I said I would text you to make sure you weren't already working on something, he took my phone and said it would ruin the surprise. That you weren't a housewife, as if I thought you were."

"Is he in a better mood today? He seemed like it just now." I was hoping so.

"He is... though we started the day with Dirk calling him. They talked the entire drive to Dallas. Dirk is doing fine, too. Apparently, he'll be in Berlin this weekend seeing some old friends. He misses all of us, but he's glad to see Niko again... more than he thought he would be."

"He's been sparse with me over the phone, so I'm glad he was comfortable telling Landon that," I said, thinking about how awkward Dirk could be with me. He always had those moments, even if they had grown fewer. He tried to hide things, but I was never really sure why. He wasn't as shy about being my nephew anymore, but there were still times when I saw him pull away from it or any of his relations to my family. It didn't surprise me that he was more comfortable telling Landon things because that was a relationship he'd chosen. I was one he couldn't get away from, and I came with more baggage.

A second later, Landon was back, carrying our dinner, packaged nicely in one of those insulated bags. I knew when it was on the table, it would still be warm enough that no one would need to reheat anything.

"Carey, dinner!" I called out. "They're home!"

Carey was there quickly, and we set the table while Heath went to change out of his suit and Landon unpacked dinner. By the time Heath was back, we had everything ready.

"So, what does Teagan have going on? He's back Sunday, right?" I asked, remembering how Carey had mentioned it to me. "Is he doing all right with everyone?"

"It's going well. He's agreed to head a team for my

company, so..." Heath trailed off, chuckling. "You don't care about this, do you?"

"Not the business stuff, no, but knowing he's okay is something I wanted to hear." With a smile, I waved for him to continue, then started eating.

"He's not working all weekend, right, Dad? You wouldn't make Teagan do that," Carey said before he could tell us more.

"No, not at all. He has a couple of meetings tomorrow, but both of those are for his own clients. He's finished with what I needed. He's going to visit the Market after, then take another night in the city to relax," Heath explained. "Teagan hasn't gone in some time, and he wanted to look around."

"That's the... pocket dimension or whatever, right?" Carey's curiosity was clear. It surprised me that she had to ask. She was so knowledgeable about a lot of supernatural places and things I figured she would know more about it than I did. I tried my best not to go at all and didn't care to make it a regular thing. Too many supernaturals from all over the world, too far from home, and a bit complicated to get access to since it required a specific type of currency to get into the Market. I always used Heath's stash when he wanted to take me.

"The Market is a pocket dimension with doors all over the world. It's the biggest supernatural marketplace in the world. It originally was a fae black market and many of the fae still consider it as such. However, for other supernaturals, it's more of a...." Heath paused, clearly trying to find the best world for it.

"It's like a magic mall," Landon said before shoving a piece of steak into his mouth.

We waited for him to chew and swallow, Carey clearly wanting to hear more. Heath seemed to be willing to let Landon give the explanations. Landon looked around and, realizing what he had done, he sighed as he put his silverware down.

"It has different places to eat or relax, foods from all over the world tucked between shops started by hundreds of different supernaturals. The buildings look like they were plucked from different places during different time periods, all of them different shapes and sizes. There are a few castles, temples, a skyscraper, and more. Inside those buildings or attached to them are doors. Most of them will lead to random broom closets if you aren't supposed to be using them. You can only exit the Market from the place where you were allowed in. Only the people in charge are rumored to use it for traveling around the world, leaving through whatever door they want. Each door has someone working at it. Dirk and I have gone for stuff before. We've also gone just to hang out... before he was a werewolf, and we had to keep that secret. Couldn't risk running into someone who recognized him. I would take you, but I don't think Pa would appreciate it."

"I wouldn't," Heath confirmed. "It's only for my pack business unless someone has their own coins to get in. Teagan has his own supply. I gave him more to pay for the others, so he didn't burn through them."

"How does he get them?" I asked, frowning.

"He's an expert in supernatural law. He has a small bag of them from before he joined the Dallas pack, apparently for helping others with legal troubles." Heath shrugged. "But knowing he worked for those, I didn't want him to waste them on the others."

"Maybe we can do a family trip," I said, giving Heath a look. He stared me down. I knew why taking Carey was off the table, but I disagreed a little. He didn't want her to become more entrenched in the supernatural world. I figured it was an experience most humans didn't know existed, but she could go safely with us. A few streets of living history with a fake sky in a contained world that very rarely had trouble. "It's a relatively safe place, Heath."

"She's right, Pa. The one of the few time in my life I've heard of trouble in the Market was with a Tribunal Executioner there, and it was resolved without anyone else being injured even though it almost leveled the block. The other was King Brion during the turmoil around him coming back and it was minimal damage."

Heath narrowed his eyes at Landon.

"Leveled the block..." he repeated back to his son.

"One incident in the countless years that place has existed is a pretty good track record," Landon countered.

"I'll think about it. You're just looking for something to do while Dirk is gone."

"Of course, and spending time with my father and sister is a good thing to pass the time," Landon said. "I like spending time with my family."

"Then say that a little less sarcastically," I called out,

chuckling as he gave me a playful warning growl not to call him out like that.

"Okay, Stepmother," he said, teeth on display.

"Yeah, that's weird," I said quickly as Carey laughed. It was weird. Landon was about a hundred and twenty years older than me. "I'm not your stepmother yet, and you definitely don't need to call me by that title... or any title. Jacky is fine."

With Landon chuckling evilly, we went back to eating. Once plates were cleaned off, Carey grabbed them to clear the table before anyone said they wanted to leave.

"Is there something you want, or is this to butter me up to take you to the Market?" Heath asked, giving his daughter a knowing expression.

"Neither," she declared, lifting her chin defiantly. "I made dessert and want to serve it. Don't leave."

"Dessert?" Heath mouthed at me when she disappeared.

"She wanted to bake today, so she baked."

"I'm always down for free dessert." Landon shrugged. "But you did make sure she didn't poison us, right?"

"I wasn't going to tell you I helped in case you didn't like it. You'll be sweet to Carey but not me," I admitted softly enough that Carey wouldn't hear. "But no poison unless werewolves are allergic to chocolate. I know you're not, so don't try that." I listened to her shuffling around the kitchen, rinsing the dishes, and washing her hands before she got the cake. A moment later, she walked out with the cake.

"Here is it!"

Carey put her creation in the center of the table.

"It's chocolate cake with Italian meringue as the icing," she explained, holding out a knife for someone else to do the cutting. I took it, and she turned to Landon, who showed his surprise, totally caught off guard by what Carey had done. "I got Jacky to help, but she just guided me. It's your favorite, right? I remember this was your favorite."

"It is..." Landon confirmed.

"You've been down because Dirk is gone, so... I knew you were coming over for dinner tonight—"

She didn't finish as Landon wrapped his arms around her in a hug.

I cut the cake, glancing at Heath, who only had eyes for his children at that moment. I grabbed a few small plates and put a slice in front of everyone, the biggest for Landon. We ate the cake, which turned out pretty good. When Heath finished his, he sighed.

"We'll go to the Market on Sunday as a family," he announced. "Once the others are back."

CHAPTER NINE

S unday came quickly. I woke up and got ready to leave. Carey was already up and ready to go. It was only nine in the morning, normally too early for her to be up, especially since she met Makalo, and they started staying up all night.

"They're not due back for another couple of hours," I reminded her. "You can sit around for a little while."

"Yeah, but why rush to get ready later when I can be ready now?" she countered. "I get why Dad doesn't want us to leave before they get back, but I am so excited. You know, I've heard about the Market, but they've never once considered taking me or explaining everything about it. It's just been a pack thing. I'm excited. Once they're back, I want to be out the door. I can't wait to see it."

"I'm glad you're excited," I said, smiling as I went about my morning routine. I emailed Oliver about the numbers from business the night before, glad to see Kick

Shot was still making a profit. It had never done that while I was running it. Now mostly a silent owner, I distanced myself from being the public face of the company more and more. I was becoming too well known, too infamous, and that sort of attention on a business had repercussions.

Kick Shot was my baby, and thinking about it, it paralleled the changes in my life. I'd started with a tiny shack of a bar and no one to fill it except those who wanted to drink in a small place with no judgment. I had seen my tiny bar burned down, and the new thing built in its place was completely different. It represented a different time. Something with a foundation, something worth more than sentimental value. Something that didn't try to hide from the world but rather looked like it invited the world in for a good time and good food. Just as I invited people into my world to find whatever they were looking for, be it safety and security, loyal friends to watch their backs or just a family.

Oliver and I had grown distant in the last year, but it wasn't anything against him or me. He was a young man with a goal for the future, wanting to run successful businesses and be part of something bigger, but he was still a human. He nearly got hurt once, and he had taken a life to save Dirk's. Letting him stay focused on Kick Shot and out of my troubles was better for his mental health. He liked being here, but one day, I knew he might ask to move on, and I accepted that. He would always be mine, but maybe one day, I would have a business outside my territory he could establish.

That's not a bad idea....

Nodding, I started writing down that little idea. Something in the city for him, where he could manage the mansion and live there to keep it from being a cold, empty home. Dirk didn't live with Oliver anymore, so there was no one he had to help with rent. He would probably enjoy the city more than the small town we lived in, anyway.

I'll see what he thinks. There might be some niche we can try to fill in Dallas, and he can head the project. My siblings all own multiple businesses. I can manage two. Plus, it would be nice to establish that the city is mine with something, even though it's not my official territory.

"You seem deep in thought," Heath said as he walked in, followed by Landon, Shamus, and Ranger.

"Wondering if Oliver might want to move to Dallas and try something new for me. Maybe a new bar or a lounge...." Shrugging, I pushed my notes aside. "It's a thought for another day. Do you four need the room?"

"No, they're just following me around." Heath found his favorite spot.

"Ranger lost his patience with the boys and called me. Kody didn't want to deal with them, so I called Heath. He was already with Landon. Said we could bring them here and get a break until Teagan came back to claim them," Shamus explained, grinning as he leaned on my window. "But now there are three teenagers in your living room."

"So, we're all hiding in here with you," Landon

finished, sitting in a chair opposite of my desk, Ranger taking the other one.

I gave Heath a look, but he only smiled, knowing what I was thinking. We had Carey, two teenage werewolves with crushes on her, and Landon in the same building.

Disaster was imminent.

"Well, that's nice. I was just getting the Saturday report from Oliver and started thinking. I don't have much going on."

"You want him to manage the city for you," Heath said, catching on to what I said earlier. "He'll be the head of your mansion household, keeping it clean and ready for your family if they visit and managing whatever business you set up in the city."

"He'd have staff," I promised, not liking how much work that sounded like it would be.

"Hire out cleaning services for now. Oliver can just schedule them and make sure they show up. From there, have him take point on starting whatever nightlife spot you have in mind and give him the ability to hire the underlings he wants." Landon grabbed a notepad and started writing all of that down. "You have the money for this, right?"

"Yeah, unless Hasan takes back what he gave me years ago," I said, sighing. "He could... Maybe. I don't actually know."

"Wait, you live off Hasan's money?" Ranger frowned deeply at me. "Seriously?"

"When I left after being Changed, he gave me a

substantial portion of his wealth to establish my own way in the world without needing to worry about finances," I explained. "It's grown, thanks to people smart with investments, but not by much. I've only been a supernatural for...." I had to do the mental math. "About fifteen years. I've only had that money for eleven of those. I don't think he'll take back the money, though."

"It would be a low blow," Shamus said, nodding. "Still, is it in the same accounts you received it in?"

"Yeah." It took me a second to realize what he was saying. "Oh..."

"You might want to move the money and assets into accounts he doesn't know about," Shamus continued. "For safekeeping, just in case. Clearly, you know him better than me, and I don't want to imply he would, but...."

"You're not offending me," I promised. "It's not a bad idea. I'll need to hire a new accountant since I share one with him, and I wouldn't doubt he gets reports on me." I had never considered how much I had leaned on my family to get the basics of supernatural life. In one simple conversation, I was facing the fact I could lose everything if Hasan really wanted to make that happen. "Damn."

"I know a company," Heath said, but his expression was wary. "If you're okay with sharing. I won't have access to your finances or anything."

"We'll work it out," I said, shaking my head, trying to not let this weigh on me. "We have other things to do today. We'll worry about all of this tomorrow, so we can let Carey have fun at the Market without being distracted."

"Oh, you two are taking Carey to the Market?" Ranger looked between us, his eyes wide. "Heath?"

"Jacky didn't convince him. I brought it up, Jacky was on my side, and Carey was able to convince him without even trying. That's why we're waiting on everyone to get back. You two will be in charge for the rest of the day when we leave," Landon said, looking over his shoulder at Shamus. "Ranger's already proven we made the right call. If he was left with you, the pack, and those boys, he wouldn't have survived it."

"I don't do children," Ranger muttered.

"They take practice, and you were given two teenage boys with no experience. Shamus was too busy for them, though," Heath said, clearly apologetic. "You did well. It's the last day and a weekend. No harm done."

"Harm was certainly done," Ranger grumbled. "To my house."

"Oh, no..."

"They played midnight paintball after Ranger went to bed," Heath told me, an evil glint in his eyes.

"They had their paintball guns? I didn't think they would take those to Ranger's house."

"They didn't, yesterday," Ranger growled.

Shamus was grinning behind him, and Landon wouldn't look in his direction.

I had wondered where Heath wandered off to on Saturday, snickering about something he told me I didn't need to worry about.

"What color paintballs?" I inquired innocently. "I like the orange ones... very visible?"

"Hot pink."

I bit my lip, trying not to laugh.

"All over the side of my house," Ranger muttered as though he was going to kill someone.

"We should take the whole pack once Dirk is back," Shamus said brightly, his smile not abating when Ranger pinned him with a dark glare. "It'll be fun! Jacky, you'd come, right?"

"Absolutely," I said, chuckling. "The chance to shoot some of you without it being permanent? I wouldn't miss it for the world."

"I like the idea." Heath crossed his arms, listening to Shamus break down how we would all get there, how to assign teams, and what games to play.

So, we planned a Saturday of paintball for two weeks from now, giving Dirk a week to recover from jet lag and relax after his time in Germany. It was something fun and innocent to do while we all constantly looked over our shoulders, wondering when someone else was going to come for us. Everyone in the room knew we had enemies, and we were constantly watchful. We couldn't let them deprive us of a day to have fun.

At eleven, Heath stood and pulled out his phone.

"They should be back any minute, right?" I asked, knowing Carey was probably getting antsy in the living room. "They haven't entered my territory, but I'll tell you when I feel them."

"Yeah... I'm going to see what the timeline is. They

might have hit traffic, had a flat tire, or something." Heath started calling one, frowning deeply as I heard the call go to voicemail. I watched him try again, and yet another voicemail.

"Do you think they just won't answer while driving?" Shamus asked softly. He had his phone out now, calling someone. I heard the voicemail from across the room.

I heard every call the werewolves made go to voicemail. Teagan, Fenris, Jenny, and Carlos. None of them were picking up, and texts were going unread.

"Shamus, Ranger, call everyone in the pack to come here," Heath said, glaring at his phone. "I want a head count and see if anyone has heard from them. It's not an emergency... not yet, but we have to be serious. If it's a false alarm, I'll take the heat for it."

"I'll go to Dallas and check Teagan's condo," I said, standing and grabbing my phone. "So you can keep the pack together here."

"Landon, go with her," Heath ordered. "In case there's trouble."

"You don't want to go?" Landon sounded confused as he stood. "I have no problem going to Dallas, but...." He gestured at me, stating the obvious without a word.

It surprised me, too. Heath was normally with me on every adventure, heading straight into danger without a second thought. There had never been a danger he hadn't come with me to face if he had the chance—vampires, rescuing me, the Russian werewolf pack, the fae—time and time again.

Now he was sending Landon with me.

"Do you want to interrogate everyone?" Heath asked in return. "Or deal with the boys when they figure out something is wrong, and Teagan isn't back when he's supposed to be? If there's trouble, I trust you to protect her, just like I trust you with Carey. Not that Jacky needs it as much as Carey."

That made more sense than I had considered. Heath was the Alpha. I could no longer be the perfect number one. He had to make sure no one panicked.

We weren't, not yet. For all we knew, phones were dead, left in the wrong bag, or any number of things. They could be on the road and not paying attention or getting lunch before coming back. I knew they weren't in the territory. I had been waiting to feel them enter, but they never had.

When I left the office, Carey jumped up with a smile. I shook my head and watched the worry enter her eyes. The boys weren't paying attention yet, too focused on the game they were playing in my living room, but Carey knew me too well. She knew her brother and father better than anyone.

She knew something was going on that was going to change all of our plans.

10

CHAPTER TEN

"What do you think?" I asked Landon as I drove. He tried to fight me on it, but I was behind the wheel before he had the chance to do anything but give in. I knew he wanted to protect me for Heath, but I wasn't a porcelain doll, and he knew that. I could drive and wasn't afraid of speeding.

"I'm hoping they're just running late, but let's be serious... we're enemies of Callahan and Corissa. We have no allies among the werewolves, not openly or who would help us. We're targets to the werecats who dislike your family, and your werecat allies are few and far between." Landon growled softly. "This is going to be trouble."

"Agreed. We should start thinking about what kind of trouble, who might be at risk, what the plan is...." I was white-knuckling my steering wheel, wondering if we were going to find all these werewolves alive. Teagan, Fenris, Jenny, and Carlos—four werewolves, three of them capable fighters, and two of them several centuries old. It would be a devastating blow if any one of them was dead.

"Let's see if we can find them," Landon said softly, his glare on the road ahead.

I dropped it, but my mind went in every direction. If they were murdered, was it someone trying to kill werewolves, or were they attacking our pack? If they had been taken, why and by whom? Who would help me if I lost a sizable portion of Heath's pack? Zuri, maybe. It was a bigger risk than just helping me with other werecats. No one else in my family would think about lifting a finger. They had no attachment to any of my werewolves, even if they were comfortable with me and Heath, and I couldn't even say all my family even liked my choice of fiancé.

We had no allies in other packs, thanks to Heath's situation with Callahan and Corissa. Rogue packs were considered unprotected by the overall werewolf community, the werewolf version of ex-communication. The only person other werewolves might attempt to help was Teagan, who held a special place in the lives of other werewolves as a Beta. If they did help him, they might do it under the stipulation that he joined their pack and left Heath's.

I pulled into the building's parking, specially designed underground for residents and some guests to park. The security knew Landon and me, having our names, and the few other people Teagan was willing to allow in. We saw no trouble, taking a little ticket to say we could stay for up to seventy-two hours without a problem.

Once parked, Landon led the way. I knew Teagan's building but had never gone up to his new condo. Landon clearly had, not saying anything as he hit the button on the elevator, and we went up, nearly to the top floor.

"Right here," Landon said, pointing to the door. He knocked, and I hit the doorbell, but after a minute, we got no response.

"Shit." Landon pulled his keys from his pocket, lifting one. "I got this."

"Wait..." I reached out and turned the doorknob, anxiety racing through me to find it unlocked. "Don't need a key." Pushing it open, I let Landon go in first. I looked up and down the hall before following him inside.

The condo was clean, as Teagan's home was. We moved slowly, looking over everything. There was nothing broken, nothing thrown around, not a single sign of violence or a fight. Suitcases were in the first hallway, telling me the werewolves never got back on the road to come home.

"Jacky, over here," Landon called out softly. "Teagan, you okay?"

I turned and went into the dining room. Landon was leaning over Teagan, pulling him upright. Jenny was on the floor, her chest rising and falling, but no sign of her being awake.

"Were they... drugged?" Mystified, I went to Jenny's side since Landon had Teagan. Her pulse was steady.

She didn't seem too worse for wear, just sleeping peacefully on the floor of the dining room. "Are there drugs that do this?"

"Carlos is over here, and he's the same," Landon said. He'd gotten Teagan out of the uncomfortable-looking slump and laid on the ground. "And yes, we can all be drugged, but not for long with conventional human drugs. Magical ways of knocking us out can last, though."

"Shit..." I looked around, sniffing, but Fenris wasn't there, and his scent was faded compared to the others. "Fenris isn't here."

"I noticed. Don't eat the food. Don't even sniff it too hard. We'll throw it all in plastic bags and show Pa when we get everyone back. We can't do anything else until these three wake up and tell us what happened or something gives us a sign to find Fenris."

"This is bad, Landon," I said, pushing Jenny's hair back from her face. "How long do you think they've been here?"

"Jacky... they're wearing the same clothes they were when Pa and I checked in on them... on Friday."

I looked up, meeting his eyes as horror filled me. If this had happened during dinner on Friday, we were at least thirty-six hours behind whatever had happened. Landon's concern was thick in the air as I stood up.

"Get some cold water," Landon said as I looked around. "We need to wake them up."

We tried our best. I brought in ice and cold water, but none of it woke up the three werewolves. We tried loud music, and Landon even slapped Carlos a few times, but when it didn't rouse him, he didn't try it on the others. Every moment and every failed attempt, I felt my growing panic when they didn't respond.

"Deep breath, Jacky. We can't panic yet. They seem healthy and unharmed for now," Landon said as my hands started to shake. "I need to investigate them and the condo. There might be a clue." He didn't move, though, only watching me as I figured out what to say, what my next move was.

"I'm going to call Heath and ask him how he wants us to move them. We have to get them back to the house for safety. Maybe they'll wake up." I reached into my pocket as Landon nodded. He moved Carlos closer, then Teagan, so all three werewolves were lying side by side. He looked through their pockets as I waited for Heath to pick up.

"Did you find them?" Heath asked without any greeting.

"Three of them. Teagan, Jenny, and Carlos have been drugged. Landon says they're still wearing the same clothing from Friday, so this must have happened after you two left the city, and they've been unconscious ever since. It looks like they were having dinner. Teagan was slumped over the table. Carlos and Jenny both went to the floor. Maybe they tried to get up and do something before falling into whatever drugged sleep they're in. Fenris is nowhere in the condo. His scent has faded compared to the others'. There's no evidence of violence, so whatever happened was quick and quiet. It had to be. Carlos and Jenny might be drugged, but if Fenris knew someone was going to take him, drugs or not, he would have fought like hell. He would have freaked out just under the drugs, even if he didn't know what it was. Right?" I was certain I knew Fenris that well, but I wasn't one hundred percent.

Landon nodded, looking up for a moment to confirm that.

"Yes, he would have...." Heath was already deep in thought. "It'll be hard to get them out of the building without looking suspicious...."

"That's what I need your help with. I want to get them home where I know they'll be safe with the pack. I want them in our house. We'll make space. It's only Landon and me here, and I don't think we can haul them out without looking like criminals."

"We could ask the BSA for help," Heath suggested. "They can give you two proper cover to get them out of the building to bring them home."

"I won't tell them about Fenris yet...." Nodding, I felt like a plan was coming together. Beyond that, I had a sudden nagging thought. "We should have made them call every day," I said softly.

"Each one of them has a panic button that will immediately notify the entire pack of trouble. I didn't want to treat them like children. We need to figure out how none of them activated any of their security options. Is Landon in the room?"

"Yeah." I turned on speaker phone for Landon to join the conversation.

"What is it, Pa?"

"Find their cellphones and look around Teagan's condo to see if any of his security was tampered with."

"Yes, sir." Landon was out the door in a second.

"We're going to bring their food back to see if we can figure out what was put in it, if it was the food at all," I explained, hoping I was doing enough to help at that moment.

"It needs to be grabbed, but I don't know how I could figure out what might be in it."

"Well, I don't want to ask the BSA to work on it. If one of their agents or lab people are hurt, then we're the ones responsible. Or it could be done with magic or a substance they don't know about yet," I pointed out.

"You're right about that. Perhaps..." Heath groaned. "I don't want to ask."

"Zuri? It's an option, but not one I want to run to. Not right now, not after everything she's helped me with and what's going on with Dirk. She's already been sticking her neck out for us."

"I know, which is why I don't want to ask her. There are other options. If you and Landon need help getting those three in the car, use the BSA. Put all the food in something and bring it with you. I have everyone else in the pack here. Right now, Fenris is the only person missing." Heath made one of those thoughtful hums. "Do you smell any magic? That's the only thing that could knock out one of the moon cursed for two days. Aside from severe injuries, which you said they don't have."

"Landon asked me not to sniff too closely at the food just in case, but the room as a whole doesn't smell like magic. That doesn't mean anything anymore. It could still have been used."

"It was still worth a shot."

"Landon, have you smelled any magic around the condo?" I asked loudly.

"No, but I discovered something," he said, sounding off. I couldn't put my finger on it, but it was there.

I walked out of the dining room to find Landon looking at the suitcases. It seemed he'd dragged more out as well, collecting every bag in the entire condo. There were a good number of them.

"What is it?" I asked. I knew Heath was listening intently, so I kept the phone up where it could pick up what Landon had to say.

"No one had their cellphones on them. They left them in different places. Not a big deal. But the security system was also disconnected. Look." Landon moved to the panel on the wall and opened the door to reveal the entire panel of buttons and the screen where Teagan could set up what he needed when he needed it. "Teagan had it on a schedule. At a certain time every night, it would set itself until morning. Someone turned all that off, so the system didn't record any open entrance or exit points. People could have walked in and out of this condo all weekend, and we'd have no idea. I was with Dirk when he was setting it up and explained it all to Teagan. Also, he gave Teagan a few ways to turn on or off different parts of it. The cameras were on, but...." Landon pointed up, and I turned to follow. "Someone painted over them. I have a feeling that was done when they were off, and when they came back on, it wasn't noticed. As for the panic buttons Pa wanted installed...." Landon groaned. "All three were broken. They were pulled out, leaving it impossible for anyone to hit them."

"How did you figure all that out so fast?" I asked, surprised.

"I know what to look for," he answered. "Check cameras, check panic measures, look at the security. Easy to do. There's a reason I was here when Dirk set it up. I chose the camera positions." Landon shook his head as he turned to the bags. "Now I'm trying to figure out if anything was stolen."

"Landon, do you have a theory?" Heath asked.

"Yeah, but I don't like it. It doesn't seem like it fits. This was intelligent. The timing, the sabotage... It was all too smart."

"Think about it while you both drive back with our wolves," Heath said. "Drive safe... but please, get home quickly."

"We'll try," I promised, with Landon nodding.

We hung up, and I texted Bethany to ask for some help, then started throwing all the food into containers with Landon's help. By the time we were done, I had gotten word from my favorite agent in the BSA, and she was on her way. We waited thirty minutes, Landon finding a cooler for the food in the meantime.

"It doesn't need the temperature control. It's been sitting out for nearly two days," I pointed out. "You could have just grabbed a bag."

"I don't want it to start stinking. It already reeks a bit

more than my nose appreciates, and that will seal it so your car doesn't smell."

"I didn't even notice that. I was focused on other stuff." Sighing, I sat down on the couch, looking at the three werewolves we had moved into the living room so we didn't step on them in the dining room. They looked peaceful, but I was beginning to wonder if they were really okay in their sleeping states. They wouldn't have eaten in nearly forty-eight hours, and I had no idea how we were going to wake them up. That wasn't even considering other bodily functions that seemed like they weren't happening. I didn't voice any of this, knowing Landon was probably thinking similarly.

It was uneventful in the grand scheme of things. Bethany arrived and was able to talk to the building's security people when they saw us carrying out our unconscious werewolves. She was good at smoothing things over and didn't ask questions.

"Let me know if there's anything the BSA can do to help," she said as Landon loaded Carlos into the backseat. He was the last one. "Seriously, Jacky."

"We'll see," I said softly. "Right now, let's just keep this quiet. Can you do that? If the wrong people hear about us having three werewolves drugged in one of their homes, we could end up with a bigger problem on our hands."

"I can. I won't make this a report. It doesn't need to be as far as I'm concerned. No one is hurt or dead. They're just sleeping. They had a wild party, and you two came to clean up." Bethany's smooth explanation of the events reeked of a lie to me, but it didn't matter. Humans couldn't smell lies. "But please, if there's something big coming, a heads-up would be nice."

"I agree, but no one ever gives me a warning, so it's not likely I'll know in time to give you one," I said, almost smiling. Almost.

She chuckled, but I hadn't told her just how bad this was, so I didn't hold it against her. She left, looking back to wave, and I got into the car.

"Ready?" Landon asked, turning it on.

"Let's get out of here. Teagan liked that condo, you know?"

"Yeah... he's going to have to sell it," Landon said as he started driving us home.

11

CHAPTER ELEVEN

Once back in my territory, Heath and Shamus were waiting to help get Teagan, Jenny, and Carlos comfortable. We put them in the living room on cots he had for times like this. Too much company for my relatively normal-sized house. I didn't live in a mega-mansion like the one the pack used in Dallas as a clubhouse. Or like Hasan's. He had a massive home, an entire estate with wings.

"This is bad," Shamus said, using a rag to wet Teagan's forehead as if he had a fever.

"We tried everything we could think of. Ice and water, noise... I hit Carlos, and he didn't react at all. I have no idea, Pa."

I looked around, seeing that no one else was around. Carey wasn't in the room, neither were the boys or either of Shamus's children. None of the pack was. I focused on my territory and in less than a second, knew where everyone was. At Kick Shot, probably getting something to eat to be out of Heath's way.

"That's not good," Heath said softly, opening one of Carlos's eyes. "Ranger should be back soon. He can do some medical—"

"Wow, I am stupid," I muttered, walking out of the room to grab our first-aid kit. I put it in the living room on the coffee table, then held up a hand at everyone. "Hold on." I went upstairs to my closet and found a very old bag I kept for sentimental reasons, with all my stuff from when I was an EMT and even before that, on my way to becoming a doctor. All of that was so long ago, but I hoped I could still make my way around it.

I checked each werewolf, seeing they did have reactive pupils, even if the light didn't wake them. Their blood pressures were all acceptable, and none of them was running a fever. They showed no signs of any illness or side effects from whatever was done to them.

"They're healthy," I declared, looking up to see Ranger had arrived but hadn't stepped in to help me. "Sorry. I... don't do this much anymore. I forgot I even had this thing." I lifted my old bag to show them and held it out to Ranger. "If you need it...."

"You can just leave it somewhere so I can find it later," Ranger said, sitting down on the couch. "So, we're missing Fenris?"

"He hasn't been in the condo all weekend if my nose is right," Landon said quietly, staring at the sleeping werewolves.

"I got the same impression," I confirmed.

"We should call Dirk back." Shamus sat down on my loveseat, his elbows on his knees as he studied the werewolves we were all worried about. "He could look over stuff. He's smart enough to hack things, yeah?"

"If we call him back, we're dealing with bigger problems. He's probably safest with Niko," Heath said, shaking his head.

"Is he?" Landon asked with a soft growl. "Don't you remember what Zuri said about Fenris's scars?"

I leaned back, sitting on the floor as I looked up at Landon, remembering the exact moment he was talking about.

"That Niko is the one who scarred him? That?" Frowning, I realized what Landon wanted to say. "Do you think Fenris did this? To Teagan? To Jenny and Carlos?"

"That's the idea you said you didn't like, isn't it?" Heath looked over his son.

Landon started to pace, growling softly as if he couldn't contain it.

"Yeah, it is," he finally agreed, turning to look out my windows. "The entire thing... It took intimate knowledge of Teagan's security in the condo, how we stay in contact, and how we make sure everyone is safe without needing to breathe down their necks. We only started using that one app after Arlo was taken by that werecat, so they didn't have their phones on them. It wouldn't have been hard to ask everyone to keep their phones away from dinner under the idea that Fenris wanted to cut off the technology for the evening. He's like a lot of old supernaturals. Sometimes, they need a break from the fast-paced world on their phones." Landon put a hand on the glass. "Paint over the cameras... turned off the security's auto functions. Teagan would have taught him to use it while he stayed there with him, or he would have picked it up. Seen Teagan use the code, something...."

"But this is Fenris we're talking about. That man can't plan what he wants for lunch," Shamus said, disbelieving. "He's too chaotic. He makes snap decisions, not masterminds an idea over weeks or months. He's the textbook definition of a werewolf ruled by instinct and emotion."

"That's why I hate it," Landon snapped, turning on us. "I told you, Pa. It's too smart. It feels... professional. If he could pull it off...."

"It means we have fallen for the greatest act of all time, and not once would he have lied to give himself away," Heath finished for his son. "It's well beyond what we know of Fenris, and I've known him for some time."

"I have no real evidence. It's all circumstantial. This is something others could have learned, but he's convenient. Maybe I'm just looking to blame him, or he's being framed. We've dealt with that before."

"As it stands, he's a member of this pack, and he's missing. We have three werewolves unconscious, and it must be magical. We need to figure out how to help them." Heath shook his head. "I won't blame Fenris until I have real evidence."

"What about Dirk?" Landon asked.

"I'll call him and ask him to stay with Niko," I said,

standing up. "He went to visit old friends in Berlin over the weekend, right? If he's not there, I'll tell him to get into Niko's territory as quickly as he can since the pack has been attacked. Whether it was Fenris or someone looking to grab Fenris for other reasons, the pack was attacked, and Niko is the safest person I can send him to." I pulled out my phone, walking away to make the call.

"Is he?" Landon asked again.

I looked over my shoulder at him, seeing the desperate expression of a man in love.

"He has to be." It was all I could say. I hit call and waited. Behind me, the others tried to figure out how to wake up Teagan, Jenny, and Carlos while Landon paced, drawing ever closer to me.

My call went to voicemail, and I felt the sensation of my stomach dropping just as I had when no one picked up earlier. I tried again, stepping further away from the werewolves. Dirk still didn't answer.

I tried Niko next, wondering if he could find Dirk for me.

Pick up, Niko. I need you to pick up...

He didn't, so I texted him, trying to get him to understand there was an emergency. It went unread.

Not saying anything, I went to my office, turned on my computer, and got onto the program Davor had developed for the family. I messaged Niko and tried to call him, but no one picked up. A moment later, someone did call back. A man I didn't recognize showed up using Niko's account, standing in his office.

"Hello. I'm Ansel. I am Nikolaus's assistant. He's not in currently. Can I take your message, Miss Leon?"

"Oh..." I rocked back. "Where is he?"

"He went into the forest some hours ago and said he would get back as soon as he was able," Ansel explained, putting on a professional air.

"Do you know where Dirk is? Dirk Brandt. His son. He's visiting right now. He's been living with me for a few years. I need to get a hold of them, but neither picked up their phones."

Ansel looked around and left the screen for a moment. I heard a door close, and he came back.

"Nikolaus went into the forest suddenly, but before that, he had been trying to find Dirk. He was due back and never came home. He'd done it before, and Nikolaus didn't seem worried since Dirk often did this before he was sent to work for you. As for Nikolaus's absence...he ran into the forest as he does when another werecat enters his territory to challenge him. I'm not sure the two are related."

I dropped into my desk chair, covering my face.

"And? How bad is this, Ansel?"

"We're on lockdown, Miss Leon. Nikolaus asked us to keep all the doors locked and not to leave the premises. This is standard procedure, so we're not concerned currently."

"Are you supposed to be telling me this?"

"No, but Nikolaus trusts my judgment when it comes to situations and telling his family what I might know. The coincidence that you are calling after Nikolaus and

Dirk when Dirk hadn't come home can't be ignored. Also, I've heard Dirk talk about you. If anyone would need to know something might be wrong, I think you are at the top of that list."

"Let me know when they come back...." I checked the time. "Two hours. If they aren't back in two hours, either of them...call me back."

"Of course. What should I tell them if they do come back? I assume you want them to contact you."

"That my werewolves were attacked, and I need to know Dirk is safe," I answered. "Thank you, Ansel."

"Of course, Miss Leon."

I hung up and walked back into the living room, only finding grim faces.

"I assume that could have gone better," Heath said, no one else daring to say anything. "You rushed in there, and..."

"Niko ran out of there hours ago. Into the forest, his assistant said. Dirk... never got home from Berlin, but apparently, that's common for Dirk."

"Dirk promised me he wouldn't be stupid," Landon snarled. "He wouldn't have missed his meeting time with Niko...."

"Landon, I need you to calm down," Heath said, not looking at his son. He was still staring at me. "Jacky?"

"Two hours. Both of them have two hours to get home or call me from wherever they are, or Ansel, Niko's assistant, will call me. If Ansel tells me no one has sent word, I'll fly to Germany and figure things out over there while you all figure out how to help these three."

"If we follow Landon's train of thought and say it was Fenris, what sort of evidence should we look for?" Shamus asked.

"Financial records, like purchasing a plane ticket," Ranger answered quickly, clearly falling into his experience as a former member of law enforcement. "That's the easiest one."

"See, I understand that Fenris is scarred, thanks to Niko, but flying across an ocean? That seems personal," I pointed out. "He's fine with me. It took some time and a few near-death experiences, but we're good...." I didn't want it to be Fenris. I needed this to be unrelated. "An elaborate scheme? None of this feels in character for him."

"It doesn't," Heath agreed. "But we have to consider it."

"What about these three? Do any of you have an idea about how to wake them up?" I wanted to shove the idea that Fenris betrayed us out of my mind and live in denial for a little while. I wanted the problem in front of me to be solved, and maybe they would have the truth.

"I asked Piper to find us some smelling salts. She'll be back soon. Aside from that, we might need to reach out to the hospital and get them sent up there. If this was magical in nature, they would be able to untangle it. They'll be safe in Mygi as well. I know we have some evidence to the contrary, but...."

"The hospital knows we know. They won't mess with us," I said, nodding at his idea. "Since my sister doesn't work there anymore, it's not like there are any surgeons running around committing murder."

"What?" Ranger sputtered. Shamus was wide-eyed near him.

I shook my head, not feeling like explaining.

"What the fuck is wrong with your family?" Shamus muttered. "And which werecat works there? You only have the two sisters, and one of them seems too off her own rocker to be a surgeon, but it's not Zuri."

"Human sister," I finally said. "My twin, actually. We don't really talk anymore. None of that is the point. Mygi won't care that the pack is rogue or that Heath is an Alpha outside of Callahan's control. They're neutral. They won't take sides because they don't want to be destroyed for picking the wrong one. They see what they do as greater than our politics. It rubs some people the wrong way, me included, but we can use them for this."

"And we will if smelling salts don't work. I don't want to hire some wandering witch or fae to come in and potentially mess this up worse." Heath reached out and brushed his hand over Teagan's forehead. "Why don't all of you take a walk? I'll watch these three. Go clear your heads. Shamus, do you mind if I make the boys your responsibility once they come back from dinner with everyone?"

"I'll take them, and I'll keep them safe," Shamus promised as he stood up. Ranger followed him out, his walk beginning to look natural with his prosthetic.

"Landon, don't do anything brash." Heath's words

cut through the room, stopping Landon from following the others.

"I'll stay with him." I kissed Heath's cheek as I passed him. "He's safe with me."

"He's going to want to burn the world down to get Dirk back by his side," Heath said, as if I didn't understand that.

"Just like you tried to do for me?" I asked, remembering how my werewolves were the ones who'd found me when the enemies of my werecat family finally tried to stage a coup.

"Yes."

"Landon will be safe with me," I repeated, giving Heath a long, slow kiss.

His hand wrapped around my waist, and he sighed heavily when I finally pulled away.

"Okay."

I left with Landon, walking to the trail, him following silently. Once we were over a hundred yards away from the house, I stopped walking and turned to look at the silent werewolf following me. He gave me a hard glare.

"It was Fenris," he growled.

"Get me the evidence, Landon." Like Heath, I wasn't ready to throw Fenris under the proverbial bus without it.

"If I can?"

"Then I will hunt him down to the ends of the Earth with you. You have my word on that."

He knew my word meant something.

12

CHAPTER TWELVE

HEATH

The smelling salts didn't wake Heath's werewolves. He hated everything about the situation. One of his pack was nowhere to be found on the other side of the world. Another was missing, leaving a crime scene in his absence. Three were magically unconscious, and he needed outside help to wake them.

Heath knew he couldn't solve every problem. There was no possible way. The health of the sleeping werewolves had to be his top priority. The longer they stayed asleep, the more likely it would become that they couldn't wake at all.

With that in mind, he found the number for Mygi and called after he convinced the others to go for a walk. The smelling salts didn't work, and he wasn't willing to do real harm to any of them to see if it worked. Landon slapping Carlos in an attempt to rouse him was all Heath was willing to allow in that vein.

"This is Becca at Mygi Hospital. May I ask who's calling?"

"Heath Everson, Alpha of the Everson Pack. Rogue." He knew what they wanted to know and gave it to them.

"How can Mygi Hospital assist you today, Alpha Everson?"

"I have three werewolves put under magical sleep as far as I can tell. No conventional methods of waking them have been successful, and they've been asleep for nearly forty-eight hours from what we've been able to deduce. It was potentially ingested."

"I see. Scents?"

"No scent of magic on them or the food, but they were found sleeping in the dining room. Do you know of the recent development that some have been able to hide the scent of magic from the moon cursed?"

"We have been made aware and will take that into consideration. Even without the scent of magic, it does sound like the sleep is magical in nature. Drugs are often burned out of your systems much faster than this."

"How would you like me to bring them to the hospital?"

"Flight... actually, one moment. I'm sorry. Please hold."

Suddenly, he was listening to elevator music, on hold as the lives of some of his werewolves hung in the balance. His hand tightened on the phone, but he bit back his temper, knowing there must be something that pulled her away, perhaps another life.

"Alpha Everson," a man said after the elevator music ended. "This is Director Johansson."

"Did you take over the call thanks to what happened with the Russians and Gwen?" he asked, believing they were about to pay for that meddling.

"Yes, but only to say you don't need to bring the werewolves here. I'm going to send a team to you."

Heath heard and processed that, mulling it over after an initial rush of gratitude. He knew he had to ask the all-important question as suspicion ran through him right after his gratitude.

"Why?"

"We have other werewolves here, and while we are neutral, not everyone in the building is," the Director explained. "To keep all werewolves safe, I will be sending a witch and two fae who specialize in this sort of situation. They'll be able to figure out what was done to your werewolves and wake them up."

"I thought you might be getting me back for helping Gwen and Jacky," Heath admitted.

"In a sense, I am. I'm keeping you off the property because trouble follows you and yours. I've heard things and would prefer them not to descend on my hospital. I wanted you to hear that from me and know the course of action I'm approving. We don't often do house calls. In fact, we don't do them at all."

"Well, thank you."

"It's not a problem. The team will be there in one hour. Your fiancé might want to know that our cases of werewolves from Russia coming in with signs of abuse have dropped by a hundred percent," he said, then hung up.

Heath pulled his phone away from his ear, frowning. Did Mygi Hospital know where they lived?

Probably. It seems like everyone knows where we live now.

He texted his inner circle in a group chat. He knew Landon would tell Jacky and Shamus would tell the boys. Just thinking of his son made him anxious. If there was a feeling Heath disliked the most, it was anxiety. He didn't know how to shake it because there were half a dozen reasons behind it. He was worried about Landon if Dirk was hurt or killed. He didn't want to see his son go through the terrible loss of a lover. Heath knew the pain of that all too well.

Heath's more troubling situation was the anxiety Landon was feeding. His son wanted to kill a member of the pack, and he didn't have the evidence to back it up. Landon wasn't the type to threaten werewolves. He made promises, and his son never broke his promises. The only thing Heath could do was try to keep his son honorable.

He can't kill Fenris without evidence. It sets a bad precedent in the pack. They need to know they'll be innocent until proven otherwise. Just as I did with Arlo. Landon can't say this is personal and act rashly. He can't just kill someone because he has a feeling.

Heath could think of a dozen people who would want to capture Fenris, which complicated things. Callahan was at the top of that list. That Alpha clearly had some reason for keeping Fenris alive for a long time and had been pissed when Fenris walked away. If any werewolf had the power and means to make this abduction happen so smoothly, it was Callahan.

Then why not take all four of them? Unless taking someone like Teagan seems like it's too far, especially if he has family in Corissa's pack.

Heath needed more information, and he needed it fast.

One more hour and my werewolves will be awake.

He watched the minutes tick by, and with only five minutes to spare, the others started coming back. He couldn't resist pulling Jacky to him as she came by. She sank onto the couch in his lap and wrapped her arms around him, exactly what he needed.

"What if Callahan took Fenris?" he asked the room. He saw Landon's eyes go wide.

"Shit."

"Exactly. If he did it, we're in a different situation," Heath said, sighing as he leaned his head on Jacky.

"I can have Davor hack Fenris's stuff," Jacky suggested, but she didn't sound comfortable with the idea.

Heath could smell her wariness and uncertainty. Davor was a messy situation by himself. His history with Jacky was not one of trust and fellowship as siblings. He could be cruel to her, and Heath wasn't willing to witness that, even if it was out of pain.

And that's only Davor before we get into how the rest of her family will react to this...

"No, let's try not to drag your family into this," Heath murmured.

Another couple of minutes, then there was a knock at the door. Jacky jumped out of his lap, but they were all beaten to the door by Landon.

"Is this Jacky Leon's residence? I believe there are three werewolves that need assistance." A woman stepped around his son, her fae nature clear with small pointed ears and unreal lavender eyes.

"Right over here," Heath said, stepping around Jacky to gesture for them to come closer. "In the room right now are my inner circle and my fiancé, the owner of the property." Heath pointed out everyone as he said their names.

"And these are the three sleeping beauties," another said in a deadpan tone. He had to be the witch because the last fae was similar to the first, except his eyes were a shade of teal. The witch had a bored expression, not at all disturbed, alarmed, or anything else by what was going on.

"Yes. Teagan, Jenny, and Carlos," Heath said, pointing to each as he said their names.

"Well, this should be quick. I've seen this spell before," the last fae said, rubbing his hands together. "It's a sleep spell we fae made, something we use in the hospital when we need patients to sleep and can't give them human drugs. Typically, this lasts up to three days, but the sooner they're woken, the better."

"How harmful can it be?" Jacky asked, coming closer.

"Depending on the species, they could die, thanks to

its effects, but only if left unattended for too long. Luckily, moon cursed come out of it rather quickly." He clapped his hands together and glowing lines formed between them. Reaching out, he plucked more of those strings over Jenny's body, making them vibrate.

Heath was fascinated, but he kept his distance. This was a type of magic he had never seen before. Those strings were hidden.

"What is that?" Jacky asked, leaning closer. Heath grabbed her shoulders, trying to keep her away. "I've never seen a fae do that before."

"He's conceptualizing spells as webs," the witch explained, his words still falling flat, unemotional. "Fae are weird. They do weird things. All their magic works differently, depending on how they want their magic to work."

"I'm sorry we don't live with the sad limits of humanity," the lavender-eyed one said, clearly teasing. "And it's not because he wants it to do that. He's from a line that specializes in spell weaving and unweaving. They can do complex magic like that, but it takes time. He's going to unweave this spell."

The teal-eyed fae undid lines of glowing magic over Jenny that we could all see, a frown growing as he played with them, clearly struggling with whatever complicated puzzle he was trying to understand.

"Oh, that's not pleasant," the fae finally said softly. "There's a condition to this. It's not just a sleep spell. It's a curse."

"What?" Heath stepped closer now, needing to know more. "How do we break it?"

"What makes a sleep spell into a sleep curse?" Jacky asked.

"It means something has to happen before they can wake up. Well, this one is cursed." He pointed at Jenny. "Definitely cursed. Let me check the others."

"That's not completely bad," the other fae said softly, leaning down. "Technically, we turn our sleeping spells into curses. We can't have patients waking up while someone does a silver extraction or anything."

"We set the conditions to end at good times, and we don't leave them alone," the weaving fae replied, shaking his head as he messed with the glowing lines over Teagan. "So is he...." Then he moved to Carlos, shaking his head before the event started. "Yeah, they were all hit with the same curse."

"Can you learn the condition to break it?" Heath demanded. He would go to the ends of the Earth to make it happen, he just needed to know. Information was power, and he had too little of it.

"Yes, but I wanted to verify they were all the same," the fae replied, finally plucking at some of the threads over Carlos, revealing them to the rest of us. "Luckily, it's nothing worse than time. One week. We can take them back to the hospital for supervision. They'll need to be given IVs to keep their hydration up. As of this moment, they're in temporary comas, with some... magical side effects."

"A week?" Heath tried his best to keep the growl

from his words, stepping back to keep from scaring the healers. He snarled as he stomped away from them, needing to move, needing to create that distance.

"It can't be a week. We need them to wake up and tell us who did this to them," Jacky said. "You don't understand. We have two other werewolves missing."

"I can't break the curse without two potential fail-safes going into effect. Either it kills them immediately, or it becomes permanent, and they die eventually. I don't know which of those fail-safes are in this curse, but one of them will be. Why make a curse someone can break without repercussions?" The fae was shaking his head, his eyes sad as he met Jacky's gaze.

Heath inhaled sharply, his frustration only slightly subdued by the authenticity of that look.

"Let me call our supervisor," the witch said, stepping back as he took his phone from his coat.

"Call the Director. He's the one who asked me to make this little team," the lavender-eyed fae said quickly. "He didn't want this pack in the hospital. We might need to make this a longer stay if Alpha Everson wants us to monitor his werewolves. And we should. It's for the good of the werewolves."

"Please," Heath croaked, knowing he couldn't reject the offer. "Your safety will be my top priority." He couldn't have it on his soul to be the Alpha that let Teagan, Jenny, and Carlos waste away and die when he had the people who could stop it.

Jacky stepped away from the group, pulling out her phone. She started texting quickly, but Heath didn't ask what was going on. He just needed to know if he would have these healers' help with his pack right now.

The witch stepped outside while on the phone, leaving none of them able to hear it. Only a few minutes later, he was back inside.

"Director says if we want to stay, we can, and he'll arrange us transport home once the curse is finished. We can have a week's worth of supplies dropped off for the patients." The witch turned to him. "However, you are responsible for housing us, keeping us safe, and if we wish to leave, we can at any time. We're not here because you want us to be here. We're here for the patients and will continue to give you the best advice about their care as we can, but if something goes wrong, we're not culpable for it."

"Done," Heath said without needing to consider it. "Jacky, can they stay here?"

"Absolutely," she said, looking up from her phone for only a second to nod, then went back to it. "Set them up on cots or... I knew we should have built the guest house, damn it. You can do whatever you need."

"We'll get it built," he promised, moving to kiss her cheek and start settling the healers in. He was worried about Fenris and Dirk, but he had three critical wolves in his care right now. Both of them were capable. He just had to trust them.

And trust that Fenris wasn't the one who did this.

"How did the magic hide from us?" Landon asked, stopping everyone in their tracks. "I can only smell it now."

"You could probably smell magic because I was playing with it, which was me using magic. Why you couldn't smell it earlier." The fae shrugged. "Not my place to say. The spell doesn't have anything in it that would cause it to be concealed like that."

"We couldn't smell a witch or fae that cast it, either," Landon said, a low growl beginning.

"The spell is fae. Witches do deep sleep spells like this with other means, often requiring a physical component like food or a potion," the lavender-eyed one said. "Is there any evidence of that?"

"None," the teal-eyed one said, shaking his head. "This was certainly cast right on them."

"A spell sold in an object. We've run into that before. It had to be triggered with blood from the person, and he was immune to its effects," Heath said, nodding. He liked knowing that, at least. It was something. The food could be thrown out, whatever positive that was. "Could it be cast then discarded?"

"Absolutely," both fae answered at the same time.

"What sort of objects?"

"That's something *you* can look into. Our job is taking care of the patients," the witch said, putting his phone away, staring down Heath once they made eye contact. "We're not supposed to solve this mystery for you or even aid you in it. We're here to keep them alive until the curse is over. Truthfully, these two have said more than they should." The witch glared at them. "We all know why the Director has hard rules."

"Sorry we can't be of more help," the lavender-eyed fae said.

"Those rules suck," Landon growled.

"Those rules keep us from getting in the way of *your* enemies," the witch snapped back. "We treat the wounded, regardless of who they are. We take care of the patients in front of us. That's our oath, one that transcends all the bullshit the rest of you get into. Sorry. I want to help more people in a week. Another family who wants their little boy or girl to survive a curse, too. There could be someone injured from a devastating car accident or someone clinging to life after a vicious vampire attack. It could be a member of the Tribunal or one of their family."

Knowledge was behind those words, a reminder to everyone that Jacky's own family had been at Mygi once, trying to save the lives of a few of their own, and they probably weren't the only powerful people who needed the protection of Mygi Hospital from time to time.

"You aren't the most important people in the world. These patients are, then the next. That's what I care about."

"Understood," Heath said quickly. He pinned Landon with a stare, a silent warning that if he opened his mouth to argue, Heath would be the one shutting him up. They needed these healers. He couldn't have them decide to walk out because Landon was giving them a hard time.

Landon stormed out of the house.

13

CHAPTER THIRTEEN

I stepped out after Landon but didn't chase him as he stormed off down a trail into the forest around my home. I wasn't his father or his sister. I was Jacky, he was Landon, and we had boundaries I would always respect. I didn't get nosy. The only reason I followed him was I needed my own air. I understood Mygi Hospital and the hard lines they kept about interfering. I didn't always agree with them, but I knew they could be useful.

But that wasn't what I was thinking about as I left the house.

I was trying to convince myself not to do something, to throw guilt at the feet of Fenris because he happened not to be here. I knew I couldn't fight it forever. Time was of the essence. I had to act, even as I desperately wished it wasn't him.

I thought about that night on that ranch—witches staring us down, my body under the control of a simple spell that paralyzed me into inaction. When she had tried to do the same to Fenris, his entire demeanor had changed, and he had said something so simple—Fenris wasn't his real name. Looking back, that shouldn't have surprised me. No one walked through the world with a name that was certainly a call to a being of the apocalypse. It was clearly as much of an inside joke as my own last name when I changed it to Leon. Beyond that, most supernaturals no longer used their original names. I was certain Hasan and Subira hadn't always been called by those names. I knew Zuri once went by another name, not that anyone ever spoke it if they knew it.

No, what I had been surprised by was his accent, and that continued to bother me as I walked around my house as Heath and the others focused on the sleeping werewolves. Now, knowing he spoke German, I understood the accent. Recently, having heard Niko rant at me, his German on display, I could hear the similarities. They had similar accents.

And they're a similar age. They fought each other in the war...

I went to find my keys quickly and silently, to keep anyone from questioning what I was doing. Getting into my car, I drove away from home without giving in to the urge to stop what I was doing.

My will to be wrong was strong, but I had an obligation to the safety of my family. That got me to Fenris's driveway, then through the front door. I searched his rooms, trying to find anything to tell me if Fenris had anything to do with this. Heath tried to be a respectful Alpha, something I knew his packs loved about him. He helped them, but he didn't invade their privacy without cause. He hadn't taken over Fenris's life when he joined us here, and I had agreed with that. Fenris had deserved to make his own life without Callahan shuffling him around like a problem child, and we just needed to mitigate any potential issues.

Searching every room until I got to his attic, I had to find bolt cutters in his shed to break the lock before I could pull down the ladder and climb up. I expected to find old personal treasures he was keeping safe thanks to the lock. What I didn't find was an attic full of dust and cobwebs, teeming with boxes of old things. There were no exposed beams. It was a small hall of sorts. Carpet was laid, the walls were finished and painted, and there was even a hook on the wall, where I assumed someone could hang their jacket.

There was also a door, which I found locked when I tried to open it.

"Damn it, Fenris," I hissed. I didn't want to break anything, but now I knew he was keeping some sort of secret. If it was a closet, there would be no reason for the rest of this strange, finished attic. There had to be secrets behind the door. I rammed into the door, my shoulder shooting pain through every nearby body part, but the door gave.

I knew immediately it was *off*. Fenris didn't let many into his home. He often came to my home to speak to Heath, and when he was with others, they probably avoided this small private space. I certainly never tried to invade his privacy. There were hundreds of reasons why no one would ever try to find this place, and all of them were probably why no one had noticed how different the space was from the rest of the house. The choice to put it in his attic only told me how much he didn't want anyone to ever see this place.

"What the hell." I breathed out, slowly stepping in, almost mystified by the strange room.

It was an office, which wouldn't have surprised anyone if it was in Heath's home or mine, or even Teagan's. Shamus, Ranger... anyone could have had this space—anyone but the werewolf who lived in this ramshackle old home. The walls weren't the same faded paint as the rest of the home. The furniture was new and clearly expensive. He had probably bought it right after he moved in. His desk was redwood. The hardwood floor had not a single scuff or scratch. The books were well-read but cared for on the bookshelf, organized alphabetically.

Maybe Teagan made him this? They're close...

I couldn't ask Teagan, though. He was unconscious in my living room, suffering a sleep curse that couldn't end for several days.

Taking pictures of the room, I sent them to Heath and Landon, only saying I was looking in Fenris' office. I silently wondered if they would be as surprised as I was by the space. I quickly added where I'd found it, hidden in the attic behind a locked door, but didn't ask if they had known about it. Their replies would answer that question quickly enough.

I put my phone away and focused on the room. I was

here to look for any clue that might point to the truth about our current situation. First, I went to the desk, opening drawers, pulling out papers, trying to find anything with a name or a plan. He didn't have much technology in the room, only a laptop that was locked and a small printer. I went carefully, flipping through every page and note I could find. Most of it was nonsense— notes passed to him from Teagan, letters here and there from over the years from Callahan. I read those, finding only Callahan asking him if he was okay, if he needed more money, if he liked the current pack he was in. Sometimes, those letters were chastising, asking Fenris to get along with whatever pack he was stuck in at that moment. There was one that asked Fenris to rejoin Callahan's pack.

I had a strong feeling I knew how Fenris answered that particular request.

Callahan had certainly taken an interest in Fenris. None of the letters were recent, though, many dated before the seventies and eighties.

They must have moved to email. Callahan seems like the persistent type. I'm a bit surprised he cares this much about Fenris. I knew he was always in charge of him, but there's something personal about all of this.

I kept going back, looking deeper into the bottom drawer of the desk but found the bottom. Growling, I slammed it shut and heard the wood crack and break under the strength of my frustration. With a wince, I quickly pulled it back open, and my stomach did several flips.

My accidental anger had broken the bottom, revealing a very small extra space. I slowly pulled out the documents, heart pounding as I realized I had just discovered more of Fenris's secrets.

Unfolding the first one, an old piece of paper I could smell magic on, I wasn't certain how old it was, but it wasn't like any paper I had ever come across. I put down the rest of the small stack before properly examining it. It was in a language I couldn't read, but I knew I had several ancient siblings who could probably identify and read it if I asked them. I put it down to pick up another, finding it to be in the same language. All the old documents were. I was certain Heath and Landon wouldn't be able to read them, either. I put them aside, sighing heavily.

"Jacky?" Landon called out from downstairs.

"Shit. How long have I been here?" I asked myself as I checked my phone. I had gotten several texts since I walked in, but I had been totally absorbed in what I was doing. "Up here!" I called out, letting him know I was okay. "Found some interesting things."

"Yeah, like the existence of this entire office," Landon said as I heard him moving up the ladder. "Pa asked me to come check on you. He wanted to come, but you never answered us, and he."

"He needs to be focused on the others," I said, not bothered by Landon arriving and not my fiancé. I knew Heath would pick me over the pack, but I would never ask him to put me over those who genuinely needed him, not when I could take care of myself. "I'm not upset. I should have paid attention to my phone. I was the one who decided to come here and shouldn't have given him a reason to worry by losing track of time."

"You can ease my father's worries about it when we get back. What have you found up here?"

I started pushing things across the desk towards him, letting him take it all in for himself.

"I knew Callahan used to talk to him a lot. Once Fenris was with us, he would ask Pa to pass along messages because he was beginning to worry Fenris was just burning the letters without reading them. Clearly wasn't the case, but..." Landon shrugged. "It was always the same as these... If he was settling in, if he was making any sort of friends."

"Fenris hates him," I murmured.

"Yeah, they can't be in the same room together."

"That's not the most interesting stuff, though. I assume you can't read this, but..." I showed him the papers I couldn't read. "Do you know the language?"

"No. I think it's utter gibberish, but..." Landon frowned. "The paper has to be a few centuries old, at least." He sniffed it, nodding. "Magically maintained, so it doesn't become dust. Might be the same magic that makes it seem illegible. Really fucking weird of Fenris to have, but he's an odd old wolf."

"You seem a lot calmer than you were. You don't see this as a sign of his guilt? It's certainly suspicious."

Landon made a face, putting the papers down.

"I'm trying to remain calm for my father right now. When I went back inside, you were gone, and he was about to tear me a new asshole for storming off like a child while he was dealing with three cursed members of the pack and two missing ones. He sent me in here, telling me to focus on the task instead of throwing tantrums."

"Yikes," I mumbled, looking back at all I had found. None of it was particularly helpful, but I decided to keep it. I lifted the enchanted papers and waved for Landon to leave with me. "Let's show him what we found and figure something out."

"Do you think any of your family could figure out what's on those? It might be pertinent…"

"I don't think I can ask them to help the pack like that, and I don't know if this has anything to do with Niko and Dirk yet. Neither do you. If we drag them in without solid evidence," I shook my head slowly. "It won't turn out well for us."

"Yeah."

Since we brought our own vehicles, we didn't talk much, heading back to the house. I had a feeling Landon was as lost in his own thoughts as I was in mine. We parked next to each other and went in together. I found Heath pacing in the kitchen and surprised him with a kiss on his cheek, taking the distracted man off guard for once.

"I'm sorry for not seeing your replies. Don't feel guilty for protecting these three while I was looking into stuff."

The tension eased out of him, not all of it, but enough. His shoulders relaxed, he got a hint of a smile, and the storms in his eyes slowed, warming as they met mine.

"I don't like this," he murmured, leaning closer. "I don't like when my wolves are hurting, and I can't stop it. I can't rescue them. I have to wait, and I hate it."

"They're in good hands, and they will love and respect you all the more for holding vigil for them while they're at their most vulnerable," I reminded him. "You know that."

He closed his eyes for a moment as he nodded. When they opened again, I could see he had calmed down a fraction more.

"You found something interesting, didn't you? Landon texted me as you left Fenris's property."

I took out the papers from my bag. Before Heath could react to them, a nasty, defensive hiss came from my left, making me turn to see one of the fae healers.

"Take that magic out of your house," he said, hissing again as he stepped back.

"So, we can guess it's fae in origin?" Landon said, moving between the healer and me.

"Fae?" The healer glared at the papers, not at all threatened by Landon. "Yeah, that magic is fae, and it's dark stuff." He shook his head. "I can't say anymore."

"Back to square one." I groaned.

The fae healer didn't storm off. He looked up, his glare softening.

"Don't say anything." He waved for us to leave the house with him, and we walked to the edge of the woods, hidden behind the security building on my lawn.

"It's dark magic?" Heath asked, going back to what the fae had stopped himself from saying.

"It's a bargain, like so much of fae magic. Bargains don't need to be written most of the time, locked by the pure magic of them. Not all fae love bargains. Many of us hate them, really. We can't escape them, though. Everything is an exchange. This one was so powerful of an exchange that it was written. It's part of the magic that seals it."

"Then what makes this one dark magic?" I asked, a deep frown. "Just how strong it is?"

"The reason this is so... terrible? One, that is *not* paper you are holding. The glamour for it is strong, seeing how it's masking the scent of its original form. That amount of power was probably used because someone thought werewolves or others with sensitive noses might eventually handle it... That doesn't matter, though. It's important to know it isn't written on paper. It's written on flesh."

I nearly dropped them, both Landon and Heath reaching out just in case I lost my grip.

"The flesh is probably of the one who gained a great deal in exchange for something important," the fae continued. "Their freedom. Their autonomy. Their future. Whatever you want to say. Effectively, this is the closest a being can come to selling their soul to the devil."

"And it was to a fae."

"Can you break the...curse, glamour, spell, charm, or whatever keeps us from reading it?" I asked, swallowing.

"I could, but it'll break all the protective glamours on

it," the fae said. "If you want to finally smell whose flesh it is, that would be the next course of action, but it would be an odd thing to keep hold of."

"What's the second reason this is terrible?" Heath asked. "You said one, it's flesh, but that implies there are more and are probably worse."

The fae seemed uncertain, closing his eyes as he fought some sort of internal struggle, then he rubbed his face, sighing.

"Have you heard of the legends around something humans like to call the Wild Hunt?" the fae asked, finally opening his eyes. "Well, it's not always as the legends go, as you know. They have more than one trick, though only the one is often shown to the world."

"What do you mean?" My voice shook.

"Whoever made that bargain is technically already a member of the Hunt, and they are still on their Hunt at the same time. It gave them all the power and time they might need to do it. If they want to take their time, they can, and when the right time strikes, they will continue the hunt again. The power they might have been given by the hunt, the assistance... that's never been confirmed. From stories I've heard, it's different per person. If they succeed, they can keep the power and escape the curse. If they fail and die, they join the Hunt for eternity. You would be amazed how many fail, even with all they are given to succeed. I don't know of anyone who succeeded, but there must be some out there."

"Break the glamour," I ordered, holding them out.

The fae took a deep breath, and those webs of magic appeared.

"Luckily, the glamour was placed by someone weaker than the being who wrote the bargain," the fae murmured. "Maybe the person who sold their soul."

The smell was first to come back. The magic could no longer hide it, and my denial was washed away as tears threatened my eyes.

"No." Heath exhaled.

"I'm going to kill him," Landon snarled.

Fenris's flesh rested in my hands.

"Do any of you know a Rainer Brandt?" the fae asked softly. "Because he was given fae magic, and he's probably the one who cursed those werewolves. Simple sleeping spells like that... it's a dangerous thing to give someone but it makes complete sense at the same time."

I didn't know a Rainer Brandt.

Though, I believe I witnessed him once before...

"I'm flying to Berlin. Landon, call the airport and have them ready the jet," I ordered, leaving no room for argument.

CHAPTER FOURTEEN

"I'm going with her," Landon said quickly. "I'm going to drive home and pack some things. We need weapons and gear. We have no idea what we're going to find."

"I'll come get you and drive us to the airport," I said, nodding. "We need to be in the air as quickly as possible, and making you drive back will be slow."

"Keep her safe," Heath said, his eyes on me. "And bring Dirk home alive. Bring that boy home alive."

"Of course. I'll get them home." Landon, like a good soldier, stood at attention and gave a sharp nod of confirmation to his father.

"He wouldn't be the focus," I said. "He can't be. He's not old enough."

"We don't know if that matters," Heath pointed out. He was gentle and calm as if this new threat had provided him something to stand on in the strange storm where we now found ourselves.

My fingers curled, wrinkling the dirty bargain in my hands.

"It better matter," I snarled at it, not wanting to direct my fury at my fiancé. I took a moment to collect myself, knowing I still had a lot to do before Landon and I could leave. Taking a deep breath, I looked up at the helpful fae.

"Thank you for this information and help. I promise it will never leave those of us here right now. Your employer won't know of the help you've given us nor our enemies."

"A favor, then? One for the future?" The fae was shaking as if the sudden seriousness of the situation scared him. The magic had already spooked him, but now I could see his genuine fear that he'd gotten tangled into a situation with the werecat ruling family.

"Within reason," I said softly. "From only me, not them." I nodded at Heath and Landon. "No favor asked of me can put anyone associated with me in danger, only myself."

"I can agree to those terms," the fae said quickly, his head bobbling in a nod. "I'm not... I'm just a healer with a particular way of looking at magic. I'm not a great bargainer or anything. I...shouldn't have helped at all, really."

"I truly appreciate that you did, which is why I'm giving you this favor. You might have saved lives today, and if this favor is enough, I will gladly give it to you," I said, then turned on my heel and headed inside.

"Jacky? What's that?" Carey asked as I passed her. I froze, pushing the grotesque contract behind my back.

"Nothing you want to know about, I promise. Trust me this once, and when you're older, I'll tell you this story in full," I said, clearing my throat as I watched her frown grow, hoping she didn't press for more. The nightmares she could have, knowing there was something like this in the world... As a woman over forty, I wished I didn't know.

"Okay," she finally said, nodding slowly. "What's going on?"

"Landon and I are flying to Berlin to see Niko and Dirk. It's urgent. Don't give your father too much trouble. Don't tell Makalo or anyone else about this."

"Are they in danger?"

It was one question I couldn't sidestep. I wouldn't sidestep it.

"Yes."

Unsurprised, she nodded slowly. Resolve filled her eyes, a belief in me I didn't always have in myself.

"Love you. Stay safe. Come home with them."

I blinked back tears and leaned in to kiss her forehead, having to reach a couple of inches to get to it. I was an average sixty eight inches tall, only five foot eight. She was now reaching five foot nine. My sixteen-year-old future stepdaughter, one of the greatest treasures of my life, was taller than me and would always be that way. I could remember when she was a small eleven-year-old. I wanted more years with her as she continued to grow up and find out what type of person she wanted to be.

"We'll come back. Don't you worry about that," I promised, then went upstairs to begin packing.

I packed light, knowing I would be running around the Black Forest, deep in Niko's isolated territory. I was going to get dirty, probably bloody, and it didn't make sense to waste space on extra clothes for vanity's sake. I packed enough to make it through three days, but I knew I wouldn't bother changing unless the clothes were ruined. After that, I rushed back downstairs, keeping my eyes away from anyone around, not wanting to make eye contact and get drawn into conversation. I went into the security building, intending on picking some weapons, only to find Heath already doing that.

"You got started for me," I said, stopping at his side to see what he was deciding on.

"A way to help," he said softly.

I couldn't smell his emotions and didn't fault him for it. The evidence was pointing at a scenario where we had all been played. Fenris pulled the wool over our eyes, and had been doing it for years in some cases. Someone was going to pay the price for that.

"Here," he said, putting my silver knife in front of me. "You never take it with you anywhere. Hasan gave it to you, didn't he? Take it. You're helping your brother and nephew."

Without a word, I tucked it into my bag. Oftentimes, I ended up as a werecat for fights. I was stronger in that form, could take more hits, and it made me bigger than most of the supernaturals I found myself fighting. Next, he put down a handgun, then a second. One was black, the other gunmetal gray, so aptly named.

"The black will have standard ammunition. Can put down a fae if needed. This one... It has silver loaded into it. Spare magazines over there." He pointed, and I loaded them into my bag. He reached for a standard hunting knife next. "To pair with the silver knife."

Nodding, I shoved it in last, thankful it had a case to keep it from cutting through my bag.

"I'll make sure to keep it all close," I said, looking at the weapons in my bag before zipping it closed. "I don't want to walk through the airport armed, though."

"I'm not worried. Landon won't let you run off to find Dirk unless you're prepared." He didn't attempt to give me even the weakest of smiles. I was expecting it, but it wasn't there as I stared into his stormy gray-blue eyes. I pulled back my own fury and hurt over the seeming betrayal. I didn't want to lose myself in it, and there was something Heath and I had to talk about.

"What do you want me to say to Fenris when we find him?"

"Nothing. Rainer Brandt is not a member of my pack. His life is forfeit, and there's nothing he can say to change that."

"There might be some sort of explanation. He might—"

"Why did he leave the bargain for us to find?" Heath asked me before I could finish my appeal. "Why wouldn't he take it with him to keep it hidden?"

"I... I don't know." I hadn't even given it a thought. I

had jumped into action and planned on thinking about that sort of stuff on the plane.

"He's an old wolf, Jacky. He knew exactly what actions Landon and I would take when we discovered it. He knew we'd discover it eventually or decide to check in on everyone and call Dirk back. Dirk wouldn't have come home because we wouldn't have been able to reach him, and we would have sent someone to get him. Probably you and Landon like right now. He's not going to go quietly. If he's sold his soul to the Hunt, he has to succeed. He'll kill everyone he needs to make that happen."

"He's already accounted for us," I said, swallowing. "He knows it'll be me with you or Landon. Maybe not Landon, since you normally feel comfortable leaving Landon to take on fights yourself. He's betting on the idea that he can win a fight against me, though. At the very least, he thinks he can beat me."

And he could. Fenris was stronger than me. He had proven that only last year.

"Either he's betting on that, or he thinks he can do whatever he needs to do before anyone gets there. Then he gets to find someone to hide behind, somewhere we can't reach him. We're already behind." Heath leaned on the worktable. "He knew his life was forfeit the moment he used fae magic on members of my pack."

Standing there, I thought that over. It was a brutal thought process, one that left everyone involved soaked in blood, some of it their own but not all of it. It was also a deeply understood piece of being supernatural. Like the traitors against my family and their attempted coup, there were some lines one didn't cross unless they wanted a fight, and that fight would be to the death.

I saw in Heath's eyes the fury I couldn't smell, his rage at the betrayal, but I knew it couldn't only be that. He wanted to do this himself, but it wasn't practical. He had to be here for the others—his daughter and the pack. Some of them were in the hands of outsiders, healers but still outsiders.

I had to turn away from Heath, realizing my own fury was matched. I was still doing my best to hold it back so I could think clearly, but it was there, stewing under the surface. I knew Heath could smell it. There was only so much I could do, and it was impossible not to feel it.

"I should get going to pick up Landon—"

Heath pulled me into a long kiss, the scent of his emotions finally unleashed around me as he let go of his Talent's tight control over them. I smelled desperation, anger, love, and fear. All were just notes around the center of his emotions—pain from a wound deep enough I feared Heath might not recover from it. It was that sort of wound that got infected. It wasn't real. He was unharmed, but it was there in his scent. I didn't find it difficult to identify.

It was the pain of betrayal, the pain that made people turn their hearts away from trusting others in the future.

When the kiss ended, I walked away, unable to say anything, that scent haunting my nose. I got into my car and pulled away from my home fast enough to kick up rocks.

15

CHAPTER FIFTEEN

Picking up Landon was quick. He always had a bag ready for anything, and when he jumped in, he explained that he'd only made a handful of adjustments to it.

"We need to be prepared for anything, right?"

I knew he didn't expect an answer, so I only nodded and drove fast. With my foot pressing the gas pedal to the floor, a simple bit of fae magic keeping us from getting pulled over, and a complicated mix of emotions making my chest tight, I got us to the airport in only an hour. It was very fast, faster than was safe for even us immortals, but Landon never raised an objection. While on the drive, Ansel finally reached out, letting me know Niko and Dirk were still unaccounted for. Not yet wanting to give up my plans, I told him he would hear from me as soon as I could tell him anything.

"Why the secrecy?" Landon asked.

"Buying us time. He's human, so he can't do anything

personally, but he can get the word out in a way I don't need yet." I was keeping secrets for a short time, so I could do my own research and work before getting others involved, which meant a slow release of information.

I was learning from my family.

I was focused as I found us a parking spot, Landon now white-knuckling the bar above his window. He didn't show me any fear, but my driving had been a bit wild through the parking garage.

"We should get set up at a closer runway," Landon muttered as I cut the engine and started getting out. "Something in your territory."

"Setting one up would be a nightmare," I pointed out.

"Clearly. We're a few decades late on getting away with it easily. Still, it's not impossible."

Landon grabbed his backpack while I grabbed mine. We didn't stop at security, finding a fae man hanging out by a staff door. I had never done this before, but Landon explained what to do on the way here. Supernaturals worked at airports all over the world, helping the powerful get through the mundane without notice. I knew the moment I was within ten feet of the fae that he had made sure no one would look our way. The scent of that magic hung in the air, bringing back memories of several fae encounters.

"Jacky Leon. I need to get to my jet. Has it been readied for takeoff? Can we get in the air immediately?"

"Come with me. You can take off in about an hour minutes at the earliest. It was the best we could do, and we didn't know how quickly you would arrive. Mr.

Everson had called earlier enough that the crew has gotten to the plane and started, but it's the fastest we can do."

"That will have to work," I said, following him into the restricted staff area. Not knowing my way around airports without guides, I had no idea what sections of the airport did what or what the other people were working on. Closely following the fae employee through the neutral airport territory, I didn't really care.

I couldn't smell any werewolves. I knew they had once worked here, keeping an eye on who entered and left Dallas. Heath and I had been caught by them, and Tywin had been very nosy. He had been equally nosy when I was traveling with my family. It had always been an inappropriate action. I was purposefully not nosy when it came to the airport, one of the reasons I never came to deal with the jet I'd won through conquest from the Dallas pack. I was the de facto leader of the city, the most powerful faction represented because I had chased out the previous. Dallas had always been a werewolf-heavy city compared to many others. I had no real job, but I had sway over what happened in the city, and that I did exercise.

"How have things been since the werewolves left?" I asked benignly as we headed for the hangar where the jet was held.

"It was a struggle in the beginning. We were understaffed for some time, but we fae moved more people into the city and have stabilized. The loss of the witch family last year didn't hurt us since those witches never tried to work with us. Other witches do, but we decided it was best not to have any of them in your path."

"I've had bad experiences with the fae as well," I reminded him.

"Well, here in Dallas, you only have a handful of options. There's not a single community in this city you don't have tension with. The werewolves choked out many other supernatural communities from moving. It was accidental, at least on Alpha Everson's part, but it's the truth. However, in the eyes of the fae, we have no ill will to you and yours. That was decreed by King Brion shortly after he reclaimed his throne. So, out of fae and witches, we thought you'd rather work with a fae for a moment."

"Our pack was large enough, we brought too much attention," Landon said, nodding. "Father and I never wanted to keep most supernaturals out, but we lived public lives and got a lot of scrutiny compared to other large packs in the United States. Also, our pack was large enough that even though we never wanted to fight others, we couldn't always prevent some in the pack from causing trouble. That happens in most cities, but we established a large pack faster than others could build up their own networks. It was always a bit imbalanced in our favor. A small incident became a big one quickly."

"Exactly. So, our communities are small. We're one of the few cities in the nation without a vampire nest, in fact."

"They can't be exposed under any circumstances. How some of the nests manage to operate where they do astounds me," Landon added. "Like Boston and Phoenix... or New York. Seems impossible to keep anything a secret in that city."

"The Master of New York is Isaiah, a member of the Tribunal, so he can get away with a lot. He settled in the city when it was still young," the fae replied, flexing some political and historical knowledge. "But setting up here in Dallas, we'll probably never see vampires. We might draw some rarer supernaturals now, though. Others who want distance from the werewolves or a smaller population to deal with."

The light conversation continued as we reached the hangar bay. It was a decent distraction for a moment, hearing that I hadn't totally broken the city by chasing out the Dallas pack and not allowing a new Alpha to rebuild. The others adapted and finally found space to build up their own communities, which would continue to do the city good.

Supernaturals had their own economy, and I didn't want to lose access to it, though I always made Heath the one who dealt with anything I needed from other supernaturals. I knew I would eventually allow Dallas to have a pack again. I only preemptively refused Callahan because of the recent events and didn't want to risk anything in the immediate future.

"Thank you for the conversation and for escorting us. You and your team do a great service to the family," I said politely to the fae, bowing my head. Landon pulled out several large bills from his wallet.

"All in a day's work, Miss Leon. It's an honor to work

K.N. BANET

with any ruler of the supernatural, and thank you for continuing to trust us with your travel. We hope to continue building that trust in the future. If anything happens in this city against you, let me say, from the fae staff here, it will never be one of us or endorsed by us in any way. Our King knows that as well."

"I am grateful to hear that."

"Yup. You guys have always been good to me and Father," Landon said, holding out those bills.

The fae took them and stowed them away without counting.

"I shall split this with the others who have helped get your jet in the air," he said before leaving us to head back to his work.

I was silent as I boarded the jet, the staff continuing their preparations for takeoff. I didn't know any of them, but Landon was familiar, shaking their hands and thanking them for being able to lift off at a moment's notice. As we sat down, I gave Landon a questioning look. He figured out my question without me needing to say anything. The crew was kept on retainer and took mandatory days off to get their flight hours in outside of their work for us, which were staggered so we always had the crew necessary to leave even if some were gone. All of them knew the secret of the supernatural and kept it. Landon and Heath had quietly handled it all while I had been dealing with the rest of Dallas's properties and resources. Mostly him, since his father had managed the closures and takeovers of the various businesses of the previous pack.

"Thank you," I said, trying to put the weight into it I felt it deserved. "I wasn't prepared for how much was going to come from the Dallas takeover."

"It's all in your name, with Father and me only doing as much as we're legally allowed to."

"Some of it's in Heath's name. I gave him rights to a bit of it." Shrugging, I settled in, getting as comfortable as I could. I had flown on this private jet before, but it felt like a lifetime ago. A distant memory of wanting to get to my sister and Heath following me even though he didn't agree with my decision.

It was Ranger and Sheila, wasn't it?

Shaking my head, I tried to dismiss the memory once again. Sheila was Ranger's longtime partner, both romantically and professionally. She was dead. Heath killed her when she, Ranger, and several dozen other werewolves were forced to attack my territory, particularly Heath and his family protected within my borders. Ranger was lucky to live that night, but he wasn't whole. He couldn't regrow the leg I had damaged enough to force amputation.

Most days, I tried my best not to think about that night just a year ago. Now I couldn't stop, knowing it was the night that had led to Landon and me in the seats we were in.

One attack from a paranoid Alpha, his mind breaking under the strain of the magic keeping him under control. A series of simple decisions on my part to help those who needed help. Uncovering a plot that was far too close to succeeding...

It was also the night Dirk had been bitten by a werewolf, leaving us all waiting with bated breath to see if he would wake up. He'd survived to be a werewolf.

I checked my phone, seeing that no one had reached out yet. I was hoping to hear from Niko or Dirk. Even Niko's staff or assistant would be a blessing, but I had no missed calls, no texts, not even any new emails.

"Rainer Brandt," Landon softly growled, but it wasn't directed at me. Landon was looking at his phone as he read something. "Fenris..."

"Does Fenris have a last name?" I asked, frowning.

"A long list of fake ones," Landon said, shaking his head. "Nothing telling, though. I can easily see why he wouldn't want anyone knowing his real name."

"Yeah..." Bitterness flooded me as I considered the last year. There had been warning signs. There was no missing them. I had trusted that crazed werewolf and trusted how Heath liked to run his pack. I had agreed with Heath in the end, knowing that to foster a sense of trust, we had to let them have secrets to reveal in their own time.

I had never dreamed he would end up revealing his secrets like this. Had never dreamed he would be who he seemed to be.

"How do you think they're related?" Landon asked. "Is he Niko's cousin or something?"

The plane started to move as he asked. I could only shrug. After remaining silent, I noticed Landon was frowning at me, causing me to sigh heavily.

"I don't know. Niko never told me the names of his

biological family. They're all dead. He said his father was the Alpha of the pack. His mother was human. Any of the werewolves who didn't die that night were conscripted into other packs, and he hunted them down during the War. I think...he would have seen them as giving in to the evil that destroyed their home and lives. He saw others as the traitors, not himself."

Shaking my head as I leaned back to stare out of the window, I felt the heavy sensation of guilt, a sinking stone in my stomach that made me feel ill.

"He never told me names, though. None of them have. I don't know how Rainer Brandt is related to Niko, but the signs all point in that direction. They've fought before, so Niko probably believes Rainer is dead."

"And Fenris is the one who walked away from the battle," Landon nodded. "New name, new identity—"

"New magic," I growled softly.

"And that. Then he waited, about eight hundred years of waiting, all so he could get into position to fight Niko again."

"And I handed it right to him," I said softly. I threw up a hand as Landon's mouth opened once again. "Don't argue with me. I did. I kept Dirk, didn't protect him well enough, and led to him becoming a werewolf, then I sent him back to Niko with a big red arrow... Rainer has everything he needs to bait Niko into a fight if Niko is his goal."

"There's no way he's not. Nikolaus Brandt, the Traitor, son of Hasan... and Rainer Brandt, probably originally a member of the same pack. This is a grudge match that is centuries in the making."

I heard something crack to see that Landon was holding his phone too tightly. A long line over the screen made me reach out and pry the phone from him.

"We might need that," I muttered, putting it in a cubby for safekeeping.

"You know what I thought about on the drive here?" looking unperturbed, Landon didn't argue about the phone I had taken it from him. "When he met you, I heard he tried to kill you when no one was there to back you up. He had the chance a year ago but didn't take it. You let him out of the cage, and he had the control not to do it. He worked with you. He kept working with you. He was mouthy, but he always was."

"I had given him a chance, and he gave me one... The situations were different, and I was on the same side as him, so—"

"Jacky, you had been helping on the same side of the coup the first time you met. The idea that you were helping the right side isn't good enough. Do you know what really changed?"

"Tell me."

"No one knew you were one of Hasan's children all those years ago. That came out to the public while you were in Seattle...after he tried to attack you, and Pa put him in his place."

For a second, it was difficult to breathe.

"Are you saying he conned me from the first moment

in the basement of the pack's mansion?" I asked once I could find air again. "That everything has been a lie?"

"I think we can't leave it off the table," Landon murmured. "It makes the most sense. We have no idea what sort of magic he can do, so... it could have been easy for him."

I only nodded because he was right.

I just hadn't wanted it said out loud yet, hadn't been ready for it yet.

As we took off, the city growing smaller underneath us, Landon and I stopped talking entirely. All I could think about was every smile Fenris had ever given me. Every good-natured joke was suddenly stained with the truth.

Each moment only made me angrier.

16

CHAPTER SIXTEEN

"We're two hours from Berlin," an attendant said quietly as she refilled our drinks.

"Do you want to reach out to your family now?" Landon asked as she walked away.

"Not yet," I answered before sipping my drink, my mouth and throat dry. I didn't like these long flights. I had taken several at this point, and it never got easier, no matter how comfortable the plane.

"They could send us some backup," Landon pointed out, not looking at me as he read something.

"And they will, but I know when I want to reach out to them. I know I have to, but it can't be too quickly. A werewolf from my territory is probably a threat against a member of my family. For all we know, Fenris or Rainer, whatever we want to call him, is probably playing some fucking game with them right now. Or Niko is already dead. There's no way to know. Dirk could be hurt, but unless he's been killed or pulls out of Heath's pack,

Heath only knows if he's alive or not. You and I are going to get to Niko's territory and start figuring out where we stand before I ask my family to come. We have to or... worst-case scenario, they'll think Heath planned this, and *no one* will be safe. Best-case scenario, I'm incompetent for trusting anyone, and the rift growing in my family gets worse."

"Why would my father plan this?"

It was all too easy to come up with a few reasons my family would consider.

"To get back in Callahan's good graces is the most straightforward," I said, staring at my glass of water. "To get back into the good graces of the other Alphas in North America to make a play against Callahan would be another, depending if they thought Heath was willing to go against him further. Killing a member of my family when Callahan has never been able to."

"He would *never*," Landon growled.

"I know, but you wanted to know why my family might think he would," I reminded him softly. "What I need to do is reach out to Niko's home and get someone to come pick us up. I have no idea where to find his territory, and we don't have time to look."

"You've never been?"

"I've never been to most of my siblings' homes," I said as I hit call for Niko but not his cellphone number. Not many kept landlines, but I had a secondary number for Niko and hoped that was it. His staff would pick up, I was certain of it.

"Ansel speaking."

"It's Jacky. I'm going to assume there's no update on where Dirk and Niko are, and they haven't come back."

"You would be correct. Is there something you need from me?"

"A ride from the airport. Landon Everson and I touch down in three hours. I hope I've given you enough time to put something together."

"Excuse me? Miss Leon... we don't allow unannounced guests here, certainly not without Nikolaus available to give his approval."

"I'm his youngest sister, and I have intel. Everything I tell you must be kept between us. No one else can know, not even other members of the family. Not permanently, but for now. We can't start a panic. Is that understood?"

"Of course. It's no different from how Nikolaus runs this household," Ansel replied. "We're adept at keeping secrets."

"Have you ever heard of a Rainer Brandt?"

"Brandt is Nikolaus's ancestral surname, which is why he brought it back to use for Dirk's last name, but I've never heard of a Rainer. Is something wrong? Did you learn something?"

"We have a werewolf in the pack with documents that state he may have been called Rainer Brandt at one point. Now, that werewolf is missing. I can explain more when we touch down. I think it would be easier in person." I had those documents in my bag. It was going to be a strange experience to show them to a human. He might know about the secrets, but I had a feeling he wouldn't be expecting what I had to show him.

"Thanks to the connection in name, you believe this Rainer Brandt has something to do with the disappearance of Dirk. Which would mean Nikolaus is handling it. More than that, you think he's connected to Nikolaus'... childhood."

"That's right, but since this werewolf came from my neck of the woods, we're coming to help deal with it."

"I shall... make an exception, and if Nikolaus fires me, I will expect you to fix it," Ansel said, clearing his throat. "We have a member of staff at the household in Berlin who can meet you when you land. They will drive you to the territory, and I will meet you here. If you intend on investigating anything in and around Nikolaus's territory, there will be a lot I must teach you."

"Teach me?"

"I will see you soon, Miss Leon." Ansel hung up without an explanation.

I looked at Landon, concern growing in me.

"Teach me?" I repeated softly, wondering if Landon had any idea.

"There might be other factions in the area to stay away from, hazards, magical traps..." Landon gave a half-shrug. "Dirk doesn't talk about home, and it's not because he doesn't know. He's always careful about it. There are clearly some secrets about whatever Niko has going on in Germany."

"Good point, but he could have explained that," I muttered. "Do you have a plan before landing?"

"Yeah." He grabbed his cracked phone and called his father. "Hey, Pa."

"Landon, it's good to hear from you. Jacky?"

"I'm right here," I said, smiling because Landon put Heath on speakerphone.

"Good, good. I've been watching your flight. You should be touching down soon, right? Another few hours?"

"Yeah, how is everyone?" Landon asked, leaning over the phone on the table between us.

"The healers are keeping everyone comfortable under the sleeping curse. We've moved some extra mattresses in, and everyone is doing well for now. I have the others doing tight patrols around your property, not the entire territory."

"You don't have the wolves for it," Landon said.

"No, I don't," Heath agreed. "What are you two planning?"

"We have some of Niko's staff picking us up when we land. Do you think my family will notice the flight? They must know I own this thing now, right?"

"I don't really know, but I'm learning not to... Why would they think it's concerning? You sent Dirk to visit Niko. Why wouldn't you go visit as well? Do they tell each other those sorts of plans?"

"No, I don't think so, but I'm trying to keep things quiet for the moment," I explained, sighing. "You know my family."

"Regretfully on most days," Heath confirmed, making all of us give similarly sad chuckles, each knowing that it would be funny if it wasn't sad.

"I just wanted to check in with you, Pa. Carey behaving?"

"I don't know what Jacky said to her, but she's been a boon," Heath said. Heath had a way of speaking that brought an image to mind. He was probably pushing his hand through his hair, a small smile forming, even if he wasn't particularly happy. "Helping the healers, making sure everyone is eating and drinking. She's too young to be running around like that, but she pointed out to me that she was only following my lead."

"Yeah, because you probably asked them ten minutes before she did," Landon said, shaking his head, and I was certain I caught an eye roll.

"You would be right. I need to make sure everyone is doing okay. Call me again whenever you need to. I want to know what's going on."

"We'll keep you up to speed," I promised. "Love you."

"Love you, too. Stay safe... both of you."

"We'll try," Landon said before hanging up. He gave me a sheepish smile, making him look ten years younger. It showed me a young man who might have existed if the world hadn't thrown every trouble and tribulation his way. A young man who loved his father and relied on him without shame or reservation. It was a side of Landon I didn't get to see often. I always knew it was there, but he showed it so rarely.

"I figured if I wanted to hear him, you would, too."

"I did, thank you." I patted his hand before leaning back to wait for our landing.

Secrets and Ruin

It wasn't the worst landing, but it wasn't the best, either. Turbulence made the final descent into something of a stomach churner, but we did touch down. We were taken to a hangar bay, where Landon discussed payment for allowing the plane to stay, clearly working around the law to make it happen. Once he was done, we were given a ride in a nondescript SUV by another fae to the pickup location. This one didn't explain why she was doing it instead of the werewolves or witches working around the airport.

"How is it already Monday afternoon?" I asked as we waited for our pickup to show themselves. I stared at the sky, frowning. "Aside from the obvious issue with the flight being eleven hours and the time zones we jumped. I know Berlin is seven hours ahead of Dallas and all that."

"Well, you've already answered it from the logical standpoint, but everyone does this thing where they lose track of time when shit is going on. So, here we are."

"Miss Leon and Mister Everson?"

My eyes snapped to the source and saw a human woman. She smelled nervous but grew bolder when she met my eyes.

"Good, good. I didn't know what you looked like," she said, suddenly smiling. Her English wasn't heavily accented, but it was still clear to me she was probably a local. "But you have your father's eyes, and there they are!" She clapped her hands together. "I'm Millie. I have been asked to take you to the car. Ansel said you would be here and need transport to the estate. It's something of

165

a drive, so let's move along. We *might* be able to get there before nightfall."

"Does he really live that far from Berlin?"

"He keeps a house in the city to manage his businesses, but yes, he's always tried to keep his time in the city to a minimum and his home away from the urban sprawl."

As we walked out of the airport, there was a moment of the sky above us, and she checked it and her watch.

"We probably won't get there before nightfall," she said, shaking her head.

"How long is the drive?" Landon asked as we followed her to the car.

"Just under eight hours. I can drive fast, but you know, teleportation would be nice. I wish the world would hurry that up." She seemed relaxed, all smiles now as we loaded in.

And she did drive fast, flying past people on the road. I held onto my seatbelt in the front seat, wondering if she should have slowed down or had one of us drive. We were the supernaturals with the special instincts and all that.

"How long have you worked for Niko? You seem about Dirk's age," I said, trying to think of anything else.

"Oh, well... I didn't know what Mister Brandt was for a long time. I worked at his club for a while until Dirk got me a better job for my degree with his dad. Driving people around isn't what I normally do, but I was asked because I figured out something was wrong. Dirk and I were supposed to hang out, and he never showed, which isn't like him. He was supposed to tell me all about the United States and Texas. He even said he was seeing someone, but he didn't tell me the lucky girl's name over the phone." She gave me a grin. "He's your nephew, right?"

"Ah… yeah, in a sense." I was grateful Landon was in the backseat. I wasn't sure if I wanted to out either man, but it certainly put me in an awkward position because she was clearly fishing for information.

"Well, it's nice to meet you, Millie. I was wondering where I recognized your name," Landon said. I looked over my shoulder to see his sharp smile, but there wasn't anything aggressive about his posture. "He's told me a bit about you."

"Oh, are you a friend of his?"

"Of a sort," Landon confirmed.

I quietly decided to leave this be until we were at the estate, and no one was driving fast enough to kill everyone in the vehicle. I did my best to keep the conversation to a minimum, but it was difficult to be too quiet as Millie raced through the country, leaving me feeling like my life was in danger. More than once, I tried to step on an invisible brake, hoping I could slow us down, only to be disappointed to find one didn't exist.

Finally, the sun getting lower than I liked, we turned right down a rarely used road. It was maintained but didn't see heavy traffic, and whoever kept it clear of debris didn't do that often. Tall trees towered around us, no more road signs showing up as we weaved down, Millie watching her speed. Branches littered the road, and I even saw a carcass of roadkill that had to be at least a week old.

"Are we almost there?" I asked, an assumption born of the environment around me and the road. I was confused because I hadn't yet felt the entry into Niko's territory.

"Yes, ma'am," she said, her voice suddenly low, a near whisper. "There will be a couple more turns. This is still a public road. You'll know when we get to the private drive."

I knew well before we finally rolled into Niko's territory. I received no wave of feeling or response from Niko, who would have known I was there if he was anywhere in his own territory. Territory magic was mostly feeling, a silent one-way form of communicating between the one who claimed it and the one who entered. Niko's response could have told me to leave or made me feel welcomed. Perhaps it would feel wary but willing to meet.

All I got was a sense of secrets, with an undercurrent of danger, but there was no active presence in the sensation. It was like a foreboding sign in a horror movie but without the immediate threat of the monster. I was walking into its lair, but the beast wasn't in the area to enforce the warning. I knew Niko wasn't in his territory. Even if he was trying to hide, I would have known from even the smallest shift in that feeling.

Not paying attention to the distance or time anymore, my eyes searched the trees, hoping for any sign of someone or something I recognized. I didn't know the landscape, but something made me want to look, as though it pricked my instincts in a bad way. As I searched and saw nothing, I felt restless, edgy with the need for someone or something to jump out and try to attack or the need to find something to attack. It took too long for me to realize what my instincts were trying to tell me, and it had nothing to do with being in Niko's territory.

This place is dangerous. Even Millie recognizes it, and she probably doesn't even know why...

I sniffed the air and caught the scent of Landon's growing agitation, but he was composed. Whatever we were getting couldn't bait him into doing anything, but he noticed it like I did.

"Here we are," Millie now said in the softest whisper, barely audible over the sound of the SUV.

She turned left down a dirt road, but it didn't stay dirt for longer than a hundred yards before becoming a paved drive. Now our speed could only be described as a crawl. I itched to get out of the SUV and run through the woods, wanting to find whatever dangerous thing lurked out there, unseen and unheard but *there*.

It was still a lengthy drive, but as we weaved through the trees into a clearing, the sight of his remote home came into view.

"It's time to get to work," I said, readying myself for whatever secrets Landon and I were about to stumble into while we looked for our missing members of the Brandt family.

17

CHAPTER SEVENTEEN

I wasn't sure if I should call Niko's home a mansion or a castle. It was neither and both. What I could reasonably guess was there had been a castle or keep-like structure originally, and Niko had renovated it with a dash of more modern aesthetics, sharp lines and angles to mix with the organic stone of older areas of the structure. It was contradictory and strange. There were solar panels on the roofs at all different levels of the three-story monstrosity and a few satellites jutting out from the seemingly original towers, one on each side of the home.

"Dirk never told me what this place looked like, but I wasn't expecting this," I said, shaking my head at the strange place, unable to identify if I thought it was cool and unique or the most atrocious thing I had ever seen.

"He never told me much about it either," Landon said, leaning between the front seats now to look out the front. "I hate it."

"Niko certainly... made some choices..."

"You know, there's no record of a castle ever being here. I looked after my first time visiting... only time. This is my second trip here," Millie said, her bubbly personality becoming more edgy and panicked as though she was trying to cover up her nerves. She was failing, but the effort was there.

Millie said nothing more as she drove us into the underground garage, where a line of several other vehicles waited. I could smell her confusion. It matched with her frown as she picked a spot.

"I hope this is the right one," she said, her audible swallow telling me she was more nervous than excited.

"I'm sure no one will mind." I was trying to comfort her, but I had no idea how things were run here. I was only hoping I could sway them thanks to nepotism.

As I got out, there was already someone running toward us, and I saw Ansel behind him, walking quickly but not in the same rush. Behind us, the garage doors were closing quickly, blocking all sunlight from the garage and leaving only the artificial lights above us.

"Welcome." Ansel started talking even though he was still another fifty feet from us. "Please follow me. He'll get your things into a pair of rooms I've set aside for you." He gestured at the running human, who was already opening the trunk to grab our stuff. "Dinner will be ready in an hour, then we have lights out at midnight—"

"We're not here to visit. You, Landon, and I need to talk, then we need to get on the move."

"Tomorrow. We'll talk tonight before lights out," Ansel said simply, nodding like he wasn't trying to argue, but he and I didn't mean the same things. "It's all accounted for, Miss Leon."

"Depending on the length of our talk, Landon and I will be gone before dinner or shortly after it," I said, frowning as I approached him, grabbing my backpack from the other human because I needed it. Landon had his as well, leaving the poor footman empty-handed and confused.

"Um..." Ansel looked far out of his depth now, shaking his head slowly. "No one enters the woods after dark, Miss Leon. Niko's rules are firm about that. Only he does. He's made it clear that his family shouldn't either. I know you're his sister, but this is his territory, and—"

"Why?" I demanded, closing the distance as Ansel spoke. Now I was right in front of him, and he was only a few inches taller than me.

"It's dangerous. Surely you noticed."

"We felt something, but clearly, we don't know what's going on, so if you can hurry up and start telling us more than vague warnings, I would appreciate it. My mate is missing, and I'm getting crankier by the second," Landon said, his words devolving into a frustrated growl at the end. "I'm being as patient as I can be."

Ansel looked at Millie and the unintroduced footman before looking back to Landon and me.

"Come with me. Both of you can take the rest of the evening off. Millie, a room has also been prepared for you, the same one from your last visit. Have a nice evening." Ansel waved for Landon and me to follow him before turning on his heel and heading for a door.

We followed silently, studying everything we could see. Paintings decorated the walls, old-looking ones of people I didn't recognize. I could distinctly tell when we left the modern portion of the building and entered the original castle's or keep's halls. Ansel stopped in front of a wood and iron door, taking out a large key to unlock it. He went in first, holding the door for us, then locked it behind us. We were in a drawing room or library; I couldn't tell which.

"This is the most secure room on the estate," Ansel said, moving to pull linens off a few armchairs. Landon helped him move them to a fireplace, and I watched as Ansel lit it. "Since you wish to speak immediately and want to know as much as I can tell you, there is information the staff can't hear. This is also the room with the only documents that might shed more light and provide evidence of what I'm about to say."

"Foreboding," I muttered.

Landon nodded, agreeing, but his eyes were locked on Ansel.

"I will start with the most important thing. The Black Forest is the only place on Earth that remains where our reality and the fae realms overlap into a single instance of a single location. As far as we know, at least."

I swayed under the implications.

"Excuse me?" I croaked.

"Fuck..." Landon leaned on the back of the closet armchair.

Ansel stood in front of the fireplace and waved at the chairs he had moved. "You'll want to sit down. There is more. This is a complicated situation, and I'm the only member of staff who can tell you enough to give you close to a full picture of how complicated." Ansel seated himself and waited.

I found a seat, picking the one in the middle. Rubbing my face, I tried to get beyond the small, horrified voice in my head that told me I should just leave.

"Nikolaus told me when I was being briefed that he never understood why, but the Black Forest Pack once protected this place and protected others from what could potentially come out of it. The Black Forest Pack was eradicated some eight hundred years ago during a war between werecats and werewolves."

"His pack," I said softly.

"We don't go out after dark because it would be too easy to lose the paths and find ourselves the prey of something vicious from the fae realms. Everyone on the staff knows about this, and we lock down the estate once night falls. There's a lot of iron in the structure to protect us, and there're iron tracks buried under the earth to make a circle around the estate. It drives off weaker fae if they come around, while the amount of iron in the building wards off the more dangerous ones. The original structure of this home, where we are now, is still under ancient protections I don't understand, but I know

Nikolaus maintains them. Those extend to the rest of the building as well, but they can't be updated."

"That would explain the architectural choices," I said, trying to make light of the horrifying reality of Niko's territory and his home. I wondered how ancient those protections were and where they came from. Were they done by Subira to help Niko, or were they something his biological family had created long before his birth?

"So, if you want to leave after dark, you must understand the dangers involved. We will not let you back in until dawn. If you leave the building now, the doors will lock behind you, and they will stay locked." Ansel looked around, standing again to go to a bookshelf across the room. "There are some interesting things here to read, based on their titles alone. I don't come into this place without cause or read these myself, so I couldn't tell you what they might say. This is Nikolaus's private library and sitting room. He entertains the family here, so I felt right to bring you here."

"Does Niko leave anything to help people who might be going into the forest to find him or a way out?" I asked, frowning as I considered the strange life of my brother.

"I have only seen Nikolaus entertain one member of your family since I took over the position I hold today, and he made it clear that he's never explained to anyone in the family what he lives with. Also, Dirk was educated enough to keep himself safe but doesn't know the entire situation. He never tested his luck when Niko explained the danger was magical in origin."

"Can you give Landon and me a few minutes?" I asked, letting everything sink in as I stood and moved closer to the fire. "I think we need to talk over what you've explained so far, and I need a moment to... figure out what questions I still need to ask."

Landon nodded at me when I was done explaining, and Ansel gave us a professional bow.

"I can come back with dinner and, perhaps, answer more questions if you think of any." Ansel went to the door, looking around the room as he stood in the doorframe. "I'll be back shortly."

The moment the door closed, I leaned against the mantle of the fireplace, letting the warmth engulf me.

"Landon..."

"We don't have much time. If Niko is out there, he's probably holding his own, but he grew up in the area and has lived here for centuries as a werecat, so he's more than capable of fighting off most types of fae. Dirk doesn't stand a chance."

"I know, and it's already been some days." Closing my eyes, I knew what we had to do. I couldn't bring myself to rush past the important preparation, though. This was something I never thought I would encounter. I had no idea what to prepare. "Help me think of questions. We need... anything. Information is key right now."

"We need to know if this estate is the only safe place. He mentioned something about paths. We should ask what that meant. It could have meant getting lost in the woods, but it doesn't feel like anything is that simple here."

"Right... I was thinking of asking if Niko had an emergency plan if fae did get inside... weapons, safe rooms, anything like that."

"I like that."

We threw options back and forth for half an hour and had a list when Ansel came back, pushing a tray with two meals. I began to question where his food was until he pulled a plate from the lower level and showed me.

"Are there any other safe places in Niko's territory or beyond it?" Landon asked first before taking a bite of his food. "You mentioned paths. Can you explain that?"

"Yes..." Ansel seemed a little put off by the question. Maybe it was that Landon wouldn't hold off on the conversation until after the meal.

I sniffed my drink, making sure it was proper water before I took a sip.

Landon and I waited expectantly until Ansel sighed and put his plate back on the cart.

"The roads have iron tracks under them, making them clear of fae unless you upset one enough to come for you, anyway. The paths in the woods have iron markers the fae won't move. Due to the nature of woodland trails, Nikolaus couldn't install proper tracks for the trails to keep them as safe as the roads. Too narrow, too winding, and they disappear over time. Niko tries to keep some well-worn, certain paths to other areas of the forest. Those are the ones he marked."

"Other areas?" I asked, needing more.

"You know a werewolf pack once lived in these woods. The other safe areas are old structures from the original werewolf pack. There used to be a thriving, large community, and they had multiple small homesteads in the area around this keep. Now, they're dilapidated buildings, but they can offer protection to anyone who wants to pass through. Nikolaus has been slowly renovating and rebuilding them over the years, hoping to give himself and us places to stop safely if we needed to go deep into the woods for an extended period. We don't often go beyond the perimeter, but sometimes it's necessary."

"Why?"

"We forage for plants and other organic magical material in the Black Forest that can't be found anywhere else in our world. They can be found in the fae realm, but the varieties here are unique to this place. It's a large source of income for Nikolaus and the household. We don't take too much when we go harvesting, and we only harvest one week every year under Nikolaus's protection. It's somewhat of a festival for us because we know we're safe. There are games like races, encouraging the staff to volunteer so we can have fun together. Everyone gets a portion of their own harvest as a personal bonus, which keeps many in this household going out there every year. Many of the Berlin staff enjoy the distance they have from the strangeness of this place."

"How much does a week's harvest bring?"

My curiosity was matched by Landon's as he asked that question.

"Depending on the quality of the harvest, somewhere between five and twenty million US dollars," Ansel answered quickly, clearly having memorized those numbers. "Volunteers for foraging often take home between two hundred and fifty thousand to five hundred thousand. Sometimes, someone will do well enough in a year with a good return, and we'll see a million-dollar bonus."

"And what... What is this stuff used for?" I asked, wanting to know about my brother's secret life.

"Much of it is very prized by herbalists who know what they can use it for. There are no potions of invisibility like fantasy would tell you, but these things are full of raw magic, and witches use them to power effects they might be doing through spells or to help reach a desired effect with a spell."

"We should get back on topic," I said, rubbing my temple. The world of magic was a world I still didn't fully understand. I didn't think I ever could. Every time I looked into it, it only grew more complicated. Even the witches in my family were only scratching the surface of it or had their own ways of doing things that weren't conventional, thanks to their power.

"Are there any known creatures we should be watchful for?"

"If you meet anyone in the woods, you should avoid them. Animals can't always be trusted, either."

"Even if we see Niko?"

Ansel looked haunted for a moment, his face paling

as he looked at me with an expression that scared me because I could see the nightmares in his eyes.

"Especially if you see Nikolaus. He's lived in this area for centuries. The fae here know him and will absolutely use that familiarity to mimic him better than anyone else could." Ansel's throat bobbled with a swallow. "It would not be the first time they have lured people to their demise with his face. It's the first thing we tell people when they come here. Nikolaus will never ask one of us to leave the property from outside the border. He will never beckon us like that. If it appears he is, then it is most certainly someone else wearing his face. You will not have the benefit of the iron protections to make sure it is him.

"If you see him, call to him. If he doesn't move, stay on the path and do not approach him. If he doesn't reply quickly, stay on the path and hurry back to the estate. If he walks away, do not follow and stay on the path to the estate. Nikolaus will always verify his identity immediately and will come to the path, showing he can painlessly walk on it. Only with that verification will you know it's truly him."

"Stay on the path seems like an important thing to remember," Landon muttered as he paced, mulling over what we were learning.

"And Dirk?"

"Dirk is less likely to be mimicked. The fae knew the young man had no power here over the others and that he was educated by Nikolaus about the dangers of these places. He never fell for them, and they knew he couldn't be used against us. While everyone here on staff loves the son of Nikolaus, we also trust he will follow the safety rules. We're not to save him. We're to contact Nikolaus and have him investigate.

"I wasn't here, but I know of a story from when Dirk was young. One of the footmen saw Dirk outside the barriers. It was midday, a time that shouldn't be dangerous, but he was a young child. The footman ran for Niko, hoping he wasn't leaving the boy to die. Niko was reading to Dirk in his room. I spoke to that footman. He went to show Niko how Dirk was also outside the barrier. He Changed the moment he saw the imposter fae. He killed it while it was still wearing his son's face."

"Did... Dirk see that?" I asked in a small voice.

"I don't know, but you are asking for the dangers of the woods around the estate. The fae are certainly one of them—"

"So is Niko," Landon said, not letting Ansel finish his own thought. The words rang true to me. If Niko couldn't verify that we were who we said we were, we were in just as much danger. Landon, Heath, and Fenris were werewolves who could overpower me, but they were some of the few I had met who could, and I wasn't even twenty years into being a werecat. Niko was roughly eight hundred. If he wanted anyone dead, there was a small chance they would survive.

"Yes, Nikolaus is also dangerous if you don't respect the dangers of this area. If you don't respect what he asks of you to verify you aren't a fae in disguise, he will attack first."

"Can we see what sort of equipment or gear he might have for people needing to go into the woods?" Landon was jumping back into action, which I was grateful for.

I came here for Dirk and Niko, to hopefully stop Fenris, and there was a chance we were all wrong about this. What we were hearing now was pointing to more dangers than I knew how to deal with.

"I..." Ansel looked around, unsure of himself.

"Let me ask something that will make this easier." It was clear Ansel hadn't been given any sort of plan in case he had to get weapons to fight the fae himself, so I picked a new direction of questioning. "If Niko died, who would inherit this place?"

"Dirk, of course," Ansel said, his puzzled expression telling me he had no idea what I was getting at.

"Dirk was human when that would have been decided. What would Niko have left him for his own safety? If that doesn't help find anything that can help, then does Niko have some sort of emergency plan if his family needs to go out there?"

His eyes going wide, Ansel waved for us to follow him. He walked out of the library and across the hall to an unlocked door, an ancient office. He didn't enter and put a hand in front of Landon.

"If there is anything like that, it would be in this room. Nikolaus told me to only let anyone in this space if he was dead. He specified it could only be his family, no one else. I'm not allowed to step inside."

"He's not dead, but thank you," I said softly,

approaching the desk. "Leave the door open while I do this."

I was rummaging through another desk, but now I knew there was some connection between my Fenris and Niko. Remembering that, I pulled out the desk drawers, ignoring the more benign things to get to the bottoms. It was odd because the more I looked at it, the more I realized this had to be the original desk, and Fenris's was a clone of it. Some of the styling was different, and the wood was treated differently, but the layout was the exact same. The height and its imposing nature. I could practically feel the years of the desk in front of me. It was an ancient piece of furniture, an immensely opulent piece of furniture for the time it came from.

It's an heirloom. Must be.

I was right to consider it, finding another hidden section and opening it.

"They learned this trick together," I murmured, tilting the drawer for Landon to see what I revealed. "Niko and Rainer."

"It's not a hard trick—"

"It was the same drawer," I said softly, brushing my fingers across it. "The same layout and the same drawer had the hidden compartment."

Inside the hidden compartment of Niko's desk, I found a single folded letter and a key of sorts, from what I could guess. It didn't look like any key I had ever seen, but I felt like my guess was right by the shape of it. I took both, then put everything back as it was. I didn't want to leave this solemn place looking trashed. It felt disrespectful in a way I couldn't put words to and luckily, no one made me try. Once I was done, I sat on the more modern leather chair and broke the wax seal of the letter.

"It's addressed to Dirk," I said softly. "This is Niko's will."

"He would have rewritten it if Dirk died at any point, but if he intended on Dirk inheriting as a son, it would make sense," Landon said, clearly trying to keep himself outside the room. I could see him shaking with the need to spring into action and go find Dirk now, but we both knew there was preparation. If this could help, we had to spend time on it.

I skimmed the letter, not wanting to delve too deeply into the intimate words of a father to his son. They weren't things my eyes were ever supposed to see. I was looking for other things, like the use of the key.

And I found that... sort of.

"Shit," I hissed as I got to the end of the letter.

"What is it?"

"'The key I've given you will open my personal armory, but the door is hidden. There's only one person I've ever told the location to, my brother Davor. While he and I aren't close anymore, we once were, and he'll respect this. He'll tell you what you need to know. It will have everything you need to survive living here as a human if you choose to continue doing so.'" I looked up from the letter, frustration now strong. "Davor."

"Davor... Ansel, can you call him?" Landon asked for me. "Jacky needs to talk to her shittiest brother."

"Um..."

"Do it," I confirmed, taking a deep breath. Every minute we had to wade through Niko's secrets, the less time we had helping him and Dirk if they needed it. It was going to be a rough call, and I had little time to prepare for it, but I wouldn't put it off because of my feelings. "Don't say it's me. They won't be able to smell a lie. Just tell him it's Niko. If he knows it's me, he'll have the entire family on the call, and we're not ready for that."

18

CHAPTER EIGHTEEN

Ten minutes was all the time I had to prepare to speak to Davor. Every minute, I was subjected to a war of emotions while trying to remain cool-headed enough to figure out what to say and how to say it. As Ansel reached out to Davor's household and they chased down Davor to let him know, I was pacing in view of the camera. Landon boldly sat where he could be seen, not bothering to hide.

"I think you should step off-screen," I finally said, knowing we only had mere seconds before Davor connected.

"Fine," Landon huffed, moving away to sit in a corner armchair.

"Thank you." Before I had time to look back at the screen and camera, I knew the call connected.

"Jacky? I was told Niko was reaching out to speak to me." Davor's confusion sounded angry, which the best I could get right now.

"I asked them to lie because we need to be fast and careful," I said, turning quickly to see Davor's furrowed brow and deep frown. I didn't know him well enough to know if he was concerned by the development or if he was holding back anger. I couldn't smell through the screen.

"What is it?"

"I need to get into Niko's armory. I'm going into the Black Forest to find him and Dirk. I have reason to believe a very old werewolf named Rainer Brandt is alive and gunning for Niko."

The moment Rainer's name dropped from my lips, Davor paled.

"Rainer can't be alive," Davor said in a fearful whisper. "Niko killed him."

"Who is he?"

"His... his brother," Davor said, the moment of hesitation pointing to how uncomfortable the thought was to Davor. "Not as you and I are his siblings, but—"

"An original member of the Black Forest Pack... a son of the Alpha, one of Niko's blood relatives."

"You don't understand, Jacky. Any werewolf who survived what Niko went through as a boy pledged their loyalty to the other werewolves. They and Niko feuded through the War. He hunted them down and killed them, both family and old packmates. Rainer was the oldest of his siblings." Davor started to shake his head.

"Niko said Rainer was being groomed as a boy to be the next Alpha, but also that all of them had that sort of training because they learned from their father. Rainer was already a werewolf the night it happened, but still young. I believe he might have only been fourteen. Niko would remember much better than I do."

Landon's coughing fit of surprise at the Alpha remark hadn't broken Davor's explanation, but he certainly noticed. As he finished talking, his eyes flicked as if he was trying to see around the screen.

"It's Landon Everson. He's here to assist me with this because we're dealing with an old, powerful werewolf," I said quickly, not wanting to pretend as though nothing had happened when something clearly had. "Heath is staying with the rest of the pack because some of them had been hit with a fae sleep spell."

"Why?" Davor asked, his eyes going sharper, reminding me more of the angry Davor I was used to. Now, I saw it differently. He didn't like the lack of information and confusion. He was trying to put the pieces together in a complicated puzzle where he was missing information.

I tried to find a way to explain as Landon got up and walked toward me, stepping into view. While I struggled, he jumped into the silence I left behind.

"We think he's been posing as a different werewolf for several centuries and sprung a trap to get away without us being on his tail. We didn't know if he was a captured victim or not and needed to gather more information. Jacky found what we needed to realize Niko and Dirk were in potential danger—"

"If it is Rainer, Niko is in more danger than he has been since the War," Davor said, cutting Landon off, but it didn't seem condescending or rude. He was worried. I caught it now, the fear in his voice, the concern for Niko, all thanks to the implication of one of his blood relatives being back. "Rainer was always ruthless during the War. He did a number on Niko back then."

"Davor?"

"I was there when Niko came back from that fight," Davor said softly, shaking his head. "I don't know how it all happened, but Rainer nearly killed him. Niko had been hunting him down for a few years because he learned Rainer was behind the deaths of a few other werecats and some allied witches. I don't know it all, but Niko said that fight was one of the hardest of his life. Even today, hundreds of years later, it's probably still the top of that list."

"Then he needs help, and so does Dirk," Landon said decisively. "I've killed strong werewolves. I can take him. Tell us where the armory is so we can get all the advantages we can."

"It's in the basement of the keep. You won't see a door. You'll need to use your nose or another trick to find out where the keyhole is. It's not technological. It's magical. It goes to a pocket dimension. It's existed longer than Niko and I have been alive, passed down by the pack for who knows how long. I wouldn't doubt if it was as old as Hisao. Niko updates it, but it's been there for a very long time, with that permanent door and only one key." Davor drummed his fingers on the desk. "The last time I was down there, it was at the back of the basement hallway, the dead end. I don't know if he could renovate the location of the door or could find a being powerful enough to move it. Try there. You'll smell... a draft of magic through the keyhole, like a leak."

"Have you ever been inside?"

"Once. He wanted to make sure the information would be passed on if he died without an heir. I didn't go through his things. I was, at the time, still awkward about his closeness with his biological family. He's the only one of us, until you, who wasn't a wild child when Hasan found him. The idea of a family before Hasan was an..." Davor sighed, shaking his head before he finished voicing that thought.

"Before we jump off, can I ask for some... interference?"

"Don't tell the others? I wasn't planning to the moment we got off this call," Davor said, suddenly giving me a crooked, somewhat unpleasant smile.

"Really?"

"Father will kill you if Niko is hurt right now," Davor said simply. "And while neither of you said it outright, it certainly sounds like Rainer was hiding among the Everson pack in your territory. You were harboring an enemy. Unknowingly, but you were. I was thinking of packing a bag and going to visit Niko as a cover story to hold down the estate while you two run into the Black Forest. You know the werewolf. I wouldn't be any help in that place, but I can keep Niko's humans safe and provide a place for you to run back to in case that wolf decides to try anything."

"You... You would help me like that?" I was genuinely a bit surprised.

"I don't want Father to kill you," Davor said softly. For a second of silence, we studied each other—me surprised by his admission and him perhaps trying to figure out why I was surprised.

"I thought you hated her," Landon said, breaking the moment. His nonchalant way of saying it, a casual disregard of the moment, was what Davor and I needed.

"Same." I stared at Davor as realization dawned in his eyes.

"You never read my email, did you?" Davor asked, leaning back.

"No," I admitted, unable to say more.

"I'll say it here then because clearly, it needs to be said. You gave me something no one else ever could. Closure. I miss Liza with every fiber of my being, and for a century... I was so angry. Furious she was just gone, and there was nothing we could do about it, not even bring her justice. I took that anger out on you far too much, and I apologize for that. There were a lot of reasons I thought you needed to be the target, and all of them were selfish, pushing things onto your appearance into the family when many of my problems had been brewing for decades.

"Once I knew the truth, I felt like I could breathe after a century of gasping for air. The anger subsided but didn't go away, so I started talking to someone. I started recognizing what you brought our family that day. I started recognizing who and what I was really angry with. You don't need to accept that apology, but I am going to do what I have to make things less hostile between us."

"And my engagement?"

"I..." Davor sighed. "When I learned of it, I thought of Liza. She had a big heart. She and I should have never worked, yet we did... She would have accepted your engagement without question and would have been overjoyed for you. The heart wants what the heart wants. That's what she taught me. No one denied us a chance at forever. I could never ask someone else to give up theirs." He looked away, off into the distance.

"The people you love that deeply never leave you once you let them in. I hope you and Heath find the depth of that bond when you're both ready for it. Sometimes, it takes an instant, or it can take decades, for the mate bond to snap into place, but if your heart is true, it'll happen, and you deserve the chance to experience that. I sent that email because I needed you to know I wouldn't stand in the way of it."

"Thank you," I choked out.

"It's not... It's not something you should feel the need to say thank you for, Jacky." Davor closed his eyes. "We're family, but I've been slow to heal from my own wounds—"

"And like all wounded animals, you attacked anyone who made you feel even the slightest bit threatened, even if you didn't understand why," Landon said simply, clearly not hit with the same emotions as Davor and me.

"Yes," Davor confirmed with a nod as his eyes

opened. "Again, you don't need to accept my apology, Jacky. Regardless, I will help you because the rift between us is certainly my fault, and as family, it's my obligation to help you. I owe you more than you realize. Why don't we spend a moment to make a solid plan before you both head for the armory and into the Black Forest? Once I leave for Germany, our family will know something is going on. We all knew Dirk was visiting Niko, and I don't visit Niko very often right now."

"Seventy-two hours. If you can hold them all off for seventy-two hours for me and Landon to resolve this, I will be immensely grateful."

"I can try to do that. I can tell them I'm going to head here to give Dirk security lessons because I know he handles much of that for you... So long as it's not Zuri or Subira asking, I should be able to get away with that lie. If I tell Jabari, he won't know the difference, and they'll believe him."

"Then that's the plan. Landon and I are going into the forest to find everyone and get them back safely. Thank you, Davor. For the information, and..." I didn't know how to phrase the rest.

"Stay safe, little sister. I'll work with Ansel about getting there."

I nodded and left the call on as I walked away, Landon following me.

"To the armory," I said as we closed the office behind us after holding it open for Ansel. I finally had what Landon and I needed. We moved quickly and silently into the keep's basement, heading for the back of the hall. I let Landon use his nose to find the spot.

"What do you think we'll find?" he asked as I pushed the key in.

"No idea," I murmured. "But I hope it's useful, or we've wasted a lot of time."

"Time preparing isn't wasted," Landon countered. "Even if it's not as fruitful as we want, anything is better than nothing."

"I figured you would run into the forest as quickly as you could to get to Dirk," I said, eyeing him as magic swirls and runes began to form on the wall. "I should be grateful. I want to run out there, but I want to be helpful when I get there, and I don't think I can be, not yet."

"I want to, too, but I made promises, and all of them require me not to die," he said with a lopsided smile. "My father knows I'll do what I have to to get home. I want to see my sister grow up, and she doesn't deserve to lose another brother. And to your last point... we got here and found the situation wasn't what we expected, so we needed to adjust our plans. I also don't want to get to Dirk only to find I gave up on the chance to get whatever I needed to help him."

We didn't need to push the armory door open. It faded away and revealed a large room. I walked in first, making sure there was no security system we needed to worry about, no traps to set off, and Landon followed me quickly.

"Fuck..." Landon exhaled.

I would have repeated it, but my mouth had dropped

open. It was exactly what Niko had called it—an armory. Walls were lined with hanging weapons, both iron and silver, and all of them exceptionally well taken care of—axes, swords, bows, and crossbows. I saw spears in the back, neatly organized on several racks. Armor from centuries before was on display, ready for a knight to don and race off to fight against the fae or maybe a dragon.

"Do you think all of this is as old as the keep?" I asked, looking around as I walked deeper into the armory.

"Without a doubt, but it's all taken care of," Landon replied as he made a beeline for the largest wall of swords. "We'll take both... silver for Fenris and iron for the fae. Have you ever used a sword?"

"No, not really." I had fuzzy memories of swinging one around a long time ago, but I hadn't taken to any real combat skills Hasan tried to teach me before I walked out to make my own way.

"Me neither," Landon admitted as he pulled down one of the smaller ones. "Pa never really used them, either, but I know he's handy with one. I never took to it. I'm more physical, but we should take some for safety."

"Yeah." Nodding, I tried to find two short swords I could use without accidentally hurting anyone. They were lighter, but that was because of my own strength. I decided to look deeper into the armory after I picked out my swords, finding a small section in the back that made me pause.

"Are those..." I trailed off as I looked closer. I remembered what Zuri had told me about Niko and his claws. In a glass display were leather gloves with metal, articulated claws attached. There were two sets, each perfectly maintained. My fingers drifted over the display, noting it looked like a third set should have been there.

"Those look nasty," Landon muttered as he came up beside me. "Do you want to try them out?"

"Zuri said they were made specifically for Niko. They would probably be too loose on my hands," I said, shaking my head. "And I don't know if I could use them effectively."

"Then I think we have everything we need. I have a few flashlights in my bag and a headlamp if necessary. We'll split that stuff up as we leave. I'll need to find Niko's trail if we want a chance of finding him."

Nodding, I started walking out of the armory. Once Landon and I were both out, it was as if the room realized we were done, and the archway disappeared, leaving the key in the wall for us. I grabbed it, and when we found Ansel at the top of the stairs, I gave it to him.

"Give that to Davor when he gets here," I ordered. "We're going to get our gear ready and go find Niko and Dirk. Stay safe."

"I want to remind you it's very late, well past sunset. It will be dangerous out there. Beginning your search at dawn is much safer."

"My brother and nephew are probably out there in the dark, potentially fighting for their lives. We've been here long enough. We're going to go find them now. Thank you for the assistance since we've arrived," I said, marching towards the closest external door I could find with Landon beside me. As I pushed open a door to the grounds, I felt the rush of the dangerous feeling I had previously. The fae in the trees were watching. They had been since we entered this area of Germany. The hair on the back of my neck stood up as I pondered the tree line.

Landon got right to business, his head down as he sniffed, causing his nostrils to flare as he moved. I could smell Niko over every inch of the land, and my ability to discern what was recent and what wasn't was shaken, knowing this was his territory, and he wasn't around. Landon's nose was better for this, so I let him at it while keeping a close eye on the trees.

We made our way halfway around the perimeter before Landon stopped.

"Here," he said, pointing with a swing from the house to the trees. "He left through that door and went that way." His hand stopped, pointing at a solid wall of trees.

No path was visible, only dark forest as my eyes adjusted. I looked at him, silently asking if he wanted to go in with me. We weren't going to be following the safety instructions.

He nodded, so I set off, leaving the perimeter first and entering the trees twenty steps later.

As Landon entered with me, I could have sworn I heard something laugh.

CHAPTER NINETEEN

"Did you hear that?" I asked, looking around.

"No, but in a place like this, I won't question your sanity," Landon replied, frowning over my head at the rest of the trees. "We shouldn't split up."

"Everything you see or hear, verify it with me, and I'll do the same," I said, taking a deep breath. The air, only a few steps into the trees, was already unnaturally different from the grounds around Niko's estate.

As Landon and I walked deeper into the forest, we stayed close to each other, never leaving arm's reach. I looked over my shoulder constantly, watching how the blackness of the night sank in behind us as we walked, removing my view of the estate.

"Is Niko's scent strong enough to keep following?" I asked softly, but even at a whisper, it felt too loud for the world around us. "The magic and strangeness of this place doesn't cover it too much for you?"

"Yeah, it's strong enough. There's a lot of other stuff,

though. A lot of things have passed by more recently. Nearly all of it is fae in nature, but there's some natural stuff in there, like deer."

"Yeah, I'm picking up on that," I said, swallowing. Fae. Everything smelled of fae and magic. The natural world, the earthiness of the area, and the vegetation were almost overwhelmed by the scent of fae. They complemented each other but weren't balanced.

"Perhaps we should've brought breadcrumbs. Like Hansel and Gretel, you know that story," Landon remarked, looking over his shoulder, probably seeing the same thing I did—the darkness. Not even a pinprick of light told us how to get back to the estate. We could only track our own scent.

"I don't think breadcrumbs would help us here." While the idea was a joke, I appreciated the attempt. "Weren't those stories based here? Think we'll find the house made of candy or whatever it was?"

"I have no idea, but I'm glad to see we're on the same page with our knowledge of old fairy tales. I never really cared for them when I heard them, and Pa was never the type to use them to teach us lessons, so they weren't part of my life."

"From memory, most of the lessons weren't worth all that much," I said, huffing in disdain for those old fairy tales. "I've only heard and read the tame versions. You know, the modern retellings and movies using them as a backbone. That sort of stuff."

"I watched some of those, thanks to my sister," Landon said with a smile. "She loved those movies as a kid. She grew out of them, but she's not really much of a kid anymore, is she?"

"She's not a kid, no," I agreed. "She's still young, though. She's not an adult, but she's right there, standing on the edge. I'm trying to enjoy the time we have before she gets to make all the choices I know Heath is scared of her making."

"He's right to be scared," Landon said as we kept walking through the dark. "He doesn't talk about it often enough and does his best to not outright ask her, but it's always there, hanging over his head. My head, too."

I stopped, causing him to bump into me as I saw something interesting. I planned on continuing this conversation, but at that moment, I wanted to point out the trail I could see.

"Landon, do you think that's a safe trail? Does Niko's scent head toward it?"

"Yeah, it does," Landon said, moving around me. I followed him, letting his nose get us to the path. Once we were there, we could both smell Niko much better, like something about the path held off the thick scent of fae. More interesting was who else I could scent.

"Fenris used this path," I said, going down on a knee to see if I could identify any tracks. There were no paws, something that took me by surprise. Only boot tracks and they were faded, having been stepped on by other things.

"So, Niko ran out here to chase him, and Fenris was here, probably leading Niko deeper into the forest," Landon said, sighing. "Niko's old. He would have known it was a trap, yeah? Dirk speaks highly of him, at least in terms of being a supernatural. He had to know."

"I think he would, but walking into a trap is sometimes the best option," I said, looking up at him with a shrug. "I don't think he would have recognized who Fenris was. It took me a long time to recognize you and Heath so well through my magic. I'm still trying to identify everyone quickly within the pack, so I can recognize outsiders easily, but I slip up when everyone is moving around. My theory right now... Niko would be working on the fact that Dirk didn't check in, didn't reach where he was supposed to go, then a wolf breaches his territory. He was called out, and his son was missing. He didn't stop to tell me Dirk was potentially in danger because he didn't entirely know himself or didn't think I needed to know. Niko is really private, so he might have hoped to handle it without calling in the pack."

"All solid theories," Landon said, helping me up with a single solid hand under my elbow as I stood. "You forgot that Niko was incredibly angry with you and maybe wanted to handle it himself because *he's* Dirk's *father*."

"That seems pettier than I figured Niko was capable of," I argued, frowning as I started walking, following Fenris's and Niko's scents, now mingling. I could smell the similarities now. The wildness of Fenris *belonged* in this place, while Niko smelled like he was a more refined version. In a guilty way, I was angry I had missed it for so long. They both were born here, they were from this place, and I had never pieced it together. I hated that I had missed it.

"It might not be intentionally petty, but it's worth recognizing the potential," Landon said pragmatically. "You threaten his relationship with Dirk. He was only supposed to be in Texas with you for a year. We're well past that. I don't go out of my way to ask Dirk if he plans on living in Germany again, but I think we all know he has no plans to. My father is his Alpha, and Pa loves him. You love him. You accepted him with open arms yet gave him all the space he ever wanted. You gave him no reason to want to leave and were never going to force him to come back here to Niko."

"I think you did that," I said with a small smile. "Giving him no reason to leave. You're right about the second. I wasn't."

"I made it easier for him, but if he and I didn't work out, he would still be in your bar for *you*, Jacky. He would still want to help *you*. You threaten Niko. You kept Dirk's secret from him and made Dirk feel safe enough to explore his options. You made Dirk feel like he was part of a *family*."

"And you don't think Niko did that for him?"

"I haven't met Niko, so I don't know, but... clearly, there was something, right?" Landon shrugged. "There's something making it difficult for them."

I had a feeling I knew what that was but couldn't explain it to Landon, not when he initially tried to guess, not today. It was the secret I could never give anyone.

"You look like you want to say something," a feminine

voice chimed in. I froze midstep, looking around. Landon didn't freeze, wheeling around as I spoke.

"Landon—"

"I heard it," he said, the tension of the moment radiating off him.

I looked around as well but didn't see anyone.

"Let's keep moving," I said, walking a bit faster now.

"What are you doing in these woods? Don't you know there are monsters out here?" the feminine voice asked.

"Ignore it," Landon ordered, but I didn't need the reminder. I only walked, Landon at my side, looking over his shoulder every couple of seconds while I kept my eyes on the trail ahead, hoping the scents we were tracking didn't leave it.

"Don't be in such a rush. We don't get many visitors out here," she continued. I heard rustling in the bushes next to me, a shadow creeping out too long over the path. "No new playmates or friends."

"Nope," I said as I shook my head, trying not to think about who or what was now all too interested in us.

"Not fun ones, anyway, and you seem fun." Punctuated with a little giggle, chills ran down my spine. "You should come play with me. It's much better than what you'll find if you keep following that trail. The others aren't as fun as me."

I stopped, unable to keep ignoring the voice.

"We're not very fun. We're not here for fun. We're not here for any of you fae, so leave us be. Let the others know. We're here for the werecat who claims this territory, who I've heard is more than willing to kill a fae for messing with him or his."

"Damn cat. He's not here right now, so we are. What will you give me to leave you be?" it asked, something nasty in its voice as it heard the chance for a bargain.

"Nothing. If you continue to bother us, I'll report you to the Brion, king of the fae and member of the Tribunal. I know him personally. Fought his battles with him and witnessed his second ascension to the throne."

There was a violent hiss.

"Do you think we recognize the fancy king in this wild place?"

"For your sake, I hope you do," I snarled in reply.

"No, you mean for *your* sake," it snapped.

Then I heard rustling, growing more distant for a few seconds until the forest was once again silent.

"Well, fuck," I muttered.

"Yeah, that's bad," Landon concurred. "The King Brion play was probably the best one you had, huh?"

"Yeah, it was."

We silently and unanimously decided to keep moving. After what felt like an hour, Landon tapped my shoulder.

"Was there something you wanted to say before... whatever that was?" he asked.

"No," I said quickly and immediately smelled the lie in my answer. "Something came to mind, but it's not something I can say, no matter how much I might want to."

"Been there before. I get it," he said, nodding. "No

matter how much any of us want it, there's no world where we can truly be honest with each other without suffering repercussions."

"You would be killed," I said in a small voice.

"By whom? It's not an exaggeration to say I'm pretty good in a fi—"

"Hasan," I said before he could finish with his bravado, not wanting him to think it was a fight he could win.

Landon growled as his scent filled with a hate for my father so powerful it took me off guard. I knew Landon didn't like him and had good reason not to, but I hadn't expected the depth of it. Maybe I just didn't want to see it. I was struggling every day to find a balance between my werewolves and my family and wanted to believe it was possible. I had to believe because the alternative wasn't something I was ready to face. Every time I saw the halves of my life rubbed together, it went wrong. This was just another case, and I knew that I was only postponing the fallout, not preventing it by having Davor run interference.

"I'm sorry I haven't been able to fix any of this yet," I said after too long of silence. "There's no excuse, really. If I was better, this wouldn't be how it is—"

"Don't give me that," Landon snapped harshly, stopping on the path, and turning to block me from continuing. Looming over me, Landon was a fearsome man. "Don't fucking do that."

"It's the truth."

"No, it's not. How would you have stopped this?"

"I..." I couldn't think of anything that didn't make me feel gross at the thought.

I won't treat people like criminals just because I'm scared. I won't do it. Everyone deserves a chance.

My chest was tight with pain, but I didn't speak. Landon studied me for a moment before he realized I wasn't going to say anything.

"You don't want to say it, do you? I know how I could have stopped this. Pa and I could have interrogated Fenris years ago. We could have tortured him for his entire story if we thought it was necessary. We could have, but we *didn't*. There are untrustworthy people in the world, and we both fucking know that. There have always been and always will be. Do you punish everyone, trying to weed them out, or do you give everyone a chance? My Pa and I, we give people a chance, like you. It's why you fit so well with us. You give people a chance.

"Your family would have stopped this, sure. They would have done it by punishing everyone, by being jaded assholes who look at the world as if it's against them." Landon leaned down close to my face, his intense wolf eyes holding mine in the night. "For a long time, I followed Pa's example, even when I didn't always want to. Now, I want to because it separates me from people like your family. Not all of them, but enough of them. *Him*. It's hard for me, but hard isn't impossible. It's just hard."

Landon turned to keep walking. As the distance grew, I realized he hadn't just ranted at me because he thought I was being stupid. He was absolving me of guilt.

He and Heath could have done exactly what I'd been thinking. They didn't, but Landon wasn't going to live with guilt over it. Even though Dirk was most certainly in danger.

Catching up, I felt a little piece of forgiveness and strength settle into place. Landon wasn't going to hold this against me. I didn't know how much I needed to hear that until this moment.

"Thank you," I finally whispered as we trudged down the path.

He only shrugged and continued to lead us with his nose deeper and deeper into the Black Forest. We eventually walked out of Niko's territory and left the last layer of safety we might have had.

20

CHAPTER TWENTY

I wasn't sure how long we walked before I thought to check the time. I brought my phone, not expecting service, but it had other uses. Trying several times to get it to wake up, a black screen stared at me until it summoned the power to tell me it had no power. Fear and panic raced through me as I considered what that could mean.

"Landon, check your phone," I ordered, stopping on the path. As much as I wanted not to care and press on without paying it any mind, I knew better. "Mine is dead."

"Okay..." He gave me a questioning look, stopping as well, and pulled out his phone. As the expected emotions ran over Landon from frustration to anger, I knew we had a problem. "How the fuck?"

"Yeah," I said, nodding as I swung my bag down and went to a knee with it. "Our phones are dead, but neither of us has touched them since we landed. In fact, I had mine charging in my bag for some time." I opened the bag and started looking for all the electronics, pulling out everything that used a battery.

"I have a spare charger." He didn't go to a knee like me, but he started shuffling through his as well. "Fuck," he snarled. I looked up to see how he plugged his phone into the portable charging battery. "It's dead, too."

I tried a flashlight, and nothing happened. I tried the spares from his bag. Landon tested his satellite phone, which I hadn't known about, and shook his head when it failed.

"It must be something about this place or something in it." I said, believing it was the only answer.

"You're probably right. It's the place, a space in two planes of existence simultaneously. It probably does all sorts of weird stuff to everything that stays too long. Our electronics are just a victim of this place." Landon paused for a second, so I waited for him to finish the thought, figuring I could guess what it would be. "Or something in this place. I don't know what sort of magic every fae can do. I don't think anyone does."

"You're not wrong, but we would have smelled something doing any more magic. We would have caught the presence of a nearby creature."

"Did you hear anything?"

"Nothing close enough to put me on edge. Didn't hear any sort of whispered spell, just rustling and moving about, but that could have been small animals. If something was closer than twenty or thirty feet, I would have said something."

"I didn't smell any increase in magic, like a release for

a spell cast or something," Landon said, helping me put everything away. "I refuse to think every witch or fae in the world knows that trick, whatever the hell Emma's family in Dallas did."

"Agreed, especially out here. This place feels... isolated from the rest of the world. Their disregard for King Brion makes me wonder if fae royalty even come out here or know about it. Either they don't know, or it's a problem they never wanted to solve."

"I bet it's the first. You could ask when we can use our phones again. You know another fae," Landon pointed out as we kept walking. "Maybe he could help." Landon trailed off, clearly thinking about this potential plan to get fae help here.

My thoughts elsewhere, it took me a moment to catch his meaning.

"Oh, his son Cassius," I said softly, nodding. I didn't think I was a friend of Prince Cassius, the son of King Brion. We'd met under bad circumstances. He hated his father. His wife had died during the short time we were both tied up in the king's fight to get back into power. "I mean..."

"If you're not comfortable with it, so be it. He's fae."

"I don't ever think about reaching out to him because we weren't close and I don't want to remind him of when he lost his wife," I admitted. "But it's good to remember because if we need fae help with the fae, he's definitely the only one I would ever consider." I snorted, annoyed at myself. "I didn't think to call him about what happened to Teagan, Carlos, and Jenny. I could have mentioned it as an option, even if we didn't go with it."

"Pa and I can handle the pack. No reason for you to make yourself owe the man a favor for that," Landon said, once again giving me a dismissive shrug. "Without our phones or anything electronic working, he can't help us here. The only reason I would consider giving him a chance to help us is because of how you and Pa have talked about him. You respected him."

"I do respect him. It's not a bad suggestion. Didn't matter in the end because I owe someone else a favor now," I reminded him.

"Yeah," he mumbled, sighing. "Hopefully, it's nothing bad when it comes back around. If it is, you got us. We'll back you up."

"A bridge we'll cross when we come to it. He didn't seem like a bad guy. He could lose his job for helping us, so it was only fair he asked for a favor in return." I looked around the dark forest, my eyes having fully adjusted now. It was still dark, the night weighing in on Landon and me like an oppressive wall, but I could make out more now than when we entered. I saw nothing, but still, my eyes scanned the trees, hoping for a sign of my family and hoping for no signs of any fae.

"A stranger versus one you know, though..." Landon pointed out.

"A guy who likes his job as a healer versus a fae royal who was despondent from the loss of his wife the last time I saw him. For all I know, Prince Cassius could ask me to kill his father or something insane like that... and we both know how much I like being involved in fae politics." I gave him a frustrated look.

"I won't argue. I was looking at it one way, and you were looking at it another. I didn't think a fae prince would be a big deal, but you do. I get why."

"Why wouldn't I? Brion steamrolled your father and me by blackmailing us if I didn't force Heath to help me, and he did that even though I've heard he and Hasan used to be *friends*."

"You and Prince Cassius exist in a similar space politically," Landon answered simply. "Child of the ruler looked at as the next in line or a route to get things done or make something heard by powerful people. Might not be as bad a king."

I didn't have a response, except it didn't change anything, and I didn't think I needed to say that to Landon.

"It feels like this path never ends," Landon whispered.

"Can you tell how long we've been walking? I was trying to check when I found my phone dead," I said, looking around. I was getting tired, which didn't make sense to me. I had been ready to walk all night when we entered the forest.

"No. Can't really see the sky, thanks to all these trees, and that's all I can do. I don't want to go off the path to find a clearing. If we lose the path, I might not pick up Fenris and Niko's trail again." He groaned and reached into a small pocket on the side of his bag. "Lemme see if this even works."

"What?" I looked around, making sure we were still as alone as we had been for some time. That didn't mean we were actually alone, but nothing was getting close again. He tapped me, and I turned back toward him to see him holding a compass. It was spinning wildly.

"Bad to worse," I growled softly. "We can't even properly navigate."

"I think it means we've reached the area of the forest that is in both planes," he said grimly. "I don't believe the estate was, but I'm certain we are."

"Anything else you want to try?" I asked, crossing my arms in frustration.

"Nope. That was my last bet of anything that might help. Normally, I don't even need to look at it. I find it hard to get lost."

"Why did you want to try it now?"

"Truthfully? Curiosity." Landon shoved it away. "It would have been useful if we're led off the path at any point."

There was nothing else to do except keep moving and hope we could find anyone. Neither of us spoke again, but I caught Landon looking at the sky every so often, just like I did. I figured he was looking for the same thing —the smallest sign the sun was coming up. It was beginning to feel as if we were under an endless night, and it would never end. My nose was practically numb from the smell of magic in the air that never left, and my head was beginning to hurt from trying to hear every sound around us and judge if it was a threat.

The path finally went through a clearing, and I

looked up to see the clear stars in the night sky. With the gorgeous view came a sense of dread, as though it was trying to tell me something.

"Do you think the sun will ever come up?" I asked out loud, feeling like another several hours had passed.

"It has to, eventually, doesn't it? Maybe we're just thrown off by the travel... more likely, we're thrown off by the place." Landon's own concern about it was clear now. "I don't like it either. It feels like we've been out here for at least twelve hours. Dawn should have been some time ago."

"Should have been, yes, but it won't rise right now," a woman said, not in the same oddly feminine voice from before. It hadn't sounded human. This one did.

"Yeah? You want to tell us why?" Landon snarled without looking, still walking forward.

I stopped, though, wondering why the voice sounded familiar. I turned toward it, seeing a pretty woman who reminded me of Alvina, Queen of the Fae. She didn't appear to be dangerous, but I knew not to believe that. Her long ears and ethereal human form made me think she was Sidhe from Oberon and Titania. In a beautiful gown, she seemed out of place, belonging in a palace, not this thick, dark forest. She looked at me, our eyes meeting as she walked through the clearing. Landon's curse at my pause told me he realized I wasn't following him anymore. He was quickly by my side again, but I was looking at the fae, wondering if she would ever answer.

More importantly, I wanted to know what she wanted and how to get her to leave.

"You already know the answer," she said, smiling at Landon, the eye contact with me broken off for a moment.

"Who are you?" I asked since she didn't want to give Landon a proper answer.

Slowly, she lifted a hand and snapped her fingers. A spectral steed appeared, materializing out of the air, and she gracefully climbed on it, making me realize I could nearly see through both of them. They were in color but not solid, which disturbed me more. A moment later, a man on his own horse rode out of the tree line. Interestingly, he seemed completely human, dressed in riding gear. The timing of it made me wonder if she had been expecting him to come any moment.

"The hunt continues, love. The hunter has lost his quarry for a moment but still has the bait," the man said, as if he was just reporting an interesting bit of news. "What have you found?"

"I don't know. They're not my concern," she said, smiling at him. "I found them interesting for a moment, but... they clearly don't belong here and certainly don't understand it. Easy prey for something during this long night."

Something predatory rose up in me, and I knew without a doubt that my eyes went from my human hazel to werecat gold as they narrowed on her. She turned back to us to say something and paused as her eyes met mine, clearly caught off guard by the change.

"Or perhaps not easy prey," the man said, now intrigued.

"Definitely not," Landon growled. The man chuckled as if Landon was a small child, and he felt like indulging said child, but the woman continued to stare at me, ignoring their exchange. Her surprise shifted to confusion and perhaps anger.

"Where have I seen those eyes before?" she asked so softly, I could have sworn she wasn't really asking me. Then she snapped out of whatever she had been thinking about and turned to the man, her horse moving instinctively beneath her. There was no sign of a bridle or reins, and she was sitting bareback.

"Let's enjoy our long night," she said, the horse jumping into movement. Her husband followed, both disappearing as they hit the tree line.

"And here I thought things couldn't get worse... or stranger," Landon muttered.

"They ride with the Hunt," I said, needing to say it out loud, hoping I wasn't insane, hoping Landon also realized that.

"They sure fucking do, and we're in their neck of the woods. At least we learned something. Dirk and Niko are still alive."

"Yeah, let's—"

A howl filled the night, and we both started to run toward it, following in the footsteps of the spectral riders. By the time we reached the trees, it cut off abruptly.

21

CHAPTER TWENTY-ONE

Fighting through the underbrush and scaring every bird in the trees, Landon and I ran toward the howl.

"That was Dirk," Landon said as we moved, keeping in step with each other, him just ahead of me, close enough to reach out and grab. I had no idea if he was doing it intentionally because I was running as fast as my legs could take me through the thick forest.

"Are you sure?" I asked, hoping we hadn't both been tricked by the fae. I wasn't going to take any chances, though. A wolf howled. It was either Fenris or Dirk, and I was perfectly fine with finding either of them for very different reasons.

"I will never mistake another wolf for him," he huffed out as we ran, each word accented by a footfall or a breath.

"Do you know how close he was to the howl?"

"Close enough," Landon said.

Small branches and twigs broke as we tore through them, some clipping us, but the sting wasn't enough to slow us down. We didn't trip. Whether we ran in human form or our cursed ones, running through the woods came naturally. An understanding of the earth beneath us and its hazards made me look down occasionally and assess the next portion of the run.

Finally, we skid to a stop, not leaving the treeline, as something interesting came into view.

"We were told there were other structures," I said, breathing hard as I surveyed the small home or shack in the clearing ahead of us. There were no visible windows, and I couldn't see the door from our angle. It had to be a single room. I had no idea how someone could put two rooms in such a small building.

"He's here," Landon said, breathing just as hard as I was. "Dirk is here."

"You can smell him?" I certainly couldn't. Not at all. "Or see him?" I kept looking around, but there was no sign of Dirk anywhere.

"Smell. Back me up?"

"Of course. Let's get our boy," I said, nodding. Landon slowly stepped into the clearing, looking around warily. From a desperate run to sudden caution, Landon adapted to the change in our environment, and I followed his lead. We weren't slow crossing the open field, both of us putting our backs to the house as we moved around it to find the door. Still, I couldn't smell Dirk and had to trust Landon's senses.

"This could be a trick," I pointed out quietly, hoping no one except Landon could hear me say it.

"Have to risk it," he said, stopping as we reached the only door in or out of the shack. There was a massive lock on it, something old that probably weighed more than a pound. His nostrils were flaring as he inhaled deeply. "He's in there."

I wanted so badly to believe it, not stopping him as he began to fiddle with the lock.

"Can you pick it?"

He wasn't using anything, just fiddling with it like he wanted to see if it would break if he yanked hard enough.

"Father always thought that picking locks was a skill I didn't need." Landon smirked at me as he let his bag fall to one side, hanging on his shoulder. He pulled out a small kit and started working. A moment later, it clicked, but Landon growled when he tried to pull it off.

"Nope. Not opening. Might be rust, but I should be strong enough." Landon yanked, but nothing budged. Without needing to ask, he backed away, and I took his place.

It was tough. We'd heard the click of the internal mechanism. It should have released, but it wasn't giving in to us. I snarled as I fought with it, hoping to rip it off by taking the door with it if I had to.

"Must be magically locked as well," Landon said, growling deeply.

"Yeah, that shouldn't give us this much of a fight," I said, huffing as I stepped back. "We did the physical lock. What would be used to unlock it magically?"

"The key is the obvious answer," Landon said. Before I could say anything, he lifted a fist and started knocking on the door roughly. "Dirk, can you hear me?"

Listening closely, my mouth dropped open when I heard a groan. I gestured for Landon to say more as I prepared to throw my entire weight into the door.

"Dirk, if you're in there, we're here for you... me and Jacky. We're out here in this fucking forest to find you. Say something." Landon stepped away, and I threw all my supernatural strength into knocking the door down, meeting a similarly supernatural barrier that didn't even let the door rattle.

"Fuck," I hissed as I went back to try again.

"Go away. I won't fall for tricks," Dirk said, clearly groggy. Even muffled by the building, his speech was a little slurred and thickly accented.

"Are you in there taking a fucking nap?" Landon snapped. "Get over here and open this fucking door."

"Stop pretending to be him," Dirk said, his words muffled. "You're not him."

I looked at Landon and shrugged. Even in this bad position, Dirk was smart. He couldn't see us and thought we were fae trying to fuck with him. It served us right.

"There's a solution," I said simply, walking back to the door. "Dirk Brandt. This is Jacky. What can I say to make you feel comfortable?"

"You can't be Jacky. She doesn't know about this place. How are you pretending to be them? Did you shuffle through my dreams? That fucking asshole told me I was going to be safe here until he was done. I hope Niko rips his fucking head off and finishes this shit. I want to go home. No fucking fae forest in the backyard at home."

Tears flooded my eyes. Home was in Texas, then. There was no fae forest in our backyard, and I was never going to let one pop up. He could trust me on that.

"Dirk, if you're not going to listen to me and give me something, I'm just going to say stuff, and if Landon hears something new, then... oh well." I was warning him. There was only one secret Dirk kept that only I knew, aside from the person who forced him to keep it.

"You don't know—"

"When you were young, you snuck around Niko's home to see a visitor. You'd never met the family he kept telling you about because he didn't want to expose you to them yet. You knew one was there that day, though, and you really wanted to meet him. Niko couldn't run interference because he had stepped out of the house to see to something." I was telling the story to give Dirk time to stop me, to realize I was the Jacky he knew, not a fae using my voice. He didn't stop me, though.

"You found Hasan, ruler of the werecats, and he was larger than life, the patriarch of our family. He has that impression on everyone when they meet him for the first time." I paused, hoping he would stop me, but still, he said nothing. "It was that day when you learned you had a human's chance of joining your father's immortal family... low, heartbreakingly low. Hasan told you that you shouldn't even try, or it would just break Niko's heart even faster than if you grew old and died."

Beside me, I could smell the sudden rise of Landon's

fury. It filled my nose, almost clouding my mind with its intensity, but I had to get Dirk to hear me.

"In a single conversation, he destroyed the relationship you had with your father," I continued. "You started pushing Niko away by acting out and trying to find your own way because you didn't want to hurt him. If you made him no longer want you, maybe it would be fine, and he could move on faster."

I heard a thump on the other side.

"You were guessing during that last part," Dirk said, clearly believing me now. The accent he had gone, he was now talking in that general American English I knew from him. Now, instead of the slur, I could hear the pain he was in through his words. "I don't know how to open the door. I'm unconscious every time he locks me in here."

"But you come out sometimes?"

"He lets me out to walk the trails, refreshing my scent and forcing Niko to keep fighting because I'm still alive. He keeps a weird silver rope, so I can't run. There's silver in my blood, too. Can't Change in here to fight back when he comes by. Makes me feel really weak and tired."

"You howled earlier." Landon leaned on the door beside me. "What happened? What stopped you? You must have been out here because you sound so muffled in there. I would have noticed that in the howl."

"Niko has probably been watching us for a while. He attacked while I was out on my fucking leash. I got knocked over but tried to slip the rope and run. In the end, I couldn't get the rope off, but I could run. I made some distance, but I couldn't find a path in time to know the way home. Niko had to have needed to retreat to figure out *his* weakness...and I was caught. Right before that fucking bastard threw me back in here, I got his hand off my mouth to get that howl out. The last thing I remember is the stone coming toward my face too fast. Can't imagine what that could have been."

Dirk's sarcasm in that last line told me he still had fight in him. That was what I needed to hear. What struck me as odd was how Dirk didn't confirm who had taken him, and I didn't want to ask. Names could be powerful, and in some tales, saying the name of the thing would summon it.

"He wants you alive, but he's slamming your head on the wall? Isn't he afraid the silver will stop you from properly healing? If you die accidentally, his entire sick plan is done for." Landon snarled every word as if he was insulted by the stupidity he saw in the action.

"Wasn't the first time. He's an asshole. He's so much fucking meaner than..." Dirk trailed off with a groan of pain. I couldn't hear much for a moment. "Sorry. I was standing up, and it made me dizzy."

"Dirk, I want you to wake yourself a bit more and shake that off," I ordered. "We don't know where he is. We haven't seen him or Niko. We have to get this door down or open and get you out of here. The moment it's open, we're moving. We can't lose any more time."

"Yeah, yeah," he said. "While you figure it out, can I ask why it took you two so long?"

"I love you, but it's been less than a week. We moved

as fast as we could on what little information we had," Landon said in confusion, matching my own feelings.

"Less than a week?" Dirk asked softly.

Horror filled me as I heard his questioning. There was something terrifying about listening to Dirk question, not just some facts, but his entire reality. He didn't believe us. Or he did and had to come to terms with how different it was from his own.

I scrambled, not wanting to think about the possible magical reasons he would think it had been longer than a few days. We learned of what might be happening on Sunday and left for Germany. At *most*, he was missing for a couple of days before we left. At most, he was in these woods for only four or five days. I was certain of this. I knew Landon was certain of this.

So, I gave him a more reasonable explanation.

"You're under a lot of stress, going in and out of consciousness. With the silver in your system, you must feel miserable, and it probably feels like it's been forever since you've felt okay. We're going to help you."

"Yeah, that must be it," Dirk said, calmly accepting my reassurance, his words exhausted but relieved by my explanation. "Must be."

"Jacky, I don't know what to do about this door," Landon said, leaning on the stone.

I heard his anxiety. His need to get through the last obstacle between him and Dirk was clear, and it was against something neither of us could solve, not with force. Magic was definitely the answer, but we couldn't wield it.

"I have an idea, but it's a bad one," I said, hating that it crossed my mind. "I would rather we continue to fight against the door, but...."

"We should wait for him to come back and take Dirk out? Same," Landon said with a nod. "Dirk, will you rest up before then?"

"Don't get eaten by anything," Dirk said.

Catching the first smile in his words since we had gotten here, I wished I could hug him and tell him everything would be okay.

"I don't get eaten," Landon replied with a vicious smile only I could see.

"Maybe in the rest of the world, but you're in the forest of the Big Bad Wolf, and he eats everything. You're off the path...a fatal mistake, Niko liked to tell me growing up."

"Then I'll be the hunter," I said with a growl as Landon frowned at Dirk's words.

Landon's eyes went wide as he finally caught the reference.

"I fucking hate this place," Landon finally muttered. He quickly shook off his feelings and looked at the door. "We're going to make ourselves a safe place to watch and wait. We won't be far, Dirk. You hear me? We'll be in range. We're not leaving you here."

"Yeah, I know. Thanks for coming."

"Always," I promised.

Landon nodded, then closed his eyes. Touching the door, he leaned in and put his forehead on it.

"Love you," he whispered.

CHAPTER TWENTY-TWO

L andon and I retreated quickly, heading into the trees but never out of sight of the shack that held Dirk.

"He'll smell us, but he's insane, not stupid. He'll smell us so I have an idea," Landon said, pointing up. "Let's make a ring of our scent around the clearing so he can't stop at the end of the trail. Then we'll climb up and try to stay out of sight."

"I like it. Let's not waste time."

We got to it, moving fast to make our scents surround the clearing as much as we could, leaving no tree or bush within ten feet of the clearing untouched. There were no paths in or out of the clearing. The emphasis of staying on them made the lack of them more disturbing here than I would have thought in my territory. We caught scents of all sorts, from fae to natural beast. I could smell Niko's investigation of the clearing, creeping around the edges like we were. Nowhere did I smell Fenris or any werewolf. If it wasn't for Dirk telling me he had been shoved in there by Fenris, I wouldn't have guessed either of them ever came by this way.

Eventually, we reached a decent tree to climb that gave us a view of the shack's door. It wasn't my first choice, but Landon's logic was sound. If Fenris thought to check the trees, he would check the easiest to climb first. We would have time to react if that was the case.

Climbing as high as I felt comfortable, nearly twenty feet in the air, I could just barely see the shack through the leaves. Landon stopped underneath me but was still over fifteen feet up.

"I couldn't smell him," I whispered. "Dirk."

"Could you smell our traitor?" Landon asked, now worried more so than he had been when we found the clearing. "It was really clear they had both been there. Niko snooped around the clearing a bit, but he was probably doing what we are right now."

"I could smell Niko," I said, frowning. "But neither werewolf."

"Must be magic," he said, his distaste for magic not hidden. "A cheap trick of our traitor given to him thanks to his...deal."

"Yeah. Let's just keep watch—"

"Will you tell me more about what you said to Dirk?" he asked before I could cut the silence I would have preferred. There was something boyish to the way he asked, but I could smell his fury, which had moved into the background of his scent while we talked to Dirk about getting him out. "While we have the chance?"

I was reluctant to say anything. Since the night Dirk became a werewolf, he and I had been treading the fine line of our freedom and keeping family secrets. I had been doing it for longer, but that night had been the closest we had come to exposing something we *knew* would get people hurt. Landon had been smart that night. He'd asked but had heard my warning and never pried after that. He knew what secrets could do and respected that.

Dirk had forced my hand tonight. I was the only person who could ever know that story. No fae could replicate it without going through my memories, and it seemed very far-fetched they would go through all that trouble to capture or consume Niko's son.

Even though Landon now knew what Hasan had said to Dirk as a boy, I had been careful not to say it was Hasan's Talent to smell it on a person. That way, Landon knew but couldn't *know*.

And I can't break that line of defense right now. Not here, with so many predators hiding in the shadows.

"When we're safe," I said, knowing there would be no getting Landon off it now. He knew Hasan had hurt Dirk and would never forget that. Eventually, he would need the entire truth, and it was better if I handled it over Landon simmering in fury until Dirk revealed it. That way Dirk couldn't be implicated in its reveal, and no one could claim Landon used his relationship with Dirk to convince Dirk to tell him.

I had a snowball's chance in hell of making Hasan see

it that way if he ever discovered that his secret was known by someone outside the family, but I had to try.

I had to have hope, even when it all felt hopeless.

"Does Pa know?" Again, there was something boyish in the way Landon talked. Not the steel wall he normally presented, but instead a somewhat vulnerable, younger man.

"No."

He didn't respond. I looked down to see Landon was looking at the shack, his expression unreadable from my position. Finally noticing the chill in the air, I wrapped my jacket around me tighter.

The wait was quiet. I don't know how long we sat in shared silence. I was able to calm down a bit, but with that calm came the real exhaustion of the long day. We had slept on the plane, but since then, we'd had a long drive and an even longer walk deep into the forest. I was struggling but didn't want to miss our chance to get Dirk or let Fenris get the jump on us. Even worse, I knew sleeping where I was would only be asking for more trouble to find us. I forced myself to stay awake and alert because there was no other option. Even fighting it, knowing the stakes of our situation, my eyes threatened to drift closed.

A horn blew, shocking us both. I felt the tree rock as Landon caught himself before he was startled off his branch. I held the trunk, wondering who or what had decided to do that.

A moment later, I saw them. The couple was back, riding their horses through the trees and under us as they moved. They avoided trees, but the bushes and other undergrowth didn't touch them as she raced a length ahead of him. They stopped in the clearing near the shack, almost out of sight, thanks to the thick trees.

Moving down slowly to see if I could find a better gap, I ended up on the same side of the tree as Landon, where he had a prime view.

The man said something in German, making the woman laugh. Her horse pranced around as though it was enjoying the night as she was. She stopped beside her husband and began to say something but was cut off by a third speaker in German.

I recognized the voice—Fenris but not. The accent didn't seem unnatural when paired with German, but I recognized it.

He slowly came into view, walking up to the riders. He was different. His posture was more upright and proper, holding himself with pride and class even though he wore casual clothing that needed to be washed, the mud stains apparent from our hiding spot in the trees. He seemed unafraid of the riders, crossing his arms in annoyance as the husband said something.

I can't believe Fenris. No, not Fenris. Rainer. That is Rainer Brandt, and I don't know him.

I wished, darkly and full of regret, I'd had Dirk teach me German. He might have hated it, but it would have been nice.

Rainer dropped his arms, putting his hands on his hips as he listened to what the riders had to say.

When Rainer laughed, I began to shake. There was

something terrible in it. It wasn't Fenris. It wasn't my wild, mad wolf who proved even the most traumatized of warriors could find a new life. This wasn't the man who would say dirty jokes and laugh as everyone turned red. He wasn't the man I'd fought beside.

The laugh was one of a man who had no love in his heart, no joy in his life, and no hope for his future or anyone else's for that matter.

Maybe my Fenris is still in there...It couldn't have all been a lie, right?

"Well, if they're watching, and they probably are, I'll switch to something I know they understand," Rainer said with a clap of his hands. "This isn't about you, Jacky Leon! Landon, take your father's slut home and keep her there."

Somehow, Landon was silent, even though the rage in his scent told me he wanted to be anything but.

"You can have Dirk *Brandt* back when I'm done," Rainer continued, not bothering to hide his derision for Dirk's last name. "Unless Nikolaus or either of you does something stupid. I don't need to kill everyone in the forest tonight, but make no mistake. I will if I must."

I heard bark crack and reached out to touch Landon's hand. He released the tree trunk to grab mine, squeezing a bit. Rainer was being an asshole. It was fine. I wasn't insulted, and he didn't need to be insulted for me. It was a waste of our time to get upset with his words.

"You know them, then?" The man seemed surprised by the development, and I couldn't help but wonder what role the riders were playing in this.

"Yes, I do," Rainer confirmed. "But they don't know *me*...though they should know better than to continue involving themselves. They should know that much."

"Then we shall leave you to continue your hunt. We will continue to enjoy the long night, watching." Turning her horse, she bolted into the trees, once again disappearing with her husband.

Rainer was left the only remaining visible person in the clearing. He turned to the shack, sighing.

"I guess we might as well make this fun. Jacky likes *fun*." He went to the door, and with a simple wave of his hand, it opened. I couldn't make out what I saw in the darkness, straining to make out any detail to no avail.

Landon was shaking beside me, leaning forward to see anything, but like me, once Rainer went inside, it was impossible.

"Get up," Rainer ordered, his words loud enough to leave the shack. "You know they're here, don't you? Your favorite auntie is here, that werecat no one likes. So is Heath's favorite son, the one you think you're in love with. I know they came right up to the door, pup. What was the plan?"

"Does it matter?" Dirk dared to ask. His voice was much weaker, not only in volume but strength. I started to move down, but Landon had the restraint to stop me. He was shaking, but he held my bag, forcing me not to move. "And they have names. You know them. They know you."

"It doesn't matter, not really." Rainer sounded okay without an answer, but a thud accented by Dirk's groan of pain made it clear he didn't like the disrespect. His chuckle was menacing as another thud made me wince. "They don't know me. Remember that."

"It'll be hard to forget," Dirk managed to say, a bit of defiance in his words. I had to focus to hear them. They were so weak now. "How weak that fucking was."

"I should have killed you the moment I heard your fucking name," Rainer snarled. "You're lucky I need you."

"An eight-hundred-year-long grudge, and the only thing you could think of was using me as bait. Yeah, you do need me," Dirk spat back, some fire coming back.

Stop taunting him, Dirk.

"Hopefully, Everson teaches you to mind your tongue one day. I don't think your lover will appreciate it when you lose it for your smart mouth." Rainer growled. "I'm tired of managing you. Go. Run for it, kid. That's what you wanted to do earlier, wasn't it?"

"What?" Dirk's surprise matched my own.

"Go," Rainer snarled, making my chest rumble in the trees.

Dirk stumbled out of the shack, looking over his shoulder as he limped. He had a black eye, a busted lip, and a few nasty bruises already forming on his face that his days of beard growth couldn't hide. I couldn't imagine what he looked like underneath his dirty clothes.

My heart sank, but Landon's grip was strong, so I couldn't run to him. It was all I wanted as I saw Rainer appear, standing in the doorway.

"You grew up in these woods. You should know how

to get home," Rainer called, smiling viciously. Only his scars made me think of the Fenris I knew. Everything else about his face, the expression he wore... reminded me of the Fenris who had lost his shit and attacked me the first time we met, but it was multiplied tenfold in its intensity.

Dirk stopped at the treeline, looking back once more.

"He won't fall for this," Dirk called out.

"He won't need to. If he doesn't come, you'll be dead. So will your two little saviors."

My heart started to race, adrenaline waking me up. Landon released me, and we both started climbing down the tree.

"You just said you wouldn't kill them if they didn't get involved," Dirk said, stepping backward ever closer to the tree line. Landon and I hit the ground, soft landings for both of us.

"We both know they won't take that deal," Rainer said, his expression unmoving.

I wasn't the first to Dirk. Landon was grabbing Dirk's arm.

"You've got that right," Landon snarled, pushing Dirk toward me as I broke free of the trees.

"You have three hours, one for each of you," Rainer said as I grabbed my nephew and pulled him to follow me back into the trees. "Then I start hunting. You better hope my brother comes to me first." As we started to run, I heard Rainer's bitter laugh. "You better hope he loves you more than he did his first family! His real one!"

23

CHAPTER TWENTY-THREE

I didn't need a second warning. The hair on the back of my neck rose at the thought of being hunted by Rainer Brandt. Something about him made every animal instinct in me want to get the fuck away from him and stay out of his territory.

"Dirk, I've got you," Landon said from behind us, me pulling Dirk as quickly as he could go. "If you need to slow or stop—"

"Fuck that," Dirk groaned, keeping up with me now that we'd gotten moving. I let go, seeing he was doing fine with this, at least. He was clearly in pain, but he was moving mostly normally. "We need to find a safe spot."

"He's a wolf. We need to be slow and trick up his nose," Landon fired back.

Dirk didn't reply, groaning as he pushed himself to get ahead of me. When we reached a game trail, he skidded to a stop.

"What are you doing?" Landon asked in a frantic growl. "We keep running."

"No," Dirk said, shaking his head. "I need to...," He started looking around, but he didn't finish his explanation for us. He wandered down the game trail a little too slow for my comfort, his eyes scanning around us.

"We didn't see Niko moving around," I said, wondering if he was hoping for signs of his father or would see him in the darkness. "He would have caught up or picked the fight with Rainer by now if he was close enough to hear all of that."

Dirk looked up at me, pale under his bruises.

"Don't say his name," Dirk said softly. "Don't."

"Yeah, names have power and all that," Landon said, grumbling at Dirk. "Why are we slowing here? A game trail is too easy. We'll get caught, and we're not making enough ground."

"I need to find something." Dirk went back to his search.

"What?" I dared to ask. No matter what direction we went, we would eventually leave the forest. That was geography. "And why?"

"I can explain later. Just let me do this," Dirk said, shuffling through bushes around the game trail. He wasn't using his sense, at least not the way I knew most moon cursed did. He wasn't sniffing for a trail. He was looking, his eyes darting around the forest, not at the ground but into the distance of the dark place.

"Explain now so we can help," Landon said, his growl

telling me he was ready to pull rank when Dirk didn't say anything. "Damn it, Dirk!

"It sounds ridiculous. I need you to trust me," Dirk snapped. "And I've never done this before."

"You grew up here." Landon's agitation was a little reasonable, but I was beginning to find it hard to bite my tongue as the werewolves got snappy.

"Yeah, I did. As a *human,* and I *never* went this deep into the forest. I'm a werewolf now. It's...." Dirk shook his head finally. "Niko knows how to explain... can try, though. It sounds ridiculous. I haven't even seen it before, so I'm not even sure if it's real, but I have to try."

"We trust you," I finally said, giving Dirk an even look. When he nodded, I turned to Landon and slashed my hand, a warning to cut that shit out, or I would be the one he could get snappy with. Looking a bit shamed, he bowed his head slightly in respect. Dirk missed the exchange to continue his search.

We followed the game trail for some time, Dirk setting the pace.

"There," he whispered, his voice full of awe.

"What do you see?" Landon asked softly, mollified by my interjection and warning.

"The werewolves, the Black Forest Pack, left their own magical trails in places they ran repeatedly. Their own safe paths, Niko said. When he became a werecat, he would feel them but not see them. I hadn't seen it before, but," Dirk ran up to a point and stopped, looking at something I couldn't see, his hand dancing over it. "He was right. I thought he was bullshitting me." Dirk looked over his shoulder. "He said he never heard of a werewolf getting lost when they stayed on the path. *This* path. The others are for everyone else. We reached the game trail and I figured game trails change over the years, but perhaps one of the wolf trails might be nearby, evidence it was always a good hunting area or something."

"A different path," I said, almost not surprised. I stepped closer but couldn't see or feel anything. When I looked at Landon, he sniffed, shaking his head as he got nothing.

"There's only one problem with this." Landon crossed his arms as we started following Dirk, leading the way down his invisible trail. "He'll know these, too."

"Yeah, and he's bad, but we've got bigger problems," Dirk said over his shoulder. "If you get lost out here, you're going to wish he killed you and not something else. Or you might just find yourself another lost soul, going in circles until you starve to death and become one of the many bad things that stay here. Securing our way out is the first priority, not trying to get as far from him as possible. This trail might even lead us to somewhere safe to bunk down."

"And Niko can feel them. If he catches our scent, he'll know we're on a safe way back home, not getting turned around," I said, seeing how Dirk was thinking. His logic was sound, and I couldn't think of a different idea that wasn't even more dangerous in a place I barely understood. "He won't be distracted by our safety as outsiders or his son."

"Exactly. Then he can handle his brother, or he can follow us home and leave that asshole to rot out here."

"That asshole will catch up to us," Landon said, looking over his shoulder as I looked back to check on him. "Jacky and I followed the fucking paths, and it felt like we walked most of a day, and the fucking sun still isn't up."

"The Wild Hunt has always been ridden at night," Dirk said. "The sun won't come up out here until the hunter and his prey are separated, or one of them is dead."

"Separated?" I needed to know more about that possibility.

"I think if the sun comes up, the hunt is over, but the sun doesn't come up right now. I'm wondering if Niko leaves the forest, he might be free of this, and his brother will have lost his game, therefore, lost the hunt. That's only a theory, though. I can't say for certain. The killing each other part isn't. The riders made it very clear that Niko's brother had to kill him now. He started this, so it was time to finish it. If he died instead of Niko."

"Who are they?" I couldn't resist asking as we jogged. "The riders."

"I don't know their original identities, but from what I gathered, they're watching him, ready to claim his soul when he fails or acknowledge his release from the bargain when this is over. I've only seen them come by a couple of times, and normally, it was just to watch us from the trees. Do *not* attack them if you see them. I don't want to know what they're capable of. Not even he wanted to mess with them, and they're not exactly nice. He's not capable of controlling his temper unless it's with them. With them, he's on his best behavior."

"So, they could be random people claimed by the hunt, and this is their job tonight, or they could be very powerful." I didn't like not knowing. That was too wide of a margin to feel any security or make a proper plan to get around.

Dirk nodded over his shoulder, keeping us moving. He was moving a bit slower, probably trying to keep us going in the right direction. I had no idea if we were going deeper into the forest or back toward a safer area.

I trust Dirk with my life. I trust Landon with my life. I can't throw indecision into this now. We can't stop moving, or we'll get caught no matter what we're trying to do.

I kept repeating that to myself as Dirk ran in the lead, me in the middle, and Landon taking the back, running just slow enough not to clip my heels.

"Can I Change? Perhaps it might help," I asked after some time, getting the words out between breaths. Dirk's head shake didn't come with a response, but I didn't pry after that. We could find a spot to stop later and hopefully talk it out.

We reached a river, taking me by surprise because Landon and I hadn't crossed one when we trudged through the forest to find Dirk.

"Shit!" Dirk snarled as we skidded to a stop at the edge of it.

"What is it?" Landon asked, looking at Dirk with a frown. "What's going on?"

"We can't cross this," Dirk said, stepping back. "Never cross the water without a bridge."

"Reciting an old rule of Niko's?"

"There are things that live in the water," Dirk said darkly. "And I'm not going to find out what tonight."

"Where does the path go from here?"

"The other side, but whatever connected where we're stopped and where it starts over there is gone. There might have been an old bridge here or maybe a fallen tree a long time ago that the werewolves used to safely cross," Dirk said, pointing directly across the water to the other bank.

"Geography changes over time, too," Landon pointed out softly, nodding. "Do you think we could find another or maybe one of the human paths?"

"We might be able to," Dirk said, followed by a growl of frustration. "But the longer we spend off a safe path, the more likely we are to never find one."

I leaned over the water, looking up and down the river for any natural crossing, but there was none in view.

"Dirk, please don't panic. So long as the three of us stay together, we can find a way," Landon said quickly and quietly as Dirk's breathing grew heavy.

"Don't panic? Do you know how many years I lived down here with Niko and followed every rule? Even at my worst, I never fucked with this place. Even when I was human and barely knew what was really going on, I knew this place was *bad*. Niko would always get this haunted fucking look in his eyes whenever—"

"I'll make a bridge," I said, cutting him off as I turned away from the river to find the closest tree that might work for what I needed. I had no idea if I was actually strong enough to do it, but it was the best option. It was a physical solution that didn't require us to aimlessly wander in the forest. I didn't pick the tree for its size or sturdiness. I needed it to come down, and if it wasn't the most stable bridge, we'd just be careful over the water.

"I'll help," Landon said, moving to my side. "Dirk, take a deep breath. Together, we can solve this. Remember that. We're pack. This is what we do."

Dirk only nodded, watching us get behind the tree I wanted. Landon pulled out his sword and started to chop into its side, and while it wasn't made for that job, the blade held up and did some work while Landon provided more power than a human ever could. I started pushing once there was even the smallest notch, hearing creaks and cracks. Landon kept chopping, and I snarled with anger as I kept trying to push it over. With a roar, I felt the final snap, and the tree began to come down, its top crashing into other trees. I climbed up the side, adding more weight and trying to bounce it down.

"Jacky, don't be a fucking idiot!" Landon roared up to me.

Branches broke, and the tree started falling once again. I was assaulted by branches as we went down. Shaken on landing, I bounced a few feet from the fallen tree and sat up while Dirk and Landon ran across it.

"You are insane," Landon snarled as he yanked me up. He started pushing the log, growling with each step. Joining him, we were able to shove it into the river, hopefully stopping anyone from using it behind us.

Just in time to hear a howl.

"Do you think that was an hour, or—"

"He's begun his hunt," Landon said, answering my question before I could finish it. "That was the last of our three hours."

24

CHAPTER TWENTY-FOUR

"There!" Dirk called out, pointing to the left as we ran. Veering hard, my foot slipped, and I struggled to maintain my balance as I followed him.

I had no idea where we were anymore. We had left the river behind and kept running because that was our only option. We didn't have time to play tricks on Rainer. We could only keep moving and hope we reached anywhere safe before he did.

Dirk pointed out a shelter in the middle of another strange clearing where the treeline was all too clean, and nothing grew except healthy, normal, albeit long, grass around it. As we slowed and stopped in front of it, I was breathing hard, knowing if I sat down, I didn't think even adrenaline could keep me awake. I was running on fumes. My eyes were strained, open for too long against their will. Blinks took too long, making me fight not to blink, or I could collapse.

I looked at Landon while Dirk investigated the old

building in front of us, not going too far. Landon seemed to be in a similar shape—deep bags under his bloodshot eyes, his chest heaving and drenched in sweat. Dirk was still in rough condition, but he had at least gotten sleep recently. I had no idea how long Landon and I had been awake. There was no way for me to figure it out since the unchanging night sky told us nothing.

"What is this?" Landon asked before I could.

"One of the pack's old buildings," Dirk said, touching the front door. "Still protected from the fae around it. That's why the clearing is still here, instead of being engulfed by the forest and taken over by the fae."

"When did you finally learn all this? You were saying you didn't know much about this place when you were human," I said, trying to straighten up.

"Niko started telling me a lot of it on the drive down from the airport. He was pissed, saying he would have prepared to take a werewolf back to the Black Forest if he had known one was coming. He explained all the things I had never asked growing up, and he never offered to tell me. He didn't know if it would apply to me since I...Well, it's been eight hundred years since the pack existed, and they lived more in the forest than he does now. They even often took humans out there. I was never as exposed to it.

"When we got here, he took me out in our human forms, and we realized I was...like them, the old pack. Too much exposure to this place adapted me to it, I guess. If I had never become a werewolf or come back, I probably never would have known."

As he finished, I could tell he was getting uncomfortable with the implications of what he was saying, what it all meant. He shifted his weight anxiously, trying to hide the pain in his leg as he fidgeted. He was looking more at the old building in front of us than at Landon or me.

"There's no judgment from us," I promised as I walked to him, ignoring how my own muscles were screaming for a break now that we had stopped once again. He pushed the door open and went in first. Landon was behind me, gently pushing me to go in behind Dirk.

"He's hunting now. We can't stay for long," Landon said as he closed us in.

"I know, but I'm hoping." Dirk ran a hand over his head, wincing in pain as he brushed a nasty bruise on the back. Landon started looking him over, carefully not touching, but Dirk stepped away from him. "I'm hoping Niko catches up. If we give him just a little time."

"Dirk...." I didn't know what to say to that,I had no idea how to even begin finding Niko, not in this place, not if he didn't want to be found.

"If any of us make the mistake of falling asleep, we could all pass out and get caught out by *him*," Landon said, shaking his head. "Dirk, I know you—"

"You don't know," Dirk said quickly. "You have no idea, Landon."

"Then tell me," Landon pleaded, stepping closer. "Please tell me, Dirk."

"It feels so stupid to say, but I finally thought he and I

had a chance again," Dirk whispered, desperately looking between Landon and me before he continued. "He was angry I kept it a secret. He was angry Jacky helped, but... My being a werewolf, knowing he and I could have forever to be a functional family. He was happy about that. After a couple of days, he was talking about how he didn't want me living with all this and wanted to know where I wanted to live. He would visit me, even if it was Texas...with you. I didn't tell him it was you specifically yet, only that I met a guy, another werewolf, and he was excited to hear that. He wanted to meet the person who was really keeping me in Texas. Then this happened."

Landon reached out and hugged Dirk. I turned away as the boys kissed, not wanting to intrude on their private moment.

"So, what Jacky said was true," Landon whispered.

"Yeah," Dirk confirmed. "Every bit of it, even her own guesses about how I behaved."

"Hasan drove a wedge between you and Niko on purpose," Landon growled softly, protectively, and even a bit vengefully.

"It's his Talent," I said so Dirk didn't have to.

"Driving wedges?" Landon snorted. "That's just a skill—"

"His ability to smell for the markers that indicate how well someone could survive the Change," I corrected. I watched Dirk as I spoke, and he didn't react to Landon finally knowing the truth, not even in fear for Landon's life. So, I decided to reiterate the stakes.

"If we survive what's going on here, you have to keep

that to yourself. I haven't even told Heath. Hasan, or any of my many siblings, would kill you for knowing. It's a viciously guarded secret. I didn't know for several years," I explained.

"He..." Landon seemed more surprised than I would have figured but was properly stunned. "Fucking wow. Of all the assholes who get a Talent like that."

"Did you tell Niko about it yet? That day?" I asked Dirk, knowing there were a lot of things to resolve, and I believed that had to be one of them. Niko needed to know why they didn't have the relationship both of them had clearly wanted. Not to blame Dirk but to remove the blame from him because it was Dirk who had pulled away. How else was a child supposed to behave when he was told he wasn't, and would never be, good enough? He was protecting himself and his father.

"No..." Dirk admitted, closing his eyes. "I figured if we were getting past it all, it didn't matter. No reason to get between Niko and Hasan. It feels like a shitty thing to do."

"We'll put a pin in that and come back to it later," I decided, nodding.

Landon nodded as well, his expression telling me that the conversation wasn't over, only postponed.

"We don't have to. We just need to find Niko so he can get out here with us," Dirk said, pleading for me to hear him on this. "We can't... I can't let his brother kill him, Jacky. Niko could probably kill his brother now that I'm not in the way, but he'll be hurt, and in here, he'll be a target. The stronger fae here know who he is and how long he's been in their business. They'll finally have a chance to get rid of him in a way the rest of the family will never be able to solve."

I opened my mouth, then closed it, wondering just how I was going to do it all—save Dirk, save Niko, get out of here with all of us alive—all before my family decided they had to get involved and put themselves at risk in this place. We didn't have enough time to wait on Niko to find us, not before Rainer got to us. If Niko was healing somewhere, he might not even know we were here. He could have been asleep and would find out about Rainer's game with us too late unless the howl had woken him up.

I looked at Landon, who sighed heavily.

"We're going to do something I'm not going to like, aren't we?" he asked softly.

"Your father would be angry with me if he heard what I'm about to say," I said, feeling tears well up in my eyes at the very prospect. This could very well kill one of us. I could never see Heath again. Or I would limp out of the trees and fly home without his last son.

"Let's hear it," Landon muttered, straightening up like a general ready to hear his orders.

"We can't avoid Rainer *and* help Niko." Dirk growled at the name, but it was said and done, so I moved on. "It's impossible. At the end of the day, this fight is between them. We could keep running and try to beat him back to the estate, but that's unlikely. We're drained, Landon. We haven't slept. We're running on whatever fight-or-flight response we have. We'll drop from exhaustion before we get home, then we're dead.

Just the idea of avoiding Rainer is impossible at this point."

"Yes," Landon confirmed, upset I was forcing him to admit it. He would have tried. I knew he would have. "Say it, Jacky, so I can tell Pa this was your idea, and I didn't encourage anything."

A tiny, hopeful part of me wanted to smile.

"We have to be offensive," I said, swallowing my fear of what that entailed. "We can't run back and pick a fight, though. We'll lose that. We have to catch him off guard by setting a trap. If he falls for it, we can get a killing blow. If he dies, the hunt ends. Niko will know and come looking for us. We'll be on our way back to the estate." I put my hands together. "If we don't get the kill, he'll hopefully still be trapped, and we can keep moving. Niko will find him, kill him, and come to us."

"Or Niko shows up for the fight or before we trigger the trap."

"Either of those works as well," I confirmed, nodding.

"It's stupid," he said, shrugging.

Dirk's jaw dropped, but he stayed silent.

"Do you really think you can't beat him?" I asked, wondering if Landon didn't have the confidence in himself I always thought he did. I knew Rainer was stronger than me, but I had believed Landon was now more powerful than him. Heath was a strong enough Alpha to order him, and Landon had manhandled him before in front of me.

"The magic throws out everything I knew about him," Landon said, beginning to pace. "I don't know what he's capable of anymore, and that worries me. Plus, while killing him is something I would very much like to do, saving Dirk is the priority for me. What's the point of killing him when the guy I love is killed in the process? I can go after him later or just wait for the Hunt to take his soul. If he doesn't get what he wants, he dies, anyway. Why risk it?"

"Okay." Crossing my arms, I leaned on the back wall.

"But I like the idea of trapping him. The question is... how?" Landon pulled him back to his side and kissed Dirk's cheek, who leaned into him at the touch.

"Now I get to tell your father you encouraged this," I said quickly, making Landon chuckle.

"Damn, caught. I like the idea, though. It's what I was thinking, but..." Landon shook his head. "I know the chances of success are low. We need a way to trap him. I know a way to weaken him and slow him down enough for a fight, but it's not really a trap. It's an ambush."

"I will take any plan," I said, pressing Landon to continue.

"We brought silver and iron of every weapon we could carry. We confuse him with our scents in a place where we can't lose the paths. Here works well. We empty all our ammunition in him to slow him down and weaken him. The silver should be fatal, but he's juiced with fairy magic, so I don't know how effective it is against him anymore. They like silver."

"And moon cursed like iron, unlike the fae," I said, nodding.

"So, we use it all," Landon continued. "Once he's properly fucked up, we rush in with swords—"

"I can Change, and Dirk could shoot," I said, hoping for that idea. I fought better in my werecat form. There was a reason werecats were considered one of the strongest supernaturals in terms of raw physical strength.

"I actually don't want you to," Landon said, frowning at me. "We don't know what sort of magic this place has. Dirk and Niko grew up with it and adapted to it, but I don't feel comfortable considering my own Change right now. If I lost control," Landon shook his head. "It feels wrong."

"You have good instincts, Landon. Neither of you should Change. Not here, not with everything going on." Dirk slid down the wall, forcing Landon to stop holding him. "I would love to. Running on all fours, we're faster, but I can't do it, thanks to him."

"What exactly is wrong with it?" I asked, leaning down. "Please, Dirk. I don't understand, and I need to."

"It's nothing specific. Niko gave me a rule. I followed it. Sorry. You'll notice even Niko's brother isn't using his wolf form. Niko wasn't either when I saw him."

"Something feels off. It's my recommendation." Landon looked at me evenly, almost daring me to ignore his recommendation.

I glared at him. He was capable with weapons, and I could shoot straight most of the time, but I didn't trust myself with a dagger or knife, much less a sword.

"Fine," I said, giving up on it for now. If they weren't comfortable, I wouldn't push it. I didn't get the same vibe.

Everything was bad. Everything felt bad. Changing forms didn't seem as if it would change that except to put me in a better position to fight. "Landon, I like your plan. Do we want to set it up here?"

"This is probably the best place we have for it. We can spread our scent around, and make him wonder where we're hiding. He'll probably think we're hiding in here. He's not a fool. He's an old wolf. There's a chance he'll figure out what we're doing, but hopefully, he won't be able to stop us until it's too late. He'll want to investigate, even if he thinks it's off and that something will happen. In the end, we're the stupid ones for trying this, but it's all we have."

"This is a serious question...What's the worst that could go wrong?" I asked, looking mostly at Dirk.

"The fae get more involved," he answered immediately. "I bet they won't choose sides. We're in their territory, and they get hungry."

"I've never heard of so many fae who actually eat people," I said, sighing heavily. "I knew some were out there, but this feels concentrated."

"Why wouldn't it be? They have easy access to humans who might go camping or hiking or cars breaking down on the side of the road at night while driving past. It's prime hunting territory, and it appears...very little oversight." Landon made a face. "I can smell them. Everywhere, all the time, and when I think one of them might be watching, my hair stands on end, but I can never see where they are."

"Yeah, that's normal. Let's just hope they don't get

involved, and if one does...don't engage. Get away from it, ignore it, anything."

"We had one try to talk to us early on. It said there were worse things deeper in the forest, but we haven't really seen anything except the riders since." I frowned. "They've had plenty of time to bother us."

"Something to theorize about later. Let's get this ambush set up," Landon said. "We don't have much time. Who knows if he's running full speed or taking his sweet time."

CHAPTER TWENTY-FIVE

W e worked fast, jogging around the area and dividing up our weapons so Dirk was also armed. He was more skilled than I was with half the stuff I was carrying, so it made sense, even though he was struggling through his injuries from Rainer and the silver in his blood. Once Dirk was armed, and we had everything as ready as we could make it, he let Landon look over his injuries again. There were bruises on his ribs and abdomen, splotchy things that made me growl softly in anger as Landon revealed more scattered on his back.

"He took out his anger on me a couple of times, like right before he let us run," Dirk admitted. "That was the only time he didn't apologize right after it happened. It was insane, and I didn't trust him to look me over when he tried."

I narrowed my eyes at him.

"Did he...act like Fenris instead?" I asked, not wanting to believe it was even possible.

"I wouldn't go that far. One time he ranted about how the Black Forest Pack was gone and couldn't come back, but another time, he promised not to kill me because I was the only werewolf left who had any claim to it." Dirk shrugged, and pain flashed on his face.

"You saw him at his meanest. He's erratic, though. That's why I'm so fucked up. I could never really tell what I was about to get. He was hard to read...I kept wondering why Fenris had done this. I hadn't realized he was never really the werewolf we knew. Before it all started, I told him if he took me back to Berlin, no one would have to know about this. That you'd forgive him and guide him to healing from whatever happened to him."

"I'm so sorry," I said, choking on the words. I meant them, but they were hollow, meaningless. I'd let this happen to Dirk. I was the one who had the wool pulled over my eyes. Even though Landon tried to tell me this wasn't entirely my fault, guilt was still eating me alive as I looked over what had been done to my nephew.

"Hey, at the end of the day, Niko was the one who didn't make sure he was dead," Dirk said, giving me a half smile that didn't brighten his expression at all.

"Poor taste," Landon muttered.

"Yeah, but I had to try," Dirk said, leaning back on Landon. "I'm sorry I never told you more about this place. Niko never wanted it floating around, you know, living in a magic forest that most people really want to believe is normal."

"We all have secrets, but you know all of mine. Everything I am, I share with you. I only hope one day, we can be in a place where you feel you can do the same with me. I don't need to know everything. I just want you to know you can trust me with anything," he whispered.

My ears couldn't help but pick up what Landon said.

"I do. That's why I wanted Jacky to tell you the last big thing I knew I had to hide," Dirk whispered back.

I looked around the clearing. Leaving them, I walked the perimeter twice before either of them broke the silence.

"What is that?" Dirk asked, his volume well over Landon's hushed one.

"I think it's..." Landon's awe couldn't be missed.

I looked around, wondering if they saw anything I didn't, but as I opened my mouth to ask them what they were talking about, they were staring at each other, wide-eyed, and they seemed to be in their own world.

"Is that what the mate bond feels like?" Dirk asked.

Landon's sudden grin was all I needed to know. Turning away when he yanked Dirk into him, I took one more lap around the clearing before clearing my voice, but they had already broken it up.

"We should get into our positions," I said gently.

"Yeah," Dirk said, his cheeks a little redder from a blush than from his injuries.

"Jacky, are you sure you want to be in the house?" Landon asked, eyeing me and the shack.

"Someone needs to be," I reminded him. "If it's empty, he'll know it's wrong. He knows I would never go back and leave either of you, but I would send you two back and stay by myself. You're both better with all that than me." I waved at the firearms.

In reality, I had one last thing I wanted to try. Rainer was a monster, and I couldn't figure out what had gone so sour between him and Niko. I had a feeling there was nothing I could really do about it, but I knew fae magic and identity was a finicky, complicated thing that took on a magic of its own. He had pretended to be someone else for a long time, who acted very differently now. I wanted to poke around until I gave my boys the signal to open fire.

I watched them go into the trees together, knowing Landon would split off once Dirk was in position to take up his own. They couldn't sit together. It was risky, especially for Dirk. Apart, they could cover every side of the house, removing Rainer's chance to use it for cover. I just needed to keep Rainer focused on me before he decided to go to find them.

Going into the shack, I closed the door. There was an old nursery rhyme I couldn't stop thinking about. It wasn't Little Red Riding Hood, but rather, the Three Little Pigs. Two didn't make houses good enough to stop the big bad wolf from blowing their houses down and eating them. One made his house of brick, and it was able to withstand.

This home was made of stone with a wooden roof. It wouldn't hold out against the wolf hunting us.

I couldn't sleep even though the thought was very tempting. I leaned on the back wall, keeping on my feet, trying to fight the urge to curl into a ball. I checked my phone without thinking, reminding myself that it was still dead and there wasn't much I could do about that.

I heard the softest break of branches. It could have been an animal, but I knew it wasn't. The night air filled with something primal, making my guard come back up as I knew another predator had entered the clearing. There was a reason I had walked the perimeter. It wasn't enough to mark something I would consider my territory, and doing it as a human was normally just foolish. It was just enough, though. The land gave me a whisper of something coming.

A werewolf but also not. There was some fae about him now, something I had never noticed before in Fenris. Rainer was truly something different, and I had no idea how he'd hidden it for so long. I only had a few theories but didn't know if anyone would ever find the truth about what this werewolf had done to himself.

Pushing off the wall, I went to the door when he was only a few feet from it. I could hear him sniffing the air. I yanked it open to see Rainer there, his eyes landing on me quickly.

"Jacky Leon," he greeted, smiling cruelly.

"Rainer Brandt," I said in return.

"So, you know. Did the boy tell you?"

"No, I found the contract in your desk." I pushed the door open wider, far enough that it caught on an uneven section of earth and didn't swing closed again.

His eyes went wide for a moment.

"No, you couldn't have...I brought it." He reached for his pocket, snarling when it was empty.

"You know I'm not lying. You can smell that."

"I remember." He shook his head, focusing on me once again. "Where are the other two?"

"They're not here," I said, swallowing. Not technically a lie, depending on the definition of *here*. Here being the old building. My finger twitched. I wanted to give the signal, knowing both of them would be panicking when they realized I didn't intend on giving it quickly.

"You didn't," Rainer chuckled. "You are here to fight me to let them get back to the estate. Insane. You can't win, Jacky."

"I know. I have to try. They're the future."

Rainer's expression went hard.

"There is no future," he growled softly.

"Maybe not for you or me or Niko, but they will have it. I can't believe you beat Dirk. You were happy for him and Landon once. You made your jokes, but—"

"I was never happy for Dirk," Rainer snapped, fury in his eyes. There was no lie in the scent, but that didn't make any sense. It couldn't make sense.

"Yes, you were," I said softly. "Do you remember the last thing we talked about?"

"I don't care," he snarled, but I caught the confusion in his scent. The only thing I could think was he didn't remember. He had no idea what conversation I was referring to.

"Can I speak to Fenris?" I finally asked.

"No," Rainer said, teeth bared, but I saw a twitch of his lips. "No!"

"He was real, wasn't he?"

"You don't know—"

"I knew King Brion as two men. Fae magic is weird about identity, Rainer. You created a second one, and it became its own identity, didn't it? Without your ability to use fae magic—"

He moved fast, a hand grabbing my throat. With a simple tug, he pulled me off the ground and slammed me into the wall like a ragdoll before I could do anything. My feet dangled helplessly under me as I fought.

"He was never real!" Rainer screamed in my face.

"He's working against you, isn't he? That's why you don't have your contract," I struggled to say, clawing at his hand.

He whacked me against the wall again.

I never gave the signal. The first shot went out and pierced Rainer's neck. He let me go to throw a hand over the wound as the next three rounds hit him in the chest and back. All four shots hit before my feet touched the ground. He wasn't stupid, though. He tackled me into the building, realizing I was the enemy he could kill, then he would hunt for the guys.

"You stupid fucking bitch!" he roared, slamming me three times into the ground with my shirt, stronger than Fenris had ever been. I snarled and tried to claw for his eyes, a vulnerable spot. No more shots rang out as he attempted to beat me to death into the dirt floor of the old building.

It was like being a child, knowing there was no way I could overpower Rainer.

When another shot was fired, it was close. My ears rang as it went off, and Rainer roared in pain, jumping off me to turn around. My vision was blurry as I tried to see who it was. Rainer jumped for the other attacker, who had to be Landon or Dirk. He missed, and the body came back between us, still unloading whatever he was using into the wolf.

I had to get up, I knew that, but I was exhausted. I was so fucking tired, and now everything hurt. Why didn't it seem like the bullets were doing enough? Why wasn't he dropping?

"Jacky!" someone said, pulling me off the ground. "Damn you. You always show up where no one expects you." I was barely conscious, big spots dancing in my blurry vision, unable to see who was speaking.

"Dirk! Take her! You, follow. I'll hold him off and catch up!"

CHAPTER TWENTY-SIX

HEATH

H eath's foot was tapping anxiously as he watched the healers care for his sleeping packmates. He hadn't heard from Landon and Jacky in days, not since they landed in Germany. He knew that probably meant they were busy and focused on the problem at hand, but that didn't mean he liked the lack of contact. It only meant he could rationalize it, which helped him keep his growing anxiety from giving him a temper.

"Dad, it's five in the morning. What are you doing awake?" Carey asked as she walked into the kitchen.

"It's five in the morning. Why are you awake?" he asked in return, frowning at his youngest.

"I got up early to make everyone coffee. People have been staying up all night and staying over. You have a lot of patrols going on. I figured no one would have gotten coffee started again and wanted to help out."

Guilt stabbed him. There were a lot of things he had wanted for his daughter and the life he had wanted to provide for her. While he respected her instincts and ability to be so caring and good in some of the worst situations he could imagine, he had never wanted her to be in that role. She was the child in the house, not an adult. They were supposed to be getting up early to help her and make sure her world kept spinning. She wasn't supposed to be comforting and caring for anyone in this house or in the pack. They should have been doing that for her. This morning, more than any other, that reality stabbed him in the chest and forced him to feel the pain of his own failures when it came to his daughter.

"Go back to bed," he said gently. "I'll make coffee."

"I don't think I could get back to sleep now, even if I wanted to," she said, shaking her head. "If you make the coffee, I'll make eggs and bacon—"

"Carey, you don't need to take care of us."

"I want to," she said, not looking at him as she walked to the fridge.

"Please. I don't want you to look back on this and think about how you had to always do this for anyone in the pack or your family—"

"Dad, it's all I can do!" she snapped, slamming the fridge shut after she yanked out the eggs. "It's already Wednesday! Jacky and Landon haven't called. Teagan, Jenny, and Carlos are still stuck asleep. I need to do something. I hate not being able to do anything. *Please.*"

Heath reached out to her, taking the eggs to put them on the counter. She leaned toward him, and he knew that was the permission he needed. He hugged his daughter, holding her for a short time before she started to cry. He swayed, making her rock side to side, mimicking how he'd rocked her when she was little, hoping the gentle motion would help.

"They're strong and smart," he reminded her and himself. "If anyone has a chance of helping Dirk get home, it's them."

"And...Fenris?" she asked, the scent of her fear and anger filling the space.

"They can stop him," he promised.

He was careful about who in the pack knew. They were still calling him Fenris, and Fenris was still a member of the pack. Heath wanted to know when the wolf died. He wanted the light to go off in his head. He thought it was interesting that Rainer Brandt hadn't removed himself from the pack. Every werewolf had a choice to be a part of a pack or not. There was no order that could force that, though it was difficult for many to break it without the help of a new Alpha taking over. He highly doubted that was Rainer's problem.

He was still the type of wolf he was, inaccurately named Enforcer for PR reasons. They thrived alone, without the connections of a pack, because they didn't trust the connections of a pack. They didn't trust anyone or anything. They could be brought back only so far, and some things would never come naturally to them. They couldn't be Alphas.

He remembered the broken-hearted day he realized Landon had become one, that irrevocable step that other werewolves had forced in him, no matter how much he and Richard tried to protect him.

"Yeah," she agreed, nodding against his chest. She pulled back. "They can, and they'll find out why he did this."

"They will," he promised, kissing her forehead. "I won't ask you to do anything, Carey. If you want to help, you may. You will also go play video games, read, and enjoy your life, even if it's hard. You're not hurting anyone by doing that."

"I'm not a child, Dad. I have two hands—"

"But you are," he said, refusing to let her think otherwise. "You can help cook breakfast, a useful skill you should keep practicing. One day, you'll live on your own and need to cook for yourself. But you won't wait on any of these werewolves or on me. Is that clear?"

"Yes, sir," she said, grabbing the eggs again. It was an utter lie, but he was tired and stressed. She was going to do everything in her power to help until she was ready to call it a day. He would get back to her later when he gathered the energy for that confrontation.

Instead, he cooked with her, making sure the eggs were cooked thoroughly, and the bacon could satisfy everyone's preferences. He fed the healers silently, putting down plates for them. They gave soft thanks as he walked away and went back to their watch over his packmates as they ate. He put out larger serving plates for the other members of his pack, knowing they could manage it without leaving someone hungry. He then held a plate out for his daughter, making her frown.

"Go eat in your room," he said. "Spend the rest of the morning making sure your homework is done. You can't fall behind if you still want to graduate early. Then you can do whatever you want with your time."

"One more year," she said, nodding. "You're right. I can help by getting high school out of the way as soon as possible."

He watched her leave, screaming internally at the idea that his daughter would be graduating in a year. The timing of her early graduation was difficult to pin down, thanks to the school switches she had to put up with, but now they knew for sure when she would be done. She was a full grade ahead in her primary education. Furthermore, his motivated daughter was only two classes away from having enough credits to complete her first semester of college before she had even been accepted to any.

I'm running out of time.

He could feel it in his bones.

Reaching for his phone, he tried to put it out of his mind. He sent a group text to everyone in the pack who was available, telling them to come in and get breakfast, then he went on autopilot to get through the morning. He smiled and said good morning to his werewolves as they came in for food. They asked about Teagan, Jenny, and Carlos, and he gave them the simple update that no one was awake yet. There was no update from Jacky and Landon. Dirk was still missing and unreachable.

"I'm about to start calling again," Heath said to Shamus and Ranger once the rest of the wolves were focused on the food.

"Heath, if you need to go after them, I can manage

the pack as necessary," Shamus said with solemn confidence. Heath knew he had the capability to stand in when needed. He might rely on Shamus for that soon, but he didn't want to jump the gun.

I sent out my best werewolf, my own son. He'll stop at nothing to help Dirk. He's madly in love with him and knows how to fight a werewolf like Rainer. Jacky isn't a pushover, anything but. The fae magic is a complication, but I trust that Jacky and Landon can lean on each other.

His worry was because he loved them, not because he thought they would fail. His worry was that they would get hurt, and only one of them might come back in the end.

Heath was better focusing on the worry, but he had to conceal the rage. The pack knew he was angry, but he didn't want them to know just how angry he really was. The bitter betrayal they were facing was something Heath could have stopped. He knew that. He could have shipped Fenris back to Callahan or denied him joining them in Jacky's territory.

I'm tired of being betrayed.

Inhaling, he nodded at Shamus's offer.

"It's in consideration, and you will know if and when I need you to step up to do that."

But if anything goes wrong, I'll kill you, and I don't want to do that.

He didn't say that, couldn't say that. He hated himself for thinking it. Letting them eat in peace, he went into the office, going to Jacky's computer. As it was waking up, he tried to call everyone's cell phones.

Everyone went straight to voicemail, something that had started the night before. Heath felt the same panic he had the first time Jacky's phone did it the night before. He hated it. His heart pounded uncomfortably in his chest as Landon's phone also went directly to voicemail.

I need…

He looked at Jacky's computer and closed his eyes, trying to fight off the urge to reach out to anyone else. He didn't want to involve her family. It would go from bad to worse. There was only one person he actually had faith in from his experiences with them, and he finally broke.

Zuri. I can try Zuri. I have to try something.

He unlocked Jacky's computer and went to the video and conference call program he'd seen her use. He was now online as his fiancée, and the distaste of his actions made him feel ill, but he was getting desperate. He found Zuri's name and clicked it, starting a call. His hand was shaking when he let go of the mouse and looked at the screen on Jacky's wall with a camera on the top.

"Heath! I'm surprised to see you calling." Zuri was sitting as she greeted him, her husband and mate in the background, bouncing their son as he walked out of view. Her smile faded quickly. "Something must be wrong. Where's Jacky?"

"Jacky is in Germany with my son," he said to explain why it was him and not her sister.

Zuri's eyes went wide.

"Did something happen between Niko and Dirk?"

"Something is probably happening to them," he said, swallowing his fear. "I should start from the beginning.

Please understand that I don't think anyone has all the information right now."

"Explain," Zuri ordered.

Heath was grateful it was the order of a concerned family member and not another werewolf. There was no power in it, which kept him from losing his cool.

"A group of our werewolves was in Dallas this past weekend for one of them to get some of his own work done. He requires a protection detail, and he always took Fenris—"

"The scarred one." Zuri nodded.

"Yes." Heath continued what he knew of their weekend, finishing when Jacky and Landon discovered the three under a magically induced sleep and Fenris gone. " It was fae magic. We didn't know what fae would have wanted to do this or what their goal was. Mygi sent healers to tend our unconscious, and we tried to start untangling what happened."

"Somehow, this is connected to Niko and Dirk in Germany," Zuri said, her lips pressed into a fine line as she stared him down. "Or Jacky and Landon wouldn't have gone there."

Heath nodded, knowing he had to explain the rest.

"We didn't know if he was taken hostage. How could anyone know what I'm about say." Heath's regrets couldn't be hidden as he told Zuri about the secret office in Fenris's home and the contract Jacky had found in his desk, watching Zuri go from concerned and angry to downright furious. She was right to be angry with him. He hated this entire situation. He hated how he'd missed it, never saw that Fenris wasn't who and what he said he was. He was supposed to only have werewolves in this territory who his fiancée would be safe with, and he'd failed her. He'd failed his family. He'd failed the other members of the pack.

He hated himself the most at that moment. Zuri's fury was only a confirmation that he deserved that hate.

"I see." She nodded. "And what did this fae contract for power tell you?"

"It was for one named Rainer Brandt, but it smelled like Fenris. He sold his soul to the Wild Hunt in exchange for power. We believed he's hunting Niko. It's the only rational explanation, which is where we get into Dirk and Niko. Once we knew something was happening, Jacky reached out to Niko and Dirk. Neither answered. Ansel, Niko's butler I believe, said Dirk had never returned from a weekend trip to Berlin to visit friends. Niko ran into the woods for something. Neither had been heard from."

"So, the game had already begun," Zuri said, nodding as she absorbed everything he said. "Jacky and Landon then went to Germany, leaving you to protect the others. You haven't heard from anyone since."

"That's right. I'm sorry—"

She lifted a hand.

"Why?" she asked.

"For not knowing who Fenris was and for never looking into him further. This was my oversight, and I've brought a valid danger to both our families."

"If I was a younger or stupider person, I would agree

with you. I would say we're both to blame. How could I not recognize one of Niko's blood family? How did I miss it?" She gave me a hard look. "Or we can blame Jacky, who our father has told to remove all the werewolves from her territory, regardless of who they are, but darling Jacky likes to see the best in people. She denied an order from our father to keep all of you and now gave someone a way to get revenge on one of us."

"You can't blame her," he growled. He wouldn't allow it. "I vouched for every werewolf we brought in and promised her I would keep them in line. I promised her I would deal with them before they could do anything."

"I'm not blaming her. I'm telling you why you can't blame yourself," she said, her expression softening. "Just like I won't blame myself. I never met one of Niko's blood family, so I would have no idea what they look like. My oversight. Niko has killed a lot of werewolves. The idea that one of his biological family survived is the least likely scenario. We knew he wanted to kill all of them who ended up on the other side of the War. We talked softly about how he was tracking another one of them here and there or when we would see him come back from one of his personal missions, half beaten and bloody from a fight. But we never joined him. An oversight made by our entire family."

"How does that mean you're not blaming Jacky?" He didn't care about himself.

"Because at least you and Jacky committed your oversights out of the goodness of your hearts and not the quiet neglect most mistakes in my family can be blamed on. I'm going to call Niko's home and try to get hold of someone, anyone. Perhaps one of his staff can give you the update you need, and I can figure out how the family might help...without making all of this worse."

"I should have—"

"No, it was better you told me first," she said simply.

Heath saw a third account enter the call, Zuri attempting to contact Niko.

It wasn't Niko that answered. It was Davor.

"Zuri!" Davor smiled, but Heath felt something was off. Why was Davor there? He didn't like it. It took two seconds for Davor to see Heath, and his fake smile fell into fear. "Alpha Everson."

"Davor, brother...." Zuri leaned in. "What are you doing at Niko's home?"

"Covering for Jacky," he answered quickly, scared of his sister even though there were probably thousands of miles between them. "Jacky and his son, Landon, went into the Black Forest to find Niko and Dirk. I don't know all the details, but I know. I know who's out there and some other stuff. They reached out to me because I was a secret keeper for something of Niko's. She's going to be so disappointed that I wasn't able to cover for her longer."

"You didn't want the rest of your family to realize what's wrong," Heath realized, his eyes going wide as he figured out what Davor meant.

"Yeah," Davor said, nodding. "Would you want them to?"

"It took me days to get desperate enough to call Zuri.

They haven't gotten in touch with me in days," Heath said quickly. "Have you heard from them?"

"No, I haven't," Davor said, shaking his head. "I wasn't expecting to. Out there... things go wrong more often than not. They either come out, or I finally call in the entire family. Tomorrow morning is the deadline."

"Why?" Zuri snapped. "What do you know about that place? What don't *I* know?"

"Only what Niko told me, and he was always really sparse with information. It's the Black Forest, and it's the only place he knows of that the fae realm and ours exist in the same time and place. It's dangerous."

Heath rocked back, finally understanding the horrible reality of what he had sent his fiancée and son into.

CHAPTER TWENTY-SEVEN

I woke up groggy. Before I even tried to move, my head hurt. My back hurt.

Trying to move made everything hurt.

"Hey, woah," someone said softly, touching me.

I hissed viciously, knowing I wasn't anywhere safe enough to be touched by people while I was in pain and half-asleep.

"Jacky."

Finally realizing the voice was masculine, I blinked and tried to see who it was, but something was over my eyes. I went to yank it off, but it was removed before I could.

It was Nikolaus, son of Hasan, looking far worse than I had ever seen him.

"It was you," I realized, remembering the last few moments before I went unconscious.

"I'd been tracking him, realizing he was doing something different from his previous attempts to kill me.

I wasn't far behind him. I didn't think he was going after you...or Dirk...or Landon Everson," Niko said, his face schooled, but his tone told me he was more than a little annoyed by the surprise of all of us being in the forest.

"You couldn't smell Landon or me on the trail?" I wanted to hit him. How could he miss that?

"I can't smell anything. I've had to track him through physical means, something I'm grateful my father taught me to do. He hit me with a nasty bit of fae magic when this got started. It's dead." He flicked his nose, leaning back as he realized he didn't need to hold me down anymore, and I wasn't trying to attack him.

"Hasan never taught me to do that," I said, sitting up with a groan.

"My father, not our father. If someone in our family is going to teach you to hunt game, it'll be Subira, and her techniques are different from what I learned growing up," Niko explained, his expression shuttered and unreadable.

"I see." With a nod, I started to swing my legs off the bed, growling as I put my feet on the ground. "There's nothing broken, right?" I asked, wanting to know if I shouldn't do this.

"No. Head trauma, but I think you've gotten more than used to that," he said, leaning back further. "You want to tell me what you're doing here?"

"He's my wolf," I said softly. "He's part of Heath's pack."

"No. He can't be. You can't put Rainer within a hundred kilometers of a werecat without him hunting them down. That's why I knew I had to hunt him down during the War. I don't know how he hid this long, but that doesn't matter. There's no way he can be your wolf or one of Heath's. He'd never work with one of us or anyone affiliated with us."

I remembered the day in Dallas when he had made his grand appearance into my life and sighed.

"Yeah, that's how I met him," I whispered. "But he went by Fenris. That's all anyone knew him as."

Niko's eyes went wide.

"You think I would lie to you?" I asked him, giving him an annoyed look. "He's my wolf. We didn't know who he was, and it seemed as if he was getting over some shit. Clearly, it was just buried deeper, hidden behind the falsity that was his life as Fenris. Fae magic stuff. I hate it."

"Oh..." Niko slumped a bit. "I see."

"So, when Fenris disappeared, we investigated because three other werewolves in the pack were hit with a sleeping spell or curse. He was the only one missing. For a little while, we wanted to believe he might have been taken hostage. Then I found his blood bargain with the Wild Hunt, written on his very flesh. It smelled like Fenris, but it was for...," I gestured at Niko, beckoning him to say it.

"Rainer Brandt," Niko said, nodding slowly.

"Yup. Now, where are the boys?" I asked, pushing to my feet, hissing in pain as my back let me know it didn't appreciate all the moving.

"Sleeping in the main room by the fire. There's only

one bedroom here, and they wanted you to have it. I didn't argue with them. You took the brunt of Rainer's anger."

"I tried to talk to his other identity, the one I had a complicated friendship with. He didn't like that," I admitted. "I was supposed to give them a signal. I wanted information."

Niko shook his head, clearly not agreeing with my choice.

"Where are we?"

"A safehouse," he answered simply, leading me out of the bedroom. I was still dressed in what I had been wearing. "You've been asleep for about six hours. They've been down for five. I did some explaining before they dropped."

"And now you'll do it for me," I said casually, expecting him to tell me everything.

"Yeah...." Niko was in front of me but moved out of the way to reveal the quaint, homey living room with a warm hearth in the center. I went toward the couch I was behind, looking over to see one of my boys. Dirk was on the couch, a blanket tucked over him. Landon had a pillow and blanket on the floor. Both made no sign that I had disturbed them.

"They needed the sleep," I said softly, reaching to brush Dirk's cheek. As my fingers grazed my nephew's cheek, Niko's growl warned me of something I should have remembered.

Landon was right, then. Maybe I shouldn't assume the worst.

I looked at my brother, seeing the eyes of his werecat focused on my hand.

"He's not property," I said, not pulling my fingers back. "He's not only yours or only mine. He's a grown man who gets to decide who he wants in his life."

"You kept an important secret from me about my son, one that only came about because he was with you, and you don't know how to do anything with a modicum of care. Forgive me if I don't think you're the best person for him right now."

You have no idea what secrets your son has me keeping from you, Niko. And for that, I am sorry. There's one I really do wish you could have, but they aren't my secrets to give you.

"I thought you wanted a world where werecats and werewolves could finally live together peacefully, more unified than we have ever been," I said, finally pulling away and straightening to stare down my brother.

"I don't do it at the risk of my loved ones."

"If none of them wanted to be part of the risk, they can leave my territory any time. Dirk has certainly been reminded of that. I don't keep him chained in my home, locked under Heath's orders. Sometimes, good things, the right things, need to have some risk," I countered. "You're just angry with me right now because you want someone to be angry with." I thought about it for only a second before I said something else. I couldn't take it back, but I said it anyway. "And you don't like that Dirk has found a life worth living while he's been with me."

"Damn it," Niko snarled, stomping to the open

kitchen. "I knew you reminded me of her, but I never thought..."

"What?" I asked, demanding to know what he was mad about now.

Grabbing a bottle off a shelf, he pulled out the cork and took a swig, not replying for a moment. He glared at me and took another drink.

"You remind me of Liza sometimes." Niko put the bottle on the counter, slowly spinning it around. "But where she was sweet and kind, you are a baseball bat with nails. She would say the same things, but the way she went about embodying them was on the other end of the spectrum."

"Ah." I didn't know what to say to that. I'd been told she and I couldn't be more different. I'd been told I wasn't anyone's attempt at replacing her. I'd been told she was sweet and innocent. I never thought anyone would say she and I were similar. No one talked about her, not nearly enough. It was a wound that was only recently cleaned and could start healing. Davor showed me how rotten and infected it had gotten and how healing could finally repair the damage.

"Yeah, it bothers me, but it's not a bad thing." Niko took another drink. "She was, and still is, my favorite sibling...from both families I've been part of, she's my favorite."

"I'm sorry," I said, walking closer. "I would love to talk about this more, but I need to know what our next step is with the werewolf out there hunting us down.

You're his target. How did you get away? Did you injure him?"

Niko shoved the cork into the bottle and put it back on the shelf behind him.

"I was able to push him off, but between getting all of you out of that and him deciding to retreat, thanks to his injuries, there was no way of killing him. Rainer has always been a damn good fighter. He wants to kill me, and thanks to that, he won't be so risky as to get himself killed for nothing. Even though I was stronger as a werecat than he was as a werewolf, he gave me hell during the War. It almost doesn't surprise me that he's the one that survived."

"And he made a deal to kill you," I pointed out. "With the Wild Hunt itself."

"Yeah." Niko stared at his hands on the counter.

"Now is the time you tell me everything that's going on," I said, leaning on the counter opposite of him.

"The Black Forest Pack had deep ties with the fae. I don't know when it started. I was too young for that education. I would have learned the deeper secretive history when I was about to be a man. I don't know if there was a bargain struck, or perhaps the werewolves originally decided it was a good place to stay, only to discover the fae, but the pack was very...isolated. My biological father, he would say we weren't like other packs. This was our world. The rest of it didn't matter. He hated the War and didn't like how other packs kept asking us for help, not caring about what we dealt with in this place. It was a strong pack, but it was strong to deal with this place, not werecats.

"Instead of hosting other Alphas, we hosted fae political leaders, keeping peace treaties with them to keep their own in the deepest parts of the forest. The Wild Hunt is something that encompasses all fae. It's shown up all over the world, and the legends around it are different everywhere. For example, there are legends about Odin, the Norse god, leading it, so..." Niko shrugged. "I've never encountered it before. I do know anyone can be a victim if they aren't careful."

"And? You and Rainer?"

Niko growled softly.

"Rainer was my eldest brother, and when he was becoming what we now call a teenager, he was invited to private meetings with my father. He saw other packs ask us for help more than I did. Then the pack was attacked and destroyed. We didn't talk about what happened afterward. I was angry and believed I hated him. My brother was fighting for the werewolves who'd killed our parents and destroyed our home. He hated me in return because I was a werecat and, therefore, the enemy. It was a youthful hate that didn't have the maturity to listen to the other side or even recognize it."

"So, you fought and thought you killed him."

"We fought here, actually," Niko said softly, putting his elbows on the counter. "In this forest, running between the ruins of our family home and the homes of those we considered friends. Fae watched us as we clashed, staying out of the turmoil because they knew the

War was exposing more than just the moon cursed to humanity. Even the most feral of fae don't want humans to know where they live and hunt. They need the secrecy to continue killing the way they do."

"Is that why they're avoiding us now? I noticed not many fae have tried to bother us since we got here."

"Probably. The fae here are...a bit stunted. Everything happens all at once to them, and they ignore the passage of time in the human world. They want to continue living as they did a thousand years ago, free of interference."

"And you killed your brother in this place, or so you thought. With the fae watching and his rage to come back and kill you, too strong an emotion for some of them to resist."

"I have no doubt whatever my brother was feeling after I left him to finish dying out here was enough to call the Wild Hunt to him. That much need for revenge, that much hate. That would do it, I bet. Among other things, I bet that would do it."

"They gave him a deal worthy of an immortal supernatural—all the time in the world and some fae power."

"Yeah, and I get why they would. Claiming a soul like that for their menagerie? He would be better than any fae hound. He would be able to do things some of the fae can't. They played the long game with him, even when they probably didn't need to."

"It gave him centuries to get more powerful for when he inevitably fails," I pointed out.

Niko sighed, nodding as he put his head in his hands.

"Tell me more about this place, how it's kept us safe, and what you want to do next. I don't like standing still like this."

"I made this safe house years ago but often use it to get out of the house when I want some peaceful private time. It's difficult to find and doesn't use anything from the Black Forest Pack. I recreated some of the security measures, and I have some..." He reached to the shelf again, picking up a stick of something. "I light one of these before coming out here, obscuring my scent on the trails. It's just some of the magical plants of the area, with thick smells that really confuse the senses, nothing special. I keep one lit here. We can use this to try to get the three of you out of the forest." He put it down between us. "Eventually, he'll find us here, but it will be hard for him. He won't move out to attack all four of us until he's healed enough. I think we have another few hours before he starts to try."

"The three of us? You're coming, too," I said, crossing my arms.

"I can't leave him out here. He's mine to deal with," Niko countered, shaking his head. "He's rabid and needs to be put down. I thought I put the entire pack to rest centuries ago. I was wrong. Now I need to finish it. His immunity to our silver weakness is a major problem, and he doesn't have the fae weakness to iron. It'll be hard, but it has to be done."

Holy shit, he's immune to silver?

"And if he kills you?" I demanded, trying to keep my voice low, but I wasn't certain if I did a very good job.

"Says the forty-something-year-old who thought being his rag doll was a good idea," Niko snapped. "Do you really think you have a better chance than I do?"

"I think you couldn't kill him eight hundred years ago, and you don't know him now," I fired back. "But we do, and there's a chance my wolf is still in there."

"You need to stop being fucking naïve, Jacky." He pointed at me, then at himself. "Do I want peace between werewolves and werecats? Sure, but I'm not a fool. I know a monster like Rainer would never allow that sort of world to exist. You should figure that out, or you're going to get someone fucking hurt. Oh, wait, you already *have* by trusting a wolf who was out of his damn mind!"

"Fenris had a chance!"

"Fenris was never *real*!" Niko roared, his volume matching mine.

"Dirk, your parents are fighting," Landon mumbled.

"One of those is your future stepmom, not mine," Dirk said, muffled by his pillow.

"That was mean." Landon groaned.

28

CHAPTER TWENTY-EIGHT

I turned around to see them pushing to sit up from their respective sleeping spots. Landon looked at me, throwing the blanket off and getting up. He seemed uninjured from the fight before I was knocked unconscious, which I counted as a blessing. Dirk looked healthier as he got up as well, a little pale, but the rest was good for him.

"Good...morning?" I said, feeling guilty.

"Yup, sure is. You're alive. That's good. Had us scared," Landon said as he walked over to us at the kitchen's bar, which looked over the main room. "Please don't scare me like that again. I don't want to be the wolf who tells my pa that you died."

"I'll do my best," I said, not sure if my best was ever enough. Most of the time, I scraped by with a bit of luck and hope.

"Yeah, that was bad." Dirk came up on my other side, leaving me flanked by my wolves. "Niko, be nice to her.

Fenris had us all fooled, and she's run into fae magic, what it does with identity, and all that weird shit."

"She got you Changed into a werewolf, then abducted—"

"I got myself Changed into a werewolf, and your brother abducted me. We've already had a talk about the first. It's not up for debate now. As for Rainer... We had Fenris, and he was getting better. He was easier to deal with every day. Even Zuri didn't realize he was your brother, so how was anyone in Texas supposed to know?"

"Fenris wasn't real," Niko repeated.

"He was real enough," I angrily retorted, glaring at him. "Just like Brin was real before he was forced to fully remember his life and identity as King Brion."

Niko lifted his hands, and while it was a sign of defeat, his expression didn't match it.

"Fine. All of you can continue living in whatever fantasy you need to if it helps you sleep at night. It doesn't change the fact that all of you are going to leave this forest, and I am going to kill Rainer, so this can be over and done with."

"Niko, we can help." Dirk stepped around the counter, but Niko stepped away.

"No, you can't. This isn't your mess to clean up, Dirk. I won't put it on your shoulders. It's something I should have been more careful about. My decision to leave Rainer out here and not checking if he was properly dead was my mistake."

"You were half-dead yourself, from what you told us earlier," Landon said, shrugging. "It's a pretty common mistake people make when they need to find shelter and heal themselves. Better to keep living another day than stay in a vulnerable position and possibly die to another threat."

"Rainer was a powerful werewolf for one so recently Changed," Niko said, staring into space. "Even for what he was."

"He must have been holding back for years," Landon said, beginning to pace. "I can overpower him...or thought I could."

"It's probably more complicated than that," I said, clearing my throat nervously. "Brin couldn't do the same things as Brion. He could still tap into it at times, but he was less powerful in general. That's what made King Brion's return complicated. He needed to avoid his enemies while shedding the limitations of his identity as Brin. Fenris was the face he wore while in...." A light bulb would have lit up over my head as I put another piece of the puzzle into place. "Callahan."

"No, let's not even get into that," Landon said, waving his hands as he shook his head.

"What?" Niko's curiosity had an edge to it. "What does Callahan have to do with any of this?"

Landon threw his hands in the air and went back to pacing.

"Callahan moved Fenris around a lot, trying to keep him out of trouble. Fenris was too powerful for most Alphas and had to resort to respecting them out of his own effort rather than properly falling into a pack structure. Callahan didn't want to keep him close. They didn't like each other, and Corissa apparently hates Fenris, but why go through all the effort for a broken wolf?"

"He was pissed when Fenris decided to stay with my father," Landon added. "But he didn't force Fenris in line right there. He just let it happen."

I looked at Niko to see if he was putting this together.

"The only conclusion I can come to is Callahan knew Rainer Brandt, and he's been helping him hide all these years. They crafted a fake identity for him and a mostly fake story for his past when he came back from his fight with you. Fae magic can be tricky, and it saw the need for this identity, so it made it the truth for that werewolf, and his lie couldn't be detected. It wasn't a lie to *Fenris*. Rainer became something in the background, a foundation for Fenris, but Fenris became an individual of his own. That's why he could learn not to attack me every time he saw me. How he evolved, changed, and...became his own. He was healing from the trauma of Rainer, trauma that wasn't really his." I put my hands on the counter.

"I don't think Fenris or Rainer really knew what was happening because this is weird fae magic. King Brion was even a bit annoyed, if I remember correctly. It was a couple years ago."

"I heard what you said to him. Do you think they might have figured it out? Rainer and Fenris?" Landon asked, stopping his pacing next to me.

"I...don't know?" I wished I had more for them. I wished I could be more confident in what I was saying.

"Most of this is based on theories. I've seen this kind of play out under vastly different circumstances. Brin and Brion were on the same page, or Brin sort of disappeared without a fight. I don't know if Fenris and Rainer are. Rainer thought he had his contract on him, was *convinced* of it. I found it in Fenris' house back in Texas. All I could think was Fenris did that... for us."

"Jacky, don't get your hopes up for Fenris," Landon said carefully.

"It's not a bad theory, though," Dirk said, seeing my side.

"It wouldn't be hard to figure out what triggered Rainer to come back in full force if this is what we're going with. He met another Brandt. He met Dirk, and Dirk is my son. I know you've tried to keep that quiet, but Rainer would have noticed it rather easily. With that obvious connection and a hunter's mind, Rainer saw a vulnerability he could finally exploit. He just needed to bide his time."

"I asked him about that. Initially, he guessed because of who Jacky is and confirmed it, thanks to me. It was the way I walked, the way I talked." The scent of Dirk's guilt caught my attention. "Sometimes, he claimed to smell the Black Forest on me. Every so often, especially in my wolf form, he thought he caught it."

"It's not your fault," I promised him, looking over my shoulder to meet his eyes.

There was a long silence until Dirk nodded, his eyes never leaving mine.

"You know, Callahan probably thought Rainer had

lost his mind over the years," Landon said, breaking the moment. "He would have seen Rainer slowly become this other person who was always broken. Not angry and wanting vengeance against his brother, but properly *broken* because he didn't have a full identity. He had a construct of half-truths and half-lies he was made to believe, thanks to the magic Rainer had bargained for."

"That's dark," Dirk mumbled.

"The fae have their fair share of darkness," Niko said wisely. "In fact, the progenitors of the Sidhe, Oberon and Titania, are counterparts, one of the light and one of the dark. Forever bound together, forever wanting the other, but never able to be with the other. It's a really common trend in the mythos. Sun gods and moon goddesses are very common in many religions around the world, spanning all of history. Even now, Sidhe, who still follow the oldest bloodlines of their kind, say they are creatures of the light or dark, and their powers can *almost* be divided as such. There are powers less easy to classify and some that can't properly be named. And that's just the Sidhe. What we call fae is really a wide variety of peoples and creatures from that realm."

"We don't need the entire Fae 101 class today, Niko." Dirk's eye roll could be heard. "Why don't we get to how we stop all this?"

"It's easy. I'll escort you to the estate. We'll use these to cover our scents." Niko pulled down the stick thing from earlier. "Once I know you're all secure at home, I will hunt Rainer. You will heal, tell everyone you're okay and that I will be okay, and no one is the wiser. The family will never need to know this insanity happened."

"Davor knows we're out here and about Rainer," I said quickly, shattering his plan in one swift sentence.

"I'm going to come over this bar and strangle you," Niko said, dropping the stick to the counter. "How, of all our siblings, did you end up telling Davor?"

"We illegally read your will to get the key to your armory, and Davor had to tell us where it was hidden," I explained. "We needed weapons. We had just learned what this place really was."

To his credit, Niko didn't come over to the bar. He glared, oh how he glared, but he didn't attack me.

"You just can't stay out of anything, can you?" he asked softly.

"Dirk was in danger. I was prepared to leave you in this forest," I hissed, finally unbottling the anger over the sequence of events that led us to this place. "You didn't tell us Dirk was missing when he went missing. You didn't tell us a werewolf breached your territory. You never bothered to tell anyone what the fuck was out here. You, a part of the family for centuries, never told anyone what was happening here. You just ran off to do it all by yourself without even leaving guidance for anyone to help you."

"My life and secrets are mine," Niko growled.

"You want to keep your secrets? Fine, but you don't get to put Dirk in danger to do it!" I snapped, pointing at him to enforce the accusation I laid at his feet. "So, I breached your precious privacy and took what I fucking needed. His life matters more than your fucking secrets. You both could have fucking died out here, and no one would have known!"

Landon reached for me, pulling me back toward the hearth. I didn't fight him, letting the distance between my brother and me grow, leaving poor Dirk standing awkwardly in the middle.

"Let's leave this for when we get out of here," he said. "Let's stay on task. I know the one thing we all want is to live through this. Davor knows. He's been trying to hold your family off. He said three days was probably the best he could do. We have no idea how long it's been."

"Niko can tell the time," I muttered.

Niko pulled out a pocket watch.

"It's...Wednesday at noon," he said before tucking it away. "Electronics don't work out here. That's mechanical, no battery. I have to tune it sometimes when I leave because it'll get a little off, but it always keeps ticking. There's some minor time dilation here, nothing serious. Yes, I want all of us to survive this. Yes, Jacky and I can shelve the conversation for after."

"Good. I don't think we can sneak out of here. I bet he'll be on top of us before we get close to the estate," Landon said, letting me go and moving to stand in the middle with Dirk but not blocking my view of Niko. "How far away are we?"

"Ten-hour jog in human form at a reasonable pace, nothing supernaturally fast," Niko answered stiffly. "You're right. He'll be faster than our pace and could very well catch us if he figures out how I'm confusing our scents. I can hold him off while you three keep going. You'll be on a safe path home. I would need to kill him anyway after taking you home."

"Tell me why Dirk said not to Change," I asked quickly, narrowing my eyes on Niko.

"If you want to test the Last Change in a place where fae can manipulate or amplify your emotions, you are more than welcome to," Niko said sternly but not enough to hide his sarcasm. "Or maybe you want to become one of their playthings in a beast form, which plays into some of their magics. You would be more vulnerable. Or maybe you don't want thumbs, which are very useful in this place. There's a number of ways being a normal moon cursed in this place could go wrong. The Black Forest Pack had their pack connections. They could communicate and protect each other from threats. You can communicate, but I don't know if it gives you the connection they used. It was an adaptation of theirs."

"Like?" Landon was asking now.

"They could literally protect each other from the manipulation of fae magics in wolf form," Niko explained. "Dirk doesn't have his pack here, and he's the only one who would be considered the type of wolf that could do it. So, he shouldn't Change. Neither of you has any of the defenses that pack developed, and they aren't something I can teach."

"Sounds like you had a pack full of Talented werewolves," I pointed out.

"Maybe they were. Maybe they weren't. We're our own type of magical being, supernaturals, thanks to our cursed existence. For werewolves who have been exposed to this place for too long, things changed. Wolves are highly adaptable creatures."

"Yeah, but I get it. I don't Change. None of us should. Fine. Do you?"

"I can," Niko said cautiously. "I don't choose to every time I'm out here."

"So, you must be a bit different from the normal werecat, huh?" I crossed my arms, waiting for a response.

Niko's face went flat, expressionless against my prying.

"I might have a Talent," he finally confirmed softly.

"And you never told anyone."

"I might not," he continued. "Maybe it's just an adaptation to this place."

"Sneaky."

"I grew up with fae in my backyard. I learned, or I died. Get mad at me for my secrets all you want. If I didn't have them, I would have been dead a long time ago."

CHAPTER TWENTY-NINE

There was never a consensus about what we would actually do. At Niko's words, there was a silent agreement that we would let him take charge of the situation. He was right about a few things. He had grown up here and lived here for several centuries alone, with only his own wits to protect himself and his people. If there was one person who could put us on a safe path home, it was him.

We were low on ammo, but we all had weapons beyond that. I stuck with the swords I had picked from Niko's armory. Landon had his as well, along with his collection of firearms. Dirk had all the firearms Heath had sent with me. We would be ready for a fight if Rainer showed up.

Niko was pulling on his gloves as we walked out the door. His claws, I had heard them called before. I had seen the missing pair in the armory and knew he had them, but seeing him wear them made me realize just how deadly they could be. They didn't impact his ability to do much, the mechanical, articulated silver knives coming off the back of his hands. He seemed right at home wearing them, as if he did so every day.

"Zuri mentioned those," I said, nodding down at them. "When she met Fenris, he gave her some lip. She said she would finish what your claws had clearly started."

"I haven't used them in a long time," Niko said, adjusting a small strap on one. "They've always been my weapon of choice in human form. Davor designed them, and I took to them quickly. No one else in the family wanted to try them." He looked at me as I studied them. "Would you ever want to give them a try?"

"I...don't know," I answered, unable to take my eyes off them. "I'm not like the rest of you. I don't know how to use a bunch of different weapons. I can shoot, but...." I gave him a half-shrug, admitting I was self-aware of this weakness. "Heath wants me doing more hand-to-hand training, but I'm busy and would rather live my life than train to fight in a way I don't want."

"Pa also doesn't push you too hard because he doesn't want to hurt you," Landon said while he and Dirk were getting their final preparations done. "But hey, I only know how to stick things with the pointy end when it comes to swords, so don't beat yourself up over there."

Turning to Dirk, Landon winked at Dirk. Dirk snorted and started to chuckle, covering his face, waving his free hand, and slashing the air.

I looked at Niko, smiling broadly, only to see him

watching the werewolves with a distant look as though he didn't know if he was allowed to take any joy from it. Or maybe he didn't feel included. This was complicated, and I was the sister who got to watch it flourish while he'd missed it for years.

He shook it off, and acting like he didn't see it, he pulled out a stick and held it to me.

"Light that, please. Dirk, this one is yours. You and Landon will take the lead once we're on the path. Jacky and I will take up the rear, listening for Rainer. He'll probably come up behind us. We're not going to take this at more than a walk."

"Are you sure? I can jog—"

"You took a bit of a beating. I could only make sure you weren't going to die. I don't know if you have a brain bleed or anything. Dirk still has silver poisoning because I can't remove that from him. He'll need days for it to pass out of his system naturally. Strenuous activity is a bad idea for both of you."

"You remind me of Jabari," I decided, lighting the stick with a lighter. It was like a thick piece of incense, with a cloth wrapped around the bottom, probably to keep from burning someone's hand. Once lit, I wanted to cough and sneeze at the same time, the scents too much for my nose and the smoke too thick for my lungs. Dirk wafted a hand before he took it, making a face. It smelled like the Black Forest, matching its uneven fae magic over the natural scents, just amplified beyond imagining.

"That's awful," Landon complained, also trying to

beat back the smoke. "Thank God you didn't do this coming into the forest."

"I thought this would be resolved quickly when I came out here to get Rainer," Niko said, taking a deep breath, the smell not bothering him at all. "I didn't even know it was Rainer until I was near the edge of my territory and reached where I first noticed his entry into my territory. Just thought it was one of the new werewolves sniffing around the forest."

"Well, it worked in our favor," I said.

"And we're all thankful for that." Niko mumbled. Leading us away from his tiny cabin, the forest grew around it, making it seem as if it was a reclaimed ruin once I was a good twenty feet from it.

"You *really* remind me of Jabari right now," I said again, following him with Dirk and Landon right behind us.

"I've never felt closer to him than I do right now," Niko said as he pressed onward, following little markers, he must have put down. When we reached the path, he waved for Dirk and Landon to go ahead of us and let them set the pace. It wasn't a leisurely stroll, but it wasn't fast either. It was the same pace Landon and I had tried to set. There was urgency, but not enough to really get our heart rates up.

Mine didn't need physical activity to race. Now that we were away from Niko's safehouse, we were back in immediate danger.

"You can't be that disappointed that Landon and I

came to help you and Dirk," I finally said, breaking the silence with my brother.

"I'm trying to think about how things will go back to normal after this," he said, staring into the forest away from me. "I know you mean well. You wanted to help Dirk, and he was missing. Some of the werewolves of your fiancé's pack were cursed, and one of them was gone. But now, you know too much, and I've only trusted Davor to know even a little about this. Now the rest of the family might find out. I've enjoyed my private life being private for a long time, enjoyed that my secrets were mine, and no one else had to get involved with them."

"Why? Someone in the family would have understood and tried to help you. Maybe not all of them but some of them." I spread my arms, meaning myself, but I was certain about Zuri as well, even Jabari. The twins were reliable. And he trusted Davor. If he had let Davor a little closer, maybe things wouldn't have played out the way they had.

"This belonged to my biological family, and even though it's mentioned, it's not a favorite family topic. You don't care. Zuri and Jabari might not. Subira's not the type of magic user to deal with this."

"Hasan," I finally realized, wondering how I could be so stupid as to not figure it out. "He doesn't like you talking about your biological family."

"He knows I stay here because I was born here. He knows something is different about the place, but he's never dug deeper. It wasn't his problem or his business, and once the War was over, he lost interest. He got his island and pretty much stayed there, not caring much for the world's mysteries anymore. If he knew I was risking my life here all the time for the hopes and dreams of my dead werewolf family, he would tell me to find a new territory. Then I'm caught in between wanting to honor one father's mission and respecting another father's orders. Keeping just enough held back so they never really understood was always the easiest way. I only let them visit my territory when the magic wasn't strong enough to feel at the estate. Oftentimes, I would only see them in Berlin while doing business there. I got very good at keeping one world from meeting the other."

"You think Landon and me being here will lead to the family finding out," I said, sighing. "Sorry about that. Dirk's life, and yours, means too much to me to keep them out of it, not permanently."

"Why did you even try to buy time for us if you don't care about them finding out about any of this? The entire family could rip Rainer to shreds, but you ran in here with a young werewolf. Well, not young to you, but young to the rest of us."

"I..." I took a deep breath. "I do care, but not about the same things. I knew if Hasan heard that one of Heath's pack was here and a threat to you, it would be another blow-up fight and could lead to someone getting seriously hurt. He could blame Heath, and there would be no way to convince him otherwise. I wanted to resolve this without needing to have those discussions. *Again.* Davor thinks Hasan will kill me if you get hurt, so he agreed to play defense and keep anyone from looking too closely. We have time to make sure not all your secrets are exposed. We're running out, but there's time."

"Fair," Niko conceded.

"I'm here to save my mate and maybe kill a werewolf who betrayed my father," Landon said from the front. "Your family can shove it. I have my own priorities."

"Why didn't Heath come and order Rainer to get his shit together if your father can control him? Most honorable Alphas do executions themselves." Niko was more confused than judgmental, so I didn't react to him.

"Rainer Brandt is not a member of our pack and doesn't deserve that treatment," Landon growled over his shoulder, not caring if the words were out of confusion. "Beyond that? Fenris was capable of ripping himself out of packs without the help of another Alpha to override the previous one. Rainer probably finds it easy. My father would walk out here, attempt it, then lose the authority. Pointless when he could have spent the time in the one place I don't excel, which is taking care of his pack as a good Alpha should. Which is where he is. It wasn't even a discussion. We both knew where we could best help everyone involved."

"Another fair point," Niko said, nodding. "Dirk only has good things to say about Heath, and he's been nothing but fair and amicable the times I've met him. It's good to know he's not doing this for the slight, but rather because there are more urgent priorities for him to manage, like the health and safety of his weaker pack members."

"He trusts me and Jacky to get things done."

Niko glanced at me, almost disbelieving when I didn't feel he should have been.

"I do get into a lot of trouble but find my way through it," I pointed out. "It's not a new thing."

Niko smirked, and I felt like I was finally getting somewhere with him. With the help of Landon and Dirk, we could actually start seeing eye to eye.

Landon was still looking back at us, his eyes on me.

I held his gaze until he looked forward again, watching the path ahead of us.

"Dirk said you were considering visiting him more often, no matter where he ended up. Have you ever considered leaving this place permanently?"

"I've thought about it and have left a couple of times, mostly during wars. I don't want to be bombed. Somehow, the forest survives, the core of it, the fae part. I keep coming back because of that. Unless something severs the connection, the world still needs someone standing between humanity and the fae that live here. I don't think anyone ever can break it, but I always hoped."

"You hoped a bomb, or several, would drop on it and make it gone for good?"

"Yes. It never happened, so I returned."

I frowned, seeing an uncomfortable truth about Niko. My withdrawn, distant brother, who never really fit in anywhere, I saw him. He'd lost his biological family to the War and gained an adopted one, but they could never really fill the space, and some of them made very little attempt to. He'd lost his closest brother to the death of

Liza, and Davor was only just beginning to come out of the deepest of his grief from that loss.

Niko was alone. With the secrets and ruins of his first family and his second family never accepting him fully, he was utterly alone. Dirk had been one of his few chances at having a family who loved and accepted him for everything he was, but then Hasan broke that too. I didn't care if it was intentional on Hasan's part or a complete accident, driven by whatever he was dealing with at the time. Hasan had done it, then Dirk had left Niko, too.

Then, if none of that was hard enough, now Niko had a long-lost brother back in his life—something a lot of people might have been happy to learn—not to reconnect or rebuild what they had both lost. No. Rainer wanted a fight to the death, and he had waited eight hundred years for the chance.

I'm sorry, Niko, that you've lived this alone for so long. Is that why you want to finish this alone?

I didn't have the courage to ask him, not sure he would appreciate that I thought he was lonely.

30

CHAPTER THIRTY

HEATH

"Perhaps we should discuss what happens when you're forced to tell the entire family," Zuri said diplomatically.

Heath had had to step away from the earlier call, and Zuri had agreed. Once they knew the immediate danger of where he'd sent Jacky and Landon to help Niko and Dirk, there were things they had to deal with. He needed to compose himself and had done that by focusing on his daughter and pack. They still needed him calm, able to control the situation they didn't know was unfolding. He was certain everyone could tell something was wrong, but none of them asked, letting him hyper-focus on them and their needs.

Even Carey didn't give him an argument when he asked her to keep to her room and out of the way. It wasn't because she was underfoot. He knew she was safe in there and not dealing with werewolves on edge. She knew that, too.

Three hours later, he was standing for the second call. This time, it wasn't only Zuri on screen. Jabari filled up much of the room behind her.

"I was going to raise the alarm. Multiple family members in danger and missing, but we know the area where they should be. I would have explained to everyone what dangers they were walking into if we decided to do a full search." Davor seemed just as exhausted and scared as he had earlier. "I'm doing my best, Zuri. I'm sorry."

"None of this is your fault," Zuri said fiercely. "None of it. It's no one's fault, truthfully. This is the consequences of war. Over the centuries, we've all made our choices, and those choices have their ways of coming back to us. We must deal with them now, but that doesn't make our original choices mistakes, not always. You are doing well. You made promises to Jacky and, before that, to Niko. You have been loyal to them in regard to those promises. There's nothing shameful about that."

"Thank you. I needed to hear that," Davor said, visibly relaxing.

"Now, Mother is off for a walk with Aisha and Kushim, taking care of the kids. We need to figure out how we're going to act. I don't want to mobilize the family too soon. It would be a disaster. With the fae involved, I almost want to ask Mother if she'll join us."

Jabari made a choked noise, and Zuri looked over her shoulder at him.

"What?" she snapped.

"If we bring Mother, we bring everyone. Aisha, Makalo, Kushim, and Amir. I know Kushim was a warrior for a long time, and Aisha isn't a pushover, but neither of them would be enough to protect Makalo and Amir if someone decides to take advantage of our absence. We're in a bad position, and I don't want to take the risk. They can hide in Niko's house while we're out in the Black Forest, but I want them close by so we can protect them."

"That's your paranoia talking, but I understand," Zuri said, nodding as she rubbed her temples.

"I just want to know if anyone can reach Jacky or Landon," Heath said, sitting down to put his head in his hands. "Please."

"I wish I had that magic, but I don't."

Zuri was apologetic, but it left Heath wondering if he was going to see either of them again. They would both be furious if he left Teagan, Jenny, and Carlos defenseless. He was the last defender of the pack and territory now and couldn't move everyone, so he could chase after those two.

"You know Dirk is a werewolf, right?" Davor suddenly asked. "Father is going to hate learning that when I have to ask everyone to come here to help."

Father. Hasan. Damn it.

"Ha." Zuri nearly bubbled with laughter as Heath's head went up. "Yeah, everyone in this call knows.

"I didn't do it," Heath said quickly, wanting to make sure that was clear. "Neither did Landon. He was mauled during the attack on us by the Dallas Pack last year."

"You're right, though. Father will hate finding out." Zuri groaned. "He, Mischa, and Hisao are the only ones who don't know now, it seems. I take it you could smell Dirk in the house?"

"Yeah, but it didn't cross my mind to care, not with everything else happening. I knew a werewolf had already been here, Landon, so it actually took me a minute to realize some of the wolf smell was Dirk and not him."

"It's something to note because Father will notice it immediately, Hisao as well. Mischa might take a minute, but I dread the moment she realizes, almost more than I do when Hasan learns."

"Sister..." Jabari stood and came closer. "You know what this means, right? There's no way we're getting through this without ending up in Germany. Already, I don't like that Davor wouldn't have reached out to us for hours. I want to go now. Two of our siblings are in a land we don't understand, but it's clearly dangerous. If we go, though, everyone will wonder why we're all congregating in Germany to bother Niko and Dirk without making it a family affair or why we've left our regions unattended without an explanation."

"This is going to be a mess," Zuri agreed.

Heath was watching Davor at just the right moment, seeing his eyes go wide.

"What?" he asked, hoping the werecat would trust him enough to say something.

"Hasan just messaged for Niko. I forgot I was using his account," Davor said, licking his lips and shaking a bit. "He apparently tried to reach me. My staff at home answered and told him I had left to visit Niko and Dirk to teach Dirk some things to help Jacky."

"You normally don't make those sorts of mistakes, Davor." Zuri seemed worried now. "Tell him—"

"He knows I'm on a call with both of you, but he really means Niko, not me. He can see it active. He has that privilege on his account—"

Heath moved to disconnect but wasn't fast enough, cursing at himself for getting complacent.

"Don't go, Everson," Hasan said mildly as he appeared on the call.

Heath let go of the mouse, and back away from the keyboard.

"Hasan," he greeted, inclining his head a fraction to give some respect to the ruler of the werecats and member of the Tribunal.

"I wasn't expecting this. I was expecting Zuri, Niko, and Jacky," Hasan said, crossing his arms. "Anyone care to explain?"

"Father, why don't you just disconnect and let the adults handle things?" Zuri snapped. "You know, the adults who don't spy on their children or each other."

"What is going on?" he growled softly. "Where is Niko, and what the fuck does Jacky think she's doing, letting a werewolf use this program? Why didn't either of you put a stop to it? Go get her, Everson."

Heath didn't move, putting his hands in his pants pockets.

"I can't," he answered honestly.

And I would never. Not for you, not while you're taking that sort of tone with her.

"Can't or won't, wolf?"

"Can't," Heath repeated.

"So, Davor is pretending to be Niko, Everson can't get Jacky, and Zuri...you're involved. By the way, it's your involvement that really told me something was going on."

Zuri hissed, glaring at her camera. Heath hoped all that anger was only for Hasan because it forced him to remember he wasn't the strongest person on the call. He was very much the weakest.

"And Jabari, don't think I don't see you behind your sister."

"I wasn't attempting to hide. No reason to," Jabari said with defiance Heath wasn't expecting. He knew the family had its problems, and everyone seemed to be on a different side, but the blatant disrespect from both Zuri and Jabari was more serious than Jacky had explained to him. Perhaps she didn't see it the same as he did, with loyal children of his own. If Landon suddenly started treating him that way, Heath had the good sense to be scared.

"Davor, now that I have found you, how are you feeling? Is visiting Niko's home helping this year? You normally find these months difficult."

"I'm much improved, Father," Davor whispered.

"That's good to hear. I was disappointed to hear you wouldn't be visiting me this year, but if you've improved enough to visit your brother, that is wonderful news. It's good to see you and Niko rebuilding your relationship as brothers."

"Thank you, Father."

"Now, onto the rest of this little mystery I've stumbled into."

"Father, just leave." Zuri was sitting with a regality she hadn't had earlier.

"Where's Jacky, Everson?" He completely ignored his daughter.

Heath knew if Davor was the easiest emotional target, then he was the next Hasan could threaten.

"Heath, you don't have to answer that," Zuri said quickly. "I would recommend you hang up and leave, but I know why you can't right now."

That was good. Heath knew if he didn't produce Jacky or a reason for her absence, he was likely to find Hisao or Mischa coming for him in the next twenty-four hours. They would either get the information Hasan wanted or finally end the perceived werewolf problem permanently.

"Then you tell me, Zuri."

"She's in Germany with Niko and Davor," Zuri said.

"Is she?" He seemed surprised, even a bit amused, but something rang off about it to Heath. "Why is that a secret?"

Heath could almost understand Hasan. He didn't

like that he could understand even a fraction of Hasan's behavior, but there was something about Hasan at that moment. How each of them would have reacted to this situation was what set them apart as men and fathers.

He was a father who wanted to know where some of his children were and found they were missing. Seemingly, he had reached out to Davor for a good reason, to check on him, only to find that Davor was somewhere else.

Heath didn't like when Carey tried to pull a fast one on him. The only reason he could find to fault Hasan for his behavior was all of Hasan's children were grown adults, many who had been or were parents themselves. Hasan was a bully when he needed to be, a truly monstrous and mean man who wanted to be in control all the time.

"One of you better start talking," Hasan said simply, standing slowly and moving back. "I *know* something is wrong. You are only going to make everything worse by continuing to hide it."

"Fine." Zuri closed her eyes in frustration. "But you have to promise you won't lose your temper on Heath or Jacky or Davor or Niko...or anyone else for that matter."

"I'll do my best, but if you're about to tell me that one or more of your siblings are in immediate danger-"

"Jacky and Niko," Zuri said softly. "It's Jacky and Niko."

Hasan's snarl made his desk, and everything on it shake. Picking up a book, he threw it as he paced around his office.

"I'll start from the beginning," Heath said, seeing Zuri's eyes go wide. "We sent Dirk to see Niko. Shortly after, I had some werewolves spending some time in Dallas so one of them could conduct some business. He always takes another one of my wolves for some time off his property and two more for protection."

Heath continued to explain until he reached the last time he heard from Jacky and Landon after arriving in Germany. Davor spoke up then, explaining his own role, how Jacky and Landon had ended up reaching out to him while at Niko's. He explained how he flew over to help them and give them a chance to settle this before it got worse. Zuri continued about when Heath had reached out to her.

By the end, Hasan was standing very still in the middle of the room.

"The Black Forest is fae territory...," he whispered, his microphone, wherever it was, almost not picking him up. He looked over, his eyes liquid gold, that shade only Jacky shared with him. Heath liked them more in her. "Zuri, you hate me right now. You have your reasons. We don't see eye to eye on many things right now, and you are by far one of my most opinionated children." Hasan closed his eyes for a moment, taking a long breath like he was counting to three, then he exhaled slowly. When his eyes were open again, they were brown.

"But I love every single one of you more than my own life, and the only thing I've ever wanted is for all of you to be *safe*. You have actively been keeping their situation a secret from me and requested I leave before I learned what was happening. That's crossing the line. When Jacky and Niko are safe, this family is going to have a long discussion about things while we're together in Germany. The *entire* family." Hasan walked up to his desk and reached out. "And if you're thinking about it, Everson. No, my family doesn't need your assistance nor the assistance of anyone from your pack. You stay right where you are. Your safety is *not* guaranteed otherwise."

He disconnected.

"We'll bring all of them back, Heath," Zuri promised softly.

"You have our word," Jabari agreed. "He won't hurt Landon. I will stop him myself if I must."

"Thank you," Heath said, knowing he had to accept that. "We should have been more careful."

"Should have been but weren't. He's normally not glued to his desk. It was bad timing. I normally feel very safe on here. Let's just say that I won't anymore," Zuri said, leaning back in her chair. "It is what it is."

"Does he really want the *entire* family?" Jabari asked, crossing his arms. "Children, mates... Mother?"

"I don't know, but we're going to assume yes and follow his orders," Zuri said, looking at her twin. "I want Mother with us for this. I want Kushim at my back and Aisha at yours. This will hurt no matter which way you look at it."

Heath sank back in Jacky's chair, smelling her in the fabric when he turned his head. He wished he could go, but that was only putting his few allies in Jacky's family in a worse position.

"Thank you again," he said. "I've never felt this useless before."

"Every time you and Jacky went on some adventure, we were all stuck feeling the same," Zuri said, giving a weak but real smile. "We've got her this time. Promise."

CHAPTER THIRTY-ONE

There was little conversation on the walk. Niko and I looked over our shoulders at every sound, knowing Rainer could be catching up to us.

"Three in the afternoon," Niko said as he checked the time.

I looked up, seeing only trees that nearly blocked my view of the night sky.

"Will we eventually see the sun again before this is over or..."

"I hope so. I think it's because we're still in more fae areas of the forest, but I could be wrong. It could be a spell cast on those involved in the hunt."

"I don't think it's the latter. It seems other fae recognize the long night, as the riders have been calling it."

"Then it's something to do with the fae realms, I guess."

"Is it possible to lose yourself in the fae realm here? Like enter it and not come back?"

"Yes."

"Thought so," I said. "Let me guess. Stay on the paths, and that won't happen."

"Exactly." Niko nodded, putting his pocket watch away. "Have you enjoyed your visit to Germany?"

"Don't...be funny right now," I said, giving him a look. "No. Not at all. This is awful. I thought I didn't like fae stuff before, but now...." I hissed at nothing, unable to stop my lip from curling in a snarl.

"Yeah..." Niko sighed. "I understand that."

"Do you? You've lived here for eight hundred years. There must be something you like here."

"Only because I think it's necessary to protect the world from what this place is."

"Bullshit. I know you said earlier you would love for it to be destroyed, but that's your only way out. Hasan used to be good friends with King Brion before he disappeared. You could have told Hasan to talk to the King to let him know about this place and make a deal to protect the surrounding area. You had options, and you chose to take none of them." I shoved my hands into my pockets. "I've been thinking about it for a good portion of this walk. Our family is a lot of things, and one of those is politically powerful. You had choices, Niko. Why did you never take them?"

He didn't answer. I could tell he didn't want to, his eyes going from human to werecat as he kept his mouth firmly closed.

"It's not like you fell in love with a fae, is it?" I asked.

"No, definitely not that," he said, rolling his eyes. "I sleep with people. I don't let them get closer than my guest bedrooms."

Wow.

"Okay, then. So why—"

"It's not your fucking business, Jacky," he snarled, stopping with a twist to block my way. "It wasn't before you walked into this forest, it's not now, and it won't be after this is all said and done. It will *never* be your business. Stay out of it."

I was startled for a second, then I stepped around him. Landon and Dirk had heard and stopped, looking back at us.

"Keep moving. We're fine," I called, ten feet back with Niko, grabbing his bag and pulling so he would keep moving.

"You sure?" Dirk asked, frowning.

"Yup!"

Niko fell back in step next to me, but now there was tension between us that I couldn't shake.

In front of us, Dirk stopped, looking into the trees.

"Hey, what's wrong?" Landon asked. Niko and I were quickly there with them.

"I thought I heard...dogs?" Dirk said, frowning as he tilted his head to the side. "I guess none of you heard it, and it's gone now."

"Then we'll keep moving," Niko said, pushing the werewolves to walk. "Just something out there messing with you. Don't let it."

"Yeah, I know."

"I have a question," Landon was a little more panicked than I would have liked.

"What?"

"Paths don't normally disappear, do they?" he asked, looking over his shoulder at us. He moved out of the way as Niko went to see what he meant. I was right behind him, looking quickly at the rest of the path, then around us, trying to remain watchful.

"It's not *gone*, but it's been damaged," Niko said, going down on a knee. "Damaged enough that the forest started to reclaim it as quickly as it could. I ran this trail only a couple of weeks ago..." Niko got up and waved for us to keep moving. "We can't stop, though. I can see where the trail used to be. We'll stay on it until we find where it picks back up again."

"What about the other trails?" I asked, looking between him and Dirk.

"They'll guide you, but they don't keep you safe," Niko answered.

"This is a trap," Landon said, not moving as Niko took a step.

"Clearly, but we can't stop here," Niko growled.

"No, you don't understand. When Dirk and I were walking, before he heard something, the path still looked normal, all the way in view. None of this was here. It was the proper dirt path."

"Then this must be an illusion," Niko said, nodding. "Okay. Stay within arm's reach of each other. Don't look into the trees."

"We're trying, anyway?" I didn't like it, but I didn't like anything about this place.

"If there's an illusion over the path, something did it that the protections don't work against," Niko said softly. "Meaning, whatever did this isn't fae because the paths are protected from the fae and their magic. They can still do things off the path that might lure someone off them, but they can't directly spell or charm anyone on it."

"What can override the path's protections?" Landon asked.

"Witches," Dirk and Niko answered at the same time.

"Because of the state of this place, the smell of fae magic could easily hide the smell of a witch's," Niko continued, giving Dirk a proud look before focusing again on our predicament.

"Are there witches out here?" I asked, looking over my shoulder cautiously.

"There used to be, but the pack did their best to handle those who used this place as their home. I killed one in my first century living here alone and haven't seen one since then. They were old witches who used the innately magical environment to extend their lives and power their magic. Stories like Hansel and Gretel were based on them. They didn't eat children. They only stole their life force as their own. All those potential years the children could have had would become their own."

"Were they a coven or something?"

"They were loosely connected," Niko said, pausing in the middle with a thoughtful expression. "Whether they trained each other or developed their techniques with each other, I don't know. What I do know is they don't belong here." He looked at each of us. "They work like the fae in one aspect. They will lure you to them. Just stay close. Jacky at the back, then Landon and Dirk. I'll be in the front. Grab onto something on the person in front of you."

Going to the back, I grabbed Landon's shirt. He was holding Dirk's belt, and Dirk had his hand on Niko's bag. Niko started walking, moving faster than our pace when Dirk and Landon were in the front.

Straining to look around the group, I couldn't see where the path properly picked back up. My anxiety had my heart racing and my ears echoing the drumbeats of my heart so loudly, I could barely hear the forest around me or the footfalls of my companions.

My foot hit something, and, feeling like an idiot, I fell, bashing my knee into the ground.

"Fuck!" I snapped, pushing back up.

"You okay?" Landon asked, grabbing my elbow to help me up.

I looked down to see what had tripped me, seeing the root moving back out of the way as I did.

"Oh, no," I whispered. "Landon, we have to run." I scrambled back to my feet and pushed him. "Go!"

He turned around, but Dirk and Niko weren't there. They were nowhere in sight.

"How..." Landon trailed off, sniffing hard, his brow furrowing as he did. I joined him, walking quickly, but it was as if Niko and Dirk were never with us at all.

"What?" I looked around wildly, unable to comprehend what had just happened. "We were together. I tripped. You helped me up. It took less than ten seconds."

"We obscured our scents, but I could still smell everyone when we were next to each other. I could smell him as I helped you up...or thought I could." Landon hovered beside me, his hand holding my bag firmly, and every time he moved at all, I felt it.

Searching the surrounding trees, I looked for any sign of them or life at all and swallowed when I saw a light through the trees on my third pass.

"Landon..." I pointed it out.

"Are you fucking kidding me?" he growled.

"Run," I said again, turning to take off. Landon was of the same mind this time. We hauled ass, heading directly away from the small building with the light emanating from the window. I made it ten feet before I stepped into something and found myself flung into the air, hanging upside down. I couldn't move. My arms dangled as though I didn't have the strength to move them. I couldn't curl up and attempt to free myself. The rope on my ankle holding me upside down burned as if it was silver.

"Keep running," I roared at Landon as he skidded to a stop and looked up, his eyes wide. "Run!"

"I can cut you down!" he growled, running for a tree. I swung, losing sight of him for a moment, then getting it back as he reached the trunk of a tree.

Then she stepped out and blew something in his face, smiling as he thumped to the ground.

I didn't know who she was, the young woman wearing modern hiking gear as she stepped over his body. Her clothing made the entire situation only more surreal. Nothing about her seemed like the old hag in the forest who lured children to eat them. If I didn't know any better, she looked like any experienced hiker, confident in the terrain around her and carrying everything she needed with her. Her brown hair was pulled back in a tight bun to keep it out of her face. She was just a woman who knew what she was about.

Behind her, Rainer stalked out of the darkness.

"I was worried you wouldn't be able to manage this," he growled.

"I've spent centuries hiding from your brother, perfecting my illusions and craft. Have more faith," she said, smiling at him. "You need me more than I need you."

"Are you sure about that?" he asked, leaning over her.

"You would have never found me if I didn't want you to," she purred. "Remember that, and let me get to work." She casually waved him away.

Rainer took a step back, looking down at Landon with a sneer. I snarled as he brought a foot back. He stopped, his green eyes jumping to me. Whatever he was thinking, he didn't kick Landon while he was unconscious before disappearing back into the forest.

I was dropped from the trap and slammed into the ground with a groan, but it didn't shake off the strange paralysis though. Everything hurt as she stepped over me, clicking her tongue as though she was doing an inspection. Sighing, she tilted her head to match the orientation of my own, and I couldn't help but wonder what her deal was or what she had planned for us.

"Why?" I asked, knowing I could at least talk. "Why are you helping him?"

"Do you care?"

"Yeah."

"It's rather simple. I made a deal with him a long time ago." She pointed at me. "That's where you come in, and him." She threw a thumb at Landon. "You're in the way, it seems. Easy enough thing to solve, along with a few other things. Now he just needs to fulfill his end of the bargain."

"And what's that?"

"Get rid of the Black Forest Pack," she answered simply. "*All* of it."

32

CHAPTER THIRTY-TWO

S he took us to her home, which reminded me a lot of Niko's safehouse, the cabin hiding in the forest.

"How did you separate us from the others?" I asked, wondering if keeping her talking was enough to stay alive.

"Illusions are important. I've watched how the fae do them because they can make masterful ones," she said, chattering as if she hadn't had company in some time. She tended the fire in her hearth before sitting down at the table near her little kitchen.

"What are you going to do to us?"

She put her head on her hands, studying me.

"What do you think I'm going to do?"

"I honestly have no idea. I've met a lot of witches who can do very different things. You don't seem like the type to prey on kids, though. I've been told there were a few witches out here like that at one time."

"I'm half-fae. I don't need to prey on children." She

smirked. "I'm immortal. I was at least granted that." She chuckled. "My mother and her husband were very jealous when they realized I had inherited the very thing they had always wanted. They did exactly as you described. They even tried to use me for it. I killed my father when I escaped during their attempt. Later, I tricked my mother into a situation she couldn't get out of and let Nikolaus Brandt kill her for me."

"If you don't need to do that sort of magic, then why," I didn't understand. "Why did you want to destroy the pack?"

"Because they didn't care if I was living a normal life or not. They didn't want to help me," she answered, her eyes suddenly flat. "They made that very clear when I went to them for help. I could have tried running and leaving this place forever, but the War made me believe this was the safest place for me. I was a girl, and this was my home. The bad things in it weren't only my parents but also the werewolves who wanted to kill me for existing once they realized what I was. An aberration, something that shouldn't have existed. I didn't know what else to do. When Rainer approached me. Well, our goals aligned. At least they did at the time, but bargains don't care about the changing of the seasons or the hearts that agreed to them."

"I'm sorry you had to grow up like that," I whispered honestly, feeling all too much pity for her.

"It is what it is. Now, I have to live with Rainer being back, and since he's back, I have to fulfill my end of the bargain, and he has to fulfill his."

"He made a lot of bargains, it seems."

"He has, hasn't he? The one he made with the fae. Simple and effective, that one." She huffed. "Ours is more multifaceted and looser than that one. I provide him all sorts of things he wants or needs to go after those who stood or stand against him, so long as his old pack is destroyed in the end. Which, again, is why I have the two of you now."

"What do you plan for us?"

"Truthfully? Rainer didn't give me any directive. Foolish of him. He said to get you both out of his way. I don't really have any use for you. Killing you would be the easiest, but...I spent some time out of this place, and I'm not totally ignorant of the world. Someone would come looking for you, then it would get so messy."

"That's. Very pragmatic of you."

"I'll probably hold you until the hunt is over. Either Rainer has killed Nikolaus and our bargain is fulfilled, mostly, or Nikolaus kills him, and there's no reason for me to keep you here."

Mostly? Oh, shit. Rainer has to die, too, doesn't he? She's wily, though. She's smart. She clearly doesn't want to be part of this anymore. A mistake she made as a child... Maybe I can work with her.

"Nikolaus isn't part of the pack. He can't be," I said, hoping she was willing to listen. "Rainer is using you to kill his brother, but Nikolaus was never a proper member of the Black Forest Pack. Rainer is the last member, and he's the only one left. He doesn't need to kill Niko."

"On what grounds?" she asked, frowning. "I love a loophole When I get to use them. Tell me."

"Nikolaus was human when the pack was attacked. The magic of an Alpha werewolf only works on other werewolves. Niko might have been his father's son, but he was human. He was claimed by the pack, but in the eyes of the supernatural, he wasn't a proper member. He's a werecat now, not a werewolf, so he couldn't be a part of any pack now. The magic is different."

"I see..." she whispered. "How do you know?"

"I'm a werecat, and I'm in a relationship with an Alpha werewolf. His power has no sway over me. We both like it that way."

"Why do you care about this fight if not for the Black Forest Pack?" she asked.

I remembered what Nikolaus told me, how the fae here had an issue with time. She was dressed so modern I figured she was more in touch with the world.

But she's still half-fae, and maybe she just gets clothing and stuff. Maybe she's not actually engaging with the world and noticing it.

"Nikolaus is my brother, adopted, claimed, whatever you want to say. The werecat who Changed him also Changed me," I explained. "He's part of a different family now, and we'll do anything to protect him. Or avenge him if we have to."

"What does that mean for me? I won't be the one who kills him," she said, blinking.

"You're stopping us from saving him," I reminded her. "When Rainer's terms were faulty."

She stood and started to pace, occasionally stopping to look out her windows.

"What will your family do?"

"Hunt down everyone involved and kill every single one of them." I went with honesty, though I could easily see how it might come off as overconfidence, given the situation. "I don't want to fight you, though. I want to help Niko and leave, and the only person who has to die is Rainer. I don't want to *ever* see this place again. You can stay here and live out eternity here for all I care."

"Could they? Your family?"

"Three of them are witches of great age and power. The others range in age from eight hundred to over five thousand. So, probably."

"My options are...I can take your word that Rainer is using a loophole or maybe even just a misjudgment of the situation and free you because I would no longer be beholden to him. Doing so would remove me from the wrath of your family because they would see me as a being to blame for the death of one of their own. But I'm left with Nikolaus, who still stalks these trees. However, if Rainer does succeed, he will know I betrayed him. Well, he and I would have things to work through, anyway."

"I can make you one promise," I declared suddenly. "If we succeed, Nikolaus will leave."

"Can you promise that for him?" she asked, narrowing her eyes at me.

"I don't need to promise he would like it or agree, but

I can promise that our family will want him to leave this place, and he'll finally have to let it go."

Maybe it would be a bit easier when he knows your story. It's worth a shot. I'm sorry, Niko. I have to do something.

Staring at each other for a long time, I could see her thinking it through. She was half-fae, half-witch. I didn't know what that meant for me. I knew fae were bound by bargains and deals. There was magic to them, but while she was immortal thanks to her fae blood, I didn't know if she was swayed by her fae side.

She reached for something, revealing a jar I couldn't see, and came to me as she scooped out what looked like lotion. She knelt in front of me and rubbed it on the burn the rope had left. I felt it spread, able to turn my ankle first and wiggle my toes next.

"Give it a moment to take full effect," she said, stepping back. "You and I will finish discussing the terms. I will give you what you need to wake him up, then I will leave. You will wake him up and will not come after me. I will leave a sign of what direction you must go to find the others. You'll need to hurry. Rainer will already be on top of them, if not fighting them."

"What made you decide?" I asked softly.

"I'm beholden to my bargains, and technically, I have gotten you out of his way. He didn't preface how long or to keep you permanently out of his way. The problem with your loophole is it only helps me. Rainer believes Nikolaus *wronged* him. You missed that part. I can feel that." She lifted a hand and waved it around the back of her head. "But it's good to know Nikolaus doesn't have to die for the bargain to be settled for *me*. He's not a werewolf, therefore, not part of a pack. Good to know. There's only one member of that pack left alive, and perhaps, you can manage that. My bargain with Rainer doesn't stop me from bargaining with anyone else."

"Can I ask a little more while this stuff kicks in? Like, how did you and Rainer end up in this bargain?"

"Rainer was angry with his father. We had seen each other when I asked the pack for help when my mother was trying to get me back. He spoke up for me. So, when he was finally tired of his father, he came to me, and I let him find me. We were..." She rolled her eyes. "Silly children coming into our own power, and there might have been feelings there. He hated his father as much as I did but for different reasons. I assisted him in getting back at the ones he believed wronged him or stood against him so long as the Black Forest Pack no longer existed by the end of our bargain. We didn't talk about it as much as we should have. Again, we were a couple of stupid children.

"I'm certain now that he had some way to get around what I had asked for, but it never came to pass. All I ever truly wanted was to live undisturbed. I could never fit in the world beyond this place, nor can I truly feel at home in the fae realms. This, halfway place is all I have, the only place I fit. It's all I ever wanted. I just wanted to live here in peace. I thought he could give me that."

I could see the tears in her eyes and smell the truth in her emotions. This was no act, as far as I could tell. She had only one home, and others were always fighting in it. Her home, quaint and small, was all she could build for fear of being discovered and attacked.

"Why did you never try to kill Niko yourself? Or talk to him?"

"He scared me, and when Rainer disappeared, I thought maybe...I could just forget about the entire ordeal," she said as she twisted her hands together in a way that looked painful. "Maybe he would just ignore me if I pretended he wasn't here. Maybe it would be okay. Then Rainer came back, and I knew we had to finish this. I had made the bargain to help him do it."

"Thank you. I think we're ready to make this bargain," I said, trying to smile.

She straightened, nodding. Fae magic filled the room, swirling around, slightly off from what I normally felt, maybe because of her half-fae status. Fae magic, no matter how it felt, always knew when a bargain was about to happen, though.

"I, Jacky Leon, also known as Jacqueline, daughter of Hasan, promise not to harass you here in the Black Forest, to never come back with the intent to disturb your peace and the life you have here so long as it doesn't threaten my own or the lives of anyone I claim as mine. I promise when Rainer Brandt is dead, Nikolaus will begin his preparations to leave the Black Forest and the surrounding area and be fully out of the area within the year. I will not send any of mine back here to take any sort of action against you for this incident." I paused, thinking about what else to add, and remembered what she said about her end of the bargain with Rainer. "And I promise Rainer Brandt will die before I leave the Black Forest, forever more freeing you of the bargain you have with him and dismantling the Black Forest Pack you knew once and for all."

"I, Adalni, promise to release you and yours and no longer interfere in the affairs of werewolves or werecats related to you. I will stay in the Black Forest unless need pulls me from it, and in those cases, I will not partake in the magics of my mother and will return once I have gotten what I need." She made a face. "I'm not sure what else you might want to ask for."

"Would you be willing to work with someone to keep this place safe for humans?" I asked. "I'm not trying to trap you here. Just make this agreeable enough to get out of this mess."

"I promise to work with whoever might honorably wish to uphold the safety of this place, for all its inhabitants and guests," she said, nodding.

The fae magic knew that was the last thing we needed.

"This will wake him," she said, placing a tiny pouch on the table. "Just a pinch. Flick it or blow it on his nose. Then hurry. Rainer didn't want me to act until he knew for certain he could get to his brother quickly."

Then she left the house, grabbing her pack and a cloak as she went.

Both my legs were working now, so I moved, heading to the table. My fingers still felt odd, but every second that passed, they felt less awkward. I grabbed the pouch and was able to get a pinch of the powder inside, then looked at Landon on the floor and sighed.

"We're never coming back here. Promise," I said as I knelt beside him and blew the powder over his nose.

He jerked up, nearly hitting me, but I pulled back just in time. That led to me falling on my ass, hitting my sore back on the couch.

"What? Jacky?"

"We need to leave." I was already getting up. "Rainer is going after Niko and Dirk. We have to catch up."

"Explain and run," he said, jumping up.

I followed him out. Adalni had left the red cloak hanging on a tree branch over one of the many small trails that wandered away from her home, and I knew what she intended.

"That way," I said, taking off at full speed.

CHAPTER THIRTY-THREE

"Could this get more complicated?" Landon said between breaths, running down the trail right behind me. I jumped over a log and looked back.

"I don't know, but I've got some ideas for what happens after we finally deal with Rainer," I called back before turning back ahead of me.

"I can't wait to hear them!"

Everything in me didn't want to run, but the motivation that we could be too late to help Niko and Dirk was enough to keep me moving at top speed.

We heard the fighting before we saw it. I saw a tree go down, the crack of its trunk snapping, sounding like thunder.

"Dirk!" I screamed, hoping he would call back.

With no response, I kept running down the trail until I had to get around the felled tree. I knew Landon was right behind me, but I looked back just to make sure since we had to get off the proper path. He was entirely focused on something beyond me, and I tried to find it.

As we reached a thinner portion of the forest, I saw Niko first. He had clearly taken hits, his nose bleeding and leaning too hard to the left as if he was dealing with some broken ribs.

I looked for Dirk, hoping to see him, and saw Rainer come out of the trees, brushing himself off. He was glaring at Niko, not yet noticing Landon or me.

Stepping back, I grabbed my werewolf before he could jump into the fight.

"Find Dirk," I ordered.

His jerky nod told me he could handle that. He stayed mostly in shadow, running around the thin area of forest instead of directly into view.

I stepped into the starlight, the area not having enough tree cover to make it the same inky, perpetual blackness as the rest of the forest. It wasn't a nice clearing, but it was close enough.

"Rainer!" I screamed, getting his attention off Niko for a second. His green wolf eyes flicked to me, narrowing as he snarled at my appearance.

"You. That bitch couldn't keep you for even an *hour*?" he growled.

I kept his attention long enough so Niko could dive in for an attack, his claws raking across Rainer's thigh. Seeing Niko move, I realized just how deadly he must have been when he was in practice with his weapon of choice. Rainer retaliated, moving faster than Niko.

Amazed by the show of speed and strength, I watched him catch Niko in a grapple, spin, and throw my brother into the trees. When he was done, he curled his fingers, and I watched as he did the very thing I knew only Fenris could do. He partially Changed, his face becoming a little more animalistic, his nails growing longer. He didn't take it too far, still mostly human, but there was certainly a thread of wolf through his appearance now.

How is he so strong compared to Niko?

Rainer ignored me and went for where Niko had landed. I finally found my feet again and rushed to tackle him, and felt as though I hit a wall. He went down under me, but Rainer was *solid*. He wasted no time grabbing me and throwing me, sending me rolling through bushes until I hit a tree.

As I surged to stand again, Dirk was next to me, grabbing me. I yanked away from him as Landon tried to grab me as well.

"We have to help Niko!" I yelled.

"Where is he?" Dirk asked.

I pointed to where Rainer was stalking. Niko finally revealed himself, struggling to stand, favoring his left leg, and breathing hard.

"I got this," Landon growled.

Before I could say anything, a shot rang out. Rainer moved preternaturally fast, the shot grazing his ear when it should have gone into the back of his head. He snarled over his shoulder, and I wondered if there was even a man left in him now. Landon fired again, three rapid shots, but Rainer moved out of the way of all of them. The best Landon got was another graze to Rainer's arm. Rainer focused on his brother once more, who was trying to overcome his injuries so he could continue the fight.

What the fuck is he?

"You're going to hit Niko!" Dirk yelled as Landon tried again.

We need a real plan.

"Landon, you and I are going to distract Rainer. We need to give him the fight of his fucking life. Dirk, run for Niko the moment we have his attention. Take Niko and keep moving. Get him all the way home, okay?" I grabbed Dirk's shirt, pulling him closer. "Okay?"

"Okay." Dirk didn't need to tell me he hated this idea. His pale face and wide eyes told me everything.

He doesn't need to like it. He just needs to do it.

Landon ran, getting between Niko and Rainer as I moved to get on his other side, making him look between us. Rainer spat something in German that sounded insulting before switching back to English.

"You are fucking stupid. You could go home and leave Niko here to die, and no one would ever have to know," he growled, his eyes flicking between us as he walked slowly to try to get us both in front of him. I kept moving left, trying to circle, while Landon forced him to split his attention.

"Enough of this."

He lunged for me first, faster than I could manage, and grabbed me as he had in our last encounter. This time, Landon was close enough to grab him from behind, his arms around Rainer's torso, screaming as he tried to pull Rainer off me. Not as dazed this time, ready for just how strong this werewolf was, I pushed down, fighting to stop him from lifting me to bash me down as he had before. I kicked up, making him snarl, drool dropping down. Landon made ground as I felt my nails become claws and sliced them over Rainer's wrists and arms. I tried to claw his face, but he yanked it back, giving Landon the leverage he needed to change his hold and get an arm around Rainer's neck.

With control of Rainer's head and neck, he twisted the werewolf off me as if he was trying to hold a bull by the horns. Scrambling to my feet, Rainer reached back and grabbed Landon's waist. He threw both of them back, hitting the ground hard and knocking off Landon's grip. By the time I was running for him, he was jumping away from Landon, who was in pain but didn't seem as if he'd be down for too long. I tried to tackle Rainer again, but he was ready for me this time, catching me as though I was a child roughhousing with an adult.

"Just give me Nikolaus," he snarled before tossing me down.

I blinked several times to get rid of the blurriness in my vision as Landon fought with much more skill than I had. He traded blows with Rainer, ducking and weaving punches in as he tried to keep from getting hit.

Pulling out the silver sword, finally remembering that I had it, I ran up behind Rainer as Landon kept him focused on their fight. I went for the stab, but it skimmed across his back, leaving a line of blood across his shoulders. He swung back and tried to backhand me, but I was just out of his reach. He knocked the sword from my hands, so I jumped onto his back, trying to tear out his eyes. He seemed larger now, thicker, broader. Fur was beginning to grow over his skin. He stopped me from taking his eyes as Landon drew one of his blades and sank it into Rainer's stomach, making the wolf scream. He grabbed my wrists and pulled me over his head, sending me into Landon.

As we struggled to get up, Rainer pulled the blade free and dropped it.

He was looking properly like a monster now, snarling with blood dripping down his maw as his green eyes seemed to glow. He continued to grow as he looked around. He hunched over, his arms reaching the ground and providing more support.

"Jacky." Landon whispered, pulling me back as he slowly backed away as well. "Have you ever seen it before?"

"Seen it? No. Can I recognize it? *Absolutely*."

Rainer was entering his Last Change, becoming the impossible-to-leave form, which completely blurred the line between beast and human. The final price of being a moon cursed—losing complete control of the curse and forever being a monster with a killing urge that couldn't be stopped.

"Where's Niko?" Rainer the monster snarled, somehow still able to form words with his new jaw. They didn't sound right, but they were understandable. "Give him to me!"

I looked around, not seeing Niko or Dirk anywhere.

"Gone, it seems," I answered. "You'll have to deal with us before you can have them."

"So be it," he growled, beginning to stalk toward us.

"Got any ammo left?" I asked Landon as we steadily backed up. The moment we moved any faster, Rainer would attack purely on instinct.

"Nope. None of it helped, anyway, and his Change just healed everything we did."

"But he won't Change anymore," I pointed out. We were buying time. If we bolted, he would pick one of us, but by moving slowly and together, we still had options. I'd spent enough time with my werewolves to pick up some of their tricks. We kept our eyes on him, his gaze flicking between us, unable to decide which one he wanted to focus on, or maybe he was making sure we didn't know.

"No. No, he won't," Landon agreed.

Rainer finally jumped, aiming directly at us. Landon and I split, running in different directions to let Rainer land where we once were. I grabbed my silver sword. I knew I could use the steel one, but I wanted to keep that one in reserve in case I well and truly lost the first. Across from me, Landon grabbed something more interesting— one of Niko's claws.

Rainer went for him first, managing a sharp turn. I ran to cover the distance as Landon ran for me. Right as we met, Rainer began his leap from where Landon once stood. I shoved Landon to the side right before Rainer landed, knocking me down, but I kept my grip on my only weapon. Before he could do anything, Landon sliced the claw, raking across Rainer's chest and throat. He pulled back with a howl of pain as blood sprayed on me.

With every bit of strength I had, I thrust upward, driving the blade deep into Rainer's upper abdomen, right under his apparent rib cage beneath his tattered shirt. He reared back farther, twisting away and leaving the bloody blade still in my hand. Landon dove for him, sinking the silver claws into his chest as I got back to my feet, very tired of being knocked down. Rainer grabbed Landon, and I heard bone crack as he pulled the claws out. Rainer threw Landon, and I lost sight of him.

"Landon!" I screamed as Rainer turned to me. He was bleeding, and in reality, he should have been bleeding out, but I watched as the bleeding slowed, and he kept standing.

Landon didn't reappear, and I snarled, feeling my bones crack as my nails became claws. My canines grew longer in my human mouth, and I hissed as Rainer started for me.

In a perfect world, Fenris would still be in there, and I could try to reason with him. I would have fought for him. Tonight, I was fighting just to keep the fragile world I had, and Rainer was going to destroy it.

Rainer lunged for me, and I met him, snarling as our hands met. I somehow held my feet, pushing deep into the earth. I kept my fingers locked as we met, and for a moment, I could have sworn I saw a sparkle of surprise.

That surprise made sense. I had learned this trick from him. It tapped into the power of the curse without taking it too far. He might have lost control, but I hadn't—not yet. It terrified me, but tonight, I embraced it. We stayed in the stalemate until one of my legs went out, and he slammed me down. I was faster now, though, kicking him off my good leg before I touched the earth and drove into his knees, knocking him down.

We rolled on the ground, each trying to get the edge and be in control, kicking, punching, and clawing at each other. It felt like an endless struggle.

I was still the weaker of us, though. He finally got me on my back, hands on my throat. He wasn't trying to strangle me. He was trying to break my neck. I strained, trying to maintain control, trying not to give that to him.

Suddenly, a sword swung out and met with the back of his neck. It didn't get all the way through, meeting bone that refused to give way. With another howl of pain, he let go of me, staggering back. Landon was there, panting.

Standing, I followed Rainer as he tried to retreat, trying to ignore Landon. Rainer was stumbling from the injury that hadn't killed him, but it certainly broke something. He looked at me, and for a flash, I knew it was Fenris, not Rainer.

"Rebel...I'm—"

That nearly stopped me. So nearly.

He gurgled, blood coming out of his mouth, unable to finish what he was going to say. Shaking his head violently and hitting himself caused him to stagger into a tree. He looked back up, snarling, and it was once again Rainer, trying to get ready to fight again.

Jumping on him, I grabbed him as Landon had previously. I remembered how the vampires had tried to kill me years before and grabbed Rainer's bottom jaw for more control, ignoring the pain as he sank his fangs into my hand. He was weaker now. I kicked Rainer's legs out from under him and held him to his knees.

Then I twisted as hard as I could as the monster screamed and howled. I twisted as bones cracked, then snapped.

Then it went silent.

Dropping the body, I stepped back, feeling as the Change pushed back, my hands returning to normal and my canines receding to a normal size. I was pretty certain the only things that didn't return to their natural form were my eyes.

Starting to shake violently, I looked at Landon.

"In a perfect world." I whispered, wondering how long I had been crying.

Landon dropped the sword and the next thing I knew, he was holding me as I started to sob. The only thing that knocked me out of my grief was the sounds of hounds growing louder in the silence left by Rainer's death.

"Oh, shit," Landon whispered, pulling me away from the body. Once he stopped, I pulled back and turned to see what was happening.

The hounds were running, spectral and fast. Above the body of Rainer Brandt stood a spectral version of him, his back turned to us. He bowed as the riders followed their hounds. It was like a wave as they ran over him.

When the wave was gone, so was he.

Moments later, I looked up, watching dawn bring the light back to the Black Forest.

The Hunt was over.

CHAPTER THIRTY-FOUR

L andon and I couldn't move very quickly as we struggled to get to the path, hoping nothing else decided to try us before we could leave.

"Here!" Adalni called, waving from the sunlit path thirty feet from us. "This will lead you home."

Landon tensed, and I touched his arm.

"Do you trust me?" I asked him.

"After everything? Yeah, I trust you," he said, relaxing. "You're family. Got to trust family. At least our family."

Smiling weakly, I led the way to Adalni. She gave us space as we limped onto the path.

"Nikolaus and the other one are well ahead of you on the same path. You might catch up with them before nightfall. You still have some distance back, but as you get closer to his home, it should get safer for you."

"Thank you," I said graciously.

"It wasn't what we agreed on, more help from me, but

it feels right to do," she said, lowering her head. "Thank you for freeing me from the mistakes I made as a scared and angry child."

Giving her a similar bow, we started walking home, Landon and I holding each other up. I knew Landon and I would catch up to Niko and Dirk, but I wasn't going to rush and hurt myself. I was tired and knew Landon was the same, never trying to hurry me. So long as we kept this pace, we would be fine.

I knew we would be fine until I saw a man on the path, walking toward us. He once had red hair but no longer. It was now platinum blonde. His familiar face was gaunt, and there were bags under his eyes, something I didn't expect from a fae. I figured they always looked perfect.

"Jacky Leon, it's been some time," Prince Cassius of the Fae greeted as he gave a small incline of his head. He didn't come within ten feet of us, but that didn't stop me from smelling the alcohol. He was cleaned up, but he had clearly been in the bottle before someone asked him to come here.

Still doing that, huh? Poor guy.

"It has," I said, nodding slowly. "Landon, this is Prince Cassius. Prince Cassius, this is Landon Everson, Heath's son."

"We've...been in the same room before," Landon said, nodding. "But it's nice to see a familiar face."

"I bet. On to why I'm here. I have a fast way for both of you to get back to the home of Nikolaus, son of Hasan. They have already been collected. I've been walking for three hours to find you two. You are really out here. Bad place to be injured and stumbling around."

"Paths are safe," I told him, pointing to the path he was standing on. He was fae, and I was told the paths were protected from fae. "Or I was told they were."

"They probably are," Cassius mumbled, shrugging. "Fae in places like this follow very strange rules. Let's go."

"How is this going to work?" I asked, stumbling after him, letting Landon hold me up as he tried to walk in step with me.

He pulled out a cell phone and texted someone.

"My brother, obviously," he said, not looking at us as he spoke. "He's gotten stronger, but he needs an anchor, and I'm his favorite anchor."

A door appeared out of nothing in front of us, Cassius standing between us and it. It swung open to reveal Rian. Cassius stepped aside and waved us in, then followed. Rian closed the door and exhaled a deep breath.

"I'm hungry," he muttered. "Hey, Jacky."

"Hi, Rian," I said, giving a genuine smile as he relaxed against the wall.

"We're not here to socialize. Your father reached out to mine with some demands. Apparently, there are some unpaid debts, and Hasan called them in," Cassius explained, frustration and bitterness dripping from him. "Debts my father couldn't pay himself, so he forced us all here to help him."

"I exposed his daughter to something dangerous,

which you got yourself involved in, and you threw such a fit about protecting her and her lover in the name of your late-wife, I thought it was only fair you helped with it," King Brion said, walking into the room. "Jacqueline, daughter of Hasan. If there's anything you want to say to anyone here before you see your family, now is the time. Now that you two have been retrieved, we will be leaving to see what we can do about containing this little pocket of fae. Your brother was told by your father that under no uncertain terms, he is to withdraw from this place permanently. If he attempts to say anything about staying, remind him that I am taking over on the condition that no more moon cursed stay in this region."

I scrambled mentally, then jumped into action, knowing what I needed to tell him.

"There's a half-fae, half-witch named Adalni living out there. She's never found another home, and all she's ever wanted has been to live in peace there, King Brion. She made a bad bargain as a child and helped me as a way of undoing that damage. She still got what she wanted in the end, but she would have rather it been forgotten."

"I see."

"She's promised to work with anyone who will honorably uphold the safety of the Black Forest for its inhabitants *and* its guests," I continued.

"Good to know. I will probably have her educated and see if she is fit as a representative for the area. That makes things much easier for me. Anything else?"

"Did you always know about the Black Forest being a

place where the fae realms and ours meet and become one?" Landon asked, his tone flat enough to be disrespectful. So flat that it was accusatory.

"I did," King Brion confirmed.

"Why didn't you ever do something about it?" I needed to know, considering he was fine admitting the potentially severe mistake he had made.

"I had done something about it. I made a deal with the first Alpha of the Black Forest Pack to contain the fae here from causing too many problems for humanity. There are a lot of troublemakers out here." He smirked. "That was the condition for the werewolves to use the territory as their own and kill my people if they were threatened. But that bargain was released some hours ago. I wonder why?"

He smiled as if he knew what Landon and I had just done. Perhaps he'd heard Dirk or Niko tell the family what happened and figured out what it all meant.

"I hope this sets you and my father even," I said finally, lowering my head to bow to him.

"It does. You and me as well." He wagged two fingers at his sons and walked out. They followed, neither looking happy.

Landon and I sagged into each other, but I knew I couldn't relax yet.

"My family is here," I said softly.

"Yeah, I caught that," he said, groaning. "But I want to see Dirk, and don't give a fuck about your family."

Nodding, we went to leave through the same door as

the fae royals had. As I reached for the doorknob, it swung open, and Zuri stood there.

"Jacky!" she exclaimed, throwing her arms around me. "We've been so worried."

"How long have you been here?" I asked, leaning into the hug, trying to find the strength to return it.

"Let's see. It's late Wednesday, maybe a few hours? The princes found Dirk and Niko quickly. They were much closer to Niko's estate. We didn't know if they were going to find you and Landon. They're both resting now, and Father has agreed to give everyone until the morning to talk."

"Talk?" I asked softly.

"He's using this as a chance to have a family meeting," Zuri explained, ending the hug and pulling me along. "Come on. Let me get you in a guest room. Landon, you'll be sharing with Dirk. It's a full house, but you two live together, correct?"

"And we share a room there as well," Landon said, staggering as he tried to walk. I reached for him, but I wasn't the one to catch him. Jabari was there, and Landon snarled at him.

"Don't give me that shit. You don't have many allies in this house right now. Neither of you does. Don't snap at the ones you do," Jabari growled as he hauled Landon to stay on his feet. "I'm helping."

"Landon?" I asked.

He gave me a look that would have killed anyone in his pack and probably made his father take a few steps back. I just gave him a weak smile as Zuri and Jabari half-dragged us through the house. Jabari unceremoniously opened a random door and released Landon, who limped inside without question. Zuri grabbed the next door down on the same side of the hall and pulled me into the room.

"How bad is this?" I asked as I stripped off my old, ruined clothes, covered in dirt and blood. In the clean home, I could very much tell how I smelled. She reached into a dresser and pulled out a clean set of pajamas.

"Heath reached out to me." She handed me the pajamas and led me into the bathroom attached to the guest room. "He and I learned about Davor's involvement. We were trying to figure out how to handle the situation where the family would come here and help all of you, what to be prepared for, that sort of thing. Our father stumbled onto us, figuratively. It was a case of bad timing, and that's all there is to it. It was Father who decided to contact King Brion." The shower was already on by the time she stopped talking, and she tested the temperature. "You are more purple than I have ever seen you, Jacky."

"Last Change werewolf hopped up on fae magic and desperate to kill his brother," I explained as I stepped gingerly into the hot water.

She stayed for the entire shower, then helped me out. I was weaker by the minute. My head hurt. I was exhausted. Sinking into my sister as she held a towel around me, I took a shaky breath.

"Thank you. Who all is here?"

"Oh, everyone," she said, helping me dry off. "Mother

and Father, all of our siblings, Kushim, Aisha, Makalo, and even my baby, who won't remember this. Mother, though, has been wandering the grounds with Niko's permission. He's never given her free rein here, and she's using the chance to expose herself to magic she doesn't often get to see or feel. You might not see her."

"Think she'll be at the talk?" I asked.

"I couldn't tell you. She's been hard to read recently, and that's saying something," she answered. "Sit." She moved me to the vanity, and I sat as commanded. I didn't care that I was naked with only a towel wrapped around me as she brushed my hair. My eyes started to drift closed.

"Jacky, I need you to understand how serious this is. I know you just got done with something that probably seemed like hell on earth, but this isn't over yet. Our father is on the warpath. He is *furious*. Do you understand?"

"He's always angry at me these days," I said, sighing heavily.

"If you don't say exactly the right thing, I can't promise you'll get to go back to your territory," she hissed.

That made my eyes snap back open, going wide at the thought.

"Landon and Dirk? They can make exceptional hostages against Heath Everson," she continued. "The only reason Dirk might get off the hook is he's Niko's son, but Niko is also in a lot of trouble with Father for never telling the family exactly what he's been doing here and why. He's been meddling in the affairs of another supernatural in their own territory. He's not a werewolf, so he didn't meet the requirements of the bargain King Brion made. He should have *never* come back here."

"He didn't know," I said, shaking my head.

"That's already been explained, and King Brion took no insult, so he's clear there. Father is still furious that he told none of us in eight hundred years."

"Did Hasan ever *ask?*" I demanded. "Did *anyone?*"

Zuri sighed.

"Probably not. I never did. I don't think any of us did, though Davor's in a bit of trouble for knowing some of the basics without alerting anyone. When I was talking to Heath, I told him I would never judge either of you for giving Fenris the chance you did. That none of this was either of your faults. At least you came from a place of love and acceptance. Goodness. Most of the mistakes our family seems to make are from the quiet neglect we seem to perpetuate. That's how this got this far." She stopped brushing my hair and stepped away.

"Get some sleep, little sister. I'm going to reach out to Heath for you and let him know you are safely back and asleep. Father won't tolerate you talking to him right now."

"And here I was, waiting to ask," I said with a soft growl. I had been waiting. Zuri was being really pushy about getting me bathed and ready for bed. I didn't fight her because I knew she was thinking about it as well. I didn't want Heath to see me looking the way I had.

"Tell him I love him," I finally said, swallowing back the pain of not getting to say it myself.

"I will. Tomorrow, you have Jabari and me in your corner, and we'll do everything in our power to make sure our father lets you go home. We'll be meeting in the grand dining room for breakfast. Breakfast and a family meeting. Someone will come get you so you don't get lost."

"I don't like when you're scared, Zuri," I finally admitted, staring at her reflection in the mirror.

"I'm not scared for me," she said, leaning down to kiss my cheek before walking out.

I slipped into the soft, clean pajamas. I thought of Rainer's final moments as I closed my eyes.

CHAPTER THIRTY-FIVE

A soft knock at the door was the only warning I had that my time had run out.

I woke up early, earlier than reasonable, and found some clothes to put on. Either Zuri had quickly bought something for me, or Niko had kept my sizes stocked in this room. There was everything from undergarments to a perfectly fitted pair of jeans and a tee, the exact blend of loose and clingy in the right spots. I even found a new jacket, a supple leather that had been pre-worn, so there was minimal stiffness.

I was over forty and had no business wearing leather jackets as if I was still in my twenties going to rock concerts, but I couldn't resist pulling it on and letting the normalcy comfort me.

They can take my leather jackets from my cold dead hands.

The small defiance made me feel stronger as I struggled with sore muscles and bone-deep exhaustion that made itself more apparent every minute I was awake and moving around. I found my bag and tried my cellphone, seeing it was still dead. Part of me had hoped getting out of the deepest areas of the Black Forest would magically recharge it. I knew it was a pointless hope, but I couldn't resist trying it, anyway. I put it on the charger, knowing if I got through breakfast, I would be able to use it. If I didn't get through breakfast, I probably wouldn't see it again.

Zuri had made the stakes of today very clear. Things had been brewing for a long time, and today would be the day to see if our family could survive the pressure.

In a way, the timing couldn't be more right.

Walking to the windows, I threw open the curtains, letting the early glow wash over me. It was an east-facing window, and while it was probably a thoughtless thing, I was never more grateful to see the sun rise and usher in a new day. The light returning to Landon and me yesterday had been overshadowed by pain and the reality that we still had to get out of the forest. This morning, I savored it. There was always something wonderful about a real sunrise after a painful experience. The world kept moving. It didn't burn down. It didn't stop. The sun would continue to rise, and I would get a day to enjoy the light before the night returned.

The moment was shattered by a soft knock at the door.

Time to face the music.

I didn't take anything, not my bag or a weapon. Nothing.

I swung the door open to see Aisha, Jabari's mate. In her arms was little Amir, a smiling, babbling toddler. Hovering behind her was Makalo, as many back home knew him, the boy Carey spoke with for hours. He was the spitting image of Jabari, only inheriting some coloration from his mother.

"On kid duty?" I asked, trying to smile. "You're here for me, you have Amir for Zuri, and Makalo is following you around, looking out of place like only teenage boys know how."

Aisha chuckled.

"You can have a sense of humor at the strangest of times," she said, holding out a free arm, an invitation for a hug that I took quickly. I had to be careful of Amir, but he knew what was happening and planted a wet, sloppy toddler kiss on my cheek.

"Hi, Aunty Jacky," he said, his little smile making me want to break down into tears.

"Hi, Amir," I said, kissing his forehead before dropping the hug. "And hello, Makalo. Can you stop getting taller? Is that a possibility?" I looked up to see his face as he gave me a sheepish smile.

"I don't think so." He shrugged.

"Such is life," Aisha said with a chuckle. Aisha was a few inches taller than me, and Makalo was taller than her. He would probably be a giant like his father. I heard a doorknob turn but knew Aisha was about to say something, so I ignored it.

"We're here to make sure you're awake and you are. Dirk and Landon are in the next room—"

"I've got it from here, Aisha," Jabari called. I looked around her to see him walking down a hall. His door clicked shut on its own.

"Are you sure? Jacky can walk with us. Or we'll wait on everyone."

"No, it's fine. That one is probably hungry—"

"Yes!" Amir said, nodding his head once with a smile.

"Okay," Aisha said, meeting Jabari for a quick kiss. "We won't cause trouble," she promised, but the way she said it was more of a warning. If anyone started trouble, she would definitely join in.

Makalo waved at me and followed his mother and cousin down the hall, leaving me alone with Jabari.

"Are you mad at me?" I asked, crossing my arms in expectation.

"No," he said, sighing.

"Do they know how bad things are?" I had a feeling Aisha did, even if Jabari didn't tell her, but Makalo could potentially see things about his new family he wasn't prepared for. That would make me feel guilty sooner rather than later.

"You know Father and Aisha despise each other. They have from the moment Father learned about Makalo. Makalo isn't ignorant of the tension and what's been causing it."

"I'm sorry for all of this," I said, swallowing as I met his stare.

"It's been a long time coming. Father is used to control, and he hasn't had it for some time. We've never openly defied him this much. We've never fought, not like this. It's not only you, either. I threatened him when he lost his temper when Aisha and I called a family meeting to talk about how she and I ended up in our situation and Makalo. Remember?"

"You said something like seeing if his handful of centuries on you made him powerful enough to beat you when you were one of the best warriors in history and never stopped being that. Or something." I could remember the explosive argument very well. The day had been traumatic. For once, it hadn't been a mess I caused.

"Accurate enough. Zuri went and had a child without saying anything to us, hiding the entire pregnancy. Mother didn't even tell him, but he's more willing to forgive our mother. Davor and Niko were keeping secrets that are still very raw." He gestured around.

"Yeah, more Niko's secrets and Davor was trying to be a loyal brother, but that won't change anything, will it?"

"Probably not. He's losing control. We're supposed to be getting Dirk and Landon right now, but I wanted to say a little more to you before we go face the family."

"I'm listening. Do we want to take this into the room?"

"No. Our families are the only ones in this hall. Rather, those of us loyal to helping you are staying in this hall. Those who are more inclined to agree with Father are staying in the same hall as him."

We're divided into factions now?

"Okay, then. Wow." I closed my eyes for a second,

pinching the bridge of my nose. "What did you want to say?"

"That no matter what happens today, you are my sister," he said, pulling my hand down gently, but I knew if I fought him or tried to pull away, I would lose. "Look at me, Jacky."

I peered up, wondering what was wrong.

"I will pick you over him," he said once he knew he had my attention.

I didn't understand the intensity and didn't like how uncomfortable it made me, but I wasn't sure if it was what he was saying or how he was saying it. I only nodded, trying to end it as quickly as possible.

"Thanks," I said as he released my wrist.

"I needed you to hear that. Go knock on their door. I don't want to be attacked the moment it opens."

"Dirk and Landon wouldn't," I said, walking quickly to that door. I knocked, looking at Jabari. "They're good men. Landon is respectful—"

"He promised to gut me when I shoved him in there last night. I don't want to hurt him, but I don't know if I could avoid it if he launches himself at me the moment he sees me."

"Maybe you shouldn't have shoved him," I said, shrugging.

The door swung open to Landon standing there, his eyes fully werewolf, his nostrils flaring in agitation.

"Time for breakfast," I said, remaining calm even though he wasn't. I looked around him. "Dirk, time for breakfast!"

"Coming!" Dirk called from beyond the little entry hall of their bedroom.

I took two steps back to the other side of the hall as Landon came out, holding the door open for Dirk. I saw the moment he realized Jabari was there.

"I'm your guide to the grand dining hall," my eldest brother said, the epitome of a lazy, unthreatened cat met with a snarling dog. Landon didn't bother him at all this morning, probably because he had the chance to prepare for the aggressive nature Landon often embodied when around Jabari.

"I can sniff it out," Landon muttered, shaking his head. "Jacky—"

"Just. Be nice for me. He's on our side, and he's not that bad."

"She's right," Dirk said as he strolled out, waving a hand at Jabari. "I was telling you earlier that today is going to be a mess."

"You were about to answer my question when she knocked." Landon turned to Dirk, and the hostility faded into something more neutral.

"I haven't seen Hasan yet, no."

"He knows Dirk is a werewolf. He hasn't spoken to anyone except to give orders and hear updates," Jabari explained from his place ten feet down the hall. "Everything that's been said has gone through others. The only person he's spoken with privately was King Brion about the Black Forest and what they were going to do about it."

"Not even Subira?" I asked, thrown off.

"Mother has been wandering, keeping to herself. This is an...intensely magical place, and Niko gave her leave to explore his estate thoroughly. King Brion said she could go up to ten miles from the estate but that the risk was her own to take. For all I know, she spent the night sleeping out there to understand it better."

"Zuri said she was acting weird."

"Father wasn't expecting her, either. He said to bring the entire family but, for some reason, thought Mother would choose to stay in Africa with our children and mates. Not a wildly off-base assumption, but this time, it was an incorrect one."

Jabari started walking, maybe feeling Landon was calm enough now. He stopped with Dirk separating him and the feral Everson.

"Immortality looks good on you," he said to Dirk, patting his shoulder. "Nephew."

"Thank...thank you," Dirk said, clearly taken off guard by the sudden attention and acceptance from Jabari. Niko and Jabari weren't close, and Niko had kept a lot of secrets from the family. Dirk had never been exposed to many of them for years.

"Back to Mother and Father, one is dealing with her magical place in the world, and one is angry. They are like most long-term relationships and far from perfect," Jabari said to me. "I don't think I need to tell you which siblings to be careful of today, right?"

I shook my head but saw Landon and Dirk both needed to know more, Dirk even tilting his head to the side.

"Mischa and Hisao," I said quietly. "Mischa is explosive. Hisao—"

"Hisao follows orders. He has one personal rule, which is not to fight his own family, but Landon, you're not family. Not in his eyes nor the eyes of our father. Maybe one day, but not yet."

"He's my mate!" Dirk snapped, suddenly pushing himself in front of Landon. "Of course, he's family! Even if not as my mate, he's Heath's son and—"

I looked up at Jabari, his expression unreadable.

"Jabari?"

"I can't confirm anything I haven't heard myself," he said quickly. "Just watch yourselves with those two. Don't sit near them. Don't let them corner you. If you need, move toward Zuri or me. We're more than capable of shielding you. Jacky, you should worry more about Mischa. She can fight dirty."

He started walking, and I realized he went from my brother to my general in a few short moments, and I hadn't caught the transition. It had been so fluid, so easy for him.

I looked at Landon and Dirk, who moved to flank me,as if Heath were there to inspect us and make sure they were positioned correctly. Without another word, we followed Jabari on the march toward the fight I had tried to avoid since this all started.

36

CHAPTER THIRTY-SIX

J abari led us through the mansion, and this time, I
only saw the modern half of it. I had been too out of
it to pay attention the day before, but since I had
returned, I hadn't seen the old keep section. He waved off
Niko's staff and opened the double doors himself. I
walked in behind him as he swung them both open, and
they stayed open long enough for Landon and Dirk to
come in before they started to swing shut again.

I found Hasan first before looking around the room
and taking it in to find my best position. He was the most
important person here. He stood on the other side of the
large room, hands in his pockets, staring at framed
pictures on the wall. I had no idea what the pictures
were, unable to see them, thanks to the angle, but he
found them interesting enough or a good distraction, so
he didn't have to look anywhere else.

Seeing that he was at least relatively calm and
distracting himself, I looked around.

The grand dining hall didn't have what I expected, which was a long table where everyone could sit together. There was evidence one had been there, but this morning, there were tables to the side, filled with enough food for the family, and other tables for seating scattered around the room in a semi-organized fashion. Niko and Davor were sitting together in the center, while Zuri, Aisha, Makalo, and Kushim were sitting at one near a wall, giving them line of sight of the entire room. Amir bounced in Zuri's lap, but I watched her hand her son back to Aisha and stand. To my left were couches near a large fireplace. Mischa was lounging on one of them, staring at the ceiling. In a far corner, there was a grand piano tucked away, and Hisao was leaning on the wall behind it.

I was just about to pick where I needed to sit with my werewolves when the room noticed I was there.

"Jacky, it's good to see you up and moving," Niko said as he pushed himself up unsteadily from his seat at a table in the middle of the room. "It's a bit chaotic in here. I had it set up as a sitting room for Dirk's visit. A good place to keep food out and relax and chat without moving all over the house."

"It's lovely," I said softly, unsure of my own voice. Mischa sat up like a rubber band that snapped, but I didn't let her stop me from meeting Niko at a good middle ground, not taking myself farther than a third across the room. He looked me over, his eyes taking in every bump and bruise that might have been peeking out from under a sleeve or on my neck and face.

"Nothing broken?" he asked, leaning in to say it quietly.

"No, I'm fine. We're fine. He's dead." I knew he needed to know. He probably already assumed, but that confirmation made him visibly relax. "You?"

"One of those hits reminded my back that it had been broken before," he said, closing his eyes in pain. I had no doubt he was feeling the memory of that pain. "After scuffles for days, he came into the last fight feeling fresh, and I wasn't."

"Well, you're alive and home. Though it won't be your home for long, huh?"

"No, no, it won't be," he murmured, shaking his head.

I could smell his frustration, the fight in him to figure out how to stay even though he had a lot of people telling him he couldn't. This was no longer his fight or his business, but he had made it his duty for centuries.

"We'll talk about it another time. I think they're hungry," I said, shoving a thumb at my werewolves, who hadn't followed me so far into the room. Niko looked around me and gave a wry smile.

"Secret about men, we're always hungry," he said, chuckling as I rolled my eyes. After a second, he realized the problem, looking at the tables, then at our two werewolves. "Let's set them up some plates."

I looked back and pointed for them to sit at the table closest to the door we had entered through, claiming that area of the room as our own. It left us with the twins and their family closest to us and far from the silent fury building across the room.

Niko and I piled food onto three plates. I desperately needed to eat as well. The last time I had been able to eat anything had been whatever we could scrounge up at his cabin and safehouse. I sat down with my werewolves in silence as Niko slid them their own plates.

"Makalo, let them eat," Jabari grumbled from their table. I looked over and saw Makalo was already halfway out of his chair.

Niko asked something in German, and Dirk's reply was fast, putting his fork down with a piece of ham still on it. He and Landon had started eating immediately, while I hadn't even picked up a piece of silverware. While my stomach told me it was well past time to eat, and I would pay for waiting until later, the room was too thick with tension.

Dirk stood up, saying something else in German, and Niko laughed, a real one, breaking something in the room, even relaxing me.

"Come," Niko said, wiping an eye.

I finally figured out what was happening as Makalo moved away from the table. Nearly a man, he stood like one now, holding his hand out as Niko and Dirk drew closer.

"It's nice to finally meet my eldest cousin," Makalo said with a smile. "Makalo, son of Aisha."

I didn't know the significance that Makalo picked Aisha over Jabari, but I knew he was close with his mother. Jabari didn't seem insulted, so I didn't think about it.

Dirk reached out, going in for the handshake Makalo offered.

"Dirk Brandt, Niko's son and member—"

"Do not touch my grandson."

Hassan's voice rumbled through the room.

The silence left behind was all-consuming. Niko's face relayed all the shock any father would have to hear his child rejected so publicly. Jabari didn't look surprised, but he was pissed. Zuri didn't hide her own anger nearly as well. Aisha was horrified.

But the really important ones were the young men left with that between them. Makalo kept his hand out, but his smile was gone, clearly working through the turn of events that just ended what should have been him getting to meet one of his most reclusive family members.

And Dirk.

His face blank as he let his hand drop and took a step back, collecting himself. He shut down, reminding me of the young man I had met, sent to me by Niko, unwilling to reach out and touch the world, not wanting to be close to anyone or anything.

Seeing that made me stand up. Landon was up at the same time. I looked at Hasan, seeing his gold eyes across the room pinned on Makalo and Dirk.

"I was never good enough for you, was I?" Dirk asked before anyone else knew what to say. A few gasps told me no one had expected him to say that.

"I don't know what you mean," Hasan said, his voice no longer holding the power it had, the flip switch to mild.

"Yes, you do. I can smell the lie from here," Dirk snapped.

"Dirk, don't. Let me handle this," Niko said, finally jumping into action, putting his hands on Dirk's shoulders as his son turned squarely toward the family patriarch.

"There's nothing to handle, Niko."

"There is." Niko shook Dirk and turned toward Hasan, keeping Dirk behind him. "He's my son, Hasan. He's not nothing to you. He's my son, and he's family."

Hasan didn't even take his hands out of his pocket, staring down Niko.

"No werewolf will *ever* be a part of my family," he said, laying down the law.

"I was never a part of your family," Dirk said, stepping away from Niko, even going so far as to throw a dismissive wave in Hasan's direction. "You made that clear years ago. I think the only reason I'm surprised right now is you're finally willing to say it in front of Niko. Took you long enough."

"Watch your mouth with me, wolf," Hasan growled.

I didn't know what to do or say. I looked at Niko, and something shifted in his expression, a thought coming to him as he looked at me.

"Father, what is he talking about?" Niko asked, breaking my stare.

"We met!" Dirk told everyone, pointing between him and Hasan. "Years ago, when you went off to deal with something and he was visiting. I found him and bothered him. I was a stupid kid—"

"You still are," Hasan snapped. "Stop wagging your tongue before I remove it."

"You want me dead right now, admit it," Dirk retorted.

Landon did nothing, made no move, only standing there, giving Dirk silent support.

Hasan made a choice at that moment, and it was simply to give no response.

That was the only response anyone needed.

Zuri pushed to her feet, knocking their table around, drinks spilling, and glasses rolling off to the floor. Amir made a sound as though he was about to cry, only to be quickly comforted by Aisha. Jabari stopped Zuri from storming toward her father, keeping her on our side of the room.

He stopped his sister, but he couldn't stop me. I was walking, the rumble in my chest growing as I stopped in the middle of the room.

"You're a monster," I accused. "You condemned that young man before he even understood what you were doing, and you made him the guilty party in it."

"Unless you want to admit to telling werewolves something they shouldn't know, you should mind your tongue as well," Hasan warned, taking slow steps to the center. When he stopped, we were ten feet apart, glaring at each other.

"Well, I never needed to tell Dirk, did I? You did that all on your fucking own when you told him he would never be able to join this family. Maybe you should have watched yours."

"That's evil, Father," Zuri snarled. "Even for *you*."

"It's my information to do with as I will," he countered. "And if the people who know can't be trusted, they need to be handled."

"If you want Dirk, you better be ready to kill me," I hissed.

"What of you, wolf, Landon Everson, second son? Will you put yourself in the line of fire to save Dirk?"

"Absolutely. My mate matters more than you," Landon said. "He mattered more yesterday, he matters more today, and he will continue to matter more than you tomorrow."

"You seem to be very confident in his worth," Hasan said, tilting his head to the side.

"Bigots aren't worth much, so it's not like he needs to clear a very high bar when it comes to being better than you," Landon explained as if he were reading it from a dry textbook. His tone only made the context much more impactful.

"Bigot?" Hasan's gold eyes narrowed.

Hasan had just opened a can of worms he didn't want to have. I stood there, the wall between him and my werewolves, letting Landon finally say his piece.

"Bigot. Do you need a definition? I'll teach it to you while explaining why you are one. You are unreasonably attached to the belief that werewolves are your enemy and beneath you, and therefore, you go out of your way to be prejudiced against or antagonistic toward anyone who happens to be a werewolf, whether or not that werewolf has done anything to you." Landon snorted when no one immediately said anything. "What? Did I say something none of you knew? Is this new information? Surprising, though maybe it's not. I have a lot of experience with bigots. I've met more than my fair share, so I guess they're easier for me to identify—"

"Your father isn't here to back you up, boy," Mischa hissed.

"I know," Landon growled, sounding all too pleased. "Which means he isn't here to remind me to be polite. Do you know what your father reminds me of? He's every parent who has kicked their gay kid out of the house. He's every racist I've ever met. He's every bit the piece of scum my mother died fighting against, and they weren't fucking werecats. They were just shitty *humans*, and he's no better than the lot of them. Crack open a fucking history book, bitch, and find out who your father *really* is."

Mischa lunged off the couch fast and hard enough to send it sliding ten feet across the floor, but she didn't reach my werewolves. Zuri blocked her path and shoved her back. There was nothing said as they glared at each other, but I knew the sides. Mischa was defending the honor of her father. Zuri was forcing all of us to hear the painful truth.

"Did that hurt to hear, Hasan?" I asked, turning my gaze back to him. "Was it difficult?"

"You are my daughter, and you will distance yourself from the werewolves immediately. You can return to your territory when they have left. I won't take any action against Dirk as long as I can verify he has told no one—"

"I told Landon," I said, facing that now before it

could come out later. "Because your secret was keeping them from being happy together. That's how insidious and awful you can be, and you refuse to even see it. You said something to a child and destroyed everything Niko was trying to build with him. He distanced himself from his father and turned his back on trying to grow close to the family. It took me years to begin unraveling that damage, and I didn't even know what the cause was until the night Dirk became a werewolf. And through it all, after destroying his chance to be a part of this family, you were still standing in the way of him finding one who truly loved him.

"You won't even apologize for it, will you? You won't take any responsibility, will you? All you care for is your fucking secrets, yet you are here with one goal this morning...berating Niko for keeping his own! We haven't even gotten to *that* yet!"

"He—"

"Don't give me excuses. The next thing out of your mouth better be an apology. Then you're going to take a walk and won't come back until you are ready to accept that Dirk, that young man back there who just went through hell to help his father, is one of the *best* of us. And he's mated to an amazing man who is loyal to a fault to the people he cares about. Landon will walk through fire for the people he cares about, and right now, you are the fire. He won't be alone, though. If I have to fight you to go home with them and go back to our lives, I *will*. I just killed one monster in disguise! I'll go for a second!"

"You could never win, daughter," Hasan said, stepping closer.

"Winning isn't the point," I snarled. "If you're going to destroy everyone and everything I care about, you're going to have to kill me to do it."

Hasan took another step closer, his chest heaving as he approached, each step as slow as the one before.

"You want to throw away Dirk for surviving something you never thought he could, but you forgot that you should have given him something to *live* for," I continued, refusing to stop now. "You gave him hopelessness. That werewolf back there? He gave Dirk something to *live* for. Landon and Heath have been better to that young man than you have ever been, then you toss him aside like he did something wrong. It's not *Dirk's* fault you never cared about him." I stopped for a second, breathing hard as another thought came to me. "It's not *my* fault you never cared about *me*."

He stopped his slow approach, jerking back.

"You never cared about my thoughts or feelings. You never cared about what I wanted in life. You indulged me when it *suited* you," I said, blinking back tears as the truth rushed out of me. "I was an indulgence of a daughter, like adopting a pet, another member of the prized collection." I swept a hand over my siblings. "But I don't want to be part of your prized collection. I don't want to spread your ideals all over the world at the expense of my own. I don't want to live with your hate. Werewolves will never be part of your family?" I scoffed, wiping my face. "Fine. If Dirk doesn't have a place in this family, then—"

"You are my *daughter!* I made you!"

"I don't have a place in this family," I finished. "I don't *want* a place in this family. Jacqueline, daughter of Hasan, is no more."

"Stop this right now!" Hasan roared over me.

"I will be Jacky, daughter of—"

"Everyone down!" Zuri screamed over us.

The room rocked as debris flew.

CHAPTER THIRTY-SEVEN

I covered my head as a wave of power ripped through the room, destroying every piece of furniture. The moment the last piece fell, I turned to see if Landon and Dirk were okay, to find them and Niko standing shell-shocked in the middle of a clean circle. Something had circled them and stopped the debris from hitting them.

Looking for the twins, I saw Zuri lower her arms, a staff suddenly in one hand. Her breathing was labored as she turned to check on those around her. Makalo was checking on his mother, who was paler than normal. Amir started to cry, shattering the silence, and Kushim took the young boy, bouncing and cooing to him, rubbing his head and whispering the saddest thing.

"I'm sorry, my little man. I'm sorry. Never again, I promise," he murmured to his son.

Zuri closed her eyes, though that didn't stop the tears from escaping.

I pulled my eyes off her, feeling the guilt, only to find

Jabari near her. Jabari was holding a staff as well, his eyes on me, and he nodded.

"I will pick you over him."

Those words came back to me as I stared at him.

Trying not to think, I saw Mischa was on the ground but not bleeding. Hisao was still in the back of the room, also not bleeding.

Finally, I looked back to Hasan.

He was standing there as though the room hadn't just exploded around us.

He was bleeding.

A thin red line was forming on his cheek, along with dozens of others. He ignored all of them as the blood hit his white shirt and tan pants, staining the fabric.

He looked over my head, and I saw a flicker of relief.

"Subira, are you finally going to help me talk some sense into our children?" he asked.

"I will get to you *last*," she said. There was no hiss or growl in her words, but the rage made the hair on the back of my neck stand up.

Hasan gave no reply. Everything about the subtle changes in his posture and expression told me he wasn't expecting that reply.

I certainly hadn't been.

"Zuri, Jabari, and Makalo. Exceptional magic. Thank you for providing your assistance. I'm sorry you had to." Subira was once again the kind soft-spoken woman I knew her to be, her words echoing gently with the power she controlled.

"It was...faster than expected, but you trained us

well," Zuri said, sounding every bit the dutiful student and daughter she excelled at being.

"I never told any of you when I wanted you to use it practically," Subira said, sighing. "I hoped it would never be my fault. We'll talk more about it later. Little Amir, it's okay. I was being scary. Kushim, step out with him. You can stay where you can hear."

The boy sniffled, but there was no more crying. I heard the fast footsteps of his father taking him out of the room.

She started walking, but I couldn't bring myself to turn around and face her. Glass and ceramic pieces crunched under her feet until she stopped.

"Are both of you boys unharmed?" she asked softly. They must have nodded because there was only a long silence before she continued. "New mates. You should be off enjoying your newfound connection with each other. I'm sorry you are here to witness this. No child or grandchild of mine should ever have to see this. If you wish, you may step out. You are safe on these grounds. You are safe in this family and from it."

I saw Hasan choke on something he wanted to say, his Adam's apple bobbing with the words he forced himself to swallow.

"Not without Jacky," Dirk said.

"Exactly," Landon confirmed.

"You are good men," Subira said. "Niko, you have raised a wonderful man."

"Thank you. Jacky helped."

I bit my lip hard, fighting the emotion those words pulled up.

"If you want to enjoy a life with the son you raised, be comfortable leaving the past behind. The past is supposed to inform your future, not dictate it. You will lose him if you keep trying to cling so hard to it. Okay?"

"I understand."

"Mischa, Hisao. Are you both okay? I had no intention of harming either of you."

"Yes, Mother," Mischa said, groaning as she pushed herself off the ground finally. "Just fell."

"Yes, Mother," Hisao said from his corner.

"Good, good."

The footsteps grew closer to me, and I saw her come around me out of the corner of my eye. She turned, stopping right in front of me, ignoring Hasan entirely. She held a staff as well, her staff, one I had seen before. She smelled of magic. She was such a small woman, something I always forgot when I wasn't near her because she was such a big presence in whatever room she decided to be in.

She also looked very young today, even though the world seemed to be on her shoulders.

"You have very little reason to hear me out right now," she said, her words suddenly less sure than they had been to everyone else. "You may tell me you don't wish to, and I will proceed to let you finish what you intended to say. I will not judge you or love you less for making that decision."

"I need to hear you," I whispered. I did. I wanted to

know this woman. I wanted to understand her. I was done with Hasan. He would need to move heaven and earth to convince me to ever give him another chance, but I wanted to know her before I cast any judgment. She wasn't without her flaws, but she never actively hurt me. She was accepting when Hasan wasn't. She was love where he was control. She was gentle while he was firm.

But she was never around, not for me.

I needed to hear her now.

"Very well." She squared her small shoulders as if she was about to face the firing squad. "I knew something was keeping my children from being as happy as they deserved to be. Your rebellion, my twins' conspiracies, and the anger in Mischa. The loneliness of Niko. The grief of Davor, I knew there was something connecting all of them. There was a time when Niko lived here and wasn't so lonely. There was a time when Davor wasn't full of grief and pain. There was a time when Mischa loved passionately more than she raged. There was a time when my twins respected and loved their father instead of wondering why they still agreed to follow him.

"I woke up one day, and it felt as though the world had tilted on its axis and left me wondering why. What had happened? I continued on like I have for thousands of years. Nothing I had done had changed. I saw that my family had changed, which meant I had to change. I had to prepare myself for a difficult truth and thought I had time. When I didn't. I'm sorry. I'm so sorry for that, Jacky."

I couldn't find anything to say. I needed just a little

more. I needed her to tell me she knew what was wrong here. I wanted desperately to tell her it was okay, that I could forgive her, but he was standing behind her, full of anger as she talked to me and ignored him.

"I'm sorry I trusted a man who made me promises five thousand years ago, and I missed how he had changed as well," she finished.

"Subira," Hasan finally said. Only her name, a plea and an order. It was a question and a statement. He just said her name, and it was a million different things.

"He's not the man I fell in love with. He's not the man who raised our twins. He's watched all of our children grow. And, I'm sorry for not seeing that I had to protect you from him. It is a mistake that won't happen again."

I nodded, dropping my head as she reached up to touch my cheek.

"The human tradition you follow is that a man gives away a woman in marriage, correct? Well, he cannot stomach the idea of your love for your chosen. I will gladly step in if you'll have me. Heath Everson makes you happy, and therefore, he makes me happy. That's all I've ever wanted. He is more than welcome in my heart as a son—"

"You can't—"

As Hasan went to interrupt her, Subira lifted her staff and slammed it back on the floor, puncturing the hardwood floor. A second later, Hasan was sliding across the floor as magic filled my nose.

"I *can*," she snarled. "And I *did*."

Hasan hit the wall with a hard crash that cracked the drywall. He stood up, not seeming shaken at all, but didn't walk forward.

"You." Hasan paused to snarl, his eyes closed as he refused to look at us for a moment. "You can't mean that."

"I do," Subira replied, hissing over her shoulder. "With everything I am, I have meant every word I've ever said, Hasan, son of No One."

I gasped. So did a few others in the room, including Zuri.

We all knew who Changed Hasan. We knew, but I had never heard Hasan ever introduce himself with werecat naming. He was always Hasan, ruler of the werecats, member of the Tribunal.

"Now, you will wait patiently while I talk to *my* daughter." She turned back to me. "You have *every* right to disown Hasan. No one will ever challenge you. No one has leave to question your judgment. I saw it too late, my brave girl. I saw too late that he was always asking you to be someone you aren't as Jacqueline, daughter of Hasan. I do not want you to feel like you aren't loved by this family. I love you, and I'm sorry I have taken so long to do what must be done. The hardest thing I have had to do in a long time." Subira took a shaky breath.

"So, I ask you, as an imperfect woman, to allow me to continue to love and cherish you. I promise to be in your life, to celebrate your love, to accept you for all you are. You cannot and *should not* tolerate a life as Jacqueline, daughter of Hasan, but maybe you could tolerate this family as Jacky, daughter of Subira. I would like to try. It would be the greatest honor you could give me."

"I..." I saw this woman now—ancient, powerful, and more than a bit heartbroken. The man she'd loved for thousands of years had broken something in their family. It had been difficult for her to see it, but she didn't shy away from her mistake in that oversight. She was pleading with me. She wanted this family just as badly as I had for so long. Her love never wavered because she said her love was unconditional, and she meant it. I could smell the truth of her love mixing with her magic. She hadn't seen that Hasan's had been so conditional.

Hasan's problem, not hers.

"I would be honored to be Jacky, daughter of Subira," I finally said, tears flooding my eyes as I let my head drop.

"Thank you, my brave girl. The gift of your heart will always be protected. I promise this." She reached for me, wiping my tears with her free hand. "Now, it is time for some changes in this family."

She tapped her staff again.

"Jabari, Zuri. Attend."

I heard them move, and suddenly they were flanking me, each holding their staffs.

"It is time for me to deal with you," Subira said, turning around to face her mate. "You broke your promise to me, Hasan, son of No One."

"I broke it?" Hasan walked closer, his gold eyes bright with anger. "I promised to build a world that is safer for our children than it ever was for us. I did that and continue to do that. If that means I need to keep our children from acting recklessly and endangering everyone else in this family, then so be it."

"You also promised me that our children would be happy," she snarled. "Do any of them look happy? I ignored you for too long, living in ignorance while I attended to our greatest secret while you drove our family into ruins! You even rejected our grandchild! You would cast him out into the cold!"

"I will *never* claim those werewolves. He is no grandson of mine, and Heath will be no son. I will never—"

"They are part of this family—"

"They killed Liza!" he roared, shaking everyone. "They will never be part of this family!"

Even Subira was silenced but didn't seem surprised. As if she'd found something interesting, a piece of the puzzle to put into place, she approached Hasan, the scent around her full of new understanding to pair with her anger.

"Dirk Brandt, Landon Everson, and Heath Everson did not kill Liza," she said, her words far gentler, a calmness flowing off her, even while she was furious. "They didn't do that. Dirk wasn't alive. Heath and Landon were on the wrong continent. They helped Jacky when he tried to hurt her."

"They're werewolves," he growled, not moving any longer.

"What happened to peace?" she asked.

"I gave it to them, and they killed my little girl," he snapped, the answer obvious to him.

My little girl. She was his favorite. Like she was Niko's favorite. Like Davor fell so in love with her, no one else would ever be enough.

I was in the shadow of a greatness I could never overcome when it came to her memory, but I didn't curse the woman. I just wished I could be seen without her over my head.

"She was something special, wasn't she?" Subira asked. "Liza was everything none of us could ever be. In their own way, our surviving children are warriors. She could never get comfortable with a hunt on the full moon. She was sad when I asked her to kill a fish we caught together. She believed if everyone was good, the world would be good. She was good, wasn't she?"

"Yes," Hasan choked out.

"Do you know who else believes that?" Subira asked, tilting her head as she studied her mate.

He didn't answer, his nostrils flaring as his eyes shot to my face.

"The funny thing, Hasan, is you seem to be drawn to children who fill some need of yours. You never did it intentionally, but you did it. Maybe it's the lack of intention that makes you blind to what I can see so easily. You found little Liza and all her goodness as we finally enjoyed peace together as a family. You could finally indulge the want of having a child who would never know violence like the rest of us.

"She believed so completely in your peace that she was incapable of violence. She wanted to see the world as something better than even we could imagine, and we both loved her so dearly for that. It was what we wanted when we finally saw eye to eye as mates. We wanted a better world for our children, and Liza. She was every piece of that."

"You don't need." Hasan growled as he clenched his jaw. It took several moments, but we all waited for him to continue. "You don't need to remind me."

"I do, because we lost our beautiful girl, and you locked your heart to everything she ever believed in. I can tell you why you were drawn to Jacky."

I remembered what Niko said as Subira continued.

"She believes in the same better world Liza did. *She's* willing to fight for it. It's not *her* fault you closed your heart because of a death nearly a century before you met." Subira pointed back at me as she drove that point into Hasan. "You are punishing her for your cold heart. You are punishing her when you Changed her, not realizing you *need* her. *We* need her. We are blessed to have the chance to be her family. She didn't choose us. She has been giving us a *chance*, Hasan, and you have been taking it for granted at every turn."

"What would you have of me?" he asked, finally pulling his eyes off mine.

"You will remain on the Tribunal. You will remain the ruler of the werecats. *I* will be in charge of this family. You will not argue or fight it. If you need something from one of our children, even if it is to speak to them about the weather, you will go through me. I will have a home built in my territory for the family to visit. You may visit me as much as you please, but I will not indulge your need to hide on your island any longer. I believe a visit to my home after so long might be a healthy reminder of a time we were once united and why we were."

"I can't call my own children? Talk to them?"

"No," Subira said, lifting her small chin and making herself the most powerful person in the world. "Your children have been the army by which you have ruled this world. I have heard these words spoken about you both by outsiders and our children. I heard them, and they broke my heart. You know why. I never thought you would actually become him, but when I walked into this room, I didn't see the warm, dutiful man I fell in love with. I saw a warmonger. I saw hate. I saw someone I recognized, but it wasn't my mate."

Hasan dropped to his knees as his face finally showed the horror and pain I could smell.

"I would never hurt you," he whispered. Truth. Painful, sad truth.

"You hurt me every time you hurt our children. You will not have access to them until you have healed the wounds you have let fester for too long and can remember the man I fell in love with."

Also true.

She turned away from him and looked over us.

"Any questions?" she asked of us.

There were none.

38

CHAPTER THIRTY-EIGHT

My plane had more people on it than expected. Jabari and Makalo were escorting us home. Jabari's excuse had been that Makalo needed to begin traveling and seeing more of the world. Niko was also on the plane, but that one had been more expected. He had nowhere else to go. Following his son was the only plan he could think of.

"Are you going to make a territory nearby or be a rogue?" I asked him as I sat down with a drink in hand. We were nearly at Dallas, everyone else sleeping, so I decided to take my chance and get this out of the way.

"Probably a rogue while I scout the surrounding area to find something close that won't encroach on your territory. Something where I can get a lot of land."

"You can help me manage Dallas," I said, smiling at the thought. "I have a mansion there."

"A werewolf mansion you won when you kicked out the pack," he reminded me.

"Jabari would tell you it doesn't matter how I got it. It's still mine now."

"Jabari gave you the deed of a vampire nest," he said, rolling his eyes. "He thinks conquest is still a perfectly acceptable thing."

"For the building and the land it's on, but it's up in Washington. That's not close to Dirk."

"Clearly." Niko gave me an annoyed look.

"Look, I'm sorry about everything. Rainer, your home, your territory. All of it," I said, leaning back in my seat. "You know that, right? Even if Brion didn't tell you to leave, I was going to have to drag you out. I made a deal. Remember how we got separated?"

"So, there was a witch?"

I explained to him everything I knew about Adalni, watching him absorb it, his expression changing as I went. There was curiosity but also some pain as he heard how the woman had lived, thanks to the pack. I then explained what King Brion had told me.

"He told me that part," Niko said, looking out his window. "It was about space, not about the greater good or anything like that. It was a job, not a purpose. Rainer being alive kept the bargain going."

"We never had the chance to talk to Hasan about how Callahan had been hiding your brother," I said, crossing my arms in thought as I looked out my closest window. Texas was going to be underneath us soon.

"No one talked to Hasan about much of anything when it came to what we actually went through and probably won't for some time if Subira has her way, and she will." I could smell how grateful he was for that and found myself feeling much the same. "We should tell her, though."

"She shooed us out of Germany pretty quickly. I think she wants to get home herself."

"She wants to stabilize," Jabari mumbled, sitting up with his eyes barely open. "We'll have to build her a home from scratch. There are things to do if she's going to run the family instead of Father."

"Are you going to build it with your bare hands or something?"

"No, but contractors who qualify to work on something like our mother's home are probably hard to find." He didn't look excited. "Only the finest for her."

"Okay, Jabari, son of Subira," I said, smiling as he narrowed his eyes on me. I was trying to tease his momma's boy attitude, and he knew it.

"Absolutely. Our mother is amazing." He got up and went to the bathroom, leaving me and Niko alone with our sleeping family members.

"I am sorry," I said again, catching Niko's eye. "About Rainer." I thought he would give me a platitude of dismissal or, like many others, tell me this wasn't my fault. What he ended up saying took me by surprise.

"I'm sorry about Fenris," he whispered.

It brought tears to my eyes.

Jabari said nothing when he came back out. The pilot let us know we had thirty minutes until landing. We started waking up, each taking one of the three still sleeping. Jabari got his son up, and Niko got Dirk. I was left with Landon, who was by far the snappiest of the three.

"We're almost home," I said, lifting my hands in a symbol of peace. "Almost home."

"Did you call Pa?" he asked, rubbing his eyes. He had passed out the moment we had gotten onto the plane.

"I let him know we were coming but that I was exhausted. He told me to rest up. Did you know our wolves woke up the day after Rainer died?"

"No. That's great," Landon said, stretching.

"The curse wore off early thanks to its caster not being an extraordinarily powerful fae, so it faded after his death. The healers figured it out rather easily and told Heath. Everyone is doing fine."

"Perfect. You know, I couldn't have had a better partner through this. Thanks."

"Thank you," I said, patting his shoulder before I took my seat for landing.

We shuffled off the plane, and I felt the immediate relief of standing on my home turf once again. I threw my bag down and jumped at Heath the moment I saw him. He held me, not putting me down.

"Never again," he whispered. "Not both of you. I can't take it. If I had lost even one of you, I would have been destroyed, but the possibility of losing both of you..."

I kissed the man until his son made a gagging nose. Turning around, all the men who followed me home were staring. Only Makalo didn't look entirely grossed out. He wasn't even looking at us. He and Carey were talking and looking at something on her phone.

"Teenagers," Heath muttered in my ear.

I chuckled, glad that teenagers were the scariest thing I had in my immediate future.

We loaded into my car and Heath's truck, trying to fit everyone. We couldn't unless people rode in the bed of Heath's truck, which Jabari agreed to. It wasn't a lack of seats, but the size of the passengers that was the problem. Heath ended up with Makalo and Carey in his truck and Jabari hiding in the bed. I had Dirk and Landon in the back and Niko riding shotgun. It was tricky because there were multiple conditions. Niko wanted to ride with Dirk. Dirk wanted to ride with Landon. Carey had to ride with her dad, and Jabari promised to keep his son close. Heath wanted to ride with Landon because I had to drive, but there was no way all of them were going to fit in Heath's truck.

It was a fun problem to have, a sudden fullness to my life I hadn't expected when I left for Germany, chasing a man who took us all by surprise.

When we got to my home, we tried to figure out where to put everyone. Jabari muttered about just building a big guest house in my territory instead of making him rent a vehicle to use the mansion in Dallas. I gave up, telling them my room and Carey's room were off-limits before going to find some quiet. Heath followed me, and I knew he had something to say.

"Yes?" I asked, sitting on the edge of my bed.

"When Teagan woke up and I told him everything,

he asked me to drive him back to Dallas. Apparently, before all of this, just last week, Fenris had Teagan put something with his will. Teagan didn't think much of it. People do things like that all the time as people become important to them. Teagan kept it confidential because he knew Fenris needed to be trusted."

"Yeah..." It still hurt. Even with everything that had exploded in my family, thinking of Fenris still hurt so much, and there was no one who really understood. Heath was the closest, and I was glad to be back to him, but he hadn't been there for those moments when I knew it was Fenris and not Rainer, and I didn't want to burden him with them.

Heath went to his bedside table and pulled out an envelope.

I took it, seeing my name written on the front.

"He left me a letter with his will?" I asked, swallowing the painful need to cry right there.

"He did." Heath leaned down to kiss my forehead. "You believed in him. Through it all, his history, his behavior, you believed in him, even before I could bring myself to. I haven't read it, but I can see why he left it for you. Now, I'm going to leave you to read it. Or, not read it."

I nodded, letting him leave me to this private thing. I gently tore it open, trying to make sure I could preserve it later.

JACKY,

. . .

IF YOU HAVE THIS LETTER, *I lost control, and I'm definitely dead. You, Landon, Heath...you would never let me live for the betrayal. It started when I realized who Dirk is. I can't tell anyone. It's like there's magic stopping me. There must be. It doesn't matter. I'm finally figuring out why I am fucking crazy.*

You showed me something else, and I've been trying to live that life you want. It's a really nice thing, you know. Good people around you, all of them. Good things to fight for. With you, I finally fought for good things.

I know this thing in my head won't let me stay in your good world. It will always be there. I'm going to enjoy this as much as I can, but I am losing myself. I wish I could warn you, but I can only get away because I know Teagan's too noble to break the rules. I black out. I don't know what's happening.

I'm sorry I can't stay in your world. I'm sorry I can't join you. Keep giving people like me chances. Keep changing lives. You're pretty good at it. I think you'll get the world you want one day if you keep trying. If anyone can do it, it will be you.

Fenris

SLOWLY PUTTING the letter to the side, I cried and let it go—all the pain of his betrayal, all the hurt of losing him. That mad, wonderful wolf.

I will. I'll keep trying for you.

When the tears dried out, I stood. Folding the letter and putting it back in its envelope, I put it in a drawer of my bedside table and took a deep breath.

Two of my brothers were downstairs, probably still fighting over who got to sleep on the couch. Dirk and Landon probably left Niko with us even though it would have been more than reasonable for them to take him to their place. They had the space. Carey was probably hanging out in her room with Makalo, even though I said it was off-limits to all visitors.

Opening the door, I headed downstairs. I looked at my family, and for a moment, I wished I had known Fenris was part of it before all of this. After a few moments, I realized the important part.

I hadn't needed to know he was part of my family through Niko. He had been from the moment he decided to join us here.

"Are you okay?" Heath asked me from the bottom of the stairs.

"I will be." I took his hand and went to spend time with the family I had left, knowing very well that I still had a lot of work to do.

DEAR READER

Thank you for reading!

It's been a rough year for Jacky. It's been a rough year for me. I can only say at the end of this book that maybe things are looking up for both of us thanks to the support of those who love us and support us.

I hope you all have those people to support you too and if you don't right now, know that I support you from here, behind my books.

The year has been hard. Harder than I can say to anyone, really. My confidence has been rocked and my bedrock stability been shattered and I'm trying my best. Just like Jacky always does.

I can't tell you exactly when the next book will come. It will definitely be this year as things continue to improve slowly.

Hopefully July 2023

Life has been really hard, so if you want news about when the next book has a preorder or is released, please sign up for my newsletter!

Knbanet.com/newsletter

And remember,

Reviews are always welcome, whether you loved or hated the book. Please consider taking a few moments to leave one and know I appreciate every second of your time and I'm thankful.

THE TRIBUNAL ARCHIVES

The Jacky Leon series is set in the world of The Tribunal. Every series and standalone novel is written so it can be read alone.

For more information about The Tribunal Archives and the different series in it, you can go here:

tribunalarchives.com

ACKNOWLEDGMENTS

I'm very bad at giving really public praise. I shower people in praise in private. But that's not everyone's love language and that's okay.

So this little page shall now be dedicated to everyone who helps me get these books from the concept to the release and beyond. From my PA, to my editor and my proofreader, to my wonderful friends helping me through the hardest moments. To my husband, who doesn't read my books, but loves that I write them and is willing to listen to me talk about them for hours.

And to you, the reader, for without you, I wouldn't have anyone to share these stories with. I'm a storyteller at heart and you have given me the greatest gift of listening.

I love all of you. Thank you for continuing to go on this journey with me.

ABOUT THE AUTHOR

KNBanet.com

Living in Arizona with her husband and 5 pets (2 dogs and 3 cats), K.N. Banet is a voracious... video game player. Actually, she spends most of her time writing, and when she's not writing she's either gaming or reading.

She enjoys writing about the complexities of relationships, no matter the type. Familial, romantic, or even political. The connections between characters is what draws her into writing all of her work. The ideas of responsibility, passion, and forging one's own path all make appearances.

☐ facebook.com/KNBanet

☐ instagram.com/Knbanetauthor

☐ bookbub.com/authors/k-n-banet

☐ amazon.com/K.N.-Banet/e/B08412L9VV

☐ patreon.com/knbanet

ALSO BY K.N. BANET

The Jacky Leon Series

Oath Sworn

Family and Honor

Broken Loyalty

Echoed Defiance

Shades of Hate

Royal Pawn

Rogue Alpha

Bitter Discord

Secrets and Ruin

Volume One: Books 1-3

The Kaliya Sahni Series

Bounty

Snared

Monsters

Reborn

Legends

Destiny

Volume One: Books 1-3

The Everly Abbott Series

Servant of the Blood

Blood of the Wicked

Tainted Blood

Tribunal Archives Stories

Ancient and Immortal (Call of Magic Anthology)

Hearts at War

Full Moon Magic (Rituals and Runes Anthology)

Made in the USA
Columbia, SC
05 April 2024

34044627R00252